I0695092

A Study of Shattered Spells

A STUDY OF SHATTERED SPELLS

CHINTOR'S LEGACY • BOOK I

JOSIAH DEGRAAF

ANDREIA PRESS

Published by Andreia Press
Ambridge, Pennsylvania.
AndreiaPress.com

ISBN: 978-1-966510-00-0 (special edition)
ISBN: 978-1-966510-01-7 (hardcover)
ISBN: 978-1-966510-02-4 (paperback)
ISBN: 978-1-966510-03-1 (ebook)

Interior illustrations by Abian van der Meijden.
Cover design by Damonza.
Maps by Rachael Ward and Aaron Williams.
Chapter header design & typesetting by Jamie Foley.
Special edition art by Cheryl DeGraaf.

For permissions contact Andreia Press: inquiries@andreiapress.com

To my students and fellow teachers at MCA,
thank you for showing me what it means to be a teacher.

Content Note

Dear friend,

As a fresh-out-of-college high school teacher, there was a lot I was unprepared for. Working with students in the classroom has been one of the highlights of my life. And yet I also found myself navigating tough issues that, as a new adult, I wanted to be better equipped to navigate.

My goal in this novel was to both depict the joys of teaching and explore some of the real challenges new adults face when they're now in positions of authority with responsibilities to help the more vulnerable. As a result, *A Study of Shattered Spells* references and deals with issues like bullying, abuse, and sexual harassment. There is not any explicit sexual content or language in this book. But there are several frank conversations about these topics as the protagonist deals with the aftermath of these problems and seeks to be a good teacher.

I have done my best to approach these sensitive topics in as honest and careful a manner as I can. I'm never a perfect storyteller, however, and reading a depiction of these sensitive topics could be uncomfortable for some readers.

For my teen students who may be picking up this book: while this is an adult novel, I did write it in a way that would be appropriate for high school-aged readers. That being said, feel free to put it aside if you find it to be too much.

My prayer is that this novel will give you an intriguing look into what life might look like behind a (fantastical!) teacher's desk while also empowering you to face the brokenness of the world with confidence. Thanks for picking up this book, and I hope you enjoy the story.

In Christ,

HELGOLAND S
ENDRISH NATION
SHENDI MOUNTAINS
SHERANG
CHINTOR
RIZADE
TALUM
VALAN RIVER
INLARU
ANOR'S PASS
THE NA
BAYLIN
KRAZ
TO THE FAR SOUT

THE THREE
KINGDOMS
MAPPED
IN THE PRESENT ERA
THE GREAT STEPPES
THE KALDIAN WASTES
KALDIA
KALINANG
KHOLOGURA
URLAGAINU
NEPADAIAH
DAMANAR RIVER
PATINE
KAMALIN
OLD ARDITEN
BOSALIN
TAKLIN
RI
IRTIN

PROLOGUE

MOST PEOPLE STAYED INDOORS
during a blood moon.

But Kalina let Riyad pull her through the leafy foliage of the jungle.

"I promise you," he said with a grin, "you're going to love this."

"You don't need to impress me." Kalina followed her husband up the narrow path. "Just being with you away from the camp is more than enough for me."

"And I'm still trying to exceed your low expectations." He pulled her a little farther, and then the trail ended at a rocky crag overlooking the small town beneath—and the expansive war camps to the east. The moon bloomed large and crimson on the horizon, like a long-languishing note on the strings of a cello. It cast an uncanny glow on the lines of tents where their fellow troops slept.

Kalina shivered without meaning to. She still remembered what the old friar had preached. *The One Who Was Not breaks free from his cage when he paints the moon in his colors.*

"I promise that doing this during a blood moon wasn't intentional," Riyad said. "If you'd rather go back..."

She turned to him. "I don't care about superstitions." *Never mind the knot in my stomach.* "I just need to be away from that camp."

Riyad sat on the rock. Kalina curled up next to him, resting her head underneath his scraggly beard. They stayed there a long while, watching the moon rise while nocturnal creatures began to awake in the jungle behind them. She tried to shut out the images of gleaming arrows that squirmed into her mind.

"You still thinking about Caldera?" Riyad asked.

Kalina swallowed. "She would have gone on leave today. She was so excited to see her family again."

"I know." His wheatish-brown hand closed around hers. "This war has taken a lot from us."

"I keep replaying that battle." Her heart thudded. "I was so close to synergizing with you."

He squeezed her hand. "You played beautifully. It's not your fault."

"Maybe I shouldn't be up here. I should be down there practicing for tomorrow's battle."

"Have you ever heard of the dangers that come from practicing too much?"

"That's a schoolkid myth."

"I don't know. I think the two of us being together up here does far more for your inner peace and ability to play well than spending a fifth hour practicing."

Kalina pulled at a blade of grass. "I just need to figure out how to synergize before we lose any more friends."

"Hmm." His beard tickled as he turned his head to kiss her hair. "Do you need me to remind you again that you're only human? We're attempting to do something no other mage has done before."

A tear slipped out. "What if Padini is next?"

"The Kaldian archers won't hit her too." He hugged her tighter. "And even if we lose again, we'll work through those challenges together. Because you're not responsible for everyone."

"I know," she lied. "I just can't help but feel uneasy, like something terrible is going to happen again."

"You sure that's not the blood moon talking?"

"It's a bad omen for a reason."

"Well, we're going to prove it wrong. Just a few more weeks of practicing this new way of synergizing, and we'll change the scope of this war. You can't rush innovations like this. Isn't that what you used to tell me?"

"I did." Kalina rested her head on his shoulder. "And I know you're right. I'm sorry for bringing this up. I really do want to enjoy this moment with you."

Riyad chuckled. "One of these days, I'll get my optimism to rub off on you."

"Sounds wonderful."

"Just watch. You and me together...our magic will be unstoppable."

She exhaled and tried to pretend she could hold on to his optimism. Their magic would sweep away the Kaldian forces. He could go back to teaching, and she to researching. She just had to do a little bit better, and she'd finally master synergizing with him.

Tomorrow.

The blood moon appeared to darken. *Must be a trick of the eyes. I've told myself for years it's just a superstition.*

Her gut told her, though, that this blood moon was trying to warn her. There would be a cost to ignoring it.

KALINA DIDN'T UNDERSTAND WHY people called her an optimist. The label hardly fit. She just believed that people could change.

Admittedly, though, people didn't always think clearly when thousands of lives were on the line.

Battalions of pikemen clashed on the dried-out rice paddies surrounding the siege-weathered city of Inlaru. Opposing mages played their trumpets. The ground between the two rivers shook. But the Kaldians hadn't successfully opened any sinkholes yet. The air crackled with energy from the violinists engaged in their own magical efforts to strike soldiers with lightning.

Kalina looked past all the dueling mages. They weren't the largest threat to winning this battle. She focused on the gun cavalry the Kaldians had released from the reserves.

Gun cavalry had shattered their battalions for the past four years. Rizadian mages couldn't deflect bullets like they could arrows. Nor did Rizade have the means to shoot back. While they had recovered a few Kaldian guns from previous battles, they couldn't trade with the East for gunpowder like the Kaldians could.

Today, however, the sight of the enemy's dreaded technology filled Kalina with excitement.

Commander Kay had stared in shock when she'd told him their rigid general had actually agreed to try something new. *Will General Mahd follow through on it? His track record raises questions.*

But so far, she hadn't regretted her optimism. *And I won't let what happened eight months ago happen again.*

Kalina dashed around the pods of mages standing with her on the hill. Her brown tunic, only partially secured by the fabric band encircling her waist, flapped around her thighs. She tried to ignore the cacophony around her as the mages unleashed the powers of the universe with their instruments. If only the competing melodies didn't sound so ugly. *But if ugly is what it takes, I'll direct music repulsive enough to scare off livestock. Anything to save lives.*

Kalina slid to a stop by one of her drummers. His quick notes pounded in her ears. She concentrated her magical sensing skills. The otherwise-invisible energy he channeled from the drum to control the Substance of Fire sprang into her vision. If not for him, the Kaldians would have ignited an inferno among their ranks.

"Signal General Mahd!" she shouted into his ear. "The gun cavalry are coming."

A quick nod from him and a moment later, a bright red light erupted from his drums. It didn't last longer than a couple of seconds. But it would alert the general to the gun cavalry if he hadn't seen them yet.

Now to see if he will reward my trust.

For years, Mahd had insisted they could only stop the gun cavalry by directing all the mages' efforts toward them—a textbook approach to handling threats. But the textbooks hadn't prepared for bullets, and the Kaldian mages knew how to defend their cavalry. Ever since the accident eight months ago and her subsequent promotion to mage commander, she'd been itching for the chance to do something different. *Something to make up for my failure to synergize when it counted.*

Kay's words rang in her ears. *"Your career will be on the chopping block if this fails!"*

A red light flashed from the command tent. *Mahd plans on following through.* Kalina ran a hand through her hair. *This should excite me.* But instead, her breath came out quick and tight.

Because now, it's all on me to show how even older tactics can become new again.

She scanned the battlefield. The gun cavalry were galloping toward Rizade's northern flank—where Commander Kay's battalion fought. She could sense most of the Kaldian mages focusing their efforts on shielding the cavalry. They expected her mages to attack them, as they'd done for years.

But the Kaldians had left the rest of the battlefield wide open and ripe for attack.

She ran to one of her flutists. Quick arpeggios up and down rolled into her ears. "When you get an opening, help our southern battalion against the river," she said into his ear. "Just a small wave breaking over the enemy to disrupt their formation."

A quick nod from him, and she ran to the violinists. "We're sending a small wave over the Kaldians next to the southern river," she whispered into an aged violinist's ear. "If you have the chance to send lightning through it, do so."

The Kaldians had drained the rice paddies three months ago when they began the siege to ensure Rizade's violinists couldn't electrocute soldiers in the paddy waters. But they couldn't move the rivers.

Kalina pivoted toward the north. The gun cavalry had almost reached Commander Kay's battalion. A few of her mages feinted to attack them, but the rest focused on the unprotected battlefield.

Where are our cavalry? Her entire plan rested on bringing back the traditional cavalry charge to counter the Kaldians' guns with steed and spear instead of magic.

Worry knotted her stomach. She and her husband had loved joining Kay's soldiers around their campfires before the accident. Their optimism and laughter in the midst of this Ternion-forsaken war had been refreshing.

If my plan leaves them open to attack from the Kaldian guns...

She ran back to the drummer. "Send the signal again!" she yelled. "We need our cavalry!"

Mahd wouldn't have reverted to his old ways and changed his mind about following my plan...would he?

In the south, everything worked as planned. A boulder propelled by one of her brass players smashed into a battalion. And, just as she'd coordinated, a small wave sprang out from the southern river and cascaded into the enemy ranks. A flash of lightning electrified the water.

Yes!

She almost leapt for joy as scores of Kaldians fell.

Then the gun cavalry arrived in the north.

The Kaldian battalion opposing Kay's pulled back so the gun cavalry could fill their place beyond the range of the pikes. Guns roared. Bullets tore into Kay's flanks as the Kaldians executed their familiar maneuver. She knew it by heart. Each frontline horseman discharged both of his pistols before falling back to reload while another freshly loaded horseman took his place.

The rotating circle of death.

Kay's battalion haltingly moved forward. *An attempt to charge the cavalry?* But few men had the courage to run toward blazing guns. Dozens of frontline soldiers dropped.

Where are our cavalry?

She scanned the battlefield one last time. And then she saw them. Down at the *southern end* of the field.

Why are they there?

The cavalry charged the Kaldian battalion that the boulder had fractured.

No. Her hands leapt to her mouth. *What are they doing?*

Rizade's opposing battalion had pulled back to give the cavalry room to move in. But the cavalry's spears couldn't reach far enough. They slammed into the wall of pikes.

She could hear the horses' screams all the way in the back reserves.

Her mouth went dry. Rizade had still won the ground closest to the river where they'd used the wave attack. But they wouldn't easily take the battalion north of it with all the horses' bodies barring the way.

The Kaldians had caught on to her new strategy and shifted their magic to protect their troops.

Now Kay's men had no support. His battalion fell apart amid the barrage of the guns. And the gun cavalry made for another Rizadian battalion while the Kaldian pikemen surged in to mop up the survivors.

Purple light began streaming from behind her—the retreat signal from Mahd's drummers.

No. Her head spun. *We still have a chance in the south. There's more to this battle than cavalry.*

Try telling that to Mahd, though. His obsession lost them most of their battles. The king should have dismissed him long ago.

But after a prophet representing the Divine Council had declared

Mahd's son would save their nation from disaster, there was no removing his military rank. *Even when he has no imagination or foresight.*

Fighting in the north caught her eye. Kay's men still faced grave danger. She could mourn today's failure once she'd protected everyone here.

"Get Kay's battalion a land bridge over the northern river," she ordered a nearby trumpeter. "Destroy it after they cross."

The other mages marched down the slopes of the mountain, playing as they went to protect against enemy attacks. But Kalina remained on the hill with the trumpeter, watching him as he focused his concentration on the nearby river.

Her chest tightened. Kay had lost so many men already. Did he still live? She knew he wouldn't blame her for the loss. Mahd's decision to send the cavalry south had caused that.

But he would have lost so many men. *Today's losses pile up by the minute.* She kicked the ground.

Notes rang out from the trumpet, and earth shot over the river, creating an improvised escape route. The Kaldians hadn't expected that move. *Knew it.* Successful maneuvers relied on three pillars: the commander's speed, the men's courage, and the enemy's strategy.

Unlike the traditional mage commander—a random noble without magic training—Kalina had actually used magic before, which meant she knew how enemy mages thought. Her prediction abilities had made her the best mage commander Mahd had ever had, even if her healed hands couldn't work magic anymore.

Kay's soldiers began to cross the bridge.

"Okay," Kalina said. "Quell their magic so they don't destroy the bridge yet, and let's move." They'd stayed alone on the hill long enough. Even if she preferred this to the dressing down she'd receive at the camp.

They marched down the hill. She lowered her head. Today should have ended in a victory.

Instead, they fell back again.

Another loss they couldn't afford against the blossoming Kaldian empire.

Kalina remembered Kay's warnings about whom Mahd would blame for the loss. *The one who proposed this new plan in the first place.*

It would have worked if the cavalry went where they should have.

But unless Mahd had changed his habit of blame shifting, he'd make her the target of his wrath.

2

KALINA HAD LONG AGO ACCEPTED
the stares she received when walking through the military camp. Even eight months later, men still whispered about the woman who had survived her instrument breaking.

She wasn't supposed to be alive. Mages whose instruments shattered while they were using them to manipulate the Substances died. One-hundred percent of the time.

Until her.

Survival, of course, poorly described what it meant to live as a woman who could never use magic again and whose husband now lay in a magically induced coma. She replayed the disaster every day, watching the explosion tear her cello to shreds and send the magic-saturated shrapnel ramming through Riyad as he played beside her.

She still felt each and every impact.

Because those pieces came from *her* cello. The one she didn't protect carefully enough, even after the blood moon's warning.

She blinked back a tear as she walked past the staring soldiers. Sure, they might call her a legend. The woman who survived the impossible. But every time she received their stares, she only remembered who still lay unconscious.

"Kalina." Kay ran to her as she began to climb the switchbacks leading to the upper portions of the camps. Jungle trees loomed high over them. "Why the *klyte* did Mahd not send the cavalry?"

"Oh, he sent them." She stopped and turned toward Kay. "The cavalry threw themselves into the southern battalions instead of charging the gun cavalry."

Kay stared at her. He always stared—it was some tic or something of his. But he *really* stared at her now while blood trickled down his forehead.

"Get out," he said. "A few men shared that rumor...but that's actually where they went?"

"I'm so sorry."

Kay started ascending the switchbacks. "I lost nearly a third of my men. But we all know who he's going to blame."

"Maybe he'll blame the cavalry. He *did* listen to my plan when you said he never would."

"And look what he did—he sabotaged it. Because people don't change. They just glut their own lust for glory, follow outdated textbooks, and resist innovation because it wasn't their idea. And if we lose—well, that must be because of providence."

Kalina looked around. "Keep your voice down." Commanders had been discharged for less. She turned around the rubber tree at the switchback.

"I don't care if Mahd hears me."

She turned to meet Kay's stare. "You know as well as I do how he deals with commanders who openly disagree with his actions."

"I know. I hate it." He sniffed and looked back at the battlefield. "I have dead friends there. And you're the *only one* willing to brainstorm solutions for their gun cavalry."

A group of twenty despondent soldiers trudged up the switchback now, and it looked like they carried some wounded men.

"I'm sorry," she said. "I'm not giving up hope in Mahd yet. But if I'm dismissed...well, I guess I should have known better than to persuade him to change." She spun, swatted away the fruit flies, and continued up the switchbacks. Kay didn't follow.

Kalina was panting by the time she reached the top of the hill. She should have directed the mages to create a more gradual slope on this hill. The ridge dividing the sprawling lower camps from the upper camps made medical runs like the one coming up behind her difficult. Perhaps she should have put the mage camp in the lower camps. But that went against centuries of pride and honor.

She kept along the edge of the ridge as she walked toward her destination. Large white tents along her right blocked out the rest of the command camp. On the left, the bodies of a few deserters hung on gallows. They didn't have many deserters, all things considered. Mahd's caution meant they lost fewer men, even if it also meant they rarely won.

The sun glistened as it broke through the leafy foliage on her left. The way it scattered its rays through the trees almost reminded her of the slow rhythm of a fugue. You could feel the power breaking through as its melodies blended together. Even so, the bent rays of the sun. In another time and place, she would have loved to lie in the grass beside Riyad and whisper about life.

Instead, the narrow tree line she walked in stood as the last remnant of the once-beautiful hillside their mages had leveled for the camps. Over the ridge, mass graves awaited the fallen soldiers. Who knew how many in Inlaru had already starved because of the siege? All this because another nation insisted on spreading its religious cult by force.

The shift from the white tents of the upper nobility to the golden ones of the mages signaled her arrival. She ducked into the medical tent. A dense maze of operating tables filled the spacious area. Several smaller tents jutted out from it to form small rooms. She passed a violinist and trumpeter playing next to a man with a severed arm. From the looks of it, they sought to reattach it.

She'd be better prepared to face General Mahd if she could "talk" to her comatose husband first. Kalina wound her way around the operating tables toward the far side tent where he lay.

She had almost got there when Mahd marched right through the other entrance of the main tent.

The gaunt general's bushy white mustache looked tense enough to win a battle with a porcupine when his eyes lit upon her. "Commander Kalina." His tone oozed everything about his current state of mind.

He's going to discharge me.

"General Mahd." She fumbled a salute. "We did break through the southern battalions."

His eyes flashed. "We're not getting into that now. Come with me." He spun on his heel and left the tent.

He always *had* been a man of few words. But did he not want to get into this *here*? Or did he not want to get into this *now*? Kalina's stomach roiled as she strode after him. She caught up about a dozen paces out. He was making a beeline for the command tent.

"I should have never listened to your plan in the first place," he said.

"It would have worked if the cavalry had shown up."

"And that's why I should have never approved your cavalry scheme. They're useless troops who don't know how to hear orders correctly. Which is why we should have stuck to proven tactics. If the Ternion had wanted this to work, it would have caused it to work."

The failure had all been due to miscommunication? She opened her mouth to try to keep the blame pinned on Mahd. *But that sometimes happens on the battlefield. Chaos undoes our best plans.* Her original words died in her mouth.

"General Mahd," she finally said. "If we try this again with a clearer understanding, it *will work.* Of course cavalry are useless against pikemen. But they *should* have what it takes to slice through gun cavalry."

"And look where this plan led us." His lip curled. "Riyad should have been the one who survived."

Color rose to her cheeks. "What?"

"You heard me right. He would have taken out those cavalry."

Kalina winced. They'd *never* successfully taken down more than a few cavalry. But...Riyad *had* always been better than she had.

"I should give you a dishonorable discharge for manipulating me," Mahd said. "Of course, you'd lose the pay that's covering medical care for Riyad, and I'd like to see that man live. But maybe that's what you get for tricking me into changing tactics. An eye for an eye."

She froze. That made no sense. She had not manipulated him. *But if he wants a scapegoat...*

Mahd stood at the crimson command tent now. "Now stop trembling like I'm some Kaldian who wants to kill your husband. He's in there."

"Who?"

"The man who came here today asking for you. I haven't told him about your failure. Be smart and maybe I'll keep that to myself. I'll have some words with you later." And with that, he turned on his heel and stalked off.

Kalina dug a fingernail into her thumb as she watched Mahd leave. He had definitely threatened Riyad's life, no matter how much he denied it.

But he…wasn't discharging her immediately? And who wanted to talk? Mahd might act like he was doing her a favor by leading her here, but she'd sooner trust a weather prediction.

The Ternion's grace be with me.

She slowly pushed through the curtain.

A great wooden table filled the large circular tent. A trumpeter had molded the table into the topography of the surrounding terrain. Little figurines and objects symbolized the various troops. During prebattle exercises, officials crowded the tent to review plans.

Now, one older man sat by himself on a stool opposite her.

He had a broad chin and unwaveringly bright eyes. He stood and smiled. She hadn't seen teeth so pristine and white in a while. *Certainly not something soldiers have.* But as he walked toward her, his eyes seemed to sparkle with joy.

"Commander Kalina, I'm so glad to meet you." Both his hands wrapped around her right one.

His giddiness unsettled her. "Thank you. And you are…?"

"My name is Bren. Head Mage Bren of Chintor Academy, the finest school in the nation."

Chintor Academy. Neither Riyad nor Kalina had even tried to get one of its coveted spots, electing for Baylin Academy as the more realistic option. Why had their Head Mage come *here*, of all places?

He laughed the kind laugh that spoke of amusement and perhaps a hint of an apology. "I take it you didn't expect a visit."

This was too jarring. "Forgive me, Head Mage. I'm sure I ought to follow customs here, but today's battle won't stop replaying in my head." *That and Mahd's threats.* "Can I help you?"

The man nodded. "Please don't apologize. I admire the work you're doing here. I have heard a lot about you."

From whom? Kalina eyed Bren closely. "Okay?"

"As you know, because of the premier education we offer, Chintor Academy has had the distinct privilege of training your general's son these past five years—the boy chosen by the elven prophet to save our country from the brink of disaster."

"Yes, Mahd may have mentioned the prophecy on occasion." She could recite it.

Emil, son of Mahd. Your choices will shape the course of this nation. For in the days of your time on earth, a great force will rise up against this nation and against the Ternion that no man will be able to vanquish. But the Ternion shall gift you with fantastic artistry with the Fabric to bend the world to your will. On the great day when you enter the battlefield, whether your nation rises or falls will depend on your mastery of war.

Depending on whom you asked, it was either the most comforting or the most terrifying prophecy in the world. Comforting because it meant they could still win. Terrifying because the prophecy suggested they *could* fail if he wasn't good enough. Perhaps that's why the Divine Council sent their prophet to them. As a warning.

Bren continued. "This is Emil's last year at school, and if he's going to save our nation, we need to provide him with the best training possible. And so I came here to see if you would consider joining our school to tutor him, along with his classmates."

Kalina's head spun. She put a hand on the table. "Does General Mahd know why you're here?"

The Head Mage nodded. "I spoke with him an hour or two ago, and he approved my proposal."

Was this Mahd's attempt to get rid of her? But that meant training his *son.*

She laughed without meaning to. "I'm sorry, but you should know that after an accident, I can't work magic anymore." She raised her hands. "I'm afraid I wouldn't be a helpful teacher."

Bren nodded and sat on the chair next to the table. "I heard about the instrument breakage." His gaze softened. "And I'm so sorry to hear about what happened to you, and especially your husband. You have shown incredible resilience. I'm sure you're not thrilled that I only know about you because of your accident. But I do know there's a lot more to you than what you've suffered."

Kalina stepped back, caught off guard by what Bren had said. "Thank... thank you?"

"I'm not here because of your injury," he continued. "I'm here because I also heard stories about what you've done as a commander. It doesn't matter whether you can work magic or not. You have the experience and skills that I know would make you an excellent teacher."

"I...I mean, I don't have any experience teaching magic." Kalina glanced toward the figures lining the topographical map. *I only know how to fight these days.* A minor tune wove through her mind.

"Your husband could teach."

She furrowed her brow. "The ability to teach isn't passed from husband to wife."

Bren chuckled. "Of course not. But you'd have some idea about what to expect. You already have far more practical battlefield experience than any of our other teachers."

"You do know I graduated nine years ago, right? I'm not even thirty."

"We've hired younger teachers before."

"What would you even want me to teach?" Not that she wanted to take this job.

"A violin magic class for our Year Threes, a battlefield tactics class for our Year Sixes, and some solo lessons for a few of our Year Sixes, including Emil."

Kalina thought about the prospect of teaching a bunch of Year Three students how to coax magic out of a violin. It sounded terrifying.

And that wasn't even considering the prophesied hero she'd need to train.

Kalina turned from the war table toward Bren. "I'm sorry. I don't think I'm cut out for that kind of work. If you're looking for mages with battlefield experience, though, there's a couple other people who may—"

"Wait." Bren stood again. "Forgive me, Kalina. I know we don't have a relationship yet, but I want to challenge your decision."

She blinked. "I'm sorry?"

"Let me lay my cards on the table. We're on track to losing this war now that Arditen is gone. The generals in the south lose ground every month. And Inlaru doesn't have much time either. Mages have used magic the same way for centuries, and our prophesied hero needs to innovate. Ever since I began looking, you're the only person I have found who has done so on the battlefield."

Kalina's heart beat faster than their drums when they were summoning flames. "You know about what my husband and I tried to do?"

Bren nodded. "You pushed the boundaries of magic further than anyone else living. And while I know our nation doesn't like change, that's what Emil needs. I've been a Head Mage for twenty years; I know what kind of person we can shape into an excellent teacher."

She cocked her head. *How can he know that?* But his earnestness was genuine.

"Come, and we'll give you everything you need to succeed," Bren said.

"Your in-laws Raz and Chineya have already agreed to provide lodging for you both. They'll take care of your husband while you're gone. And we have a committed team of mage healers to help keep him stable as well. Because we're committed to making this work."

She had forgotten that Riyad's sister and her family lived in Chintor. She hadn't seen them in years. But she remembered them as good people.

"The Ternion works in strange ways," Bren said.

Guess I didn't do a good job of hiding my surprise. She opened her mouth to again express concern. Then her gaze caught on General Mahd's banners hanging behind Bren.

"I'll have some words with you later."

Her days as a commander were over. But she couldn't stand on the sidelines. A memory danced into her mind. Those days of walking into that small kitchen with the chipped clay walls and seeing Riyad grinning at the table with the eggs he'd fried for the two of them. She had a reason to fight.

You're not qualified.

That thought rammed through the memory. Because she knew Bren was flattering her. But who else in this country would teach this prophesied boy how to innovate on the battlefield? Only this inventor-turned-commander had successfully done so.

She'd seen how many graves they'd dug when commanders wouldn't change.

Kalina spoke before she could second-guess herself. "I'm in."

3

SHE STILL COULDN'T BELIEVE
the speed of her decision.

Kalina wasn't a cautious researcher anymore. She'd learned to think with the quickness and decisiveness of a commander. Especially when her husband's future lay on the line. And so here she was, committed to teaching students for the next year.

Despite the night that had descended over the camp, the tent's ceiling glowed above her. Candlelight reflected softly off the pooling wax beneath it. And shadows danced across the overgrown beard covering her husband's face. She kept her cold hand in his as she knelt beside the bed, watching the air whisper in and out of his half-open mouth. She traced her thumb in circles around the back of his hand.

"I don't know," Kalina murmured. "Is this bad of me? I should have said no since I don't have much talent on this front. But I can't leave your life in the hands of fate."

She studied his face. If only it could show her his thoughts. Some mages thought comatose patients could still hear people. She clung to that claim whenever people asked her why she came to talk to him every morning and evening. Otherwise, she needed to explain to the soldiers why she needed him daily when they'd left their families behind. And she'd rather not have that conversation.

"You should have been the one who survived." Her voice choked, and she tightened her hand around his. "You were the teacher always encouraging students, inspiring them, and making an impact. I just played around with making lightning-based artificial lights in a guild. And I know what you would say: We adjusted to life on the battlefield, so of course I can learn this too...but it's easier to kill Kaldians than to connect with kids." Pressure built up within her chest. "You should have taught Mahd's son."

She stared at the ground. Getting along with other kids had never been her strong suit as a student. She had some weird habits, and her retorts weren't quick enough. Riyad had always told her that teaching was built on relationships. But if she had trouble building those as a kid, how could she do so as an adult?

Kalina's stomach churned. *Why did I agree to this?*

"I...I can't lose you," she whispered. "We're losing this war, and I try not to say that publicly, but everyone knows it, Riyad." Wind whistled overhead. She rested her head against his forearm. "All my hopes depend on this boy."

Rizade didn't have a tradition of cultivating expert mage healers. They had healers who could feed Riyad and keep his muscles from atrophying. But specializing had been Arditen's tradition. After the explosion, she had pulled every string possible to get one of the elite Arditen mage healers to cure him. But they had all gone to their besieged capital city. And after the Kaldians ran over Arditen's capital and conquered them four months ago...

She had spent weeks begging others to pray that the Ternion had let at least one of them escape. Then she learned that the Kaldians had conscripted them all. The only way to revive her husband was to beat them so they could free those enslaved mages.

And so, here she was. Becoming a teacher at the best mage school in the nation. *Flattery and stupid hopes have gotten the better of me.*

But Head Mage Bren's endorsement had to mean something, right?

And she knew what Riyad would tell her if he could speak.

"You're so much more than you think you are, human. And if the Ternion has put something in front of you, it's a sign that it wants you to take it."

"Human" had been his favorite nickname for her ever since their childhood days when he'd played an elf in their mock fights. And then later, a way to remind her that she couldn't do everything. *He always believed in me.*

Well, she had taken an opportunity now.

Let's hope I don't regret it.

Light rain fell around the camp. *A welcome relief for the dry season.* Kalina maneuvered around the healer's tent while a couple of soldiers carried her husband's stretcher outside. A flutist had already fed him that morning by using her magic to direct soup down his throat. Now, the one side of his mouth was turned up in that classic grin of his.

Even in a coma, you still know how to smirk, huh?

She'd have to make sure she mentioned that to him whenever he awoke.

Men with crates and belongings trudged around trying to prepare the whole camp for departure in the midst of the rain. Turned out Kalina wasn't leaving alone. The entire army was retreating.

She could see the hopelessness written on the brown faces of the soldiers who walked by.

A large crate floated through the air nearby as a lute strummed in the distance. Toward the end of the cleared plateau, pillars of earth rose out of the ground and resettled. The trumpeters were creating sinkholes and other weaknesses that would trap the Kaldians if they tried to make a camp here.

Kalina walked past the rickety outpost towering over the retreating camp. Colored lights blinked from above as the drummers in the outpost sent coded messages toward the next outposts in the Light Network.

Ahead, Commander Kay exchanged words with Padini. His head jutted forward in his trademark stare as they talked.

The moment Kay noticed her, he said one last word to Padini and then jogged over. "So, he did it. Mahd found a way to get rid of you."

"Wish I could tell you otherwise. But I guess my 'obnoxious optimism' only works some of the time." Kalina shook her head. "I'm sorry about whatever lapdog Mahd replaces me with."

Kay's lip curled. Rain dripped from the ends of his hair. "It wasn't your decision. At least you have a good job. I may not be a mage, but I've certainly heard of Chintor's reputation."

"Who hasn't?" Padini's family had paid a year's salary as a bribe to get her into Chintor Academy.

Kay glanced at some men walking by with a folded tent. "I can't believe this. Look at us. We're retreating from a winnable battle—and Mahd is sacking the best mage commander we've had." He shook his head. "I can't believe he wants you to tutor his son."

She choked back a laugh. "You're telling me."

"And you *know* how puffed up Mahd can get about his son. I would love to know what hearing that kind of propaganda day in and day out does to a kid. You know why I think this Head Mage wants you?"

"Why?"

"Because he knows this boy is as incompetent as his father. And because he's this prophesied hero or whatever, no one knows what to do with that. Just like no one knows what to do with an incompetent general who keeps the king's favor because of who his son is."

Kay still didn't get it. Mahd didn't need the prophecy. Rizade had boasted about its six-hundred-year ruling dynasty and the permanence of their appointees too long to revoke someone's position for anything less than treachery.

There is a reason one of our best-sung heroes of legend is a man who obeyed a corrupt general for years without objecting because he patiently waited for the Ternion to stop the general's evil. Kalina found the legend disturbing. Yet this was Rizadian culture.

She shrugged in response. "Maybe he'll improve. I mean, he did manage to win that border battle a few months ago."

Kay laughed. "Right. The one win that he's trumpeted at least a dozen times as proof that last war's tactics still work." He scratched his chin. "Well, your command will be missed. Teach that son of Mahd about real battles."

"I'll try."

Kay moved on, following the rest of the troops. She ignored the worry worming its way around her chest.

Another retreat of shame and humiliation. Kalina stepped aside to dodge another large crate floating through the air.

Like it or not, Mahd's son was their only chance of reversing these constant retreats.

4

"THOSE KALDIANS? YEAH, WE'LL
teach them what real magic looks like." Riyad grinned.

Kalina walked in the land of dreams and replayed memories. But who cared if this wasn't real? She would relish reliving the last hour with her husband.

"I think you mean I'll *teach them something." Kalina grinned while she finished tuning her cello. "Or have you changed your mind about using your magic to help me today?"*

Riyad strummed a chord on his lute. "So that's how you treat my musical assistance, is it?" A soft wind ruffled his beard. "It's all about who gets the glory?"

"Oh, obviously. Who cares if this helps us beat the Kaldians so long as it gives me the fame we've always known I deserve?" She flashed a smile at him.

"Goodness. You're as bad as my students."

"Only because I want to keep you humble." She blew a kiss at him. "That's how this works!"

"I don't remember that part of our marriage vows, human."

"Guess you have a poor memory then, fellow human." *Kalina ran her bow across the mahogany cello. Pure pitch sang through the air.*

Riyad looked up. "The drummers gave the signal. We should begin Quelling."

She ran her bow across the cello once more. "Ready to show them why we'll win?"

Riyad chuckled. "Let's not get ahead of ourselves. We haven't finessed our trick yet."

"No, but it's not long until we do—and then their Quelling won't stop the two of us." She concentrated on the enemy across the battlefield. "Maybe we'll even do it today."

Riyad smiled. "It's good to see you so optimistic again."

"Can't be moody forever. I can tell today has good things in store."

Famous last words.

"And there's Chintor!"

Kalina shifted, head still groggy, as the cart bumped and shook over each rock in the road. *Already?* She could have relived that memory a few more times.

She sat up and tried to get her bearings.

The town lay ahead. Unlike most cities that boasted careful planning and geometrical buildings, the town of Chintor looked like a bunch of ramshackle buildings half nested on top of each other and squeezed between the Valan River and the high cliffs of the Deep Jungle. It reminded her of living on top of a couple dozen girls in her old, crowded dormitory.

Rather fitting that my return to school would mean living in a place like this.

Rice paddies covered the plains across the river. Nearby, a flutist played a melody pulling a stream of water out of the river and splitting it into smaller streams that snaked through the air to the various paddies. Sunlight bounced off the floating streams. The farthest paddy she watered had to be half a mile away from her. Impressive. Most mages didn't have that kind of distance control.

"It's a beauty, isn't it?" Head Mage Bren gestured at the city. "I know you'll love it here." He smiled broadly, his ivory teeth glistening in the daylight.

Kalina glanced back at the overgrown city ahead of them. *Maybe.* She had expected a more impressive city, given Chintor's reputation. But she chose a polite response.

"It reminds me of my old school days."

She didn't mention how much she'd hated school.

"We can do better than what Baylin Academy offered," Bren said. He gestured to the cliffs. "Chintor Academy sits up there."

Trees and undergrowth covered the rocky face of the hundred-foot cliffs, like a wall vanquished by mold. A trail snaked its way back and forth up the green face.

"It's in the Deep Jungle?"

"There's a cleared plateau. Students aren't allowed to enter the Deep Jungle without supervision. Of course, that doesn't mean they obey." He winked at her. "You know how kids are."

I do indeed know how petty and rebellious children can be. Kalina eyed the walls atop the cliffs. "Was it originally a fort?" The cart lumbered on, passing the flutist and a nearby stream of water running through the air.

Bren nodded. "It still can be. But the school can't fit the whole town anymore."

So if the Kaldians come here, we can only protect the students.

"Don't worry," Bren said. "Here at Chintor Academy, we don't let people fall by the wayside. If war ever comes, we'll protect them. No matter what."

She frowned. Perhaps. But three years of war had taught her sentiments often failed after the first ten minutes.

She glanced at the plodding zeletor pulling their cart. The scales of the elephant-sized lizard glinted in the light of the noonday sun. Beyond it, three other travelers strode ahead of them on the bridge. The middle traveler's hands were bound behind him. His companions on either side carried a trumpet and lute on their respective backs.

The unbound travelers turned as they approached. "Head Mage Bren," the lute player said. "Welcome back to Chintor!"

Bren nodded. "What happened here?"

"Unauthorized use of magic." The lutist clapped his hand on the back of the bound traveler. "Says he has papers from another district. But he doesn't have a license to play music here. So someone's going to stand trial next week."

"I was repairing a local wall," the bound man grumbled.

Kalina shook her head. A mage could easily obtain a license in a district if they already had a license in another one and had a legitimate reason to practice magic elsewhere. Skipping that step signified ill intentions.

And she knew as much as anyone how dangerous magic could be in the hands of the wrong musicians.

The zeletor wouldn't fit in the crowded city, so they left the beast at the stables by the bridge. Two of the stable boys carried Riyad's stretcher into the city—levitating it with magic wasn't smart when crowds could jostle a mage and cause him to drop his rhythm. Bren led the way and Kalina took up the back—she couldn't let her husband out of her sight while these two teens carried him around. She felt every time the crowds bumped his stretcher in the narrow streets. And that didn't even get into her own lack of personal space. She was stuck *here* for the next year? *I might not be a complete claustrophobe, but the academy better offer more space than this town.*

Bren stopped at the entrance to one of the walled courtyards dominating the northern part of the city. Small for a walled courtyard. But this was Chintor.

I should lead the way. Kalina squeezed between the moving crowd and her husband's stretcher to reach the door and hit the metal ringer against the stone wall.

The doors burst open and her sister-in-law swooped her into her arms.

"Oh, Kalina," Chineya said. "I'm so happy to see you. My heart aches for both of you. But you're here now." Kalina blinked, a bit surprised by how elegant the colorful patterns on Chineya's tunic were. Artisan families didn't normally own rich clothing like that. But Chineya's husband *did* design clothing for nobles.

Chineya looked past her shoulder and waved toward the others. "Come on in! Don't stand out there in the street."

She stepped to the side to allow the others to come in as she put both hands on Kalina's shoulders. Her cheeks lifted into that ever-present smile of hers. "You all need something to eat after your journey." She spun to the two stable boys. "Take my brother through the door in the right corner." She gestured toward one side of the U-shaped house. "I'll have a feast ready once you're back."

"Oh," the one said. "We're not a part of them. We're from the stables."

She waved. "There's stew for half the village here. You take my brother to his room, and I'll make sure you have proper food in your bellies before you go back to work."

As they left, she turned back to Kalina. "It looks like my brother showed those human-sacrificers what kind of a man he was."

Kalina raised an eyebrow. "I'm not sure what you mean."

She laughed. "You know Riyad. Always willing to sacrifice and take burdens on himself no matter how much it hurt. Don't you think he'd feel proud about this?"

Kalina's heart rose as she watched Riyad carried off. Yes, that *was* her husband. He had always feared death less than her.

Of course, the death I'd feared the most hadn't been my own. And she knew what had put him in this vulnerable position.

Chineya's eyes softened, and she put a hand on her shoulder. "And you know he wouldn't have blamed you."

Kalina didn't say much as they made their way through the crowded streets after her sister-in-law's bountiful meal. Head Mage Bren didn't seem to mind. Perhaps he was still trying to digest all the food Chineya had stuffed them with before they left. It gave her time to roll over the same question again and again in her mind.

How did she know?

Kalina would have sworn she hadn't told anyone what she really felt about Riyad's coma. Sure, she'd cried with Riyad about this several times, but did he count in his current state? She hadn't even seen Chineya in over a year. *But she knew.* She had looked Kalina in the eyes and known the guilt she felt.

Chineya had a point. Kalina hadn't shot the klyte arrow that broke her cello into splinters.

But if I had only spotted the archer or stood a little farther from Riyad— as I should have—maybe this wouldn't have happened.

Truth was, unlike her husband, who had a track record of putting himself on the line for others, her life had been the opposite. She always got away unscathed while others suffered because of her inaction.

Just like when I knew what Qel did to my sister, and—

Kalina shook her head. She couldn't finish that thought. Riyad had told her further introspection about that wouldn't be helpful.

But she had to wonder who she was to think she could prepare a prophesied hero.

"Here we are," Bren said.

The cliffs towered high above them. Kalina swallowed. Bren wanted to introduce her to the school, but she was most interested in meeting the teachers. She wasn't a fool. Bren would only have traveled to recruit her if there was something wrong.

"There's a winding path you can take up to the academy." Bren gestured to their left. "But, of course, if you're with a lutist, there's a faster way."

He stepped onto a wooden platform lying beside the cliffs. Kalina joined him as he grabbed his lute from his back and began to pluck it. The wooden platform shuddered and then ascended as Bren telekinetically controlled it.

Her foot tapped against the platform in alignment with Bren's playing. *The problems better be with Emil, not his teachers.* She needed people she could trust for the challenges she'd inevitably face as a first-time teacher.

They reached the top and Bren settled the platform gently on the short wall overlooking the academy. She gingerly stepped off and raised her gaze to the surrounding campus.

Five large, stately buildings formed a U around an expansive lawn that appeared to fit the dimensions of a golden rectangle. They were all made of seamless stone, no doubt formed by some mage centuries ago. Two golden-rectangle-shaped buildings stood on either side, and a much longer building loomed across the courtyard.

Tall pillars lined the front of the central building with a large dome cresting the center. Architectural sculptures of the Divine Council adorned the sides of the building. It looked like the size of two golden rectangles attached widthwise. *Perfectly proportioned, as great buildings should be.* Seeing traditional geometrical Rizadian buildings again felt refreshing after spending so much time in Arditen on military expeditions with their unproportioned buildings.

And it certainly wasn't as crowded as the city below.

They walked down the stairs of the wall onto the central green. Her body relaxed now that she wasn't being constantly jostled. The noise of conversation and laughter wafted from the side buildings. She guessed they were dorms. Perhaps the one directly ahead housed the classrooms? To the left, past the dorms, were large square depressions that teachers used when training students to practice magic, similar to Baylin Academy. Of course, this place boasted a *lot* more grandeur and geometrical symmetry. Unlike the city below, this seemed fitting for a school with Chintor's reputation.

Keep your head. Kalina straightened her posture and adopted a more confident gait as they strolled across the lawn. The kids would eat her alive if she showed an ounce of fear or unease. And she wasn't an unpopular schoolgirl anymore. She mowed down Kaldian soldiers.

Kalina suddenly realized Bren was talking to her.

"...as a result, we unfortunately can't offer you much training before you start teaching," he said. "We're going to trust you to start off as best you can, and we'll offer training on the way."

No training? She bit back the shock. "You don't think I need that?"

Bren chuckled. "In teaching, you learn a lot on the job. We don't expect you to be a perfect teacher. We just need someone with experience. Even if it leads to a messy first week or month, your experience in war strategies and musical techniques will take you a long way."

So she had to figure this out by herself?

Great.

The uneasy feeling in the bottom of her stomach was growing. *The teachers here had better be the allies I need them to be.*

They walked through the towering pillars into the central academic building. Halls stretched to the sides in both directions. The floor was *tiled*—and it even formed a large fancy geometrical design of encircled triangles and hexagons in the middle of the vestibule.

Sometimes Kalina wished Rizade's architectural tastes were different. Arditen's floral designs held more beauty than their geometrical infatuation.

Bren put a hand on her shoulder. "Don't worry, Kalina. I know this may feel like a lot. But I also know you're able to deliver. And together, we *will* make a difference at this school for so many students...especially Emil."

Were her emotions written across her face today? Because that's what it felt like.

But she smiled and nodded as they turned left to the hallway.

"While you're here, I wanted to introduce you to your fellow teachers," Bren said. "I've put a lot of work into gathering the best teachers in the nation. And I think you'll like them a lot."

"Yes!" Her eager voice slipped out without conscious thought. "I would love to meet them."

If I can only make sure I remember their names…

"Elder Umar's office is closest to us," Bren said, turning to the left. "Let's see if he's in."

He pushed past the mauve curtain hanging in the doorway to reveal a closet-sized room with a miscellaneous assortment of jars, instrument parts, and tools scattered around the desk. The wrinkled man working on a disassembled trumpet by the window turned around to look at them.

"Is this the new teacher?" he asked. A smile spread across his face as he stepped toward them. She felt a note of gentle kindness in the way he shook her hand. "It's great to meet you."

She fumbled for the right words to say. "It's a pleasure to meet you as well, Elder Umar."

"Elder Umar has taught at this school longer than anyone," Bren said. "Forty-two years and counting; isn't that right?"

Umar chuckled. "I lost track a long time ago." He slowly sat in his chair. "I can tell you this job doesn't get easy. But it doesn't get any less rewarding either." He looked up at her and smiled. "I know the first year will feel impossible. But keep pressing on. The second year gets better, and you aren't as bad that first year as you think you'll be."

Unfortunately, she only had one year with Emil, so she had to make this first year count. But she appreciated the welcome. "Thanks, Elder Umar." He seemed promising as a coworker.

After a few polite exchanges, they left for the next room. Bren pushed past the curtain to enter another closet-sized room. Bookcases with sagging shelves and chipped edges lined the walls. Stacks of books and papers leaned precariously on the desk in front of them. A gray-haired woman with wrinkles under her eyes glanced up from behind the desk, candlelight glinting off her nose ring.

"Elder Jadoni," Bren said. "It's so good to see you. I'd love to introduce you to the newest member of the Chintor family."

"Ah." Her gaze flicked back to her book. "Yet another teacher young enough to be my granddaughter. Have you taught before?"

That's one way to greet someone.

"I'm afraid not," Kalina said. "I served as a commander on the front lines up until a few days ago."

"Oh. Wonderful." Sarcasm dripped from her tongue. She stood, keeping a hand on her chair, and scanned the bookcase behind her. "We're doing this again."

She wrested a book from the shelf and handed it to Kalina. Their gaze met.

"I've read every book on teaching magic out there, and this outdoes the others. Obscure, but excellent. Please return it in four weeks. And don't screw up."

Kalina hesitantly accepted the ancient-looking tome from Jadoni's equally ancient-looking bony hands with skin bleached the pale yellow of age. Jadoni sat down again, and her gaze dropped back to the book.

"Th-thank you?" Kalina said. *Jadoni clearly lacks faith in me.*

"Thanks, Elder Jadoni." Joy breathed through Bren's voice and he beamed. "We love the work you do here."

As he left, Kalina tucked the tome under her arm and followed. *So Jadoni is crotchety and doesn't like incompetence. Probably won't be an easy colleague.* She'd need to decide if she wanted to try to read the book or give it back to Jadoni tomorrow so she didn't forget her deadline.

"She's such an amazing teacher," Bren said as they walked down the hall. "I don't get to attend her lectures much, but I've never seen anyone better at teaching the lute. So welcoming as well."

Kalina nearly choked. "I'm sorry?"

"That book." Yet again, a smile broke through his lips. "How kind of her to think about that."

She eyed Bren. Had he not seen the crone's disdain for her, or was he ignoring it?

Before she had the chance to think about that too much, though, he pushed open another curtain to another room. Here, large stacks of books littered the floor, and the clear desk only had three opened books on it.

A bearded man with unkempt hair and piercing green eyes looked up as they entered. He didn't look much older than Kalina.

"Ah? And is this the new teacher?" He stood and reached out a hand. "Elder Mito. Pleased to meet you." A drawl extended his words.

"Elder Kalina," she said as she shook his hand. That *elder* part rolled strangely off her tongue. She didn't feel like she deserved the title. But she was a teacher now, and she had to own it.

"Elder Mito exudes brilliance like a prophet," Bren said. "An exceptional student of war strategy as well. You two should talk sometime."

The left corner of Mito's mouth tilted strangely as he looked at her. "You're from the front lines, aren't you?"

"I am."

He nodded slowly. "Interesting...I've always wanted to talk to an actual battle strategist. I have a lot of thoughts on the whole subject. Still haven't figured out how we're losing to a ragtag nation who wants to make everyone worship their god."

Kalina eyed him quizzically. "I mean, I could tell you the reason. For centuries, the art of war has relied on mages who can block any projectile weapon if they're skilled enough. Now, that's no longer true with Kaldia's imported guns. And we haven't found a way to stop them yet—or obtain our own source of gunpowder."

"Hmm." He studied her carefully. "Is that so? I don't have personal experience on the field, but..." He shrugged. "I don't know. It seems like an easy answer to fall back on. Why fight courageously if we can blame our losses on technology? The Ternion forbid that our country admit we need brave mages. Good thing we have a prophesied boy to save our hides."

Kalina tried not to recoil. Who did this man think he was? The Ternion knew how many mistakes General Mahd had made. But their mages had no short supply of courage.

"Well, I'm sure you'll have some great conversations later," Bren said as he put a hand on her shoulder. "It's good to talk with you, Elder Mito."

He smiled. "And you, Head Mage Bren. Pleasure to meet you, Elder Kalina."

Is it, though? She mumbled some polite response as they turned to leave the room. Jadoni hated her lack of experience, and Mito blamed her for losing the war. Umar seemed nice, but these other two didn't seem like pleasant colleagues.

The other teachers had their own eccentricities. There was Suraya—who looked about her age, had an obsessively organized room, and seemed annoyed that they'd interrupted her from work. And there was Ashinara—who seemed exuberant to see her. A bit too happy, perhaps, since she asked *so* many personal questions about her husband and already seemed intent on becoming close friends. *She'll be a handful.* Umar seemed the best of the lot.

The other teachers weren't there that afternoon. Which left her standing with Bren in the hall after she managed to peel herself away from Ashinara.

"I can't imagine a better faculty," Bren said. "And every year we lose someone, we always manage to replace them with someone better. It's such a blessing to have you helping us make this the best academy in Rizade."

He couldn't imagine a better faculty? Kalina had only been here for an hour and she already knew that, except for Umar, there was something dysfunctional about the teachers. None of the teachers at her school growing up had seemed this...eccentric. Or uninterested in their Head Mage. Maybe teachers looked like this "on the other side of the curtain." But she'd expected more from an academy with Chintor's reputation.

She couldn't figure out why Bren overlooked that. Unless he, like her, tended to put a smiling face over all the world's problems.

Either way, it had confirmed her fears: She wasn't just brought here because Emil was a difficult student. Something more was going on beneath the surface. Even if Bren wasn't ready to talk about that.

But Kalina smiled. "I look forward to teaching here with the rest of you," she lied.

"Is there anything I can do to help this transition?"

She thought for a moment. "A cello would be nice."

"A cello?"

"I can't work magic with it, obviously. But I did retrain my fingers to play music for a reason." Nothing quite lived up to the deep, reverberating sounds of a finely tuned cello. "I'd rather not lug mine up the cliff each day."

Bren smiled. "Well, I think we can find that for you. Anything else?"

"I'm sure there will be. There's a lot I'll need to do in the next week to get ready to teach. But maybe I'll know tomorrow exactly what I need."

Bren cocked his head. "I'm sorry, did you not catch what I said earlier?"

"Um...maybe not?" She hadn't been listening well while stressing about where the school's dysfunctions came from.

"I had mentioned this when we were walking up to this building, but the temporary substitute we hired to fill this position at the start of school last month quit yesterday. That's why we don't have time to give you training. You need to start tomorrow."

5

K ALINA HAD SWORN AFTER
graduating she would never again pull an all-nighter.

And yet here she stood on her first day as a teacher with bloodshot eyes. *If only Riyad could see me now. He'd probably crack some joke about how I'm cursed to always find jobs that require me to get up before dawn.*

Kalina surveyed the room of fifty wooden seats placed in a semicircular auditorium arrangement. Light streamed through the wide-open windows behind her and glistened off the shining tiles and decorative pillars. So her students would be blinded every morning. *Won't they enjoy that?* As the introductory Year Three Magic Integration Class, they'd spend most days outside once they began practicing the art of strings. But right now, they needed to review the basics of the craft. Both because she didn't know what they knew and because she hadn't had time overnight to figure out how to manage training twelve students at once.

My students will eat me alive. Not like the salvation of this country and the life of my husband depend on my ability to do this job well, right?

She shook her head. *Stay focused—you have more pressing matters at hand. Like how to greet the students as they come in.* Ashinara had tried to persuade her yesterday that she should hug each of them every day they came into class. But that sounded weird.

Kalina settled for sitting on the high stool at the front of the room and greeting them all together.

At five minutes to the hour, the first few students began to trickle in. They sent a few nervous glances as they took their seats. She tried to smile back. Today would be awkward, and they had to deal with it as best they could. She remembered all the stories Riyad had told her about what students did the moment they learned which teachers tolerated mischief. *If I show weakness, they'll pounce.*

At least she didn't have the pressure of dealing with this "chosen one" in her first class. That lovely challenge wouldn't present itself until the afternoon.

Finally, all the wide-eyed Year Three students sat in front of her in their tan tunics and black trousers. Only the wide, colorful sashes encircling the girls' waists added variance to their dress. The sash designs suggested that most of them came from rich families. No surprise there. Most farmers and artisans didn't have the funds to send their children to mage school. And while schools claimed to only test students' ingenuity when deciding whom they would train, everyone knew the children of magistrates and governors had a leg up.

Especially at Chintor.

She glanced at her desk. The sundial wasn't quite on the hour yet. But she didn't have time to waste.

Kalina cleared her throat. "Welcome to Music Integration Class. My name is Elder Kalina, and I'm going to be your teacher for the rest of the year. We'll practice how to connect the bowed instrument skills you've already learned to the ability to control energy. I know getting a new teacher five weeks into the year presents challenges, but...well, we'll work with it as best we can."

A hand shot up in the front row. *I suppose I should have expected that from a bunch of fourteen-year-olds.*

"Yes?" she asked the boy.

"Is it true you can't do magic yourself?"

Well, there it was, front and center. Kalina held up her hands. "It is."

All the kids stared at her now. Some smirked. Others looked inquisitive.

"I used to." She looked the student in the eye. "I spent four years researching new creative uses of violin magic with the Krazian Inventors

Guild and two years as a battle mage. But I lost my ability when my cello shattered eight months ago, and I've been a commander since."

Another hand shot up. "So you *did* survive your instrument shattering?"

A stab of guilt went through her when she thought of Riyad. But she pushed that aside. "I did."

Any smirks were replaced by looks of shock and awe.

"How did you do that?" This time, the kid didn't even wait for her to call on him. His large eyes widened as he stared at her, looking completely oblivious to everything around him.

If I let this precedent stand…

"Please raise your hand next time." There had to be some distance between a teacher and her students for them to respect her. "But to your question, I don't know how I survived. It must have been the grace of the Ternion. Either way, I'm here to make you the best violinists you can be, and I've talked enough about myself. Let's talk about each of you…"

Turned out, teaching a two-hour class felt as mind-numbing as it did to sit through as a student.

Kalina should have known spending a whole lesson on introductions and review would dull the kids. She still preferred bored and obedient to an animated, chaotic classroom, but she'd hoped to tie fun and obedience together. That, however, required more than a night to prepare.

Right now, she sat at a table in the small teachers' lounge alongside Ashinara and Mito. Sitting with the man who had insinuated Rizadian mages lacked courage wouldn't have been her first choice. But the room only had one table. And so here she sat with the halfway decent stew the cook had made for lunch. It almost reminded her of the signature stew Riyad liked to make during the long days of wet season.

Unlike Riyad, though, this cook doesn't go overboard with the paprika.

"…and he really needs someone to love him," Ashinara said. "He wouldn't act out if he knew he was loved."

Mito rolled his eyes. "He needs someone to hit him over the head with a club." The slow cadence of his voice made him sound bored. "Isn't this your sixth year? Privileged kids like Jacir, who grew up with the mayor of Chintor for a father, don't change unless you come down hard on them.

And besides, the boy already knows he's loved." He smirked. "I ran into him and Meliya last year, and his pants were—"

"Stop that!" Ashinara smacked his hand. "We all know what happened."

Mito side-eyed Kalina. "She doesn't."

"He wouldn't have done that with Meliya if he wasn't trying to fill some void in his life," Ashinara said. "I tell the kids that all the time: Casual intimacies won't give them what they want. If they wait for the special one like I did with Malé, they will be so glad for doing so."

"Yes, I'm *suuuuuure* hearing that will stop Jacir from acting up in class," Mito said as he leaned back in the chair. His drawl continued. "Always works for kids, doesn't it, Elder Kalina?"

"I don't have much experience with this yet." Of course, Kalina knew Mito was right. Even though she didn't know Jacir, Ashinara struck Kalina as one of those teachers who mothered her students too much.

"Ah, right," Mito said. "You just have experience fighting a losing war."

Kalina bristled. *Seriously? That's how he speaks to a colleague?* "I could recommend you to the army if you want to join our mages."

Mito shook his head as he stood. "Nah. My talents would be wasted. Now, if you hear about any commander or general positions opening up, then maybe we could talk." He picked up his bowl of stew and walked out.

Kalina shook her head. Like the king would even consider giving a generalship to someone who wasn't related to a magistrate or governor. She'd gotten lucky with her own commander position. And Mahd wouldn't be repeating that decision.

Ashinara shook her head as well. "You know, I try to give him the benefit of the doubt. I know we all deserve that. But sometimes with Elder Mito..." She shook her head again. "I don't know. He grew up in the same district as you and everything. You grew up in the Metsan District, right?"

A stab went through Kalina. Her family...well, they'd gained a reputation. Publicly accusing a friar of wrongdoing did that. *Does Mito know who I am? Does he believe us?*

"Enough about him." Ashinara put her hand on Kalina's arm. "Today's your first day teaching! How has it been so far?"

"It went fine," Kalina lied. "I mean, I don't know what I'm doing. I've never done this before. But—"

"Oh, I'm sure you're doing fine. I've been teaching for six years and I *still* don't feel like I know what I'm doing." Ashinara laughed. "Do any of us?"

For the sake of the country, Kalina hoped they did.

Early afternoon meant Battlefield Tactics Class. And that meant preparing for her first class with Emil. She should have felt gratitude that she could meet him in a crowd before the pressure of tutoring him one-on-one. That, after all, would be the real test of whether thinking she could train him was presumptuous arrogance or not.

I just want the verdict. Even if she failed, she'd rather know than deal with the question marks.

Battlefield tactics hadn't been a required course when she studied in mage school. She'd specialized in theoretical magic. But ever since the army began drafting all available mages to serve on the front lines, schools had cut the theoretical, engineering, and even medical specialization tracks. Which meant she'd have all the Year Six students in this class. And since it was a two-year course, the students probably knew a bunch of terms she'd never covered. She'd started the textbook last night and counted at least seven.

Ignorance had never felt more reassuring. It showed how limited textbooks were in preparing students for real battles.

The sundial still indicated ten minutes till the start of class when two girls flung open the curtains and walked through the doorway.

"Hi!" one of them said immediately. "Are you Elder Kalina?"

"I am."

"I'm Anvisa." She descended the stairs to the front of the classroom. "And this is Leneya. We're so glad to have you here with us!"

More names to remember. Anvisa had a ponytail and a big grin. Leneya had glasses and looked a bit more bashful. Classic talkative and silent friend pairing?

Kalina smiled. It was nice to have some people glad to see her. "I'm happy to be here as well. You girls got here early."

Anvisa laughed. "Oh, we're *always* early to our classes. But we needed to make sure we were *especially* early to this one to get to meet you. Like, no disrespect intended, but the sub we had for this class didn't know anything. Not that I missed learning new ways to kill people. I wanted to become a doctor before this all started, and I don't know what I feel about killing people on the battlefield, even if they *are* Kaldians. But if I need to do this,

I want to be good at it." She paused. "What about you? Did you find it hard to kill people?"

Kalina blinked.

"Sorry," Anvisa said. "That isn't the best 'welcome the new teacher' question, is it?"

"You're fine." She studied their faces. "Do you want my honest answer?"

Anvisa nodded. "I mean, I didn't mean to ask a question that personal... but yes?" Kalina thought she could see a glint of worry in her eyes.

"I never wanted to join the war. And yes—I did worry about that. To be honest, though..." *Should I tell her the truth?* But they needed to know. "It's disturbingly easy to kill people as a mage. When you're above the battlefield manipulating the Substances...you never see the faces of the people you slaughter. And that's what's disturbing. Because you become comfortable wiping out lives without batting an eye. It's different for soldiers on the front lines. But for mages?" She eyed both of them. "Killing will become as normal as waving at someone. And you'll need to learn how to live with yourself for treating death that way."

Both stared at her with widening eyes. Maybe honesty hadn't been a good idea. But they would have to mow down enemy troops within the year. And Kalina hadn't even mentioned the stress of the battlefield, the agony of losing friends, or the recurring nightmares that left her in cold sweats at least once a week.

"I hadn't thought about that," Anvisa said. "I mean, I guess I should have. But you're the first teacher who's actually fought before. I'm so sorry to hear about your husband, by the way. I should have said that earlier. That must be awful."

Kalina swallowed the lump in her throat. "It is. But you know how you get through it? You save lives. That's our first lesson today, because that's what we do as mages. And I'm going to give you what you need to save as many people as possible."

That sounded a bit more like a traditional teacher, didn't it?

The girls nodded. And then they began asking questions about safer topics like her days as a researcher. Anvisa did most of the talking. But Leneya did jump in a few times. Pretty soon, the room filled with students.

Kalina looked around as Anvisa and Leneya sat down. The whole Year of forty-three students sat in the spacious lecture hall. Which one was Emil?

"Welcome to Battlefield Tactics Year Two," Kalina said. "My name is

Elder Kalina, and I will be your teacher for the rest of this year. I've spent the last three years of my life fighting this war. I won't sugarcoat what it's like. And I'll teach you how to survive it. Because we don't have time for platitudes or useless memorization in this class. This is about defying death."

A couple of the boys in the second row whispered while they glanced at her. *Should I let it go or crack down on it?*

She couldn't let it become a regular occurrence. "Yes?" she asked, looking straight at them. "Is there something you wanted to say to us?"

The trio looked at her wide-eyed while trying to steal glances at each other.

Kalina waited.

The tall kid in the middle elbowed the kid on his left.

"Uh, we were wondering about your time on the battlefield," the kid on the left said.

"Oh?" Kalina kept a matter-of-fact tone. "And what's your name, sir?"

"Jacir." He pulled on his earlobe.

He was the kid Mito and Ashinara had discussed over lunch.

"And what did you want to know, Jacir?"

"I—uh—we were curious about the rumors that your instrument broke on the battlefield."

This question again? "They're true. I can't do magic now either, if that's your follow-up question."

"And you survived it?" The question flew out of the mouth of the tall kid in the middle. He stared at her with what looked like awe.

"I mean, I'm here!" Kalina said. "Do you have a name?"

A titter rushed around the room. *Did I say something wrong?*

The boy blinked and straightened in his seat. "Oh. Yeah; my name's Emil. You might have heard of me?"

Emil. Now that she knew who he was, he did look the part of a boy chosen by prophecy to save the world. Tall, lean, and handsome with that wind-swept brown hair and self-confident grin curving around the sides of his mouth. No more trace of that surprised, abrupt kid.

He was buddies with the class troublemaker?

Interesting.

"Well, Emil, next time you and your friends have a question, you're more than welcome to raise your hand and ask."

His hand shot up.

"Yes?"

"How did you survive it, Elder Kalina?" His gaze drilled into her. It almost reminded her of Kay. But he possessed a certain charisma Kay never had.

"The grace of the Ternion, of course." That's what all the friars said.

"But—but how? That isn't supposed to be possible." He paused. "No disrespect intended, Elder Kalina." He was leaning so far forward, it looked like he might slip off the rickety wooden chair.

Kalina eyed him. *You said you wouldn't lie to them...*

"Honestly? I have no idea. I suspect there's something we don't know about magic that explains how I survived. But your guess is as good as mine. Does it make a difference to you?"

A half laugh burst out of his lips. "Don't you know the prophecy?"

Her gaze narrowed. "What do you mean?"

"My prophecy. The one from the elven prophet Zedin that says I'm destined to save our nation. You *have* heard it, right?"

"Of course I know the prophecy. I don't see the connection."

"I know my dad likes to skip the last line, but I thought the Head Mage would have told it to you."

An uneasiness began to slip around Kalina like a python coiling around her ankles. "What last line?"

"After it says that we'll only win if I'm good enough, it says this: 'And on that day, your instrument shall be broken as a reminder to all that the Ternion raises up and uses whom it chooses.' You know. Killing me." His eyes glistened. "That's who I am. The guy who's going to give up his life and die young to save this country. Because we all know what happens to mages whose instruments break while they're playing them. But you found a way to survive it."

Kalina's heart thudded. Questions she'd wondered about for days finally clicked into place.

Emil cleared his throat. "I...I need to know how you did it."

BOWED STRING MAGIC

Used to control energy

→ People used to think it could only be used for warfare and for _healing_ people. Over the past twenty years, researchers like Elder Kalina have shown it can be used to create artificial lights and other new _inventions_.

→ Healers can easily _hurt_ people with this magic if they're not trained to be _careful_ enough

(Only seek healing from professionals, not other students—no matter how much Anvisa tries to convince me!)

Krem studying
xo

REMINDER TO SELF: Proposal for Year Six Capstone Project due _next_ week.

→ I know you're reading these notes, Anvisa!

6

oAS SOON AS CLASS ENDED, Kalina exited the room and speed walked toward the stairs.

I knew this had been too easy. But she'd persuaded herself that her presumption was justified, and Bren really saw the marks of a good teacher inside of her.

Her cheeks burned. How could she have known that he hired her because she was a casualty?

Bren's office lay at the bottom of the stairs. She brushed past the curtain into the spacious room. Sunlight streamed through the open windows behind his desk and glinted off the white tile floor. Bren was poring over a few pages scattered over his bare desk.

He looked up. "Elder Kalina!" He smiled broadly, and his eyes twinkled. "I had meant to stop by earlier. How has the first day gone?"

She didn't have time for his happy greeting. "When were you planning on telling me the *real* reason you hired me?"

He didn't stop smiling. "I hired you because I knew you'd be a great teacher."

Kalina shook her head. "Emil told me about the full prophecy. If you wanted me to teach him how to save his life, you could have asked, and I would have told you that I have no clue how I survived. It may have been a miracle."

"Do you believe that?" Bren cocked his head.

Kalina exhaled, momentarily derailed by his question. "No—I mean, the Ternion doesn't usually work spontaneous miracles. It's probably some law of magic we don't understand. But that's the point: We don't understand it. I can't save Emil's life."

"Okay..."

"I need to quit. I stammered through both of today's lessons, I don't have a shred of experience, I can't save Emil's life, and you could find plenty of more experienced teachers. You should have told me why you hired me, and I'm sorry I was arrogant enough to take this job. As is, I'm here to resign."

The smile faded from Bren's face. He pushed back from his desk. The chair squealed against the tiled floor. "I don't lie, Kalina," he said gently. "You *will* be a wonderful teacher. Everyone struggles their first day, and I don't believe one hard day makes you an inept teacher."

"You don't understand." Kalina put a hand on the smooth wooden desk. "The elven prophet gave us a *conditional* prophecy. We *need* to win this war." Riyad's classic grin flashed through her mind and deepened the pit in her stomach. "I came to Chintor because I thought you really saw something of a teacher in me. Well, now I know that's *not* why you hired me, and my lessons today prove everything I feared about my abilities. If I'm not the best teacher for Emil, I need to step out of the way so someone else can do it. We can't risk making me the weak link in Emil's training."

The chair creaked as Bren shifted. "You won't be the weak link in Emil's training. I hired you because I saw potential."

"And it's just an accident that you went to the one mage who survived an instrument breakage to train the boy prophesied to die by one?"

"There were *multiple* reasons I offered you this position."

"And I'm sorry, but I won't have any answers for him." Kalina walked to the window and stared out at the green yard and the wall beyond it. "If General Mahd wanted me to save his son, he should have asked me on the battlefield." *Unless he wanted to get rid of me.* "Emil needs a better teacher if we're going to win this war."

"What...what do you know about General Mahd?"

She eyed him and stepped away from the window. He knew something. But she still chose her words carefully. "He makes what he believes are the best decisions. Our king appears to believe the same."

He nodded slowly. "So if I told you that General Mahd might prefer that his son become a martyr sung into legend, would that surprise you?"

What? She stepped back. "He talks about his son all the time."

"And why do you think a general with questionable tactics has had a position of authority for this long?"

She studied Bren's expression. So he knew how Mahd had leveraged his son's prophecy. "You don't think he cares about the life of his son."

"Emil and I have had several long conversations about his family life. I am not a man to speak ill of anyone…but given your survival, I didn't think the general would let me bring you here."

Kalina understood the implications Bren was too polite to spell out.

"Listen." Bren stood and walked over to her. "I understand this is a lot to take in at once. That's why I didn't tell you about the full prophecy. But if we're going to win this war, we may need to assure Emil that we can save his life. Don't get me wrong: Emil *earnestly* wants to do the right thing. But he's also a seventeen-year-old plagued by fear…and he's had some struggles here. He lacks hope—hope to press on to the end. I didn't *just* hire you for that. But that *is* also why we need you." He paused. "You may be the only person who can motivate Emil to fulfill his calling."

Kalina wanted to sit. It felt like one of the massive drums used in war had been strapped onto her back.

"I…I don't know if I'll be able to find an answer."

Bren put a hand on her shoulder. "You just need to try. And you don't need to look for answers now. Get adjusted to teaching first. But once you do start, we'll help you find answers."

If they exist.

"Give it two weeks," Bren continued. "Many teachers struggle during their first week, and I don't want you to make a hasty decision."

Numbness settled in her mind. "I'll think about it."

7

Kalina gripped the mug of steaming tea with both hands and stared past her sister-in-law toward the handmade tapestries adorning the wall. Evening had whispered in long ago and everyone else in the house had fallen asleep. The table candle flickered between them.

"You know, I always wanted a sibling who would stay up late with me," Chineya said. She wove more thread through her handheld loom as she worked on her sash.

Kalina cracked a smile. "Riyad didn't fill that role?"

"What do you think?" Chineya laughed. "I'd rather pull teeth than try to keep him awake after sunset."

"You're telling me." Kalina laughed as she remembered. "I'd fight to help him stay awake in the evenings and he'd drag me out of bed in the mornings."

"Did I ever tell you about the day he learned to hold a conversation in his sleep?"

"So that's where he learned it from." Kalina snorted. "At first, he says he's listening to me with his eyes closed, but then his responses become short and vague, and pretty soon he's responding to me in his sleep; it drove me nuts. Of course..." She looked down at her mug.

"You'll get him back someday," Chineya murmured.

Kalina nodded and blinked away a tear. "Thanks for taking care of him today. And for all the other days you'll be doing this. I know you haven't signed up for an easy task."

"Well, he *is* my brother," Chineya said with a laugh. "And when we restore him to life, I'll have a grand time teasing him about how I'm always taking care of the baby of the family. You do what you need to do to help us beat those Kaldians."

"Right..." Doubts resurfaced like a concerto returning to its main theme. Kalina took a sip of the roasted rice tea to try and calm her thoughts. Its bitter taste felt appropriate.

Chineya took more thread out of her basket. "Is the tea good for you?"

The tea didn't matter. But...

"Sure." She turned her gaze back to the tapestry full of geometrical shapes. "I just can't see how I can stay there in good conscience."

"You're too hard on yourself. I like this Head Mage's advice: Stick it out two weeks. What's the worst that could happen?"

Kalina shook her head. "We have limited time. The Kaldians will take Inlaru soon, and that's the gateway to the rest of this country. Emil could be learning from someone who knows what she's doing."

"Don't you think the Head Mage of *Chintor Academy* knows potential when he sees it?"

"Bren may be a good man...but I think he's pretty dense to the state of the school." She paused. "Chineya, I'm pretty sure half the teachers hate him. Whether it's their body language or the comments I overhear, they don't respect him. I've never worked in a place that had this little regard for authority before. And he's oblivious to that."

"Did people not complain about their commanders in the military?" Chineya wove another thread through her loom. "Because I can tell you that happens everywhere in the civilian world, regardless of what the friars teach."

"Oh, we complained privately." She eyed the fashionable shawl depicting a legion of interlocking rings draped around Chineya's shoulders. "But we also knew how to respect our commanders in public. These teachers speak freely. Even the students speak more openly than my Baylin classmates."

"So maybe the school doesn't live up to its reputation." Chineya pulled a thread out. "That's okay. The Ternion knows we make too big of a deal about hierarchies in Rizade. Even if your Head Mage misses things, two weeks won't determine whether this country survives or falls."

Kalina shook her head and picked up her teacup. "We can't waste time." She drank more of the burnt liquid.

"And you don't think you have *anything* to offer? No novel skills you learned on the battlefield that you could teach him?"

Of course she had skills she could offer. But what she and Riyad pioneered on the battlefield was unique to who they were. It could have turned the tide of the war. But she couldn't teach that.

"Look, Chineya." She put the teacup down again. "I know you think I'm someone great and awesome like your brother, but I don't know a thing about teaching. I bored my kids half the day. And I sure don't know how I survived. Yes, I innovated on the battlefield. But that doesn't mean I'm equipped to teach others."

"Huh." Chineya wove more thread into her sash. "I guess you're right. You're not like my brother."

Kalina sat back. "What do you mean by that?"

"My brother wouldn't have given up on day one of the job."

Kalina rose to her feet. "I'm sorry?"

"Look, you can get mad at me if you want. I love you, but I'm also going to speak truth when I see it. The truth is, Riyad got up, he fought, and he didn't quit easy. That's why he kept pursuing you all those years. I thought you were the same way. You spent three years sacrificing everything on the battlefield. Will a group of adolescents scare you away?"

"I'm not scared by a group of adolescents." Kalina leaned across the table. If Chineya wasn't going to mince her words, she wouldn't either. "But unless you want to bow to our new Kaldian overlords while they sacrifice your sons to their god and leave Riyad to die, Emil needs the best teachers possible."

"Riyad didn't have any teaching experience either, the first day he taught."

"Well, it's like you said." The words dripped off her tongue. "I'm not my husband. I don't have his gifts. I don't have his experience. And apparently, I don't have his character. Happy now?" Kalina turned to leave. She had forgotten how the two of them had butted heads in the past. Despite Chineya's warmth and hospitality, she didn't know when to keep her mouth shut.

"So that's it," Chineya said. "You gave up all your dreams in order to try to win this war. But you're not willing to take two weeks to tackle a new challenge."

"Nope." Kalina headed to her room. "I'm many things, but I'm not arrogant."

"And does humility say you're smart enough to know your teaching capabilities in one day, or is that your fear talking?"

Kalina halted in the middle of the doorway and looked back. "*Klyte.*" She crossed the distance between them again in a few quick steps. "Why can't you stop this and let me go?" Her chest heaved and her eyes burned. "We both know Riyad should have had this job."

"The Ternion spared your life for a reason, Kalina."

"For *this*?" Tears spilled out now. "You don't get it. I *don't* believe the Ternion controls everything. Maybe it spared my life. But maybe it was an accident. Because throughout my whole life, I've been the casualty, not the hero. My plans never work. You know whose did? Riyad's. And now I'm in over my head with a boy whom the Head Mage just revealed *isn't ready yet.* If I fail to fix that, Riyad never comes back."

"Then don't be Riyad. Be yourself, and see if that's the teacher our prophesied hero needs."

"And what if I'm not what he needs?"

Chineya shrugged. "What if I wasn't the mother my children needed? We can't worry about what may be. We need to take on what's in front of us and laugh at the world when it throws our problems in our face. Were you a good battle mage your first day on the job?"

"I didn't have a choice."

"And you rose to meet the occasion. Look, Kalina, if this school has as many problems as you say it has, don't you think this boy needs someone who sees that?"

Kalina breathed in. Then out again. Tear lines felt damp against her cheeks. She remembered what Riyad had told her when they first became battle mages. *"It's fine to make mistakes! You're only human, and the fate of our country doesn't rest on your shoulders."*

If I'm training Emil, it kind of does.

But the fate of their country rested on Emil's shoulders even more. He knew it. And he now desperately *wanted* her in his corner. If he was already struggling to find hope and then saw her quit...what would that do to his motivation? He needed to hope again.

She knew what Riyad would say if he saw her now.

Kalina exhaled slowly. "I'll give it two weeks. But if it doesn't work, I'm out."

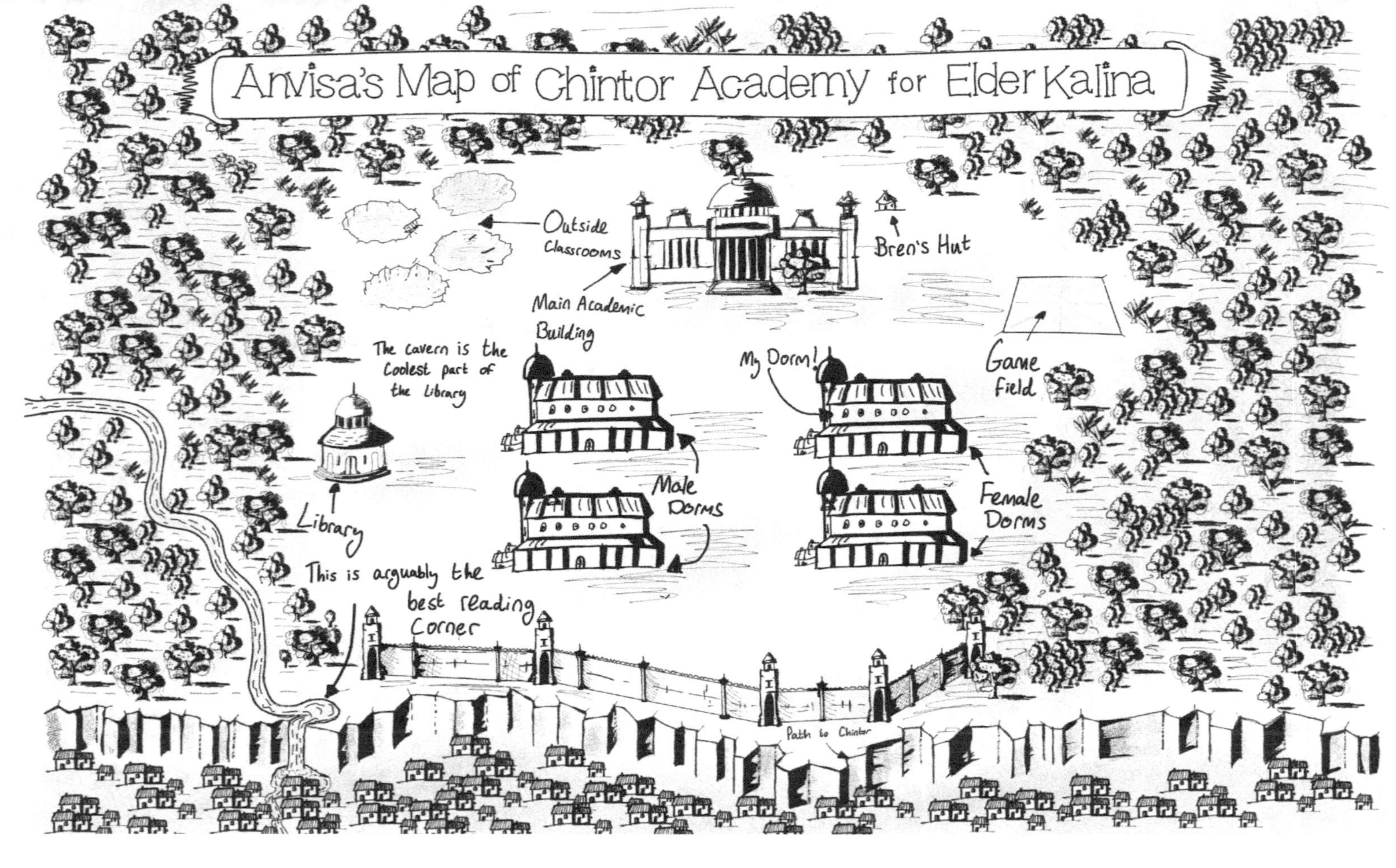

Anvisa's Map of Chintor Academy for Elder Kalina
Outside Classrooms
Main Academic Building
Bren's Hut
The cavern is the coolest part of the Library
My Dorm!
Game Field
Library
Male Dorms
Female Dorms
This is arguably the best reading corner
Path to Chintor

8

$\mathcal{I}$ REMEMBER IT AS IF IT WERE
yesterday. The first day at Baylin Academy ended in a characteristic catastrophe. I had felt sick and nauseous the whole orientation day, and had hoped it wasn't all that serious.

But then when I sat next to Riyad trying not to get distracted by him in Introduction to Repose class, my stomach revolted, and I vomited all over him.

People say they want to die from embarrassment, but if I could have gotten lost in the Deep Jungle and never returned, that would have still been a better fate. I had chosen this school because Riyad had come here, but neither of us had confessed our feelings for each other.

I didn't attend any of my other classes the rest of that day. Obviously.

And I would have skipped classes the second day if the teacher in charge of my dorm hadn't scolded me.

I was late for the first class, but I didn't share it with Riyad. I tried to pretend like all my classmates weren't staring while I stumbled to the remaining open seat at the front of the classroom.

Riyad had already told me he hated back-row seats. So for my second class, I sat in the far back corner and avoided eye contact. Maybe if I didn't look at him when he entered, he wouldn't see me.

I still stole a glance when he strode into the room.

To my horror, he headed in my direction and sat down right next to me.

I made a studious investigation of the wall next to me. But then he coughed and I glanced back to see him staring at me with that classic grin—lips pressed to hold back the smile that still broke through at the right edge of his mouth and in his shining eyes.

He held a small mug out. "Ginger tea. I heard it helps with nausea."

To this day, Kalina still didn't know how he had managed to get the mug of ginger tea for her. But when she took it out of his hands, she'd known the year wouldn't be as bad as she had feared. Not when she had him around.

And as the last of her twelve Year Three students trickled into the room, she gazed at the mug of ginger tea on her desk. There wasn't any hint of nausea today. But she could at least remember him.

"All right," Kalina said once the class was seated. "Let's do roll call. Baz?"

She sped through the list as the kids responded. It would take her some time to remember all their names. She could only remember Hanodoi from yesterday—and that's because the boy had a long "feminine" name due to his Kaldian heritage. *Odd to have a Kaldian in the classroom.* But not all Kaldians agreed with the cult that had propelled their nation to war.

"Today we're going to review what we know about the Substances and how they work." Since yesterday had been mostly introduction, this was her first real lesson. "Who can tell me what the five Substances are?"

A hand shot up. "Space, lightning, solids, liquids, and lights."

"*Energy* is a better word than *lightning,* but otherwise correct," Kalina said. "And what ties the Substances together?"

"The Fabric!" another student replied.

Kalina nodded. "The great Fabric of reality." She laid a tablecloth down over the books and supplies scattered across her desk. "Imagine it as a three-dimensional grid with lines infinitesimally close that fills the whole world." She tapped the black checkered cloth. "Like this tablecloth, these lines will bend over physical objects in their path. And every Substance relates to the Fabric in its own unique way."

She scanned their bored looks. Perhaps a more interactive approach would work. "Let's do an instrument review. What do lutes and other plucked string instruments do?"

One student in the front row groaned. "Elder Kalina, we know this already."

She shook her head. "The notes from the substitute teacher said you needed review." *And I need to know how much you know so I can adjust my future lesson plans accordingly.* That had been one of Umar's tips when she talked with him yesterday.

A student in the middle raised his hand. "Lutes control space, or the Fabric itself, and can move different objects by pulling them through the Fabric."

"Good. How about violins and other bowed string instruments?"

A student at the front responded. "Violins control energy and send it along the lines of the Fabric."

"Excellent. If you need memory help, stringed instruments interact with the *lines* of the Fabric while other instruments control what's *in* or passes *through* the Fabric. Now, how about trumpets and other brass instruments?"

A new hand shot up. "Trumpets control solid objects—that which the Fabric bends around—and reshapes them into different forms."

She nodded. "Just like the tablecloth bends around the objects on this table. And what's the one thing trumpets—or any other instrument for that matter—can't control?"

An awkward hush fell upon the room. Students looked at each other.

Kalina raised an eyebrow. "You can say it."

"But," the student in the front said, "we're not supposed to say that word."

Some of her own schoolteachers had refused to say the word even in academic contexts. They referred to it as the "unmusical substance" or something like that. But Kalina knew far too well how that metal destroyed lives. And she didn't play around with word games.

"Outside of the classroom? No, I don't want you using it as a curse word," she said. "But inside it? We can call it *klyte*, because that's what it is: the one substance in the world that cannot be affected by magic and will destroy any instrument it touches. Klyte destroyed my cello on the battlefield. And I want you to know what it is and what it looks like."

She fished the klyte arrowhead necklace out of her tunic. Padini had found it in the wreckage of her cello. People gave her odd looks about keeping it. But Kalina wanted to remind herself that she wasn't afraid of the Kaldians. And keep a means of protection in case a mage ever attacked her.

"This is klyte," she said, holding it up so they could all see its semitranslucent green color. "And if you ever see it on the battlefield or anywhere else, you need to be *very* careful. Even if it's dulled like this arrowhead. Understood?"

The kids all nodded quickly. Their sober attention was fully on her now. *How many of them have seen it before?*

She dropped the arrowhead back down into her tunic. "Moving on. How about flutes and other woodwinds?"

Another student. "Flutes control liquids—that which fills the Fabric—and moves them around."

"Good. Remember, while we can't see with the naked eye why liquids and solids interact with the Fabric differently, they do. That's why lutes can't move liquids: Pulling the Fabric doesn't move them like it does with solid objects. If the Fabric moves, solid objects will move with it, but not liquids. Finally, how about the percussion instruments?"

"Drums summon the lights and fires which pass through the Fabric," a final student said.

"Good. And what steps do you need to take to use any of these instruments and conduct magic?"

Out of the corner of her eye, she noticed the student who had complained passing a note to her classmate.

A student began speaking as Kalina thought about how to deal with it. "Mages must first concentrate to enter Repose where they can sense the magic happening around them. Then they need to mentally reach out to the Substance they want to control. Playing the notes of their instrument releases the magic of the universe to achieve their goal."

Someone memorized a textbook explanation.

At that moment, Kalina noticed Head Mage Bren standing at the top of the small auditorium. Her heart almost leapt into her throat. How long had he been there? Did he know she wouldn't normally cover material this basic? His hands were crossed as he tracked the note.

The other teachers had warned her about surprise observations. She *would* be a disciplined teacher.

"Okay." Kalina stepped over to the wide-eyed boy holding the note. "Hand it over." She had to show Bren that she could manage a classroom well. "You all should know better than to write notes in my classroom."

She took it out of his hands. As she unfolded it, she remembered how one of her teachers had handled this situation. It had put a dead stop to anyone trying it again. "Anything you want to say can be said to the entire class."

She spread the paper and read the note out loud. "The Kaldian is sweating a lot today. I can smell him from here. Probably knows he's the only person who doesn't understand this stupid review lesson. He's probably peeing himself just thinking about the possibility of being called on."

Kalina blinked. What *was* this note? The student didn't like this lesson, but all this about the Kaldians didn't make any—

Recognition broke on her like lightning electrocuting soldiers. And her gaze spun toward the red-faced boy sinking in his seat on the other side of the classroom.

Hanodoi.

The shocked gaze of everyone in the classroom rested on her.

"Why did you read that out loud?" a student next to Hanodoi blurted as she leaned toward him.

Kalina felt Bren's eyes on her.

Shame and anger boiled up inside her. She spun toward the student who had written the note. "Elrenda! Out to the hall this moment."

Kalina wanted to collapse by the time class ended. What a failure. She'd wasted her kids' time reviewing basic magic concepts for the second day in a row, and worse, she'd humiliated Hanodoi. Even if the guilty student now had extra cleaning duties, she should have known better than to read the note out loud like that.

She drew her bow across her cello, creating a note that reverberated throughout the room. Music helped her de-stress. The worn fingerboard needed to be resmoothed by a luthier. But she was thankful to at least have one at the academy, especially one with a brighter tone.

Footsteps sounded above. *Guess Bren came to share his thoughts on my awful lesson.*

But she looked up to see not Bren, but Elder Umar coming down the steps of the auditorium. He kept a lot of body weight on his wizened cane.

"I thought you weren't able to work magic anymore," he said.

Kalina shook her head. "I can't. I play because I enjoy the instrument."

He smiled. "I don't see many mages who say that these days."

"Well, music can be pretty beautiful," she said. "I know it's easy to only think about how we can use it...but it's so much more than that."

He chuckled. "I can't disagree with that." He paused. "I wanted to ask you a question about a Year Six student we both have, but I'm sensing this might not be a good time."

She shook her head. "It's...fine...I'm just trying to mentally unwind. Seems like I keep finding new ways to mess up."

Umar continued down the stairs. "You know you've only been here two days, right?" His voice had that gravelly tone of old age.

"Yeah." Kalina pursed her lips. "And today I humiliated Hanodoi in front of the whole class by reading a student note out loud before I realized it was about him. The kids bully him already. And here I am, adding to his embarrassment."

"Welcome to teaching." Umar sat on one of the student's desks in front of her. "We're supposed to be the adults who always know what we're doing. And yet it turns out that sometimes we're the problem."

She snorted. "My teachers growing up weren't like that."

Umar raised a white eyebrow. "Really? You never disagreed with anything your teachers did?"

Well. Now that he mentioned that, several memories resurfaced.

"I told myself I would never become like them."

Umar smiled. "It's difficult to handle things the right way, despite what we thought as students."

She sighed. "Sure."

"You know." Umar looked up at the ceiling for a couple of moments. "I don't remember much about my first year. When you get to my age, a lot of events blur together. But I do remember the time ten years ago I accused a student of cheating in front of his class when it turned out he hadn't. Not one of my prouder teaching moments."

She shook her head. "Sounds like me."

"But you know what?" Umar continued. "I apologized to the student, first privately and then in front of the rest of the class. I accepted the grace that the Ternion gave me, and we moved on."

"I know. That's what I need to do. I just..." She put her bow down across her knees. "On the battlefield? Mages trusted me because I knew what to do. Here, I'm faking it. And I'm worried the kids won't respect me if I admit fault."

Umar chuckled. "You know, for as much as teachers always express that fear, it hasn't been true in my experience. Teaching is built on trust. And you know the quickest way to lose that with your students? Refuse to admit fault when you're wrong. I've never seen an honest apology make students leap on the teacher more."

Kalina pursed her lips. That's the sort of teacher she wanted to be—not one who pretended she knew everything when she didn't, but one humble enough to admit her faults. It took...well, a great deal more humility than she'd guessed.

Umar smiled. "We all make mistakes. Don't let one bad day get you down. The first year is the hardest, and the first month especially so. But we all get through it."

She still didn't know if she'd make it a month, and Umar didn't need to know that right now. But he was right. She had to hold herself up to the same standards she expected her students to follow when they messed up.

She just had to figure out how in the world she would give this upcoming apology.

9

WEEK TWO. DAY ONE. SHE HAD apologized to Hanodoi both privately and publicly without killing the respect of her students. And she had made it to the second week.

Of course, she still didn't know how to teach without boring students to death.

But today she had come up with a new lesson idea. She'd hoped to spend the hour before class prepping for it. But some Year Six students had come in half an hour early. *Who knows why they like talking to me?* But she enjoyed speaking with them more than worrying about the upcoming lesson.

"...and you wouldn't *believe* what happened when Krem played his lute," Anvisa said. She crowded Kalina's desk along with Leneya and Krem. The three students made quite the trio. Anvisa and Leneya had come alone for a couple of days, but then Krem had started joining them. Kalina appreciated his addition. When it was only Anvisa talking her ear off, conversations could become tedious.

Kalina raised her eyebrow. "What happened?"

Krem jumped in. The boy was on the heavier side, and vibrant energy shone through his eyes whenever he was excited. "I made a large rock move in his way so fast that Pesh couldn't stop himself and tripped over it, and then his flute went flying! It was so dark outside, I don't think he could find it until the next day. Either way, it put an end to him chasing us."

She laughed. "Well, maybe I shouldn't be saying this as a teacher, but it sounds like you gave him what he deserved."

Krem nodded, eyes wide. "Oh, believe me, we did, Elder Kalina. He and Jacir don't send streams of water at people walking around at night anymore."

"There weren't any teachers around, I suppose."

Anvisa laughed. "Oh, Elder Kalina, haven't you realized yet what this school is like? Having teachers who supervised after hours would mean having consistent discipline."

Kalina *had* picked up on the fact that discipline varied widely from classroom to classroom. And hardly existed during the evenings. Head Mage Bren either didn't realize or didn't care.

"Maybe that's why we need you as a teacher," Krem said. "Gotta have someone with military discipline to whip students into line after hours. Right, Leneya?"

Leneya jolted, seeming surprised to be roped into the conversation, and nodded.

Kalina shook her head. "Well, I can't leave my husband alone, now can I?"

"You could bring him here!" Krem said.

She snorted. "How do you know I'd even be a good disciplinarian?" Truth was, while she *had* been a military commander, she had still seen the mages as her comrades more than her underlings. And they hadn't needed discipline.

Krem grinned. "Well, we heard what happens to students who pass notes in your class."

She put her head in her hands. *Why am I even talking about this with them?* She loved how friendly they were, but there should perhaps be more distance between a teacher and her students.

She cleared her throat and glanced up. "That...was not one of your teacher's greatest moments."

Krem laughed. "After the four hours of cleaning you made Baz and Elrenda do, no one's writing notes anymore, so I think your technique worked." He made eye contact with Leneya again.

Leneya frowned. "I don't know about that..."

There was something going on between Leneya and Krem. Krem had an interest in her. But Kalina couldn't tell yet if Leneya reciprocated.

"Well, maybe good things can come out of bad decisions," Kalina said. "Either way, class will start soon, and we're doing something new today, so I need you three to go to your seats and give me time to prepare."

She had procrastinated enough.

Turned out she only had five minutes to finish before her other students came in. Which left precious little time to gather her supplies and walk with them to one of the outdoor auditoriums on the south side of campus. Long steps descended fifteen feet into the ground around a square center as large as her classroom. The lutists had filled the bottom with a foot of sand for this activity. Good thing she was doing this in the dry season.

She didn't know if this would work. Worse, she had to try it out in front of Elder Jadoni. But she might not continue past this week, so did it matter what the old teacher thought of her? More importantly, Bren had hinted that Emil needed help, and contrived classroom assessments hadn't revealed his problems yet. So Kalina needed to try something new to figure out what his deal was.

Elder Jadoni hobbled up on her cane to meet Kalina in front of the sand-filled arena. Her nose ring sparkled in the sun. A frown creased her chapped lips.

"Are you ready?" Jadoni asked.

"Yeah," Kalina said quickly. "Thanks for lending me your students."

She snorted. "They've been begging me to let them do something fun with magic for weeks now. This gives me an excuse not to come up with something myself. Keep them busy so they don't cause trouble."

Kalina nodded. "Sure."

She stepped to the side. "It's your show."

Kalina scanned the surrounding crowd—all of her Year Six students and Jadoni's dozen Year Four lutists. "Listen up! This is the best way I can simulate war tactics without bringing you to an actual battlefield. We'll do this exercise multiple times to make sure each type of musician gets practice. Today, however, I'm testing my violinists."

They had four hundred wooden blocks scattered across the field, half painted red, the other half painted blue. "Elder Jadoni's and my lutists will control the wooden blocks on our sandy 'battlefield.' Lutists, your job is to move your blocks to the other side with your telekinesis while blocking the other team's blocks. Do *not* move the other team's blocks. Elder Jadoni will make sure you follow these rules."

She turned to the other players. "Violinists, you should already know your teams. Electrocuted cubes won't count toward the other team's total, so strike as many as you can before they cross the finish lines on either side of the battlefield. Use whatever strategies you want to electrocute the cubes but keep all lightning strikes *inside* the arena. Whoever has the most intact cubes at the end wins. Any questions?"

Emil's hand shot up. "Are you sure you don't want to give the blue team more mages?"

She raised an eyebrow. "You think your side's too good?"

Emil shrugged. "I mean...you know who I am."

The boy's swagger could be seen a mile away. At least he hadn't adopted his father's rudeness.

But she wouldn't feed his ego—even if all his classmates did. "The teams will be what I've said they'll be: your two dorms against their two dorms. No exceptions." Half of this exercise was to assess teamwork after all—and that worked best if she kept the dorm houses together.

No one else asked any questions. She could feel Elder Jadoni's eyes on her with the pressure to deliver.

Kalina took her station on one side of the arena while the two teams split. The remaining students who played flutes, trumpets, or drums lined the edges alongside her.

She eyed Emil as he tuned his eight-stringed fiddle while jesting with his friends. It was odd to see a student with a different kind of instrument from the standard five: lutes, violins, trumpets, flutes, and drums. Normally, mages waited until after graduation to learn other instruments in their musical family. And most mages didn't even bother learning something else. Kalina had only learned the cello because she joined the Krazian Inventors Guild. *But perhaps when you're a hero of prophecy, you branch out early.* She'd never seen a fiddle quite like his before.

Time to discover why you aren't ready for the battlefield yet. She gave the signal. The game began.

A cacophony of sounds erupted from both sides of the arena—each mage playing their own tune to influence the Substances. A few nearby students covered their ears. Kalina smiled. *Give them a month on the battlefield and they'll get used to dozens of discordant tunes playing at once.*

She relaxed her breathing and reached out mentally to enter the state of Repose.

Magical energies rushed around her. It was like feeling the wind, except she could sense exactly where each energy came from and what it was doing. The explosion may have kept her from using magic, but it hadn't affected her ability to observe it.

She could see the magical energies as well in Repose—the colored streams that broke from each student's instrument. But tracking the magic visually was an amateur move. On the battlefield, eyes weren't fast enough to figure out which colored streams came from what instrument. The only way to track magic effectively was to sense its effects on the Fabric with her mind.

Movement zipped below. Lutists pulled the cubes this way and that along the lines of the Fabric in their quest to get to the other side. But she wasn't testing their abilities. She shunted those currents to the back of her mind and focused on the air above.

Lightning cracked. Strikes charred the cubes below. She almost had to cover her ears because of the noise. Anvisa's and Emil's strikes were the strongest. Good thing she had put them on separate teams. But none of the mages were protecting their own cubes—just striking the other team's cubes.

Come on. You can do better than that.

Anvisa started Quelling the red side's strikes first, trying to stabilize the magnetic divide the other team sought to exacerbate to create lightning. *Good.* She was signaling to her teammates as well. So she was a natural leader. And she understood the importance of Quelling. Quelling turned most magical endeavors on the battlefield into the equivalent of a tug-of-war—both sides pulling in opposite directions to bend the Substance to their will.

The lightning strikes became less frequent as both teams Quelled opposing strikes. Cubes pressed against each other in a line as lutists tried to break through.

For several minutes, the sides locked. Anvisa barked orders to her blue mages as they tried to protect the center. On the left side of the arena, Emil still struck cubes with his lightning, overwhelming the Quelling. His regular cracks of lightning showed his prowess. But Kalina had expected more from him, given his reputation.

And then she felt it.

Emil didn't have one magical energy coming from his fiddle.

He had *three*—all targeting different areas of the arena.

For a moment, she couldn't believe it. Doing two things at once with magic took unbelievable effort. And here he was doing *three*? And winning the "tug-of-war" with each opposing Quelling mage? But she could plainly see multiple streams of magic coming out of his fiddle and its understrings.

He was in a league of his own.

Anvisa's targeted strikes began to open some lanes. But something else rumbled. A massive shift in the energies. Kalina focused on the center in time to recognize an enormous energy differential. Emil had brought all his different pitches into one singular target.

He isn't going to...

Anvisa's allies hadn't prepared for this.

Emil released the energy.

And a stroke of lightning rippled down the Fabric into the center of the arena, smashing through red blocks and blue blocks alike.

A boom shook the arena. Kalina's hands flew to her ears. But she had experienced this enough to keep the concentration of Repose.

Anvisa and her allies did not. As they stared in shock, Emil unleashed a more targeted assault on their blue cubes. Multiple bolts of lightning crashed throughout the arena. A couple of blue mages tried to stop him, but their efforts were futile. Emil's allies tried to support him, but their bolts rarely got past the Quelling like Emil's did.

The battle finished in a matter of minutes. And while the blue team managed to get seventy-two cubes to the other side without being electrocuted, Emil's got a hundred-and-nineteen. Anvisa's team never stood a chance.

Kalina stepped out of Repose and stood. Emil's team whooped and hugged him while the blue team consoled each other. Kalina glanced at Elder Jadoni and cleared her throat.

"All right," she said. "Let's gather together." She had a pretty good idea what Emil's problem was.

"Elder Kalina, did you see that?" Emil asked as he ran over. "I mean, I'm not trying to be arrogant, but did you *see* what I did?" He grinned with that crooked-tooth grin that stretched and highlighted the scar on his left cheek. He looked about ready to spread wings and fly.

She looked up at him and smiled politely. She liked Emil already, but she wasn't going to show favoritism. "We'll talk about it," she said simply and waited for everyone else to come around.

"Well done, everyone," she said once they had gathered. "The real battlefield has blood and chaos, but what you will do as mages won't be that different, and you all caught on quickly. Blue team, excellent communication with each other. Make sure you communicate a clear plan before the battle that can adjust to setbacks. You won't have time to plot new strategies during the chaos. Pay attention to your opponents—even if their endeavor seems gutsy and hard to pull off. And make sure you cover all sectors of the battlefield. You *can't* let your opponent catch you by surprise. You need to play Quelling music *before* the attack comes so you can immediately resist it. Understood?"

Anvisa answered for the group. "Yes, Elder Kalina."

Kalina turned to the other team. "Red team. Emil, do you know how many of your own troops you would have slaughtered with that move in an actual battle?"

Emil looked at her with interest. "I thought I was playing to win."

"You're training for the battlefield. This isn't a game."

"Okay. Sorry." But then he grinned. "You have to admit, Elder Kalina, that it *was* a pretty cool move, though."

"Oh, it was. But the Kaldians won't let you do that. And you *can't* kill your own troops. Which leads to my second point: You all need to learn how to work together. Take a page from the blue team's book. They communicated and worked together. I didn't see any of that from you. You still won. But out on the battlefield when put up against experienced mages, you'll need coordination."

Emil frowned.

"Would you like to say something, Emil?"

"I mean..." He glanced downward and kicked at the ground before looking back at her. "No offense, Elder Kalina. But you *do* know who I am, right?"

Kalina raised an eyebrow. "Are you more than a student?"

Some students laughed knowingly. *Good.* She wasn't sure if they'd pick up on her humor or not.

"I mean, I'm trying to be honest about who I am."

Kalina smiled. "Of course I know who you are. But even the strongest mage can't take on an entire army by himself."

Emil shrugged. "I dunno. With this prophecy out there, maybe I need to. I can't worry about what others are doing, and they don't need to feel responsible for winning like I do."

Jacir—the kid she still watched for behavior problems—clapped a hand on Emil's shoulder. "It's all right, Elder Kalina. We aren't bothered by Emil's power. He's going to shove it up the Kaldians' butts. And he's already fought off several of their mage assassins. You've seen his scar, haven't you?"

She must have had at least four different students tell her about the origin of the scar on his left cheek and how he fended off the two assassins who had gone after him and five Year Two students a year and a half ago. Instead of fleeing when he could have, he single-handedly defended the younger students and beat the assassins. A rather shocking feat for a just-graduated Year Four student.

But at the moment, that was beside the point. "It doesn't matter how strong you are," she said. "When my husband and I fought together, we were two of the strongest mages out there. And guess what? We wouldn't have won battles if we hadn't coordinated with others. Strong mages work as a team."

Emil shrugged again. "I guess."

So, he doesn't believe me.

Kalina clapped. "Thank you to everyone who participated. It will take time and experience to understand what to do, but you did well for a first attempt. We'll go ahead and dismiss class." Class still technically had another half hour, but energy buzzed through her veins after a successful simulation, and she had nothing else planned. Only one final thing to do. "Emil? I'd like to see you in my office in half an hour."

His head popped up. "Y-yes, Elder Kalina."

"Year Four students, we still have a full lesson," Elder Jadoni ordered. "Move the sand back into the open bags toward the side and put the blocks in another sack for future exercises. And be quick about it. Then we'll return to the classroom."

Kalina's students dissipated as the lutists plucked their instruments again. Sand and blocks rose into the air.

Jadoni hobbled over on her cane. "Not bad," she murmured. "I've never seen a battlefield strategy instructor do that before. Maybe more should. Though you shouldn't make it a habit to let class out early. Kids get into trouble when they have too much free time, and it's harder for the rest of us to keep our students' attention if others are running free. If you run out of material, give them study time in your room so we can keep a united front on when classes dismiss."

"Oh. I'm sorry."

"No need to apologize." Jadoni shrugged. "You didn't get the training you should have received before teaching here, so it isn't your fault. One other word of advice: Don't give Emil so much grace. He's a snotty brute, and he knows it."

What? Kalina had already noted Emil's unhealthy self-reliance, but 'snotty brute'? He'd sounded respectful even in his skepticism of her critique. *Are we talking about the same kid?*

"O...okay," she stammered.

"You'll see," Elder Jadoni continued. "When you've been around kids for as long as I have, you recognize patterns. That boy is a born troublemaker."

10

KALINA LEANED BACK IN THE CHAIR

at her desk as she waited for Emil. Jadoni's words kept ringing through her mind. Was that really who Emil was? If anyone had told her before coming here that General Mahd's son was a snotty brute, she wouldn't have batted an eye. But after seeing him over the past week, that didn't seem accurate.

Why would she say that?

Jadoni *did* seem like a harsh teacher. Both in her firm discipline and in her words. Kalina could respect someone with good discipline. But judgmental...

Well, she needed to analyze Emil herself and not through the lens of hard-nosed teachers.

A knock sounded outside the curtain, and Emil poked his head in. "Can I come in, Elder Kalina?"

"Have a seat." She was aware of how bare her room and desk felt compared to the other teachers' cluttered work environments.

Emil sat down. He fidgeted as he laid his fiddle next to him with a clink. "I'm sorry if I disrespected you by what I said." He bent over in his seat and studied the floor. "I didn't mean to challenge your authority."

Kalina shook her head. "I'm not mad at you. I wanted to talk more—and without an audience."

"Okay." He looked up expectantly.

Kalina cleared her throat. "Let me lead off with this, Emil. I know who you are. And I know you're gifted. But we need to work on your coordination. Individualism doesn't work on the battlefield."

"Okay." His facial expression was blank, though his tone spoke respect. "Thank you, Elder Kalina."

That sounded forced. "Let's start over."

He blinked. "Start over?"

"Yep." She leaned forward. "I don't know what other teachers want, but I'm not here for you to feed me what I want to hear. I want *honesty*, not mindless regurgitation. If you disagree with what I'm saying, say so."

He sat back. "Okay."

"So. Let's start this conversation again. Why didn't you like what I said out there?"

Emil fidgeted in his seat. "Look, Elder Kalina, I know you have military experience and everything..." He avoided eye contact.

"But?"

"Please don't hate me." His face looked pained. "But...is it possible there's a reason common strategies fail against the Kaldians?"

She raised an eyebrow. "Why do you ask?"

"Well, I've been on the battlefield before. About a year ago during the New Year Break, I went with my father when he besieged Kirtin. And I know I'm young, but we should have *won* that battle. Easily. And we didn't. Look at this whole war. Us and Arditen united against the Kaldians should have *easily* held them back. But now the Kaldians rule Arditen and we're alone against them."

Mahd had kept Riyad and Kalina guarding the border while he besieged Kirtin. *Pity. I wish I'd met Emil then.*

"Not everyone sticks to textbook strategies like your father does," Kalina said carefully.

Emil laughed. "I don't care if you say it. My dad's an idiot. He knows how to lead like nobody else does. But he's a terrible strategist."

Kalina wouldn't even call Mahd a good leader, but at least Emil had enough insight to see his father's poor strategies.

Emil continued. "I'm not talking about my father, though. I've talked with Elder Mito a lot and the entire army uses bad strategies." He glanced at her and then lowered his shoulders. "No offense, Elder Kalina. But I don't see how current strategies will win the day."

So Elder Mito complained about the military's strategies with students as well.

But Kalina also noted Emil's changed tone and body language. He feared her. Why?

She tapped her fingers against her desk. "So I do agree with you. I pushed for new strategies throughout my time as a mage commander. But what strategies do *you* think we should use?"

"I mean..." Emil gestured toward himself. "What I did out there. We need more mages on the front lines taking risks and acting like heroes, not bunched up in fear toward the back wasting time with coordination."

Laughter rose in her throat, but she did her best to turn it into a cough. "You think mages should fight on the front lines?"

"Well, yeah. Magic becomes more powerful the closer you are to what you're trying to control, right?"

Oh boy. "Sure, but the closer you are to the front lines, the more likely the enemy will kill you. Especially when you're in range of bullets even lutists can't stop."

Emil laughed. "Haven't you read the great war epics? I don't remember Prem or Gane hiding in the back or obsessing over what other people did. They acted like heroes and changed the world."

This time she snorted. "Prem and Gane? Emil, they're more legend than history. People don't have the abilities those men had."

"Well..." Emil gestured to himself again. "I do have a legend about me if you haven't heard it yet." He grinned. "Don't tell me you're jealous, Elder Kalina!"

She sighed. She had a hard time not smiling at youthful spunk, but he didn't need to see that. "Come now, Emil. This isn't a matter of *jealousy*. You're a powerful mage. But even good mages don't work alone."

Emil sank back into his chair. "Have you *seen* my classmates?"

Kalina shook her head. "I'm new here, so you'll have to tell me."

"Well..." Emil met her gaze. "I know everyone talks about how great Chintor Academy is and what a privilege it is to study here. 'We only accept the best,' and all that. But I need to say it: This school isn't what it used to be. We don't have a rigorous curriculum. Students *can* pass their classes while putting in minimum effort. And we *don't* have the best students."

He paused. "You all fight for our lives on the battlefield. Here? My friends only care about kissing girls, getting knuckles deep into drama, and passing enough classes to avoid a scolding from their parents. They're not studying like the future of our country depends on it. After all, Emil's going to die and save everyone, so what's the point?" He leaned in. "I know that no one here wants to admit this, but since you asked me to be honest, I have to say it: Chintor Academy lies about what kind of students it accepts."

Kalina allowed his words to sink in. *So Emil sees some of the same problems I do.* He was the first person here willing to name these particular problems. That meant something. *What else is he willing to admit about the school and its dysfunctions?*

She probably shouldn't ask that as a teacher, though.

"I've seen some of that myself," Kalina said. Which was probably too much to say as a teacher—the Head Mage wouldn't want her admitting that the school sometimes lied. But honesty went both ways.

She continued. "The mages on the battlefield won't be like your classmates, though. They give it their all."

Emil shrugged. "I think I take the motivation out of people. Why should my dad bother trying to win battles if he has me?" He looked away. "This didn't have to be the war that would kill me. But because everyone else screwed up, it has to end with my death. And I can go fight in the front lines and be brave. But I don't see the point of working with people who shove their responsibilities on me."

She floundered for the right response. There were reasons mages hadn't fought on the front lines for centuries. But should she get into that now? How would a good teacher answer him?

"Sorry. I'm not trying to be stubborn." He grinned. "No one likes a complainer, right? I gotta go out and save our country, no matter how other people use me. It's like I said earlier in front of all my classmates: Good heroes don't let other people bear their responsibilities."

The smile looked hollow. Like a piece of tree gum stretched out to disguise how little of it there was.

Kalina's cheeks burned. This boy was ready to give up his life to save this country—and her husband. She scolded him for his arrogance while he tried to hide how much it hurt to lose a chance at a long life.

He had more important issues to work through before he was ready to hear her battlefield advice.

"I understand," she said quietly. "Thank you for your honesty. I don't have anything else to say today."

Not until she understood how to address the deeper issues bubbling under the surface.

THE ART OF REPOSE

> Mental state required to control the fabric (And see the streams of magic)

—> It's like you're both still enough to fall asleep and focused enough to pass a test. Which still doesn't make sense when I write it down, but somehow I learned how to do it. Guess there's a reason it takes two years to learn the skill.

—> While Elder Mito compares it to what it feels like to pray, most friars call that comparison blasphemous.

11

KALINA COULDN'T STOP THINKING of Emil.

He lingered in her mind while she finished planning the next day's lessons. While Elder Jadoni used her lute to lower them down the cliffs on a lift. While she sat beside her husband and the sun drooped low in the sky.

"I...I don't know where to begin," she said as she held Riyad's hand. "This boy doesn't know anything about effective battlefield tactics. Just raw power. And he's too hurt to listen. He needs someone who knows how to help kids deal with grief. And do all of that in seven months."

She laughed despite herself. *Our prophesied hero parrots centuries-outdated tactics.* It sounded like a bad joke. He needed help, all right.

He needs someone like me.

She froze. Where had that thought come from? She still knew nothing about teaching. Nor about counseling grieving kids. Anyone with battlefield experience could give him what she could.

But Rizade couldn't spare any other battle mages.

"No...no...no..." Kalina sank down next to Riyad. "You know who I am, Riyad."

Yet the battlefield simulation *had* been her invention.

And no one else was here to coax Emil away from the ideas Elder Mito fed him.

The dead smile painted on Emil's lips picked away at her like a cook plucking each weblike silk strand from an ear of corn. Who knew how much the knowledge of an early death had devoured him? If she understood his hints about Mahd as a father, the boy had experienced precious little happiness in his life.

But she had survived.

There were better researchers out there. Kalina knew them. But she had done good research herself with the Krazian Inventors Guild. And no one else had experienced an instrument shattering.

This country needed someone who could give Emil hope and time-tested techniques.

While she couldn't teach well, she could provide both traits.

And it wasn't only what the country needed. Kalina recalled Emil's hollow face. She'd seen that kind of face before. Last time, she didn't act soon enough.

At least her sister still had the hope of a future ahead of her.

"I don't know if I can save him," Kalina whispered. "No mage has ever discovered how to survive breakages."

But she had to try to give Emil a reason to smile again.

For the second time that day, Kalina ascended to the academy. This time she didn't get the privilege of a magically operated lift. She had decided to stay—a week early and everything. And it was best to tell Head Mage Bren before she changed her mind.

Why couldn't he live down in the city like everyone else?

Of course, it probably *was* better that he lived up here with the few teachers who supervised the academy's dormitories. The Ternion knew the students needed that.

Sweat dripped from her brow by the time she reached the top. Muggy twilight had fallen on the cliffs. The only light came from the candles burning in the windows—although a few students had the new artificial lights powered by violin magic. Her guild had played a hand in inventing those. Bren's cottage lay behind the main academic building. She set out at a fast tempo across the green.

Kalina had crossed half the lawn when a yelp broke the silence.

She looked left. The boys' dorms were a stone's throw away. Was that just normal male shenanigans? She shook her head and turned to keep walking.

"Please stop!" Tears rang through the boy's voice.

She halted. Who was that? She scanned the open windows of the nearby dorm.

Then she saw it. Second floor, two windows down from her. Hanodoi—the boy with fourth-generation Kaldian heritage whom she had unwittingly helped the kids bully. He squirmed against some captor behind him while another figure held a burning candle toward him.

Kalina moved for the dormitory door.

She thrust the squeaky door open. A couple of boys lounging around the vestibule looked at her in surprise. She ignored them as she ran up the battered stairway. There wasn't time to find a male teacher. Why weren't the teachers on dorm duty dealing with this?

She turned at the top of the dilapidated railing and strode across the creaking wooden floor. A couple of students stood in the doorway of a room halfway down the hall—and it looked like a lot more stood inside the room.

Hanodoi's pleading was sounding more anxious.

Neither of the boys in the doorway turned. Over their heads, she could see about twelve boys in the room. Jacir held a squirming Hanodoi. Another kid with his back toward her held a candle close to the Year Three student, and a third boy stood near Hanodoi with a metal triangle in his hand. He hit it every moment or so to keep the flame hot.

"You know the code you signed," the boy with the candle said. "Put out your hand and take your punishment like a man if you don't want Jacir to kick you again."

Too many boys stood in her way. She pushed through them. "Move."

The boys staggered back, mouths open.

Hanodoi, whimpering, stretched out toward the candle.

"That's right," the boy said. "Stop acting like the rest of your kind and eat the cost for what you did."

A jolt ran through her veins. *I know that voice.*

"Emil Mahdson." Kalina's voice rang out like a bell.

Emil spun in shock, candle still in hand.

12

"EL-ELDER KALINA!" EMIL TOOK a step back.

Jacir let go of Hanodoi. The boy collapsed. And the triangle player stopped ringing the note. The fire dimmed immediately.

"What kind of klyte are you trying to pull here?" Kalina snapped.

"Elder Kalina." Emil's voice had none of the arrogance or domineering command it had possessed ten seconds earlier. He almost sounded respectful. "I didn't realize you'd be coming in here. We're just trying to uphold the code of our hall."

"The code of your hall? And what kind of stupid code exists in this hall?"

"I mean, it's a code we all agreed to," Emil said. "Everyone said they could be held accountable if they broke them."

"And what rule did Hanodoi break?"

"Well…" Emil bit his lip. "His room wasn't clean for inspection."

Kalina glanced around. The room wasn't pristine, but for a boy's dorm room? It looked fine.

"So if someone doesn't clean their room, you burn their hand." Her eyes narrowed.

"We all agreed to do some kind of courage challenge," Jacir piped up. "Hanodoi will be fine. He was just a bit nervous. And we were going to heal him afterward."

"I-I'm fine." Hanodoi stood up. "I did sign the code, Elder Kalina. It's okay. You don't need to do anything about this."

But she saw the look in his eyes. The look of a kid who worried his bullies would treat him worse if he sought help.

"Nope. This code is garbage," Kalina said. "I don't care if you want it, Hanodoi. Jacir and Emil, you're coming with me to see Head Mage Bren. You too, triangle player." She had him in class—she should have known his name. But memorizing sixty names in one week wasn't her forte.

"But—" Jacir sputtered. "You're not the teacher on duty for this dorm!"

Kalina fixed him with her eye. "Do you think I care? To Head Mage Bren. Now."

The moment Kalina dragged the trio out of the dormitory, she knew she had limited time. If she couldn't decisively end the bullying tonight, they would seek retribution.

Bren's cottage was shaped in a perfect circle. He came to the door a mere minute after she hit the knocker, looking as put-together as ever in his pristine white robe.

"Elder Kalina!" He grinned at her. Then his gaze flitted to the boys standing beside her. "Is there a problem?"

She nodded. "If you don't mind the interruption, we have a discipline issue."

He pursed his lips. "Come in."

Bren led them into the main sitting room. Colorful patterned rugs coated the wooden floor. Geometrical shapes were etched on the plaster walls. Bren motioned for the boys to sit on the couch. They did. Neither Bren nor Kalina sat.

"What's the issue?" Bren asked.

"I had come up here to speak to you about another matter when I saw these boys in their dorm holding down and forcing Hanodoi to burn his hand with a candle flame."

Bren's eyes widened. "You three had a *female student* in your dorm?"

Jacir snickered.

Kalina shook her head. "Hanodoi is a boy. His great-grandparents were

Kaldian. We talked about him last week after you observed my class." *How do you not know the name of the only Kaldian studying at the school?*

Bren blinked and nodded. "I see." He turned back to the boys. "Well? What do you have to say for yourselves, then?"

"I—I didn't realize we were doing anything wrong!" Emil blurted out. Guilt racked his face. "Prem Hall has always had a reputation for perfection. And as the leader of the hall, I had to do something about the way Hanodoi kept falling short. My dad always told me physical consequences motivated people the most. And since all the boys agreed to that at the beginning of the school year, I didn't think this would be a problem."

Kalina stared. Emil used *that* as his excuse?

Bren's eyebrows furrowed. "They *agreed* to be burned if they didn't do their duties?"

"They said we could test their courage in some way," Emil said. "It wasn't like we wanted to scar Hanodoi or anything. I knew fire scared him, so I wanted to use the opportunity to help him face his fears."

The boy had such a sincere look on his face, a model of innocence. Kalina bit back the names she wanted to throw at him and tried to act like a teacher. "You told him to stop acting like 'the rest of his kind.'"

Emil looked at her oddly. "I mean, you know his ancestors came from Kaldia, right? The people that sacrifice human beings and want to kill us? They're cowards. And I didn't think we wanted our students to be cowards like them." He paused, then his mouth dropped. "Wait—you both don't think I'm a *bully*, do you?"

She opened her mouth to respond.

"No, no—we're not saying anything of the sort," Bren interjected.

Kalina blinked. *Speak for yourself!*

"This is a bit...concerning, Emil." Bren eyed him carefully. "I don't know what kind of code you made with your hall, but you shouldn't be giving physical punishments. If I remember correctly, when this came up last year, I told you I didn't want you giving *any* punishments."

Emil bit his lip. "I know, Head Mage. But...I thought your concern was that I didn't have the authority yet. If they all signed a code saying they *wanted* to be held accountable, I thought this would be fine."

Kalina cleared her throat. "And what would have happened if they *refused* to sign the code?"

Emil glanced at her. She could see the worry in his eyes. "We didn't threaten them, Elder Kalina. I am *not* that kind of person." His eyes glimmered around the edges. "We presented these rules and asked if anyone had issues with the contracts, and no one said they did, so everyone signed them. I didn't know this would be a problem."

Of course, her heart wanted to go out to a boy struggling to keep back tears. But uneasiness settled in her chest.

"I think I'm going to want to review this contract of yours," Bren said slowly. "I don't think we want you treating other students in your dorm this way."

Emil tried to choke back the tears. "I'm so sorry, Head Mage Bren. If I had known...I mean, Hanodoi didn't mind. Elder Kalina heard him say he didn't want us to get in trouble. Right, Elder Kalina?"

Kalina wanted to explain that Hanodoi lied to protect himself. But that would give the game away. "I don't care if a bullied student says he's fine with it," she said, hoping Bren would understand what she left unsaid. "You're not behaving acceptably."

"You...you think I'm a bully?" Tears fell down Emil's cheeks. "I—I just wanted to lead like my father did. I thought I had to start doing that now if I'm going to save this country. I honestly wouldn't have done any of this if I had known you thought it was wrong."

"You're not a bully," Bren said, kneeling to meet Emil in the eye. "You..." He exhaled slowly. "I think we need to talk more about what it means to be a good leader. Does that sound fair?"

Emil wiped his eyes. "S...sure."

"Here, you need a hug," Bren said, stretching his arms out.

Kalina didn't know what to say as she watched Emil hug Bren.

Bren gave the eye to Jacir and the other kid and told them he'd better not hear them doing anything else like this. Then he sent them off to bed.

When the door closed behind them, Bren turned back toward her. *I told myself I would wait to see what he said first.* But the words couldn't keep themselves from bubbling out of her mouth.

"You let them go—just like that?"

Bren cocked his head. "Do you not agree with my actions?"

"That boy held Hanodoi down, threatened to kick him if he didn't burn his hand, and mocked him for his ancestry. He acted like a bully. We're letting him off with an apology?"

Bren shook his head. "I know Emil. He's not going to do that again."

For a moment, she considered biting her tongue. True, she didn't know Emil that well. But did it really matter how well she knew him?

"I thought certain actions deserved punishment."

Bren nodded. "I understand where you're coming from. I had similar reactions when I first started teaching. But we do things differently here than other schools because our goal isn't punishment. We're trying to change hearts. When dealing with kids like Emil who grew up with bad parents...kids like him don't need condemnation. They need love. Of course, they need to change if they're hurting others. But this isn't the military. We can extend the grace of the Ternion as they're learning to make right decisions."

Kalina pursed her lips. That hit home. But she couldn't help remembering the bullies she had faced in school. "I'm worried that he's putting two different faces on—a respectful, kind face in public and something very different in private."

Bren scratched his chin. He looked perplexed. "You saw Emil's tears, didn't you? The boy knows he messed up. And hyperscrutinizing someone's apology never ends well. Can't we give him some grace? Haven't we all done things that hurt someone else?"

Images from over a decade ago flashed into her head. Her brother yelling at her about why she hadn't said something sooner about her sister.

She swallowed and looked up. "Not intentionally—not like this." But her words felt hollow.

Bren shook his head. "Well, I'm glad you're better than the rest of us. I wish I could say the same. Most of us need second chances. Especially when you're a boy raised by the parents he had. You...you know that both of his parents were abusive, right?"

Kalina cocked her head.

Bren sighed. "Emil is pretty open about it with most of his teachers. His mother used him as a slave when he was young and whipped him regularly. You can still see the scars on his back, though he tells other students the Kaldians gave those to him. His father wasn't often around, and the few times he saw Emil, he paraded him in front of other nobles to increase his own status. The boy was half starved when he first came here."

She shook her head. This didn't excuse his behavior. But that was awful. "Why in the world?"

"I have my suspicions. But I'll let Emil share that part of the story with you when he's ready. To the subject at hand, though, I'm not asking you to agree with my decision. I'm asking you to have compassion. After his childhood, he doesn't always realize what behaviors are inappropriate. And even then, this is *very* out of character for him. He wouldn't have done this without Jacir and Pesh's influence."

That felt rather simplistic. But Bren was right; she didn't really know Emil. And would she have the arrogance to claim she could accurately judge Emil's character after a mere week?

"You know," Bren continued, "I thought of asking you to give him additional leadership training. You've been a commander. He's only seen his father lead before, and...well...I suspect you offer a better example of leadership. I hoped you might help him discover a better path. But I guess that depends on whether you're willing."

Emotions roiled inside her. Emil had tried to burn Hanodoi. But he did seem sorry. He had an awful dad. And if this truly wasn't in character for him...

Perhaps her doubts didn't matter. Even if Bren mishandled the situation, this was a chance for her to help Emil grow. Perhaps even to help him overcome his abusive childhood. And no one else here had the experience she had in commanding mages.

He may be a bully. But even bullies can change.

"I'm willing to help him. And I've made my decision too. I'll stick around as a teacher for this year if you'll still have me."

Bren smiled widely. "I'm so glad to hear that, Kalina. You're such a treasure to us here. And I know no one else teaches the kids what you can."

Sure. "Thanks." Kalina stepped back, preparing to leave.

"Oh," Bren said, "and one more thing."

"Yes?"

"What happened tonight...that should stay between the two of us. You don't need to lie if other teachers ask. But when we're dealing with offenses, I prefer to keep things on a need-to-know basis. Our kids don't deserve to have their reputations tarnished for childish mistakes, and we want to protect their privacy whenever possible. Do you understand?"

"Understood."

13

TOO MUCH HAS HAPPENED ALREADY

for this to only be the second day of the school week.

Emil grinned and laughed in the front row with his buddies as they waited for class to begin. His joy dug like needles under her fingernails. *It's all just life back to normal now?*

Hanodoi, after all, had said barely a word in all of class this morning.

Kalina stood and tried to brush that away. "All right, class, today we will begin working through part two of *Krafe's Guide to Military Strategies.*"

Emil's hand shot up immediately.

She decided to call on him.

"Elder Kalina, will we do more of those battlefield simulations? That was so fun yesterday!" Several other students nodded and voiced their assent.

He had *that* on his mind? "We need to work through our textbook today. We will do those simulations regularly, but we need to coordinate our schedule with Elder Jadoni's class."

"I think I learned more in that simulation than I did in the entirety of part one of our textbook last year," Jacir piped up.

Nope. Kalina hadn't forgotten his smug look in Bren's cottage. "You *will* raise your hand before commenting, Jacir. If you learned more in one hour than you did in the entirety of last year, you weren't paying enough attention in class. Now please turn to part two in your texts immediately."

A sigh threatened to emerge from her lips. She'd always hated teachers who were particular about the rules. Now, she was one of them.

But if boys like Jacir didn't start following rules soon, Hanodoi wouldn't be the only student bullied.

The kids remembered almost nothing from the textbook. A few like Anvisa did. But Kalina swore that if Meliya asked her one more time to explain a core concept of magical theory, she'd try to kick her back to Year Five classes.

Perhaps if Meliya spent less time trying to give doe eyes to Jacir, she would have remembered basic magical concepts.

It was a wonder she had made it to the sixth year.

Of course, Kalina didn't want to be the cynical teacher. Riyad hadn't been. The kids needed someone calm, steady, and encouraging who never got frustrated at their mistakes. *I just don't know how he pulled that off.*

Anvisa and Leneya came up to her at the end of class. Krem wasn't with them this time.

"Thank you so much for the lesson today," Anvisa said. "I hadn't thought before about how we forget about the beauty of music."

Of course, my off-topic rant stood out the most. "Well, like I said, it's one of my pet peeves. We're practicing a form of art. And yet we only ever think about what music can do for us! It wasn't until I began working as a researcher that I realized how much the way we teach magic in this country sucks the life and joy out of it. And I know this won't make you a better mage. But it can at least bring more joy to our lives." She gestured to her cello. "That's why I taught my fingers to replay this after the accident."

"Well, I'm definitely going to try to take more time to remember the beauty of what I'm creating," Anvisa said with a grin.

Kalina smiled. Solo tutoring lessons with her were the highlight of her week. The girl bubbled with energy.

"Not to change topics, but I wanted to ask a question about yesterday if it's all right," Anvisa said. "I've spent a lot of time thinking about how we could have countered what Emil did, but I still can't figure it out. You said we needed to Quell before an attack, but...how do you do that?"

Kalina nodded. "Lightning releases when mages separate positive and

negative charges on the Fabric and stretch them out over a section of the battlefield. Right now, you're thinking of Quelling as something that's only reactionary. You watch the opponent and stop him, pulling back on his efforts like a magical tug-of-war. But when you're going up against mages as strong and fast as Emil, that won't work. You need to stabilize the positions of the positive and negative charges. Think of it like planting your feet and pulling back on a rope in tug-of-war before the other team pulls. Mages can still counteract that, but this slows them down."

Anvisa nodded quickly. "How do I stabilize charges?"

Kalina walked her through the process. She wished she could have modeled it for Anvisa; her disability limited her teaching. But she guided her through practicing it, and after half an hour, Anvisa began to get a grasp of it.

"Thank you, Elder Kalina!" Anvisa chirped when they had finished. "I will definitely practice this in my free time." Leneya smiled as well. She hadn't said anything the whole conversation. She wasn't even a violinist—she played the trumpet. Did she ever talk to people other than Krem and Anvisa? Kalina racked her memory but couldn't remember an occasion.

Leneya and Anvisa left. Kalina had hoped to spend this afternoon researching how she could have survived her cello breaking, but she didn't have much time before sunset. Not that Kalina minded. She wished she had more students like Anvisa. Kalina swept up the last of her materials and hurried to her office.

Kalina brushed past the curtain and grabbed a book she'd pulled from the library yesterday exploring the technical sides of magic theory. This would be a chore. But she needed to wade deep into theory to discover how she had survived. She sank into her seat.

She had read ten pages when a knock rang outside the curtain.

"Yes?" Kalina looked up.

Elder Jadoni hobbled in on her cane. "Good afternoon. Do you have a moment?" Her brows narrowed and her voice rang with sharpness.

Bother.

Kalina shut the book. "Sure. What's the matter?"

"Hanodoi." The older woman dragged a chair two feet to the desk before sitting in it. "He acted odd today, so I pulled him aside and wrested his story out of him. Is what he said true?"

Bren had sworn her to secrecy. But if Jadoni already knew...

"That the other boys held him down and tried to burn his hand with a candle? Yeah, that's true."

Jadoni slapped her hand against the desk. *That has to leave bruising at her age.* "And Emil, Jacir, and Pesh did that to him?"

Pesh. That was the other kid's name. She nodded. "Yeah. It was awful."

Jadoni sucked in her lower lip. "If I were any younger and had any more strength in my arms, I would bring back corporal punishment for these boys. Back in my day, when Chintor actually deserved its reputation, this would be handled with the rod."

Kalina had heard stories of those days. None of them had been good.

Jadoni continued. "What happened to them?"

Kalina exhaled slowly. "Head Mage Bren assigned Emil several remedial sessions with me to talk about leadership." She tried to remember what he had done with Pesh and Jacir. "He might have other teachers talking with the other boys. I'm not sure."

Jadoni's head jerked back. "They tried to burn Hanodoi, and he wants to just *talk* with them?"

Kalina put her hands up. "Like I said. It wasn't my decision."

"Klyte." She slapped her hand against the desk again. "Every. Single. Year. I tell myself I'm here to quietly earn my retirement and get out, but then Bren pulls klyte like this, testing if I can still keep my mouth shut. He didn't even remove Emil as head of the hall?"

Kalina shook her head.

"Of course not." Jadoni's lip curled. "He'll let that bully keep hurting people until the day he graduates. As if this school wasn't messed up enough already."

Kalina's stomach churned. "If it makes any difference, Emil cried over the whole thing last night. He should have been punished, and he doesn't understand the full weight of what he did, but I do think he wants to change."

Jadoni gave her a blank stare. "Oh. You too."

"I what?"

"You also fall for Emil's klyte."

Kalina sat back in her chair. "Look, I said I wanted to punish him."

"And yet you still fall for his crocodile tears. Listen, I know you're new here and don't know anything about kids, so I'm going to give you some grace, but let me tell it plainly: Emil is a born manipulator who will put on whatever mask it takes to get out of punishment."

Kalina bit the inside of her lip as she replayed previous conversations. "That seems harsh."

"It does?" Jadoni raised a thin eyebrow. "Let me ask you this. Has he apologized to Hanodoi?"

"I don't know."

"And did he actually apologize to you last night, or did he cry about being caught?"

She blinked. "I don't remember his exact words, but I'm pretty sure he apologized."

Jadoni rolled her eyes. "That boy's run a reign of terror in his dorm for an entire year. Most dorms have a head of the hall that organizes a few social events, and that's it. He's made a whole hierarchy where there's an elite band at the top, and if you don't meet their nebulous standards of perfection, bad things start happening.

"But every time we try to nail him, he denies the whole thing and says boys who don't like him made it up. Maybe if he's feeling pressure, he'll start talking about his scar again and crying about the awful Kaldians and dying young. Yada, yada, yada. And guess who eats it up?"

Kalina didn't say anything.

"It's Bren. Every time. We can't admit that maybe our prophesied hero is a bully, can we? Especially when he looks like such a respectful young man in public. And so the other kids must be making it up. Except this time, you caught Emil red-handed."

I can almost feel the steam coming out of her nostrils. "I did."

"And yet he still doesn't do anything." She laughed. "I'm trying to start a betting pool about how many history books Bren thinks he'll be in after his death. You want to join?"

"History books?"

"You do realize that's all any of this is to him?" She waved her hands. "The man thinks he'll be remembered as one of our heroes because he was the Head Mage of the school that trained Emil."

"He's said that?"

"He doesn't need to say it for me to know it. Look at how he spends his time. Most of us have a life outside of school. Not Bren. The school is his life, and he spends all his free time corresponding with nobles about the school and Emil and playing politics. The man doesn't have real friends apart from Mito. He's the most boring man I've ever met, because everything is about ambition and fame to him.

"Just consider Emil's discipline record. He could *murder* someone and Bren would still go on about how he's still a good boy inside. And yes." Jadoni looked her in the eye. "I know I shouldn't be saying all of this. And if you try to report me, I'll deny saying any of it. But I'm too old to join in with the idolization of authorities. Bad men can still be made Head Mages, no matter what the friars say."

Kalina smiled at her last comment, even as the rest of her words sank into her. "I won't report you." *We share more in common than you may realize.*

"Prudent. Now, I'm not going to bother telling you what to do because young people like you don't listen to the elderly, but if I were you? I'd turn down this offer to mentor Emil."

Twenty-seven wasn't *that* young. But Kalina ignored her comment and focused on the last thing she said. "Why?"

"Because kids like Emil don't change." She leaned in closer. Kalina could smell her onion breath. "I've circled this sun of ours for sixty-eight years—too long, if you ask me—and I know a thing or two about people. That little bully will get you to like him so he can get out of trouble. Oh, and probably get you to help him save his skin too. Which...too bad for him. The good thing about his death is that it means he won't become the next leader of Rizade. But to get to the point, you don't have the experience to handle someone like him."

"Thanks for the vote of confidence."

"It's your life." Jadoni threw up her hands. "If you want someone to tell you you're some special person who will change the world, Ashinara's next door. I'm telling this to you straight because I'm too old to care about what you think of me. You're not as awful as I expected you to be. You kind of bore the kids, but it's your second week. And that battle simulation came from a stroke of genius. But you're fooling yourself if you think you can change Emil. Boys like him never change. And the sooner you accept that lesson, the better."

"O...okay."

Jadoni stood and grabbed her cane. "Remember, I want my book back in three weeks." She limped out of the room.

Kalina sank back into her chair.

What *was* that?

And what kind of school had she joined?

14

THE TARGET LAY A MERE FIFTY yards in front of her. Kalina eyed the bullseye past the string of her bow and released.

The arrow landed with a thump just outside the target's center.

Kalina leaned back. The klyte arrowhead on her necklace swung back and tapped against her chest. She had taken up archery after regaining the use of her hands, claiming she needed to defend herself on the battlefield. But it also gave her time to think away from everyone.

Talking with Riyad gave her alone time as well. But she also needed time when she was truly alone. Here in Chintor, the cramped archery range in the middle of the bustling city was the best she could get. Noise drifted over the walls surrounding the open corridor. But at least she could be alone, if not in a quiet place.

Her mind kept going back to yesterday's conversation with Elder Jadoni. She couldn't quite place her. Was Jadoni a bitter old woman who mistrusted everyone? Or was she right about the school?

Kalina released another arrow. This one hit right next to the other. Still missing the innermost circle.

Things *were* pretty crummy at Chintor Academy.

But there was bad and there was Jadoni-levels of bad. The woman never had a good word to say about anything. *Is Emil really the artful manipulator she claims he is?*

He had certainly made a lot of excuses in front of Bren. His parents also hadn't done him many favors in teaching him how to repent.

She released the bowstring again. This time the arrow fell even farther outside the center.

She wished she could ask Elder Umar's advice. The grandfatherly old man who had helped her apologize to Hanodoi was the one person she fully trusted at the academy. But Bren had sworn her to secrecy, and she wouldn't break her word.

Kalina had to consider the source. Jadoni understood a few things, but she also mocked Emil for his scars. She read selfishness into Bren's motives, which didn't fit. If anything, he struggled with the opposite issue: trusting people so much that he failed to realize when he gave them too much slack. If he had a hidden agenda for fame, Kalina hadn't seen it.

Bren and Emil both had problems, and Kalina didn't believe in overlooking serious faults.

The question was if she wrote them off or held hope for change.

Grace.

She released the arrow. It struck right at the edge of the bullseye.

She knew what first came to mind when she thought about that. Or rather, who came to mind. That dashing bearded man who always slipped in when she closed her eyes. She tried to avoid imitating Riyad with all her decisions. *But seven years of marriage rub off on you.*

And after Head Mage Bren's question about if she'd ever hurt someone else...

She could still remember that conversation, clear as day.

It had happened in the middle of her fourth year.

I speed walked across the rice paddies surrounding Baylin Academy. The sun shone with the intensity of a piccolo's pitch. I would miss my noon class. But right now, I didn't care. I needed to get away from it all. Too many of the elders knew about my sister's rape. And I didn't care how many extensions or cancellations they gave for work I'd missed. They knew.

Behind their smiling faces, I could see their secret judgments. Why didn't you say something earlier?

"Hey, human!"

For once, I disliked Riyad's nickname for me. I glanced back toward the academy to see him striding toward me. Water from the paddies splashed his trousers. His black hair gleamed in the sun. He had it piled on the top of his head again. My heart leapt within me.

Not the time for that. "I need some time for myself."

He kept walking toward me.

I should run. But where to? The open paddies stretched all around us.

"I said I need some time to myself, Riyad." My knees felt weak. I could feel the tears squirming beneath my eyelids. *Why couldn't he choose another time to break up with me?* "Please leave."

"Kalina." He used my name now and stopped ten feet away. "I heard about what happened."

My throat caught. *He knew.* My gaze fell from his. "Well, good." I swallowed. "Just say what you need to say so we can get this over with."

He squinted. "Say what I need to say?"

"Yeah." The pit in my stomach threatened to swallow me up. "Break up with me so I don't need to bear the terror of waiting." I blinked back tears.

His lips opened slightly. "Kalina..." He narrowed the gap between us. And before I could say anything, his arms were around me.

I inhaled sharply as I clung to him. *Don't let me go, Riyad. Please...*

After a long moment, he pulled back to look me in the eye. Tears rolled down my cheeks like the descending notes of a harp.

"You know I still love you, don't you?" he asked. He hugged me again, even tighter than the last time.

My tears erupted like the blast of a trumpet.

Finally, he peeled himself off me, and all my words spilled out. "You... you don't understand," I sobbed. "I should have known about my sister. I had wondered if...if that was happening. Every time I tried to ask her about it, she denied it. But I should have trusted the hints over her words. I was a fool, and I did nothing."

"It's not your fault, Kalina."

"Yes, it is!" My fists half-heartedly hit against his chest. "I should have known, and I did nothing and I...I...I shouldn't be here. You know that.

Mages ought to be the bastions of society. Well, guess what? I...I..." My words caught in my throat.

He put his hands on either side of my face. The look in his eyes spoke something deeper than I knew to put into words.

"You're human," he whispered. And I'd always remember those words. "That's what I've always told you. If grace was only for small mistakes, would it really be grace? What if grace is for the things we can't make amends for?" He brushed a loose strand of my hair behind my ear. "I'm so sorry about what happened to your sister. I don't know if you could have stopped it. But even if you could have, we give each other grace because we grow from our experiences. And next time, you'll know better what to do when you see the signs of abuse."

Kalina's arrow hit the target in the center of the bullseye.

She panted and stepped back, wiping her brow. Elder Jadoni was wrong. Kids like Emil *could* change. She had to believe that.

We give each other grace because people can change.

The country needed her to help Emil grow over these next seven months. The army needed a hero. And her husband's future depended on rescuing the Arditen healers.

She gathered her arrows into the quiver, ready to shoot another round.

Green light streamed over the short walls of the open range.

Kalina jolted and spun. The light came from beyond the walls of the city. The military signal for high alert.

What was the army doing here?

Nervous energy rushed through her veins like fingers slipping over the strings. She snatched up her remaining arrows and exited the range. Outside, women stood and murmured as they stared at the green light. They didn't need military experience to know what that color meant. Kalina wove around the gaping bystanders. Her worn sandals slapped against the cobblestone as she rounded the narrow street corners.

Finally, she broke out of the alley onto the only wide street of Chintor. The gates lay ahead—along with the dozen armored horsemen standing in front of them. They wore Rizade's uniform. Drums went off from somewhere beyond the gates.

A murmuring crowd kept its distance from the soldiers, but Kalina pushed her way through the civilians. She strode toward the horsemen as, on the other side of the crowd, the mayor of Chintor and a few officials came forward. The mayor looked just like his son Jacir—he even had the same haircut with short hair around the sides and long greasy hair on the top.

One of the horsemen dismounted and lifted his head. Kalina jolted, stopped dead in her tracks. Commander Kay.

For a moment, they locked gazes, and he gave a knowing nod in her direction. Then he turned his burning stare toward the mayor and nobles of the city.

"What's going on?" The mayor's words came out hot and fast.

"Six days ago, a second Kaldian army joined the first and broke through the walls of Inlaru," Kay said. "They captured the city and immediately sent their second army this direction."

Kalina's blood froze.

"We barely managed to catch up to and flank them before they reached Chintor," Kay continued. "We've set up defenses on the hills eight hours south of here. That should hold them off for some time. But they're here for the boy."

Emil.

"Eight hours south..." Shock poured through the mayor's voice.

"We're cut off from the Light Network. You may as well consider this city under siege. Prepare to send food and medical resources to our army. And strengthen the fortifications." Kay turned to eye Kalina. "The boy is our only hope."

INTERLUDE:
FROM THE JOURNAL OF EMIL MAHDSON

Elder Kalina & I had our third one-on-one meeting today. It was illuminating. She has the battle mage experience no one else here does, though I value Elder Mito's caution that there's a reason our mages & strategists lose.

But she still doesn't know how she survived. And she's still hung up on the way I lead my hall. Like that's the most pressing problem when we have the entire Kaldian army eight hours south of here.

Now she wants me to start keeping a journal to reflect on my life. She even got Head Mage Bren to assign me an hour by myself in this room each week to write in this. She promised she wouldn't read it. But I've seen my mom & Elder Crayenda play this game before. They act nice so they can win my trust, and then they use that to hurt me. I know it isn't fair to put all that on Elder Kalina. She could be one of the good ones. But how can I be sure?

At least she probably won't beat me.

I don't know what to write apart from the fact that it's been an awful year. Even before the Kaldians took Inlaru.

In some ways, I suppose it all begins with the catastrophic defeat of Arditen last year. That's when I realized I was destined to die in this war.

And that didn't need to happen.

Especially after a month-and-a-half where I watched my father make horrible decisions on the battlefield & refuse to listen to any of my suggestions.

Does he even realize that *his* failures are making us lose this war?

Does he care?

He's only ever treated me as a trophy.

Really, though, that doesn't upset me the most. I'm more ashamed about my personal failure. Because I should have finished my capstone project over New Year's Break so I could have finished all the graduation requirements a year early.

And I failed.

Sure, I still entered this year way ahead of all my classmates. And I'm playing an advanced instrument already. But I need to be better.

I feel the eyes of everyone on me whenever I leave my dorm room. Everyone expects that I'll save them from the Kaldians. It's why my dorm leaders won't bother studying experimental magic techniques with me. I tried so hard to get them to form an elite club at the beginning of this year. But it's just Elder Mito & me studying the obscure every week. Because why should they join us when they can sit back & expect me to single-handedly win the day?

They see the show that I put on for the school.

But I know the truth: I'm not good enough.

I never am.

I can fake it all I want. But the Kaldians will beat me if I can't turn something around.

As for the worst part of the past several months? I don't really want to write about it. But it seems like I should.

Leneya broke up with me.

Those words are hard to write. Even after three months. I can't get her family's farmhouse out of my mind. It was a little taste of heaven every other weekend over that month and a half reminding me what I fought for. Her parents fit the classic mold the friars always expound on: the strong husband who provides leadership & muscle labor married to the shrewd wife who manages their business. And even though they don't have much, they love her & her siblings. Nor do they treat them any differently, even though her siblings aren't receiving a formal education.

I don't know that I've ever been in a "normal" family home like that before.

They didn't base their love for me on my prophecy. They hardly mentioned it. I didn't feel like I had to walk on eggshells. Leneya always encouraged me. And those midafternoon romps we had in the barn...

It was all going great until she broke up with me right before the school year started.

She's still there when I fall asleep at night. I can see her out of the whispers of my vision. She was supposed to be the girl I went out to fight & valiantly die for.

Every time I see her, the subtle curve of her chin recalls all my old feelings.

I want to run to her. To kiss her. To hold her in my arms again & never let her go.

And she doesn't even look at me.

She just goes around telling people I'm a brute who wanted to use her. What?

I did so much for her. But I also messed up. She realized I wasn't the perfect savior I'm supposed to be. Because it's hard to keep up the pretense that I'm actually a storybook hero.

And so, here I am. Feeling the burn of her casual cruelty.

It's become clear to me by this point that the Ternion (if it exists) hates me too.

I want to die knowing I had a good life while it lasted.

Is that too much to ask?

15

THE KALDIAN FORCES SPREAD

out beyond the cliffs like a swarm of ravenous razdas, all waiting for the
moment a back was turned to descend upon their prey.

Kalina shuddered. It was one thing to know how close they were. It
was another to finally see it for herself, a month after they had first arrived.

Emil stood right at the edge of the cliff. The rest of her Year Six students
hung farther back, evidently nervous to be this close to the hordes of
human-sacrificers.

"I don't understand why they hate us so much," Meliya murmured.

"It's 'cause they're a bunch of cowardly infidels who hate the Ternion,"
Emil said.

That was certainly a part of it. But their friars also preached that they
had a right to inherit the whole land, not only the dry wilderness that
covered most of Kaldia. And that if they did so, their god would bless them
with prosperity. Just like he had already with gunpowder.

"Well, they outnumber us for sure," Elder Mito said. "Tough luck for us."

Kalina shot a glare in his direction. *That isn't what our students need to
hear right now.*

"A battle is won on more than numbers." Kalina gestured to the hills
their forces camped on. "We do have some strategic advantages."

These weren't any hills. Steep embankments made the elevation even more treacherous to ascend. Those cliffs hadn't existed originally. Rizadian mages had been at work ever since the Kaldians conquered Inlaru. Firm palisades at the top further entrenched their defensive lines.

"If I were the Kaldians, I'd keep moving and look for a better spot for pushing north," Elder Mito drawled.

"Then clearly you don't know what you're talking about," a gruff voice snarled.

Kalina spun to see General Mahd coming their direction with his two guards. For once, she appreciated his harsh gaze.

Mahd continued. "The hills run along the east until they hit the Deep Jungle. And to the west is a swamp the likes of which no army can feasibly go through. I would have thought you knew your geography."

And this is why I requested that Elder Mito accompany me on this two-day visit to the front lines. Emil had been stubborn lately in clinging to Mito's outdated tactics. Kalina wanted him to see with his own eyes how naïve Mito's battlefield theories were.

Elder Mito lowered his gaze and shrugged. "If you say so."

General Mahd shook his head and turned toward Kalina. "These your students?"

"Yes, General."

"Then all of you follow me. You'll see what we're doing to keep you all alive."

Kalina gestured, and as the general led them between the tents and the palisades, she made sure all the students followed. She noticed how Elder Mito slunk close to Emil and fell back to overhear their conversation.

"Swamps are meager obstacles when enemy flutists can drain them," Mito said. "If we were fighting a smart enemy, they would have considered that."

"We'll have scouts and flutists by the swamps to counter that." Kalina voiced what General Mahd hadn't bothered to explain. "The Kaldians aren't fools."

Elder Mito rolled his eyes and jogged up toward her. "You know," he said with more edge to his voice than usual, "traditionally there *is* a code among teachers that we don't contradict each other in front of students."

Head Mage Bren had mentioned that. But Kalina was a military commander, and Mito was filling Emil's head with garbage.

"I thought you cared about the truth," she said. "Isn't that your thing? 'Follow the truth no matter where it leads'?"

"Oh, of course. And if you put down valid perspectives as foolish, I'll have to tell Bren that you probably aren't fit to tutor our prophesied hero."

She blinked. Mito didn't have that kind of influence, did he? But then she remembered what Jadoni had said about them. How many times she saw them chatting jovially. And how much Bren bought into Mito's military theories...

General Mahd started talking again. "These are the mages who keep our forces safe."

Kalina looked up. They had come up to the band of mages in Repose, surveying the battlefield lest enemy mages mount a surprise assault. A few of the mages glanced their direction.

"That sounds like a boring job," Meliya said.

Kalina cringed. Not that Meliya's words surprised her. The girl rarely listened in class. She was too busy trying to snag Jacir's attention.

General Mahd fixed his redwood gaze on her. "And what's your name, girl?"

Meliya's eyes widened. "Um...I'm Meliya...uh, sir."

"Well, Meliya, I prefer boredom to watching my men die."

Emil stepped up on a ledge to peer over the palisades. "Have we considered using our high ground to actually drive them back and take out the enemy before they get reinforcements?"

Kalina frowned. Mahd certainly lost a lot of opportunities because of his cautious approach. But high ground gave them defensive advantages, not offensive ones.

His father waved a hand. "I'm not here to take suggestions from a *student*. Get down from there and stay in line."

Kalina bit her inner lip. *That's how you respond to your son?* Elder Mito exchanged glances with Emil. *"See,"* Mito's gaze said. *"The army is as incompetent as I told you."*

She wanted to say something. But she knew better than to test Mito's threat.

She changed tactics and cleared her throat. "General Mahd, do you think you might be able to explain why high ground doesn't give us an offensive advantage here?"

"Shouldn't you be teaching that?" Mahd growled. "I'm not here to do your job for you. We need to move on to the next station!"

Anvisa and Krem stepped protectively near Kalina, clearly upset at the affront the general had given. She brushed past them and hurried to catch up to General Mahd.

"Well, look at that," Jacir snickered to Emil as she passed. "I didn't realize our resident boy savior could be wrong."

"Oh, leave off," Emil snapped.

Kalina wrinkled her nose. Why were Emil and Jacir fighting? They always walked in lockstep. *Unless Emil has taken the concerns I shared about Jacir's character to heart.*

She caught up with the graying dictator. "General, may I have a word?"

"I don't have time to do your job for you."

"That's not what I'm asking. I think the students would benefit from hearing what I teach from a second source."

"Students need to learn to accept a general's word without questioning. Maybe you do too."

"Is there a problem?" Elder Mito came up alongside them.

Klyte.

"Yes. Both of you need to teach students to respect their superiors. Where do they think they're living, the Endrish nation?" General Mahd curled his lip. "Pure rubbish." He turned back to the students. "And here are the newer fortifications."

Kalina turned right. Soldiers were building walls in front of the wooden palisades, laying on mortar and stones to create a stronger defense perimeter.

"Took us weeks to find the right quarry. But this is what real war looks like. Gaining positional strength and biding one's time."

Emil cocked his head. "What's the plan for when the Kaldians get enough reinforcements to storm the hill?"

"Oh, we're not planning on holding this forever," General Mahd said. "We need six months until you finish your training. And we have our own reinforcements coming up as well from the south."

"But how will our troops get up here when the Kaldians hold Inlaru?"

"I *said* we'll protect you," General Mahd snapped. "All of you kids. You think that just because you're smart students, you know more than seasoned generals. Well, you're not. Leave the worrying to us and know your place."

Kalina formed fists. *How does he not see what he's doing?* All he had to do was explain that the Kaldians didn't have any other armies to spare. And they couldn't afford to abandon Inlaru with their only other army. He didn't need to make his leadership look worse than it actually was.

But no. He had to take it as an affront to his authority. And Emil would find reinforcement for the klyte Elder Mito fed him.

"One final stop before I send you to the mages for the rest of the day," General Mahd said. "Follow me. You'll see something you don't learn in school."

Kalina held her tongue. At least Emil wouldn't be tempted to follow Mahd's disastrous strategies. But her whole goal for this trip had been to subtly show Emil that Mito's strategies didn't work either.

So far, she was hardly succeeding.

General Mahd led the group to the crimson command tent. It sat on a hill so it could overlook the lines in front of them. Its tied-back curtains revealed the battle map on the table within.

"This is where battlefield decisions are made," General Mahd said. "My advisers and I determine the state of the battle from tents like this and use our drummers to signal orders to our commanders. Our superior position should scare off the Kaldians. But if they attack, we'll beat them from here."

Emil looked at the tent. And then turned and looked toward the ridges, which were a good quarter of a mile beyond them.

"You can't even see over the cliffs from here," he muttered to one of his friends.

General Mahd continued. "We've lost fewer men than any other Rizadian army. And that's because of the decisions we've made. My troops rest in the security of knowing that we don't throw away lives."

Actually, many complain that they aren't allowed to take more risks. There was a reason Mahd lost fewer men than the other Rizadian generals—he called premature retreats, which also meant they never won.

And that had its own impact on troop morale.

Jacir piped up. "A few of us have been talking about if mages should fight on the front lines. Have you ever considered that?"

Stop. Kalina stared at Jacir and the smirk playing across his face. *He knows General Mahd won't like it.* And for some reason, he seemed to want to humiliate Emil's strategies. *What happened between you and Emil?*

Because right now, Mahd was only going to hurt Kalina's efforts.

General Mahd guffawed. "Don't you learn anything in school? You may as well ask for a death sentence. I don't even leave my pikemen out there when the gun cavalry emerges. We win by saving lives for future battles. Don't you read your textbooks?"

They did, but the textbooks didn't encourage his cautious tactics.

Mahd shook his head. "I'd rather have the largest army than one that sacrifices men just to gain a few more feet of ground. It's the model we've followed for centuries. Why should we try something new?"

Kalina's remaining hopes for the field trip withered and died.

Disgust spread across Emil's face.

"So no, we don't do that," Mahd continued. "Because risks kill an army. It's why all my soldiers love me. Once you join, my goal is to make sure that *none* of you are hurt."

Emil looked at her right at that moment. And she could read the unspoken lament in his gaze.

"My father doesn't even think about me and my prophesied death."

And then he turned to the teacher encouraging him that the only reason mages didn't fight on the front lines was due to cowardice. The bond between him and Elder Mito had just forged a deeper connection.

General Mahd went on prattling about the dangers of risk-taking, but Kalina had tuned him out.

This trip had reinforced all the lies Emil believed.

16

"LET'S PRACTICE OUR MELODIES again!" Kalina raised her baton in the air.

A couple of Year Three students sighed. But a dozen violin bows still went up around her in the outdoor classroom.

She waved them through the standard Quelling melody at sixty beats per minute. The resonance of a dozen violins playing the minor melody filled the arena. *So far, so good.* Quelling melodies were always done in a minor chord. But then she signaled them to switch to a standard energy melody in a major chord at the pace of eighty beats per minute. Almost immediately, they fell apart. The arena descended into musical chaos.

She held up her hand to stop them and fought to avoid putting her head in her hands.

"Have you been practicing? You sound about the same as you did last week!"

Blank stares answered her question.

Don't flip out. She was still in a bad mood after yesterday's battlefield trip. But she calmed her breath and remembered what kind of teacher she wanted to be.

"You'll continue to fail if you don't practice," she said. "And we can't practice actually *doing* magic until you master these basic melodies. So we're going to do this again. And I expect all of you to practice for at least an hour tonight."

They were already two weeks behind schedule.

At the very least, she did know how to run startlingly effective battle simulations.

And so, for her Year Six students, battle simulations it was.

She scanned the "battleground" as wooden cubes slammed into each other. Arpeggios soared across the battlefield. Drums on both sides beat thundering notes. Lightning sparked between eruptions of fire. She hadn't let two different types of mages fight at the same time before. Flame and lightning scorched nearby trees. Burnt cubes rocketed into the air.

"Keep your strikes *inside* the arena!"

On the other side of the field, Jadoni kept a tight eye on her lutists moving the cubes. She'd surprised Kalina when she told her she was fine doing this for her class once a week. But she claimed it had nothing to do with how much her students liked it—only with how valuable the practice was for them.

Kalina had her doubts. The crone cared about her students more than she admitted.

Anvisa and her team had become a lot better at pre-Quelling the Fabric to prevent lightning strikes. Unfortunately, they still went up against Emil. And while they could resist his teammates' attempts, they had nothing against him. His lightning strikes illuminated the battlefield. And blackened cubes went flying wherever he struck.

Winning magical tug-of-war against a boy chosen by prophecy wasn't easy.

Orange and blue flames licked the left side of the battlefield. Wood cracked under the scorching heat. The drummers were more evenly matched in the fire they called forth. A group of red cubes on the edge combusted into roaring flames. But then a lightning strike from Emil blew the nearby blue cubes into pieces.

Little could deter Emil's strength from landing him another handy win.

"Blue team percussion: good defense," Kalina barked after gathering them for their recap. "Pay attention to what your stringed allies do and try to work together to dominate the battlefield. Red percussion: you need to learn when you can't make headway and switch your strategies earlier. Don't keep pursuing failed tactics."

She turned to her violinists. "Blue violinists: *great* teamwork following

Anvisa's lead. You're working together well. But you're playing things too safe. When you face tough opposition, you need to know when to take risks. The battlefield isn't about waiting for the perfect opportunity. It's about taking risks and pursuing the best available option.

And then she faced Emil's team. "Red violinists: As long as you're putting all your hopes on one juggernaut, you're not growing. Your form and tactics look like amateurs fumbling through sheet music. I don't care if you're winning right now. On the actual battlefield, you'll go up against enough competent mages that you will *lose* if you don't start working together. Understood?"

A few of them nodded. Emil didn't. The visit to the battlefield had reinforced all his negative assumptions about battle mages like herself.

Kalina sighed and clapped. "All right. Back to the classroom."

She watched as the students made their way back. Anvisa stopped when she passed her. Leneya stopped too.

"I...I tried so hard," Anvisa said. Her face screamed with repressed frustration. "But we *still* couldn't win."

"It's hard," Kalina acknowledged. "You're going against prophecy."

"But all his teammates suck, and we still can't win against them." Frustration flashed again across her face. "What am I missing?"

Kalina sighed. "There's nothing you're *missing*, Anvisa. Just keep practicing and growing. But like I said earlier, when your team begins losing, you need to stop playing it safe. I understand why you settle for moves you know will work. But when your opponent trounces you, at some point, you need to take risks and put yourself out there."

She glanced right to see her students gathering near the edge of the jungle, pointing at something in the treetops. Looking up, she saw the blue scales of a teriden crouched on one of the upper branches. Kalina blinked. While the human-sized reptiles were carnivores, they didn't hunt humans and normally stayed in the depths of the jungle.

"Back to the classroom," she said with a wave of her hands. "The teriden doesn't need your attention."

With a groan, the students peeled themselves away, Emil last of all. The teriden leapt off the branch back toward the jungle. The skin membrane between its limbs opened up as it did so, allowing it to glide out of sight.

If only Emil paid as much attention to my battlefield advice as he does to this teriden.

Kalina hurried down the hall of the main academic building, arms full of books. Elder Suraya had been expecting these back for a while. She knocked on the wall beneath her nameplate. Unlike every other teacher, Suraya didn't have a doorway to her office. Kalina waited a moment. A trumpet played from behind the wall and the stone peeled back to form a doorway.

She stepped in to see Suraya sitting behind her immaculately organized desk. Kalina would have sworn only Bren and Suraya had desks that neat and organized. Of course, Bren's desk was more bare than organized. Jadoni claimed an empty desk implied a vacuous mind. But papers and objects stacked high on Suraya's desk, all at perfect right angles.

"Hi," Kalina said. "I'm returning the books you lent me a couple weeks ago on magic theory. Thanks for letting me borrow them."

Suraya nodded and set aside her trumpet. Her ruby-red lips parted. "Of course. Did they help?"

Kalina shrugged. "Honestly? Figuring out how I survived feels like a goose chase, and I don't know if I got much. But I at least learned that most mages die from fractures because their magic redirects back into themselves, not because of some mystical reason...so I guess I need to figure out how I survived that."

"Glad you found them helpful." Suraya gestured to her bookcase. Her embroidered shawl fluttered. She clearly put time each day into her personal fashion. "You can put them back where you got them. They're in alphabetical order."

Kalina went over and began looking at the titles to slot them in.

"I heard yesterday's field trip went well?" Suraya asked.

"I suppose." She shoved a book on a shelf. "I had hoped that seeing the actual battlefield would deter Emil from some of his naïve beliefs."

Suraya snorted. "And so you brought Elder Mito with you?"

She scanned the bookshelf for *R*. "It seemed like a good idea at the time."

"That man is a character. Fits all the stereotypes of the brilliant professor who's a bit off his rocker—except without the brilliance."

Kalina chuckled. "You have any advice for...drawing Emil away from some of his ideas?"

"Emil's always been stubborn. And between the two of us? He doesn't like listening to female teachers. I worked on him in Years Three and Four, but nothing changed. We eventually let him go his own way."

She frowned. "That's what I'm worried about. We can't afford to let him use bad tactics. He'll be on the battlefield in six months."

"That's why we trust the Ternion." Suraya turned slightly toward her. "Right? The Ternion isn't going to let its worshipers fall into the hands of human-sacrificers. So it's not worth worrying about what we can't control. We're responsible for doing our part."

The words did little to quiet her uneasiness. *What if Emil's tactics* are *my responsibility?*

Well, that didn't help. Kalina appreciated that someone else saw his issues. She'd spent far too many lunches with Ashinara—who could never say a bad word about anyone—and Mito—who enabled Emil's issues. But it appeared that Suraya shared General Mahd's fatalism.

At least she could now speak with the one teacher whose opinion she did trust.

She knocked and poked her head into Umar's room. "Does this time still work for you?"

The old man's face brightened. His smile stretched back the sagging wrinkles on his face. "Always, Kalina. Please come in."

She slipped into the room and sat in the seat in front of him. "Thanks for taking the time to meet. I know I should be able to figure this out myself."

"Well," Umar said, "a normal teacher also gets three weeks of training and preparation before starting. I'm happy to offer what I can."

She fidgeted. "I don't know. I'm not a good teacher. Sure, I might be teaching the required content. But nothing works except for my battle simulations. The students always tell me about the fun things they do in other teachers' classes. I only produce vacant gazes."

Umar nodded. "I see." He paused. "How do you plan lessons?" A hint of curiosity colored his voice.

"The previous teacher didn't leave me much—just a list of topics and textbook readings. So for the battlefield tactics class, I give lectures on the textbook with anecdotes from my own experience. And for the bowed string magic class, I'm teaching them basic melodies so they can begin manipulating the Substances in Repose. But I can't get them to practice enough after hours."

"Have the Year Three students started manipulating the Substances?"

Kalina shook her head. "I want them to master their music before they try to combine that with Repose."

Umar leaned back in his chair. "Well, look. It's not my job to tell you what to do. But in my experience, students have a hard time being motivated to practice when it's all theoretical. If I were in your shoes, I'd begin having them practice using their instruments while in Repose to create energy. Perhaps bring in more exercises to your battlefield tactics class as well. Give them problems to discuss and solve. Textbooks sometimes make it sound like we're trying to impart as much head knowledge as possible. But we want practical skills. And the more you can focus on that, the better."

She nodded slowly. "That...that makes sense. I guess I worry that if I slow down to do more of that, I won't teach all the basic and intermediate melodies required in Year Three or get through the Year Six textbook."

He chuckled. "Let me let you in on a little secret: No one finishes the class objectives. The Head Mage's requirements are more a list of ideas than a definitive checklist to complete. Work through most of them, but prioritize practical learning over completing a list."

She exhaled slowly. "That would be easier."

He smiled. "It should be. Don't feel pressured to complete all those requirements." He raised an eyebrow. "And don't feel pressured to match up to other teachers. You will never be me or Elder Suraya or Elder Jadoni. That's fine. Be Elder Kalina and chart your own course."

"I know..." Kalina stared at the ground. "It's just hard at the moment. I don't have the experience you do."

"Keep pressing forward and things will get easier. Remember, the first year is always the hardest."

To be honest, hearing that's a bit cliche at this point. But she nodded. "Thanks." She looked back up at him. "I mean it. It's good to have someone in my corner."

Umar chuckled. "There's a lot more in your corner than me."

If I trusted their advice. But Kalina didn't want to complain about that with someone as kind as Umar. And if she had extra time, she could use it to plan for the upcoming weekly meeting with Emil.

The two of them had a lot to talk about after yesterday's trip.

And she wasn't sure how he would respond to the suggestion she planned on making today.

PLUCKED STRING MAGIC

move objects along the fabric

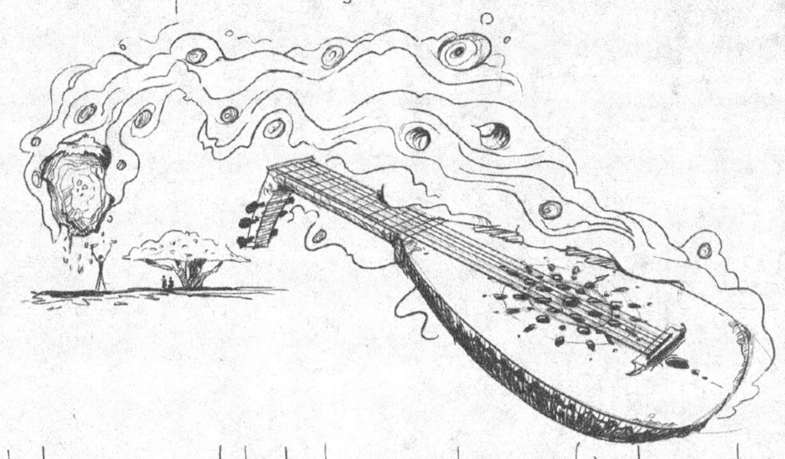

→ Lutes are used to help move heavy objects, scale
tall cliffs, make people fly (though mages can't
make themselves fly... still not sure why that
doesn't work), construct buildings (if not done
with trumpets), and obviously kill people in battle

→ Lutists can only control one object at once, so
many lutists use large boxes if they want to
move a lot of objects together

ZELETOR →

Honestly, they
kind of scare me.

17

@KALINA DIDN'T KNOW IF SHE WAS ready for her meeting with Emil.

But she *had* learned something from the failed field trip: Emil desperately wanted to innovate. It's why he kept proposing ideas to his father. Even if they didn't all work, he was at least trying. And so, after a month and a half of studying strategies every other mage used, perhaps he was ready to pioneer something new.

Emil slid past the curtain into her office without knocking. "Hey, Elder Kalina!"

"Hi," Kalina said. "Please knock in the future."

"Oh. Sorry, my bad." He plopped into his chair, put his eight-stringed fiddle down with its recognizable clink, and tapped his foot against the floor. "We didn't grow up doing that in my house."

She cocked her head. "You didn't knock?"

"Mom didn't believe in curtains. Said that people who want privacy seek to hide things." He smirked. "It's probably 'cause of my dad."

He had revealed to her a couple of weeks ago that his dad was a serial adulterer. *Go figure.*

"So you didn't have any privacy growing up?"

"Nope." He popped the *P* sound. "Great environment to grow up in. Had to be ready for Mom barging in at any moment to interrogate me about what I was doing and beat me if she didn't like it. Great homelife."

She shook her head. "Well, I'm sorry about that."

He shrugged. "I've dealt with worse."

Kalina looked at him carefully. "So. How would you assess today's battle simulation?"

"My teammates are trash. You know it, I know it, and they might know it too. They need to step it up, because Anvisa keeps improving and it won't be too long until we can't beat them."

She blinked. *Did he just admit that?* Maybe her proposal would fall on ready ears.

"What are you going to do about that?" she asked.

"I mean…I've told Jacir that he and the gang need to do better. Not that he listens to me anymore. But Elder Mito says I need to focus on my own performance, not what others do."

Kalina pursed her lips. "You know Elder Mito is not your Year Six mentor, right?"

"I know…" Emil sighed. "I guess I trust him. He knows what the heroes of old were like. And he spotted all the problems with my dad's strategies."

"I agree that your dad is a horrible tactician. But frankly? Reading fictional epics tells you jack squat about what works on the battlefield. Do you know why we don't act independently on the battlefield anymore? Because armies that worked together squashed those soldiers. There are better ways to innovate."

Emil cocked his head. "Like what?"

She studied him. "What do you know about my time on the battlefield?"

He shrugged. "You don't say much, so not a lot? Head Mage Bren says you were a good mage, though."

She nodded. "By myself? I did fine. But my husband and I together became something else entirely. Because the two of us discovered something. I played cello while he played lute. But out there on the battlefield, we discovered how to harmonize our music to affect the same objects together."

Emil coughed and his eyes widened. "I'm sorry—what?"

Kalina remembered that last day Riyad and she had played. *We were single-handedly winning the battle. And he was smiling so big.*

Then everything collapsed into chaos.

She shook away the memory. "Yes. We synergized our energies so our magical strength doubled and we could override enemy Quellings."

"But—but that's impossible!" Words flew from his mouth faster than a glissando. "Only mages with the same type of instrument can synergize. Bowed strings and plucked strings have different effects, so the cello and the lute have to deal with two different Substances! Unless you plucked both, it's impossible for them to work together."

"And yet we did."

"But—but—" He grasped for understanding. "That would revolutionize warfare as we know it! Why didn't you mention this before? Are other battle mages doing this?"

Kalina sighed. *If only.* "Remember why synergy rarely happens on the battlefield? Both partners need to harmonize their notes into a singular melody. Because of the clamor of battle and the amount of improvisation needed, battle mages normally can't pull that off. My husband and I knew each other well enough to do it. The other mages couldn't."

Of course, it didn't help that, like most generals and nobles in Rizade, mages cast skepticism on drastic innovations.

"Then why do you think I can pull this off?"

She smiled. "Because you improvise better than most. And unlike everyone else in our country who likes sticking with the status quo, you know we need to innovate. While it may be hard, I think that over the next six months, you could learn to listen to other melodies and harmonize. And if you can double other mages' efforts, you could affect *all five Substances*, not just one. With your raw strength? That would be a game changer."

For a long moment, Emil said nothing. He simply stared off into the distance, tracking something with his eyes. A fly? A whispering mote of dust? But she could tell he was considering it. *Look at that.* If she could successfully turn that failed field trip into a genuine teaching opportunity, maybe she really was fit for this job.

Then his eyes swiveled back toward her. "That doesn't make sense."

"What doesn't make sense?"

"I'm the person who needs to save this nation."

"...And?"

"They don't deserve to take the credit for my sacrifice."

She blinked. "You're concerned about who gets the credit?"

"Elder Kalina." His breath rushed out quickly. "I've already lost *so much* in life. Please don't ask me to give up a heroic legacy as well."

This is ridiculous. "I'm not trying to take things from you. If you beat the Kaldians by pioneering a new skill, people will still sing your name for generations."

Emil shook his head vigorously. "No. The people I help would take all my credit. I know how this works." His words came out in spurts, like water from a rickety pump. "People use me for what they can get out of me, then throw me away and bask in my fame."

How is this the first thing on his mind? "That isn't true, Emil."

"Oh?" His gaze dug into her. "You think the bullies at this school treat me well because of my charming personality? People like Jacir and Pesh wouldn't have a thing to do with me if I wasn't supposed to save their hide. Heck, Jacir already doesn't like me anymore." He whipped his head around to stare at the wall. "It's like my mom always said. People don't like me; they tolerate me."

"Emil." She tried to meet his gaze. "That's not true. You've told me before that your mom beat you. Don't let her lies fill your mind."

"I see it with my own two eyes." He pursed his lips. "If I fail to save this country, how many people would stick by me?"

Her heart burned. She remembered her own days as a student. Only one friend had stuck with her.

"I'd stick with you." The words left her mouth before she considered them.

His head swung toward her. "Would you?" Anxieties lined his face like droplets on a web. "Do you mean that?"

Well, now that I've said it...

"Emil," Kalina said gently. "I know I'm a teacher, so I can't be a peer friend. But I care about you. Even if you don't succeed, I won't leave you. Because you matter."

Emil's expression communicated hesitance, yet also that faint trace of optimism that told her he *wanted* to believe. "You promise?"

She blinked.

"I'm sorry. I know I should trust your word. But I've been betrayed by too many people who said things without thinking about them. And I need to know if you mean it."

She hadn't come into this meeting planning on doing this. But the boy needed someone. And she knew what it felt like to be merely tolerated. "I promise, Emil. I won't abandon you, even if you fail to stop the Kaldians."

"Okay." Emil exhaled. "Can...can I get a hug from you?"

She blinked again. "Of course." She got up and stepped over to him.

He wrapped his arms around her, and she could feel the fear tensing up his body.

Something about this feels off. Was it how different this was from his confident personality? How quickly the conversation had spiraled away from synergizing?

Kalina would, of course, return to that topic later. Maybe she didn't have to worry.

But nebulous doubt still danced just beyond the reaches of her mind.

18

KALINA WAS ON *FIRE.*

She hadn't unlocked some hidden teacher talent. Even after talking with Umar four days ago, most of her lessons still bored the kids.

But today she had gotten lucky.

The previous teacher's plans for teaching Year Three students how to manipulate the Substances had them first trying to create a spark of lightning. But her students had never used magic before. And she remembered how difficult combining Repose with music was.

That's when she had remembered the ingenious way her teacher had first taught her: not with a full-on lightning spark, but by sending energy into a small plate of raw sunflower oil to make it smoke.

The previous teacher's notes indicated that she rarely had more than two students create a lightning spark on the first day. But Kalina got half the students in her class to make their plates of oil smoke.

She hadn't expected the pride that surged through her bones the moment she saw them succeeding. *This* made the struggles of last week all worth it—to see the looks of delight in their eyes.

Still high on her students' successes, Kalina walked into the faculty lounge with the bowl of vegetable rice she had grabbed from the chef. The bite of hot spices wafted into her nostrils. It wouldn't live up to Chineya's standards. But did school food ever do that?

At the small table, Mito sat alone reading a parchment.

Shoot.

Mito was insufferable enough in a group. *I should have lunch in my room.* But she hesitated.

"Well." Mito's eyes brightened upon seeing her, and he put down the parchment. "Looks like I don't have to eat alone today. Not that I don't enjoy reading new revelations from the Ternion. But unlike our friars, I don't think this is authentic." He flicked the page. "Too many contradictions between this and the most trustworthy revelations we already have."

She sighed internally and sat opposite him. She didn't want to get into a religious debate. *If he tries threatening me again, I will cut out.* "How was teaching?"

"Oh…" He stroked his scraggly black beard. "You know how kids are. Always trying to pull something new on you." He nodded in a way she supposed he considered sage-like. It looked ridiculous. "How's my boy doing with you?"

She blinked. The man never asked her about Emil. "He definitely has skill. But he's stuck in shortsighted thinking."

Mito raised an eyebrow. "Oh?"

Kalina planted the seeds. "I want to help him pioneer some new techniques the army's ignored. But it requires him to work with others, and he's afraid they'll steal his fame."

Mito leaned in. "What are these techniques?"

"Keep this to yourself, but I know a way for mages to synergize with other kinds of instruments. Hard to believe, but I pulled it off with my husband before our accident, and I believe I could teach him to do that on the battlefield."

"Well, then." Mito nodded slowly. "That would be something, wouldn't it?"

"Maybe you'd be willing to support me in persuading him to learn this. The general wouldn't like it…but I'm willing to go against the grain of the military on this."

In truth, she doubted General Mahd knew enough about how magic worked to care. But she knew her audience.

"Hmm." He picked at a knot in the table. "Did you win any battles with this?"

"The Kaldians blew up my cello shortly after Riyad and I first pulled it off."

"Oh. I teach skills that have a longer track record than that."

Kalina bit the inside of her cheek. "You see the potential, though, don't you? We've all seen before how powerful synergizing is. And unlike most mages, Emil is actually great at improvisation."

"Yeah." He leaned back in his seat. "I kind of have to agree with the kid, though. What—he has to watch what other mages are doing and then jump on their efforts? That doesn't sound like a decisive hero who's coming up with his own strategies."

Arguing with Mito was like trying to get chickens to march. "No mage comes up with all their own strategies. They follow their commander's orders."

"And that's the problem with the modern military." Mito shook his head. "The strong follow weak imbeciles who penalize decisiveness. We need mages making bold decisions without asking permission or apologizing for them."

There were so many issues with that statement, she didn't quite know where to begin. *Have you even thought through the chaos that would create?*

She settled for something that lay closer to home. "You realize that this kind of authoritarian attitude is what leads Emil to bully kids like Hanodoi, right?"

"What?" Mito snorted. "That's not decisive heroism; that's being a self-entitled tool. And believe me, I gave Emil grief over that."

"Sure—but Emil justifies his bullying by saying he's trying to become a decisive leader. Doesn't that concern you?"

Mito rolled his eyes. "He's a kid, and sometimes kids act like fools. Don't read into it. Besides..." He looked at her knowingly. "You *do* know Hanodoi kind of asks for this treatment, don't you?"

Kalina raised an eyebrow. "What?"

He smirked. "Oh, don't tell me you haven't noticed. He asks annoying questions, intentionally fails to follow social cues, and gets upset when people make blanket statements against a culture that's trying to sacrifice us to their god. *'Not all Kaldians are like that'* and other nitpicks. The kids are wrong to bully him, but sometimes I wonder if he likes all that attention."

Her mouth dropped.

"Don't look at me like that," Mito said. "Come on now. Are you *really* going to tell me he's never asked you a dumb question?"

"Maybe," she admitted.

"Or not respected your time by asking the same thing over and over again without listening to you?"

She studied her bowl of lukewarm rice.

"Then you know what I'm talking about. Most of the kids pick on him. It's because they're kids, for crying out loud, not because they have some defective view of leadership."

She pursed her lips. They'd gotten far afield of their original discussion topic.

But it had become clear that Mito would offer no help in her attempts to teach Emil how to synergize.

Battlefield tactics class started in fifteen minutes. She was playing an old tune she and Riyad had dueted on her cello when the curtain opened.

"Oh, stop it!" Anvisa pulled Krem into the room by the elbow. "You're being a coward." A grin spread across her face.

Kalina put down her bow and leaned the cello against her desk.

"I'm not being a *coward*," Krem grumbled as he followed her down the stairs. "I just don't think Elder Kalina cares about this." He eyed her.

Kalina glanced at the curtain to see if the third member of the trio would join them. But no. Her gaze flipped back to the duo as they walked over to her desk.

"Hi, Elder Kalina!" Anvisa said cheerily. Lights danced in her eyes. "Krem wanted to ask you a question."

Krem shook his head. "*Anvisa* wants me to ask you a question. *I* want to let you play your cello."

Anvisa laughed. "He's embarrassed to ask you directly." She looked at Kalina expectantly.

Okay. Kalina glanced toward Krem fidgeting next to Anvisa. He kept eying the curtain. And yet he didn't rebut Anvisa's last statement.

"Is there something I can help you with, Krem?" Kalina asked.

"Well..." Krem's foot scuffed at the floor. "I don't know. I don't want to bother you while you're working."

So he does want to ask. "Well, you're already here. What's going on?"

He exhaled slowly. "So, um, you know Leneya?"

She knew where this was going.

"I, uh...well, I think I like her. Probably. I don't know. So I was kind of considering asking her out, but I don't know if she likes me in that way or not, and I don't want to mess up our friendship. Anvisa says I need to go for it, but I'm not sure, so I guess I'm seeing if you have any advice on the subject."

He breathed in slowly. And his gaze drifted back to her. His cheeks looked as red as the skin of a ripe peach.

Kalina bit her lip to avoid laughing at his awkward anxiety. Did most boys find it this hard to ask a girl out?

"You know," she said when she regained her composure, "sometimes we need to take our shot in life. It's like figuring out what instrument you want to play in Year One. Unless you try, you'll never know which one will fit. Personally? I think she'll probably say yes. But you'll never know unless you ask." She smiled. "You're training to go out into *battle* next year. Asking a girl out can't be more terrifying than that."

"Oh, I'd rather go to battle a dozen times," Krem said. "You don't know what it's like to be a guy, Elder Kalina."

Kalina allowed herself to laugh this time. "I'm not saying I do. I'm saying there are plenty of hard things we all have to face in life, and she'll probably say yes, and you're overthinking this. What's the worst that could happen?"

"The dissolution of our friendship," Krem mumbled.

Anvisa gave Kalina an exasperated look. "Do you *see* what I have to deal with here?"

Kalina shook her head. "Well, you're going to have to make a choice, Krem. You've got less than a year left before you all leave, and at that point you may never see her again. How much do you want her?"

"Exactly!" Anvisa elbowed Krem. "Like I said."

"Yeah, yeah..." Krem poked his tongue into his cheek. "Okay. Well, thank you, Elder Kalina." He shuffled his way out of the room.

Anvisa watched him leave, then spun toward Kalina. She ran her hands through her hair. "I can't *believe* him!"

Kalina smiled. "Sometimes people need time to work through things."

"Yeah, like *two months*? That's how long he's talked to me about her, and while I haven't told *him* this, Leneya *really* wants him to ask her out. She walked next to him the whole field trip to the battle lines. It's *so* obvious to everyone except him that she likes him."

She laughed. "Well, they're moving faster than my husband and I did. I think it took us four years before either of us admitted our feelings. We went to the same school because of each other and everything! But we still didn't say anything to each other for a while." She smiled when she remembered how nervous Riyad had been when he admitted his feelings that day on the beach. *As if I would have turned him down.*

Anvisa gave her a grumpy look. "Yeah, well, it's their last year and who knows what's going to happen with the Kaldians, and so if they're going to make something happen, they have to do it now." She sighed. "Wish me luck, will you?"

Kalina had never seen Anvisa's bossy side before. It was kind of funny. She smiled and leaned closer. "Look. If Krem likes Leneya, he'll ask her out. Give him some space. Sometimes people are more likely to make the right move when they don't have someone breathing down their neck."

Anvisa exhaled. "I'll try. But I hope he says something soon, because let me tell you: hanging out with both of them while we have this huge zeletor in the room? I'm sitting on pins and needles. It's about time they address it."

"I understand." Kalina smiled as Anvisa walked out of the room, and then shook her head. She had signed up to be a magic teacher, not a life coach.

And yet, here she was. *If only Riyad could see me now. I'll have so much to share when we revive him.*

Nor had she missed the implication of her advice to Anvisa.

She's not the only person needing a reminder that we need to give people space if we want to see them grow.

19

$\mathcal{E}$VERY MONTH, THE SCHOOL HAD
some evening social event that demanded teacher supervision.

Tonight was one of those nights.

Students milled about the central green as they waited for the dancing to start. Kalina walked between their conversation circles. The boys had all changed into the traditional colorful tunics men often wore in Rizade when not in uniform. The girls had kept their tan tunics but changed into more vibrant skirts.

She glanced left to see a group of students crowding around Hanodoi near one of the fountains, Emil among them. She frowned and walked toward them.

"I just want to know, would it be Jacirroi or Jacirroke in your culture?" Jacir asked, a grin spread wide across his face.

Hanodoi shrugged and looked away. "Kaldia doesn't have a name like that."

"I think we should go with Jacirroi." Emil smirked. "Sounds like a winner."

"You know it, Emilor," Jacir said.

Jacir and Emil are getting along again now. Kalina stepped up. "What's going on?"

Emil pivoted toward her. "Elder Kalina! We were trying to learn more about Kaldian culture. Thought we could all have Kaldian nicknames for our hall so he doesn't feel like so much of an outsider."

Hanodoi was partially hunched over. No way had Emil suddenly developed an interest in Kaldian culture. This was just a way for him and his friends to make a joke of Hanodoi. But could she call them out on it when they would claim their interest was genuine?

Kalina waved her hands. "We're not doing Kaldian nicknames here. Knock it off and leave Hanodoi alone."

"What's wrong with these nicknames?" A mischievous grin slipped out of the corner of Jacir's mouth. "I thought there wasn't anything wrong with Kaldian names."

There's that plausible deniability.

A flute began to play on the other side of the courtyard.

"The music is starting. Go ahead and join the dancing." Kalina walked off.

"But why are Kaldian names so bad?" Jacir asked again. A couple of students snickered. She didn't turn back. *I should have thought more about how to best handle this situation.*

Music twirled through the air like water bubbling over a pebbly stream. Elder Ashinara stood with Mito and Umar at the side of the green. Kalina walked up to them as the kids formed a traditional dance circle. Many of them danced with someone whose elaborate color designs marked them as being from another social class. Mage status trumped class distinctions, after all.

She remembered the way Riyad would sneak up during a dance, surprise her with that grin of his, and ask with the words he always used for that occasion. *"Hey, human—what do you say about the two of us dancing tonight?"* Of course, after their marriage, he always delivered the line with irony.

"I'm so glad to see Emil here," Elder Ashinara said. She had wildflowers tucked behind her ear today. "I'm surprised this got him away from his studies."

Kalina glanced at Emil, dancing between Meliya and Andreya. "Does he not attend school social events?"

"Not this year he hasn't," Mito said. "Works night and day so he can beat the Kaldians. It's a bit overkill, if you ask me."

"I'm glad he's happy again," Ashinara said. "He was so crestfallen after Leneya broke up with him during New Year's Break."

Kalina's mouth dropped. She stared at the boy. "He dated *Leneya*?"

"For at least a year," Ashinara said. "They were such a good couple, too. He needed someone like her to get him out of his mopey shell, and he seemed so depressed when they broke up. I know those signs when I see them. I'm glad he found someone for this final year."

Kalina couldn't believe the quiet girl who only hung out with Krem and Anvisa used to be with the most popular kid at the school. She shook her head. "Emil's dating someone else now?"

Ashinara glanced at her. "The girl he's dancing next to, Meliya. They started dating last week."

"Huh." *She was dating Jacir a few weeks ago. No wonder Jacir and Emil haven't been getting along.*

"Emil could do with someone better," Mito muttered. "She's going to dump him within three weeks, tops."

"Oh come now," Ashinara said. "Meliya *did* stay with Jacir for six months."

"I'm surprised they made it that far," Mito said. "Two days dating Jacir should have been enough. But I think she broke her record for how long she could date the same guy."

Umar chuckled. "I don't know how you know all of this."

"When you're on the younger side of life, kids share more with you," Mito said.

Umar shook his head. "Sure, but I'm surprised they tell *you*."

"Surprise, surprise, some of those teenage girls like opening up to us stoic folks," Mito said. "They think I can give them help or something when my advice is quite simple: Don't date in school. If only they listened to me."

Kalina noticed Hanodoi standing alone on the side. Did he not dance? Or had the other kids refused to let him join? The Kaldians had banned dancing after embracing the cult of the one god, but she didn't think Hanodoi held those beliefs.

"Well, I adore young love," Ashinara said. "That's when I first met my husband, and what I wouldn't give to relive those days, awkward kisses behind the dorms and all. You know what that's like, don't you, Kalina?"

Kalina bit back the ache that resurfaced as memories flashed through her mind. She looked away.

Umar laughed. "I used to have that attitude too before I married," he said to Mito. "It was probably for the better that Feneya didn't meet me earlier in life. I was a bit of a rascal in my youth. But some days when I think about her, I wish I had known her for longer than I did."

From what Kalina had gathered, his wife had died seven years ago after thirty-something years of marriage. She'd heard rumors of something going on now between him and Jadoni, but she hadn't seen anything personally. She couldn't imagine someone as kind and grandfatherly as Umar marrying someone as crotchety as Jadoni. *But perhaps opposites attract?*

"I don't believe it because I'm single," Mito droned. "I believe it because I see what love does to these kids. Emil does better work when he isn't distracted by girls. And that isn't even to mention Meliya's work ethic."

Kalina knew well enough about that. Meliya was failing her class at the moment.

Ashinara looked at the dancers and sighed. "I wish Anvisa would find someone, though. She's too talented a girl to remain single."

That's not how finding a partner works. "It seems like she has good friends. Though I wonder how much they can get a word in when she begins talking."

"Leneya used to be more talkative," Ashinara said. "But she's been quiet this year."

Umar nodded. "I've noticed the same. Her quality of work has also gone down. I suspect there's something going on in her life."

"It's the kids' unending drama," Mito remarked.

"Maybe," Umar said. "I think she also changed her social circles. I don't see her with the same kids I did last year. Maybe the breakup did it."

"Well, look at that—grandpa does pay attention to students' social lives." Mito grinned.

"I notice where students choose to sit in my class."

"I'm surprised you don't have seating charts," Kalina said. "I had to introduce those the second week."

Umar chuckled. "When you're as old as I am, the kids know better than to mess around with their classmates in class. Old age brings some advantages."

The dance ended, and the kids scattered to the tables decked with food. The cooks had worked hard in the kitchen. It almost smelled as good as

Chineya's cooking. The pungent smells of smoked teriden and some type of spicy fried rice filled the air.

Ahead, Emil ran up to Hanodoi. *Can he not leave the kid alone?* She hastened to break up whatever torment Emil had planned for the boy.

"...and anyway," Emil said as she moved closer, "I wanted to apologize for making you uncomfortable. That wasn't a very heroic way for me to act. And I'm sorry."

Kalina blinked. Had her words actually struck home?

"Uh, sure, I forgive you," Hanodoi said. They shook hands. And Emil turned away. For a moment, his gaze met Kalina's. Then his cheeks reddened, and he ran toward the tables.

She hardly had enough time to process the conversation when Jacir passed by with a younger boy she didn't recognize.

"I'm just saying that you don't need to be buddies with some overhyped hero to be a magnet. Ask enough times, and those girls get tired of saying no. They'll do whatever you want."

Kalina started. "Excuse me?"

Jacir spun to look at her. Recognition filled his eyes. "Oh—uh, hi, Elder Kalina. Like I said. Girls will do any activity with you, whether it's walking around the jungle, studying together, or joining the dance circle." He grinned. "You know how it is."

And then he hurried on.

A dozen responses leapt to her lips. But Jacir would deny all the other implications of his statement. And the Head Mage would demand concrete evidence. Their girls deserved better than someone like him.

"Anything troubling you?" Umar asked, coming up behind her.

Kalina bit her tongue and shook her head. "Let's keep an eye on Jacir."

Umar nodded.

They sat at the end of one of the long tables with two other teachers. Emil and his group sat close by; Jacir sat at the far end. Emil's friends jested loudly as they ate.

"Looks like we're around the noisy crew," Umar said.

Kalina eyed Emil. At the moment, he was the center of attention as he laughed and jostled the guy next to him, one arm still around Meliya. It looked like people liked him. But was that true admiration, or, as he claimed, a crowd of flatterers?

A couple of other teachers joined their quartet at the end of the table.

Suraya looked out of place with her typically precise demeanor in the middle of a casual dance night.

"Have you heard the news from the front?" she asked.

Everyone looked around with blank stares. Kalina shook her head. "What news? I was there at the beginning of this week."

"The Kaldians have some new weapon best described as a giant gun on wheels. They were able to shatter the fortifications from a distance and make an assault on our troops two days ago. We almost lost. By the Ternion's grace, we barely fended them off, but a full quarter of our men were killed or wounded."

Kalina's eyes bugged out. "A full *quarter* of them?" *Klyte.* They rarely had that many casualties—especially with General Mahd's cautious strategies. If the Rizadian ranks broke...she may not even have six months with Emil.

"I'm surprised Head Mage Bren let you in on this," Umar remarked. "He doesn't normally share the messages he receives."

"I think it was an accident," Suraya said. "He was pretty shaken. We need to keep this from the kids."

"Keep it from the kids?" Mito stared at her and gestured toward Emil. "That one may need to be ready for it."

For once, Kalina agreed with Mito.

Umar pursed his lips. "Suraya's right. The kids don't need the burden of knowing how dire things are. It's similar to why we don't tell them about desertion rates, how many mages have been killed by guns, or our supply-chain issues. I'd rather shield them from the weight of this war."

Kalina blinked. "They'll be fighting in it by the end of this year, though. They already saw the front lines."

Umar eyed her. "I know. They've also asked a lot of questions since then."

From Umar, even critique as subtle as that spoke volumes. Bren had approved it, though—and it did the kids no good to be fed a cleaned-up reality. Kalina searched for the right words to say.

"They deserve as normal a year as we can give them," Suraya said. "And only the Year Six students will be joining the war. I'm sure Bren doesn't want the kids knowing. The mayor of Chintor doesn't even know about this."

Suddenly, Kalina saw the situation in a different light. "Do the Kaldians know how many they killed?"

Suraya raised an eyebrow. "What do you mean?"

"Do they know how many they killed? Half of war is hiding information like that from the enemy."

"Ah. That would explain why Bren mentioned us disguising our losses. I don't get how the Kaldians wouldn't know roughly how many they killed."

"War is messy," Kalina said. "Sometimes an army retreats because the commanders don't know they won the battle. Control an opponent's knowledge and you gain the advantage." She paused. "I prefer honesty with our students. But if the Kaldians don't know about it, none of us should even know, much less the kids."

"Mahd would want his son to know," Mito grumbled.

"Emil can't keep a secret," Suraya said. "Take it up with Bren if you disagree."

Umar turned to Kalina. "I appreciate your understanding. Our stance will make more sense the longer you work here. We shouldn't lie to the kids. But they aren't always ready to handle the full truth."

Perhaps. The Ternion knew she lacked much experience with children. But how would they be ready when they were being fed sanitized truths?

20

KALINA'S LANTERN FLICKERED as she held it up to illuminate the teetering stack of books in front of her. She frowned and tapped the glass pane. These artificial lights were still too finicky to use reliably. They'd attempted to fix that during her time at the Krazian Inventors Guild. But it took time for updated technology to disseminate.

Still better than a torch with all these books.

She glanced about the cavernous recesses of the library basement. Haphazard stacks of books cluttered the dark chamber. Personally, she thought it was a terrible idea to store books in a basement. Especially one that had sunk into the ground over time. But Bren insisted their mages sealed the walls and floor before rainy season every year.

Kalina bent down near another stack. Unfortunately, none of the books that had been exiled to the basement for space concerns were organized. She wouldn't have come down here if she hadn't already reviewed all the books related to instrument breakage on the upper level.

Admittedly, this was an odd way to convince Emil to synergize. She really wanted to play the authority card—either herself or with Bren's support—to force Emil to learn this technique.

But she needed Emil to *want* to use it. Because she wasn't preparing him for the classroom; she was preparing him for the battlefield, where he'd have freedom to make his own decisions. So here she was, hoping Bren was right that Emil would change if he didn't have a death sentence hanging over him.

Kalina carefully pulled a book out from the middle of the stack and flipped through its pages. It looked like dense reading about speculative uses of magic. The chapter headers didn't contain anything related to instrument breakage. A word about Compelling in the table of contents, however, made her frown. She flipped to that section. A book with this information shouldn't be publicly available, even in a disorganized basement stack...but there it was. A whole chapter analyzing how to use bowed string magic to manipulate energy in the minds of others and Compel them to take certain actions.

She tucked the book beneath her arm. This should be in the teachers-only section of the library upstairs. The kids did not need to stumble upon books teaching uses of forbidden magic punishable by the death penalty.

She moved to another bookstack. Most of the books in it were falling apart, likely because they'd been abandoned in a musty basement. But she did pick out one book promising to tell of *Strange & Amazing Tales of Great Mages*. Maybe someone else had experienced an instrument breaking as well. This looked like a collection of tall tales. But she needed to find something that would work. And the books she'd requested from the other side of Rizade hadn't arrived yet.

Along with the two books she already had, this was probably enough for the day. She danced around the stacks of books and ascended the rickety staircase.

The upper level couldn't feel more different. Tall, neatly organized shelves loomed over the checkered tile floor. Regular sconces with artificial lights cast a warmer glow around the room.

She started to head back to the librarian's desk when she noticed Hanodoi reading in the corner.

She walked over to him. "Reading a good book?"

Hanodoi jerked, then relaxed once he saw her. "Oh—uh, don't tell anyone." He looked around. "But I wanted to read about Kaldian culture before...uh...all of this happened."

She tilted her head to see the title of the book. *A Short History of Kaldian Temple Architecture*.

"Remind me when your family moved to Rizade from Kaldia?"

"Oh, my great-grandparents did, eighty years ago." He looked at her intently. "Believe me, they left forty years *before* the missionaries came."

"I know," she said gently. "I don't blame you for being Kaldian."

"Okay, well, could be nice for others to know that." His voice cracked and his cheeks reddened. "Sorry."

Kalina shook her head. "It's normal for voices to change. Why architecture?"

He flipped the book around to look at the worn fabric cover. "Well, my grandfather was a trumpeter who formed houses. Told me all about the Kaldian temples. I guess they've destroyed most of them because 'real worship happens in nature' or whatever they believe now."

She nodded. "They razed the Arditen temples too." Before they'd done so, she had been shocked to see temples made out of mere wood and plaster while she fought in Arditen. *No wonder the Kaldians could destroy them.*

Hanodoi bit his lip. "You know...between you and me, Elder Kalina, I'd like to live in old Kaldia. Before they adopted the cult and began their holy war. I don't tell that to many people because they'd call me a traitor. But there was something beautiful to the old country. I'd love to see depictions of people, animals, or even trees in art. Not that there isn't also beauty in Rizade's triangles and circles...but there's beauty in more than that. And sculpting the Divine Council a bunch of times doesn't count."

"I understand. It must feel strange to live in a culture that only paints or sculpts eternal objects."

"Thanks for talking." Hanodoi shrugged. "There aren't many people I can talk to about this."

"I know. You do...you do have some friends, right?"

"Some. I keep this to myself."

Just then, the door crashed into the wall. She glanced across the library toward Emil sauntering in with Meliya and a couple of his buddies.

"I'm out." Hanodoi stood and walked away.

"...so yeah, I'm pretty sure I'll finish my final project four months before the end of school," Emil was bragging. His voice boomed around the library. "Going to give me that much extra time to make plans for smashing those Kaldians."

"Shh," Anvisa said from the desk next to the door. She was the student librarian. "Library tones please."

"Yeah, yeah, I know." He glanced back at his friends. "Gotta be quiet to make sure she's happy."

"Emil," Kalina snapped at him across the library.

His head pivoted. "Sorry, Elder Kalina." He looked at her with a sheepish gaze.

She sighed. "You shouldn't need me in here to show respect."

"I know. I'm sorry. I was just joking around." He glanced at Anvisa. "Sorry, Anvisa. No hard feelings?"

"Sure."

She kept her eye on him as he went with Meliya to look among the bookshelves. His friends shuffled out. Not surprising that his buddies didn't want to study. But she didn't expect Meliya to do so. *Perhaps Emil's a good influence on her.*

Hopefully he wouldn't run into Hanodoi. Kalina took her books to Anvisa.

Anvisa looked up from her own book. "Good afternoon, Elder Kalina," she chirped. "How was the Cavern?"

Kalina raised an eyebrow. "The Cavern?"

"Oh, it's what we call the basement." A light gleamed in her eyes. "Isn't it the coolest place? So many books, creepy dark recesses, forgotten tomes…I love poring through those stacks to see what secrets might be hiding down there."

Anvisa had quite the imagination. "I prefer nice shelves and consistent lighting." Kalina set two books down on the desk. "For now, I'll need you to mark these two off for me." She pulled out the third book from under her arm. "I'm taking this book into the private teacher's section." *I have a key for that room somewhere.*

"Ooooh." She looked at the book curiously. "What's in it?"

"Nothing you need to worry about. Unless you're interested in discovering what dark magic even the Kaldians would give the death penalty for?"

"Oh, I think I'll pass on that. I don't think that would lead to an enjoyable week." Anvisa wrote checkout dates on the library slip.

Kalina smiled. "Probably not." She eyed Anvisa's book. "What are you reading?"

"Oh, this?" She flipped the cover over. "*The Song of Katrina Endol.* I know I should be studying some textbook, but I can't stop interspersing it with good fiction."

"I won't judge you for that. The Ternion knows we were made for more than studying." Besides, as her weekly private lessons revealed, Anvisa spent plenty of time studying already. Kalina scrutinized the title. "That's a foreign book, isn't it?"

"Yeaaah." Anvisa sighed. "I love the story, but this translation bungles it up. I really want to teach myself Endrish someday. I've heard about all their amazing books, but the guy who translated this can't even spell right! Have you ever read any Endrish works?"

She shook her head. "I never read harder works like those. My husband did. I think he liked the Endrish authors. But I only read for escape during my school days."

"This *is* pretty good escape reading."

"My younger self would have had a hard time believing that." But Kalina smiled at her joy. Perhaps this was why Umar insisted that they avoid sharing everything about the war with students. The more they could enjoy their last year and forget the problems of the adult world, the better.

Out of the corner of her eye, Kalina saw Emil coming back, linked hand in hand with Meliya. He carried books in his free hand. What books had he wanted?

"Elder Kalina," Emil said as they came up to them, "I think you'll like my book selections." Meliya wrapped her arms around his waist.

"Oh?" She looked up at him.

"I decided I wanted to learn more about battlefield tactics than what you're teaching in your class, so I found these." Kalina wasn't familiar with any of the titles. He wasn't going to get Mito's outdated views, though, so this might be good. Even if he needed more than textbook training.

"Impressive," she said. "That's a lot of additional reading."

"That's what I keep telling him!" Meliya exclaimed.

"I know." Emil grinned. "But Year Six is too easy for me, Elder Kalina. I have *so much* free time on my hands. And you know I gotta work harder than everyone else if I'm going to save this nation."

Huh. "Does that mean you'll have enough time to learn how to better assist your teammates?"

"Elder Kalina!" He laughed. "I need to focus on beating the klyte out of those Kaldians."

Meliya giggled as she looked up at him.

Kalina rolled her eyes. "Language."

"Sorry. I meant I need to focus on beating the *snot* out of those Kaldians. Can't let them get an edge over me!" He handed his books to Anvisa. "What books did *you* find, Elder Kalina?"

Kalina didn't want to get his hopes up. "Oh, just some theory books."

"Ah." He bounced on the balls of his feet. "You trying to figure out how to save my life?"

Of course, he asked directly. "We'll see what I can find, Emil. I certainly hope so."

"Please do," Meliya piped in. "I love this guy too much to lose him." She hugged him tighter and pressed her face against his chest.

Emil winked at Kalina and took the books back from Anvisa. "You're the best, Elder Kalina. Don't worry. I know you'll figure out the secret. I'm gonna dedicate the rest of my life to you!" He waved as he and Meliya went for the exit. "Don't forget to tell me if you find something! I believe in you!" And then they were out the doors.

Kalina stared at the doors as they shut. She remembered the promise she'd made to him. He really did seem to be beginning to trust her. She smiled.

Anvisa sighed the moment the doors clicked shut. "I don't know how you do it, Elder Kalina."

Kalina glanced at her. "Do what?"

"Put up with him. I'm about ready to chuck a book at his head."

Kalina raised an eyebrow. "Really?"

"I mean, not really." She sighed again. "I don't know. He always talks about 'me, me, me,' and I don't know how you continue to treat him nicely."

"You sounded kind when he first entered."

"Yeah, because I *had* to." She shook her head. "Didn't want to forgive him, but I know what the friars say."

She loathes the boy. But why? Can I ask that as a teacher?

"Well, I appreciate you trying to show him some kindness." Kalina pursed her lips. "He has a hard calling ahead of him."

Anvisa stared at her blankly.

"Do you want to say something?"

"Look, I don't want to step outside my bounds, Elder Kalina, because I respect you and all that, but do you know how many times I've heard that from teachers? It's fine for him to skip out on group projects because he has a prophecy. It's fine for him to bully other boys in his dorm because he needs to be a leader. It's fine for him to torment his girlfriend because he might die soon."

"That's not what I'm trying to sa—" Anvisa's last statement sank in. "He torments Meliya?"

"I meant Leneya, not Meliya. And I don't want to exaggerate. He wasn't physical with her or anything." She glanced away, then shrugged. "I don't know. Maybe he was just overbearing."

Kalina had seen reactions like that before. This time she wouldn't ignore a hint. "What did he do?"

"I dunno." She avoided Kalina's gaze. "He didn't respect her."

"In what ways?"

"Well." She pursed her lips. Then she opened them again and everything spilled out. "He was always taking up all of her time and didn't respect when she wanted to have alone time with friends because he wanted to do everything with her, and he couldn't stop talking about himself and his needs, but whenever she had trouble he was never there for her, except for maybe on one or two instances, and he kept pressuring her to do physical things with him that she didn't want to do and she became really uncomfortable with him and he said a lot of nasty words when they broke up, and—"

"Whoa." Kalina held out her hands. "Slow down. There's only so much your teacher can take in at once."

"I'm sorry." Color rose to Anvisa's cheeks. "I just don't think he cares for anyone except himself."

Kalina scratched her ear. "That could be true. But I want to believe that the right people can show him a better way—and that's why I'm still kind to him. Even someone like Emil can change." *He apologized to Hanodoi, after all. Kind accountability seems to be making a difference.*

"I know…" Anvisa glanced off. "I'm sorry, Elder Kalina. I probably sound mean. But he's hurt too many of my friends, and I'm tired of seeing that."

"I get it. And I want to hear more about that so I know how to best address issues with him. So let's start from the top about what his relationship with Leneya looked like."

Interlude:
FROM THE JOURNAL OF EMIL MAHDSON

All I want is to be understood.

Is that so much to ask for?

Elder Kalina wanted to know more about Leneya. "Did you pressure her at all? How much did you care about her interests? Why would she feel like you only cared about yourself?"

I wanted to run.

Yeah, she asked them in a "nice voice" & claimed she was just concerned. But I've watched teachers play that game before. When they already believe you're guilty, they're not actually listening to your defense; they're hunting for ammunition.

I should shut up. Instead, I keep trying to defend myself because I want to believe that someone won't use my words against me.

I'm not sure I did a good job of explaining myself. "Did you pressure her at all?" I mean, she wasn't sure about kissing or touching in certain places at first. But I was so scared her reluctance suggested she didn't really love me & only wanted social clout from dating me. And I *never* forced her to do anything. If we did something, it's because we talked, I persuaded her, and both of us agreed it was the right decision. Right up until the point when she regretted what she did & blamed that on me.

"How much did you care about her interests?" I mean, as much as I could? I don't get this question. Should we all share the exact same interests in everything? Of course Leneya cared about things that I didn't. But I tried my hardest to listen to her even when she went on & on about things that don't matter.

For the last thing... "Why would she feel like you only cared about yourself?" I need help. I thought Leneya understood that. With all the responsibilities I carry, of course I've needed to focus on my studies. I'm not thinking of myself because I'm some self-entitled narcissist. I'm trying to save our people. And maybe not live a miserable life before I die.

I hate going around campus knowing there's that small group of students who hate me. All because Leneya won't stop her pity party. She's even dating Krem now & she still won't shut up about it. I swore after our breakup that I would leave her be, keep my mouth shut, and move on. And I kept that promise.

And now? Because I held my tongue, Elder Kalina holds me at arm's length.

I tried talking about it with Meliya last night. She tried to be encouraging. But I don't know how helpful she was. It doesn't help that I still feel guilty every time I'm around her. Which...I shouldn't? Sure, I broke her up from her previous boyfriend. But I knew what Jacir was like. She complained to me every week about how he forced her to do things & had fun at her expense. Even as Jacir's friend, I couldn't defend him.

She tells me how happy she feels now that she's with someone who actually cares for her. But I can't help but wonder if I deserve that. Even though I know this kind of thinking is stupid. She's been a good friend for years, I knew she was with the wrong person, so I asked her out & did it.

But I haven't gotten past Leneya yet. And every time I see her, the wound opens raw. It's so stupid. She's mocked me & turned people against me. There's no reason I should still love her.

Yet her laughter fills my mind when I close my eyes.

It was wrong to date Meliya.

<h1 style="text-align:center">21</h1>

STONES FLOATED THROUGH THE AIR,
and melodies bent the fragile blades of grass.

Kalina looked at the house their students were magically constructing in the field in front of them—and at Emil ordering all the other students around. "Should we say something?"

Umar looked contemplative. "It's funny. Normally the other students put up with Emil because he's the one who's doing most of the work. He's different when he can't do much to help."

Kalina nodded. "I was thinking when you mentioned this activity that the violinists wouldn't have much to do."

"Some years, the violinists made electric lights for the house. But that was before we removed the theoretical and engineering tracks to funnel all students into the military track." He paused. "I would normally step in when a student is pushing others around like this. But I know you're trying to work on his character. What do you think? Would he learn more if we intervened, or if we let him experience the natural consequences of his bossiness?"

She pursed her lips. It was hard to say. Over the past month, her efforts to show kindness while holding him accountable seemed to have curtailed his bullying. But it hadn't made much progress in making him willing to learn how to synergize—or do anything else that meaningfully worked with others. She also still couldn't figure out quite what had happened between him and Leneya.

"You've worked with kids longer than I have. I really don't know."

"Well, knowing those kids, they're going to say something eventually." Umar chuckled. "For their sake, I'd rather speak up first. But for Emil? Maybe he should see the results of his actions."

She nodded and turned back toward the students. Building a house from scratch was a traditional Year Six class project. A few teachers had pushed to skip it given the importance of training the students for war. But Umar had asked her if she would still organize this with him. And she wanted to give their kids a respite from the pressures of war. Too many of them viewed magic as a tool for hurting people.

So here they were, a mile outside the city on an unused field. The kids were about finished with the foundation.

"So I'm curious," Kalina said. "What got you into teaching in the first place?"

Umar smiled. "It was mostly my wife's doing. I didn't think I was cut out to be a teacher."

"Really?"

"I wanted to work construction. Something simple where I could follow orders, play my music, and leave it behind at the end of the day. But Feneya had some friends here, knew they needed a trumpet teacher, and basically forced me to teach. And...I surprised myself." He raised an eyebrow. "You *can* fall in love with this profession, you know."

She laughed. "You say that like I'm not open to it."

"Oh, I'm not assuming anything." A wry smile slipped past Umar's lips. "I'm just an old man saying things."

"Of course. And what made this old man fall in love with our profession?"

"Well..." Umar smiled as he watched the kids work. "You know, I don't think I realized at first how much I'd care about these students. I know it's what a lot of teachers say. But it's honestly the truth. You see them grow and mature over their years here." He chuckled. "And some of them certainly surprise you when you see them again as adults and what they've done with their lives. Feneya and I, as you may have figured out, could never conceive. And so something about this...well, it filled a gap."

She exhaled. "I think the kids make me most nervous about this job."

He laughed. "They like you, you know. So whatever you're doing, I think it's working."

"It's the one who doesn't fully trust me that I'm most nervous about." Kalina nodded toward the prophesied hero standing next to a group of other students. Given their irritated faces, it looked like they may have finally gotten fed up with him.

"Perhaps we should see what's going on," Umar said.

They walked closer.

"...look, Emil, if your girlfriend wanted to be able to help with the walls, she should have practiced more," one of the kids, Sez, said. "You don't know how trumpets work. Let us handle this."

"I'm leading this project," Emil said. "And I want to involve *everyone* in this."

Kalina blinked. Where had this inclusive side of Emil come from?

"Yeah, well she can do something like mold the stones the lutists excavate so we can lay them in the floor. We don't need someone like her doing the walls. So buzz off."

"I'm sure our teachers would like more teamwork."

Has Emil spotted us? He hadn't looked in their direction yet.

Sez's gaze flitted toward Kalina. "We're giving Meliya something to do. Not our fault if she doesn't like it. Take it up with the teachers." He turned and began playing his trumpet again. The other trumpeters followed suit. The stones lying on the field morphed together to create a solid wall.

Emil breathed heavily. He finally glanced toward Kalina and Umar. But he didn't say anything. He stalked toward another group of students.

"I will admit," Umar murmured. "It's odd to see Emil dating Meliya. They *have* been friends for ages, and I've wondered if he liked her. But she never seemed to reciprocate his interest. And I could never quite figure out why he liked her, given his ambition and her laziness."

Kalina shook her head. "I've wondered the same. Especially given all his rants about how lazy other students are. Perhaps love blinds him."

"Love blinds us all. Not just romantic love either. There's a reason the boy gets away with so much."

"So you see the issues as well?" She hadn't been sure if he saw how Bren, Ashinara, and Mito covered up for him.

"I..." Umar pursed his lips. "Well, I want to show proper respect. But I'm not blind."

"I understand." Eventually, she might try to tease more out of him. But his tone made it clear he didn't want to delve into this anymore today.

Kalina watched Emil as he talked with other students. Would he realize after this exercise that he needed leadership help? Or would this become another reason he blamed his classmates?

Their students ended up putting together an elegant house when it was all said and done. Emil didn't talk to her afterward. And it highlighted a growing problem. He was listening to her less and less.

Perhaps if I find a breakthrough in my research, that will get him to care less about his fame. She was passing Bren's office when he called her to come in.

Please let this be a brief conversation. Kalina walked past the curtains pinned up to the sides. "Yes, Head Mage Bren?"

"There's someone here I would like you to meet." Bren gestured to the man in tan uniform standing next to his desk.

The man turned toward her. And she would recognize that intense stare anywhere.

"Kay!" Her thoughts of research collapsed in an instant.

Commander Kay grinned like a zeletor. "I figured I had to come by and visit."

"But why?" Her heart jumped. "Did something happen on the front lines?"

He laughed. "No need to worry. Ever since our second army arrived at the Inlaru Delta, we've kept their attention divided. But...well, you never know what will happen. So the general wanted me to review Emil's performance. He's only got four-and-a-half months left, after all."

Kalina pursed her lips. *Mahd didn't bother visiting his son himself?* But perhaps it was for the better. She trusted Kay's judgment over Mahd's.

"Commander Kay asked me about seeing Emil practice," Bren said. "And I think there would be nothing better than showing him one of your battle simulations. I haven't been to one of them in over a month, anyway. Kay's only here today and tomorrow morning, so I wondered if we could pull a simulation together for tomorrow."

"Um, sure." Her mind raced.

Kay laughed. "Don't feel so intimidated. It's me. I know Emil will excel."

Except Emil wouldn't. And another commander would recognize his poor tactics. Unlike Bren, Kay wouldn't pay attention to the fact that Emil won. He would notice all Emil's failures.

Maybe that's what I need. Emil didn't care what Kalina had to say. But if a current commander pointed out his problems?

"I just told Commander Kay everything Emil has learned about successful battlefield techniques, he's learned from you," Bren said. "I knew Emil needed more than books. And he has blossomed under your tutelage."

That wasn't true at all. And Bren should know that. Kalina opened her mouth to share another perspective. But then she stopped. *Kay will see the truth either way tomorrow.*

"Okay." She forced a smile. "I'll talk to Elder Jadoni about putting this together."

REVIEW OF THE FABRIC

*Defines and governs reality.
Instruments control and manipulate it.

THE FIVE SUBSTANCES

(Each instrument type influences a different Substance)

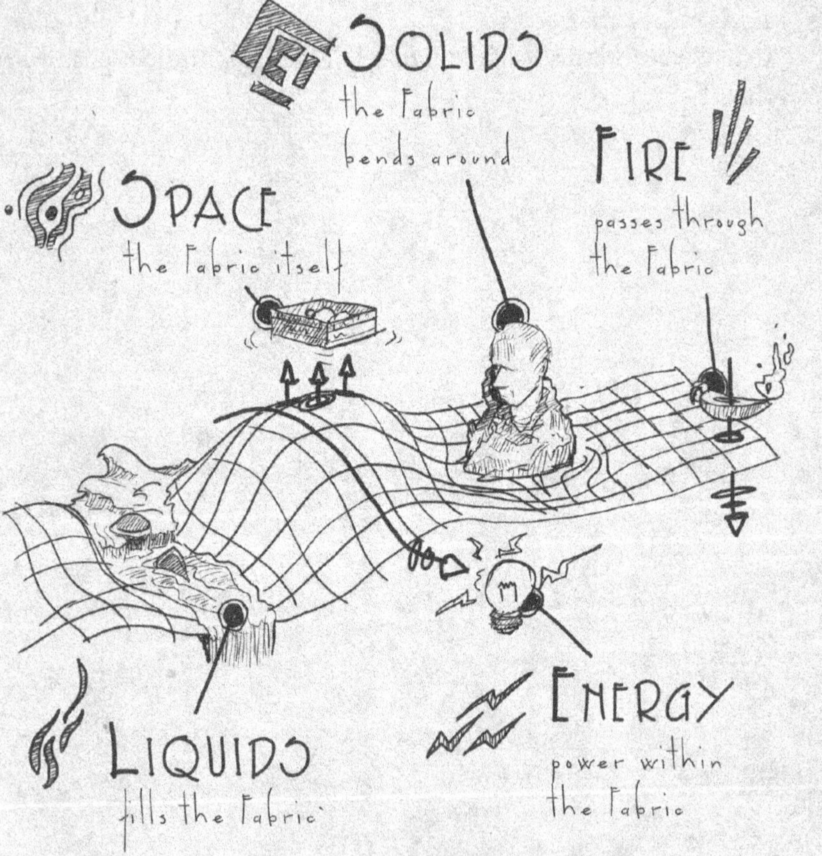

To be honest, I don't really understand the difference between "filling the fabric" and "passing through the fabric." Elder Toze says I don't need to understand that unless I want to be a magic theorist.

22

KALINA RAN HER BOW ACROSS
the strings of the cello, producing a low note for her husband lying on
the other side of the room. While she appreciated the brighter tone of
her cello at the academy, her personal instrument boasted a better-angled
fingerboard. She slid her bow back and forth to create an arpeggio that
crescendoed and ended in a long reverberating note. A musical lament for
her perfect duet partner.

Has it been over a year already since I lost you?

She had noticed the merchant stalls while coming back to Chineya's
place. They hardly seemed the same ones she saw when she first entered
Chintor. The variety of produce had disappeared a long time ago. The prices
had more than doubled. And there was a certain haggard look in the eyes
of everyone she passed.

Her hand moved back and forth more and more quickly, producing
a flurry of dissonant notes up and down the chromatic scale. She'd first
learned the dubious harmony of this piece in school as a Quelling tune. If
she wanted, she could resolve the discord into a brighter key used to shift
from Quelling to attacking. But she avoided that turn as she played.

She still had much to Quell, even if magic no longer sprang from her
fingertips.

Chineya stepped into the room with a handful of half-wilted leeks in her hands. *Does the woman ever not have food with her?* Kalina finished drawing out her languishing note.

"Your music is beautiful," Chineya gushed. "I don't want to make you stop! I wanted you to know that while the flutist came to feed Riyad twice today, the violinist couldn't make it. She said she'd come an additional time tomorrow to stimulate his muscles, though. I also wasn't able to move him around after the second time because of some city officials who unexpectedly showed up for lunch with Raz."

Kalina nodded. "His muscles won't atrophy from one missed day with the violinist. And...I'm continually impressed by how well you keep up with all his appointments. I couldn't be teaching without you."

Chineya smiled. "Each of us has burdens to bear in this war. But with a laugh and a strong arm, there's nothing we can't take on."

"Sure." She fumbled to find something else to say. "City officials coming over for lunch sounds pretty important." *Surprising as well. Most officials rarely eat at a farmer's house, much less an artisan's.*

Chineya winked. "Let's just say good home cooking breaks a lot of boundaries. Even when I have to be creative on rations. Speaking of which, I need to throw these into the stew for tomorrow, so we'll talk more later." She whisked out of the room.

Kalina shook her head. *Hospitality alone builds relationships with officials?* Chineya was something else.

She turned back to Riyad and remembered Chineya's words. *"A laugh and a strong arm."* Well, she at least had the latter. She put her cello aside, stood, and walked over to Riyad. The healers said they had to move him regularly to keep bedsores from opening. She grabbed the pillows propping him up on the right side of his body and wedged them under the left side of his back.

"Can't have you getting worse than you already are," she murmured. She ran her hand through his black curls. They had gotten so long. She should cut them soon. He had always been quite particular about his hair length.

"Do you remember that student you always complained about back when you taught?" She laid her hand against his cheek. "The one I told you I could never imagine teaching because of how many times he interrupted you? I'm feeling like I'd rather have him than Emil."

She smiled as she remembered Riyad's long rants about that student. But then...those complaints had morphed into a resolve to relate to the student and get to know him. And eventually, the interruptions waned as he began to talk to the student instead of lecture him.

If only Emil was that easy to fix.

"Why couldn't the arrow have hit us *before* the Kaldians surrounded Arditen? Serves you right for mocking them." The one time their army had fought alongside one of Arditen's, Riyad had given several of their mages a hard time about their ostentatious golden uniforms. Only allowing nobles to become mages had its downsides.

Of course, Arditen's elitism also meant their healing mages were the best in the three kingdoms. And as much as they had enjoyed jesting with their mages that day...well...

"You probably had it coming." A small smile peeked around the edges of her mouth. Maybe she did know how to laugh.

What I'd give to tease each other again.

23

TODAY WAS A DAY FOR HONESTY.

And the Ternion alone knows what will come of it.

"All right." Kalina addressed the Year Six students in her classroom. "We don't have much time, so we're going to keep this brief. As most of you know, a military commander wants to observe your performance. Don't let your nerves get the better of you. But do make full use of everything I've trained you to do. Any questions?"

A hand went up in the back. "Who's playing?"

That's what I forgot. "Violinists and flutists."

Emil looked at her. She could read his gaze immediately. He knew why this commander had come.

She cleared her throat. "He'll be here soon. Let's get going."

Kalina could feel Kay and Bren's eyes on her as she walked around the arena. She'd instructed some flutists beforehand to place a small pond in the center of the arena to give the mages more to interact with. *Let's see how adeptly they can use it.*

Anvisa barked orders. Krem paced. Most of the other students sneaked glances at Kalina. All different ways of handling their nerves.

Emil took a different tack.

"Look," he said to his team, "I know this is intimidating. But do you know whose errors he'll scrutinize? Mine. Whose success does he care about? My victories. So who bears responsibility for our victory? It's all me. We've won every single battle so far. And if we mess up today? That's on me. So don't stress it. The Ternion sent me so you don't need to fear the Kaldians. And you certainly don't need to fear this exercise either. This is my fight. Give it your best, and we'll get our tenth consecutive win under our belt today."

His words seemed to resonate with his teammates. *Impressive. Emil knows how to lead a group of soldiers into battle.* Sure, cockiness still colored his words. But in this context, it was almost helpful.

And he was the only student who was thinking about the worry his classmates were feeling, not just his own.

Kalina clapped. "Listen up!" The students needed to hear from her as well. "You've done this a dozen times before. And today is no different. It doesn't matter that we have observers. You're not going to get flustered. You're not going to dwell on your mistakes. And you're going to press on because that's what battle mages do. So stand by your team and take on whatever comes up against you. Because you have everything you need. Understood?"

She got a few nods.

She glanced toward Jadoni, who gave Kalina an approving signal. Her students stood at attention.

Kalina tilted her palms upward and entered Repose. "You may begin."

Dozens of tunes burst out around her. Streams of magic sang through the air. Blocks flew across the battlefield. The pond in the arena trembled and shook. She could sense deeper tremors in the underground streams below the earth.

And then there were the violinists. The Fabric sang with repressed energy. Claps of thunder shook the battlefield. Emil's three tones ripped the magnetic forces of the Fabric apart. Bolts of lightning charred blue cubes on the battlefield.

Anvisa and her fellow blue mages didn't try to stop Emil apart from some general Quelling. *Interesting.* Instead, they throttled his teammates, and then sent their own bolts through the Fabric. Emil still took out more cubes than they did.

A geyser erupted on the left side of the field from the groundwater beneath. Earth sprayed across the battlefield and red cubes went flying. Kalina stepped back as drops of water splattered on her face. At least Anvisa's team got something in.

Thunder pealed again, and Emil fried another clump of blue cubes.

Something strange rippled among the blue mages. Half of Anvisa's flutists focused on channeling the new geyser while the other half focused on the pond. Almost as if—

Oh.

The water in the pool surged up and cascaded in a thin wave over the red blocks while the geyser continued to splatter water across the field.

I've seen this move before.

Anvisa and several other mages hit the wave with lightning. Energy rippled through the pathway created for it. And no shortage of cubes lay in its path.

In a few brief moments, close to half of the red army was out of commission.

Emil cursed. Kalina glanced at him. He shoved one of the mages next to him. Yelled something she couldn't hear. Then he threw his attention back at the field, bringing his melodies together to throw one major lightning bolt, similar to the one he threw during the first simulation.

This time, Anvisa countered him.

A few of her mages had already Quelled different sections in the wider area. But she took it a step further, pulling the magnetic charges the other way. Trying to create a counterstrike. It wasn't a traditional Quelling maneuver. If she was stronger than Emil, this could fry her own troops. But she wasn't. And it allowed her and her mages to counter his efforts without synchronizing.

When Emil finally released the lightning, it still destroyed several cubes—but only as much as a normal student would destroy.

Emil cursed again and attempted the same strategy on the other side of the field. Anvisa met him a second time. It took several mages to keep him from decimating their side. But they held their ground. Cubes whizzed across. And then...it was over.

Kalina exited Repose and blinked. Blinked again. Then she began counting blocks. A *lot* had been hit. And the numbers looked close. She had to count twice to verify the result. But yes. Blue had forty-three unmarked blocks to red's forty-one. Anvisa and her mages had done it.

They had *beaten* Emil.

A smile stretched her lips. After such a long losing streak, Anvisa's team had finally beat a stronger mage through the power of teamwork.

And everyone would see the problems Kalina saw in Emil.

She glanced up to see the look of dismay on Kay's face—large enough that she could clearly see it despite his distance. He knew the truth. She then looked back at Emil. His teammates were circling him.

"Leave me alone!" He pushed his way through them and headed in her direction.

Jacir and another student followed him, saying something she couldn't make out.

"We failed," Emil snapped. "Enough with the recounts."

"But," Jacir said, "we almost stopped—"

"You fool." He whipped around to look Jacir in the eye. "Don't you know why the commander came here? For me! And guess who made it clear to the whole school that he *can't* save this country from disaster?"

Emil turned and faced Kalina. His face choked with naked anger.

"Ask her," he snapped at Jacir. "I'm sure Elder Kalina can give you a speech about *exactly* why I failed."

"Emil." Kalina stepped toward him.

He turned back to her. "What? Do you need to make it clear to me as well?" He bit his lip. "No. I know *exactly* how I failed." He turned on his heel and stalked toward the jungle.

She exhaled slowly. *What should I say?* Emil's classmates all looked at her.

She could hear voices coming behind her.

"We won, Elder Kalina!" Anvisa jumped in front of her, talking a million miles a minute about everything they'd done and how she couldn't have imagined they'd make it work.

Kalina glanced back at the hill overlooking the arena. Both Kay *and* Bren looked worried. She knew what she should do as a teacher. Dismiss the kids to class and talk with both onlookers about everything that had occurred.

But she knew what emotions Emil's anger tried to cover. And she *had* made a promise about what she'd do when he failed.

She turned to follow him into the jungle.

24

THE JUNGLE GOT DENSE FAST.

The academy had been built close to the boundaries of the Deep Jungle where the lone elves roamed. People knew better than to venture too far into the bush. Everyone knew what had happened the last time mages tried to clear a path through a tract of the Deep Jungle. Headless bodies had littered the half-formed path.

There wasn't any danger in going a couple of miles in. But superstitions still reigned. And people stayed clear of it.

A thorny vine scraped Kalina's arm. She ducked to avoid a low-hanging branch. Emil hadn't run into an easy place to traverse. Though the thick vegetation at least made it clear where he had trampled.

He wasn't far ahead. His head bobbed between the gaps of bushy foliage ahead of her. She stumbled over the twisted roots after him.

"Emil," she called out.

He glanced back, but kept walking. "Go away, Elder Kalina!"

"We need to talk."

He stopped and turned back again. "Missing your opportunity to yell at me?" His voice cracked.

"I'm not here to yell at you."

"What—is this to shame me for how badly I lost? Because I know that already." His eyes glistened the closer she came.

She stopped ten feet away. "You don't need to run when you fail."

"Really? Because I've seen this game played before."

"What game?"

"Oh, you know." He looked away. "The 'I thought you were so much better than that, Emil' game. 'Don't you know you're chosen by prophecy? How embarrassing to be beaten.'"

"Emil..." She struggled to find the right words. "I've *never* said any of those things to you."

"I know how you teachers act." Bitterness soaked through his words. "You think I'm some Ternion-blessed prodigy who naturally succeeds at everything. And that's not *true*. I put *so* much time into my work outside of classes because *none* of this comes easy. I've spent *hours and hours* practicing experimental magic outside of school these past few years so I can beat the Kaldians. But all my hard work and endurance must be because of the prophecy! And so if I'm not the best one out there, it must be my fault."

Kalina shook her head. "If that's how other teachers act, I don't want to be like them. I'm here to help you."

"Oh yes. 'I want to help you.' 'I want you to be a better person.' 'I'm tough on you because I love you.' My mom told me that while she whipped me because I didn't set the table right. My dad claimed that when he saw me once every six months.

"Well, you know how much of that they believed?" The words burst from his mouth. "It was all a lie so they could show me off to their rich friends. Everyone talks about wanting to help other people, but if we're being honest with ourselves, we all know it's a facade to get other people to like us." He quivered with rage. "You're here because you need me to save your skin from the Kaldians."

Tears sprang to her eyes. "That...that's not why I'm here, Emil."

"Oh? Then why did you take this job? Out of the goodness of your heart? Or to win this war?"

She exhaled slowly. "Yes, Emil. I took this job to try and save our country. But that isn't why I stayed."

His lower lip quivered as he stared at her.

"Do you know that I almost quit this job my first week in?"

He said nothing.

"Well, I did. Because between you and me, Emil, I know I'm not a good teacher. My lectures bore you all, I don't know how to grade, and half the time I'm running around like a chicken with my head cut off. Only my battle simulations work, and that was a stroke of luck."

He laughed, and for a moment, a smile crossed his face.

She pressed on. "And so you know what? I nearly quit. And you know why I stayed? Because when I looked at you, I saw a boy who wanted a good life and struggled with the loss of that dream. I know I haven't figured out how I survived yet. Even after going through dozens of books. But I'm not giving up. Because I want you to live."

Confusion washed across Emil's face.

"I know your parents were awful," she said. "But not everyone acts like them. There *are* people who care. You need to trust us. That's why Anvisa beat you. It's not because she's any better than you. But she's learned how to trust people and work alongside them. That's all I want to help you do—to trust the right people. Because none of us can do this ourselves. Not even a prophesied hero."

Emil slowly sat on a log. His breath came out heavy, and he shook his head. "You...you really aren't mad at me?"

Kalina leaned against the tree and cracked a smile. "I think you've got that market cornered right now."

Emil sighed and put his head in his hands. "You don't understand, Elder Kalina. I can't be as good as everyone else. If Anvisa can Quell my attacks, those experienced mages will squash me like a worm. I know you think I'm arrogant and selfish. But I don't have *time* to work with others and learn new skills like synergizing. Not when my own skills fall so much behind."

"No one's expecting you to win battles solo."

"Then why was the commander so disappointed in me?" His words quivered from a deep emotion. "You saw the look on his face. It wasn't disappointment in my team. It was disappointment in *me*. Because the Kaldians could beat my dad's awful strategies and arrive any day now. And *I* won't be ready for it."

"You can *be* ready if you're willing to try something new and start working with your team."

"Yeah." Emil looked up at her. "And that's why I didn't want to have this conversation. Because every time people say they want to help me, where does it all end? Pointing the finger and telling me it was all my fault. I *begged* my friends to join Mito and me in learning experimental magic at the beginning of this year. But they said no. And I'm blamed for their failings."

"That's not what I'm—"

"Yes. It is. You're just like my mom blaming me for being a bastard."

Kalina blinked. "What?"

He laughed bitterly. "Haven't you figured it out yet? My dad knocked up one of his servants. Understand why my fake mom hated me? Because the child the Ternion chose to save this world wasn't even hers. But because I had a prophecy, she had to raise me like her child. That's all my life has been—people pretending to like me when they want to get rid of me."

Where did this rant come from? But she had already learned that with Emil, whenever he felt like a failure, all the things he hated about himself sprang to the surface.

She had to pull him out of this mess. "What about your friends? Even if they won't work with you, they *do* like you."

"They like power and fame."

"Even your girlfriend, Meliya? I've seen the way she looks at you. She *truly* loves you."

He avoided her gaze. "Maybe."

"Maybe?" Kalina thought back to that day in the library. "She *adores* you."

"You don't understand." He fixed his bloodshot eyes back on her. "People want to be close to power. You're one of four people I consider trusting. And some days I even wonder about you."

"I'm on your side." Her words stumbled out. "You don't need to isolate yourself."

He shook his head and stood. "I don't want to talk about this anymore."

She stepped toward him. "Plea—"

"Leave!" And with that, he dashed off, far faster than she could run, into the depths of the jungle.

25

IT WAS THE CLOSEST KALINA HAD EVER come to figuring him out.

And I still didn't find the right words.

A deserted field met her gaze when she exited the jungle. Everyone had returned to their classes. *Who knows where my students went?* She'd abandoned them all to chase after the one. Hopefully Head Mage Bren would forgive her decision.

She jogged down the hilly green past the outdoor classrooms. Two students played their lutes to move the sand out of the arena back into bags. Particles swirled through the air as they strummed their will into reality. She used the side entrance of the main academic building and strode toward Bren's office.

Voices rang out from within.

"I'm trying to say that's the first time he lost," Bren said.

"And I'm trying to say he had no team coordination," Kay said as she entered. "I'm not a mage, but I've seen effective mages work together, and that wasn't it."

Kalina cleared her throat. "Hi. Sorry for my abrupt exit."

Kay turned, and his trademark stare rested on her. "Commander Kalina. Sorry, *Elder* Kalina. Forgive my bluntness, but what the klyte was that?"

"That's the problem I'm facing." She avoided looking at Bren. "Emil knows how to use magic. But he's awful at working with others. And today, his lack of teamwork caught up with him."

"He must have been so stressed about today," Bren said.

Kay raised an eyebrow at her. Then he turned toward Bren. "No, Kalina's right. It's not stress: The boy needs to work together with others. *That's* his problem." He turned back to her. "Why haven't you trained him to do that?"

His tone sounded harsh. But in an exaggerated way that told her he was faking it. *He understands the politics here.* This was an opportunity, not an attack.

She raised her head higher. "I've tried, Commander Kay. But he's refused to do so. He has people telling him that past heroes worked alone. And he believes that."

Kay blinked. "Who's telling him this?"

"A teacher here at the school."

He leaned forward. "On what grounds?"

"Well, he's read the old epics and thinks that if heroes back then acted solo, we're losing because we focus too much on teamwork. Oh—and because we don't send mages to the front lines."

Kay guffawed. "What on earth?" He glanced back toward Bren. "You have teachers telling kids that? That's absurd!"

Bren bristled. "The situation's more complicated than that." He shot a glance at Kalina.

Kay's laughter died. "I can't believe this. You need to shut that teacher down. General Mahd would throw a fit to learn his son is being taught to be a showman on the battlefield."

"Don't worry," Bren said, "we *will* train him to work with others. It's what our academy does."

"Well, you've failed so far. So if you're going to live up to your reputation, you should start doing that fast."

Bren's face looked like he had tasted something sour. "Believe me, Commander. I've never seen Emil out on the battlefield before. I had no idea he was that poor. But we *will* make a difference in the boy's life."

Kalina frowned. Bren *had* seen Emil out there earlier in the year. Had he forgotten?

"You better." Kay turned back toward Kalina. "The boy needs your help." And with that, he left the room.

She exhaled slowly. *That turned out better than I expected.*

Bren sighed deeply. She looked back to see him sitting down at his desk. "I'm disappointed."

"I...I am too. I had hoped Emil would have performed better."

Bren shook his head. "No, Kalina. I'm disappointed in *you*."

Her heart leapt to her throat.

He continued. "I thought we were on the same team." Concern etched his features.

"Um. Aren't we?"

"Kalina." He spoke softly, but his voice thudded into her. "I would respect you more if you were honest with me."

She swallowed. She guessed what he meant. But she wouldn't incriminate herself. "I'm not sure what you're getting at."

"We're a *family,* Kalina. I thought you understood that."

She didn't like that term. Chineya was family. Coworkers weren't. "What are you implying?"

"I value the dignity of every person here. That's why we're careful with how much we reveal about students. That's why I'm careful not to criticize you in front of others. Families cover up each others' mistakes in the bonds of love. It's what the Ternion asks us to do. But trashing a colleague to put yourself higher in someone else's esteem?" He shook his head. "I had expected better."

"I was speaking honestly about the situation."

Bren looked at her carefully. "So you didn't care at all for the commander's opinion of you as a teacher?"

"I care about him getting an honest assessment of the situation. Both of us served in the military; we care more about results than personal feelings."

"Really?" His eyebrows furrowed. "So if I gave him an honest assessment of you—that students complain about your boring lectures and that your only successful lessons are your battle simulations—would you be happy with my assessment?"

She inhaled sharply. Bren knew that?

"I don't talk about your faults because you're a new teacher. But I notice them, even if I give you grace and don't bring them up." He paused. "I wish you'd have the kindness to extend that sort of grace to others." He looked down at the letter in front of him, dipped his fountain pen in the inkwell, and began to write. He didn't look back up at her.

She felt her cheeks redden. Was he finished? She didn't know what to say to all of that.

So she left.

The conversation remained with Kalina the rest of the day.

It drifted around her mind while she ate lunch with Ashinara, half paying attention to her. It lingered while she taught the class of Year Three students that had been switched over to the afternoon slot. It screamed at her while she stayed late grading the battle tactics tests the Year Six students had taken a couple of days ago. It was stupid to keep doing tests when battle simulations revealed more about their skills. But she had to find some way to measure their textbook work.

She couldn't grade well, though, when unfinished business hung over her.

Was Bren right?

The thought burned its way across her consciousness. Bren claimed the Ternion commanded them to cover over offenses like this. And sure, the friars sometimes taught that. But there were multiple interpretations of what "grace" meant, even if the friars pretended everyone agreed. Grace couldn't mean ignoring serious problems. Lying about Emil didn't help anyone.

A niggling feeling deep inside her, though, said she had wanted to take a shot at the school.

And Kalina didn't know what to do with that.

She stepped outside the academic building and put a hand on one of the pillars. The crisp night air danced along her bare arms. Fading torches cast a pale glow over the deserted green. She hadn't realized how long she'd been grading.

She paused at the threshold. Should she go to Bren's cottage and apologize? She didn't want to. The man had lied himself, and he didn't deserve an apology.

But she *could* have brought her concerns about Mito to Bren earlier.

Her stomach twisted.

That's when she heard feet running.

Kalina stepped away from the building to see a dark form dashing her direction. The person came from the jungle. It couldn't be Emil. He had returned hours ago.

She moved farther from the building. As the figure drew near, the flickering torchlight wavered over her face. It was Meliya—Emil's girlfriend. Tangled hair streamed behind her and the look on her face spoke pure terror.

Kalina's senses went into full alert.

"Meliya." Kalina whipped her gaze around and stepped toward her. "What's wrong?"

Meliya's eyes grew wide. She kept racing toward Kalina.

The green behind her was empty. "Meliya, what's wrong?"

"No, no, no," she gasped.

Kalina stepped to the side—afraid of being run over—and grabbed her shoulder. "What's wrong?"

A wail burst from Meliya's lips and she crumpled to the ground. Her body shook with sobs.

The hairs on the back of Kalina's neck went up. "Meliya." She knelt beside her. "Is there something out there? You need to tell me if there is."

"I—I—" She couldn't talk without sobbing, but she shook her head.

When Kalina tried to put an arm around her, she scooted away and sobbed harder.

"What's wrong?" Kalina asked.

"E-E-Emil..." Her voice came out in shakes.

Kalina looked around. *Still no one.* "What happened?"

She continued to sob. She tried to speak. But she couldn't make anything come out.

"I—I..." Her breath came out erratically. "I shouldn't talk."

A chill ran down Kalina's spine. She glanced back to the jungle, but the green was still empty. "Did he hurt you? Because I don't care who he is—I will do whatever it takes to protect you."

"E-Emil..." Meliya sobbed. "I don't—I don't know what he did to me." Tears fell from her face. "But somehow he tricked me into loving him."

Kalina exhaled slowly. So...this was a breakup? Teachers said Meliya had a tendency to be lovesick and emotional. But this seemed extreme.

She spoke softly. "Sometimes we regret the people we decide to date. It's okay to realize you dated the wrong person."

Meliya looked up at her. Her black hair hung chaotically in front of her face. "I didn't decide to date him."

"You didn't decide to date him..." A dark thought slithered into her mind. *No...* "Did he threaten you?"

But Meliya shook her head. She looked about ready to crumple again.

Kalina leaned toward her. "What did he do?"

"He *made* me love him," she gasped. "I don't know how. But somehow he messed with my mind. He *made* me love him."

Oh.

Oh, klyte.

26

Kalina opened her mouth, but everything she wanted to say flew from her.

She wanted to wrap the sobbing girl in a hug. But she remembered Meliya's previous aversion to her touch. Her mind strained to grasp what had happened. Emil...Emil had *mind compelled* her.

He had Compelled her to *date* him?

Bile rose in her throat. *How long have they been dating? A month and a half? And all that time...*

She shivered. *This can't be true.* Emil wasn't so far gone that he would use mind control to make a girl date him, right? That was illegal—he shouldn't even know how to do that.

But she saw how distraught Meliya's sobs were. She wasn't lying.

"I'm so sorry." Kalina's voice came out hoarse. "That should have never happened to you."

The grim night was silent around them, without any wind or even noises from the dorms to break the sound of Meliya's weeping. Kalina stayed on the ground with her until the sobs began to lessen. Then she walked her into the academic building and into her office, where she lit the oil lamp. It cast long shadows around the dim room. She sat next to Meliya. Meliya wasn't sobbing anymore. But she still shook.

Kalina didn't say anything. Just sat next to her until she was ready to speak.

"I...I don't know when it started," she finally said. Her tears glinted in the dim orange light. "I...I don't know when any of this started. It feels like a bad dream. Did he make me break up with Jacir?" She shuddered. "I don't know! He could still be Compelling me and I don't even know it."

Kalina swallowed. "How did you discover this?"

Meliya dug her fingernails into her palm. "He...he came to me this evening and said he wanted to talk to me out in the jungle. I...I said I did." She paused. "But did I, or was that his Compelling?" Another tear slid down her cheek. "Then, while we were out there, he asked me if I loved him. Truly loved him. I...I said *yes*." She spat the word out as if it were poison. "Then he said he needed to *really* know if I loved him. And he picked up his fiddle and played a few notes." She paused. "I have never heard notes as high or as strange sounding as those. And, suddenly...I *knew*. I tasted something like sour cherries in my mouth. And I knew I had never loved him. I loved Jacir. And—" A sob ripped through her throat again. "I wasn't in control of this for the past few months."

"He controlled *everything* you did?" Kalina's mouth felt dry.

"No...well, I don't know!" Meliya turned toward her, eyes brimming with fear. "I don't think so! I *think* he just made me love him. But..." Meliya's breath came out in spurts.

"That's okay. I believe you. Don't feel the need to explain things."

"He was so upset when I told him I didn't love him." Her body continued to shake. "And when I said I'd tell someone, I think he was about to Compel me again before I threw a rock at his face and ran. You can't tell anyone else about this, Elder Kalina! He yelled at me as I ran off that he would come after me if I told others. I shouldn't have even told you, but you can't tell anyone else!"

Kalina exhaled slowly. She didn't want to believe it. Emil had been improving. *This is something rapists and seducers do. Not a kid.*

But of course, she knew Meliya was telling the truth. The taste of sour cherries was a dead tell that someone had been under Compelling. From everything she'd read, a Compelling couldn't last longer than two to three days. Which meant if he had Compelled her to love him over a month and a half...

He'd recast his spell a lot. Again. And again. And again. Forcing her mind to his will on a near-daily basis.

How many people had Emil Compelled?

Has Emil Compelled me?

The wind whistled outside.

Kalina breathed in and out again and tried to fit all the pieces together.

That same boy who broke down in the woods earlier today to tell her all the pain he had suffered. He...

She remembered how he had looked away when she told him Meliya truly loved him.

Oh, Ternion.

"Meliya..." Kalina grasped for the right words. "I...I am *so* sorry." She met Meliya's gaze and didn't let it drop this time. "I am *so* sorry."

Meliya sniffled. "It...it's not your fault, Elder Kalina."

"This should *not* have happened to you." She let the weight of those words hang in the air. "This wasn't your fault."

A sob broke past Meliya's lips. She stared down at the ground.

Kalina entered Repose. But she could see no further effects of Compelling in Meliya's mind. If only she could look at her own. But she'd need another violinist to do that.

"I looked at your mind," Kalina said. "You're not being Compelled anymore."

A gasp burst from Meliya's lips, and she looked up. Her face spoke hope for the first time that evening.

Kalina swallowed. "Meliya..." She didn't want to ask the question. "Do...do you want to talk about what he made you do?"

Meliya looked toward the wall. For a long moment, she said nothing. "We...we made out. A lot." She shivered.

Kalina waited to see if more would follow. Nothing did.

Meliya looked back at her. "We made out."

"I'm sorry. That must have been awful."

"It..." She breathed in and out slowly. "He made me *want* to do it with him, Elder Kalina. I guess he could have made me do worse, but..."

"But what he did was still awful."

She shook her head and swallowed. "Yes."

Kalina didn't have the words to deal with this.

Official law across the three kingdoms said the same thing. Compelling received the death penalty. No exceptions. If someone was willing to Compel another once, you couldn't tell when they'd do it again, and you wouldn't know it was being done to you until it was too late—unless you had a violinist check for it.

I can't fathom Emil being executed.

But she also couldn't fathom him doing this. *And he did. Time and time again.*

This was far out of her hands.

She could feel the silence surrounding this empty building in the middle of the night. It was as if the two of them were left alone in the world.

"Emil…" Kalina thought about how to say this. "I want to make sure you're protected, Meliya."

"I know," she said quietly.

"If you want to go to the Head Mage with this, I'll come with you."

She looked up. Fear washed through her face. "He'll hurt me if he learns I told anyone."

Kalina studied her expression. Terror gripped Meliya. *I'm scared too.* But…

"Will you feel safe tomorrow with Emil here?"

Meliya swallowed and looked away. "Maybe I shouldn't be making a big deal about this. I'll be okay after tonight."

Kalina frowned. "Do you really believe that?"

Her gaze whipped back to Kalina. "No…I don't know!" Sobs broke from her lips again. "I'm *so scared*, Elder Kalina. What will he do when he learns I told?"

"We'll make sure he can't do *anything* to you." Kalina leaned toward her. "We're *on your side*. He won't hurt you again."

"He's hurt other people again."

"And he shouldn't have been allowed to do that. But this goes far beyond what he's done before."

She exhaled slowly. "Are you sure you can protect me?"

"I'll do whatever it takes."

A momentary doubt flashed across her mind. But no. *Bren and I may have disagreed in the past. But he'll realize how serious this is.*

"Okay," Meliya finally whispered. "What do we need to do?"

"Are you comfortable talking with Head Mage Bren about this?"

Nervousness filled Meliya's eyes.

"If you want, I can talk to him for you," Kalina said. "I don't want you to have to do anything you don't want to do."

"Head Mage Bren scares me."

He *was* the Head Mage. "I can talk with him. That's fine. Do you want to come with me? You don't have to if you'd rather go back to your dorm. But—"

Meliya shook her head. "I'm coming with you."

27

BREN STAYED SILENT AS KALINA relayed the whole story to him in his cottage. Meliya sat silently beside her on the couch. Kalina couldn't read the expression on Bren's face. For several long moments after she finished, he stared into the distance.

"I..." He leaned back in his chair. And he again studied the wall. He shook his head. "I don't know what to say." A deep frown creased his face. "If everything I heard actually happened...well, that is truly disturbing."

After another long moment of silence, he looked at Meliya. "Are you... are you sure he Compelled you? Did he say that to you directly?"

"Believe me, I would have never felt that way about Emil otherwise." She blurted. "We were friends. But I never wanted him."

Bren shook his head. "That...that isn't what I'm asking." He paused. "How did you know he Compelled you?"

Kalina stepped in. "She tasted sour cherries afterward. We both know she wouldn't have known that side effect otherwise." She didn't like talking about Meliya's ignorance in front of her. But Bren knew her academic track record.

Bren held up a hand. "With all due respect, Elder Kalina, I wasn't asking you." He turned back to Meliya.

"I..." Meliya avoided eye contact. "He said he wanted to know if I actually loved him. I...I *told* him I did." She looked like she had tasted something sour. "But when he played his instrument, all those feelings vanished." She swallowed. "I...I think I stumbled back; that's how he knew I didn't love him. And that's when he started telling me he had just wanted to help me." Her voice caught.

"Did he say anything else?"

"I...I asked him what he'd done to me." She traced her finger along the edge of the couch. "He told me he had wanted me to see him the way he actually was."

Kalina felt ill.

Bren nodded slowly and sat back in his seat. "I see." He scratched his chin. "Is there anything else I should know about your side of this story?"

A tear slipped down her cheek. "Elder Kalina said everything else."

Kalina looked up at him. "Head Mage Bren...we don't know how many other people Emil has Compelled."

He nodded. "We...we should talk to him tonight. We need to hear his side of the story."

Meliya shifted uncomfortably.

"Go find Elder Umar," Bren said to Kalina. "He's overseeing the male dorms while Elder Toze travels. Have him get Emil and bring him here—without any instruments."

The moment Elder Umar brought Emil into the room, Kalina could tell Emil knew why he was here. While he walked with a facade of ease, his gaze darted about and his neck was stiff. A bruise adorned his left cheek. Her heart burned. Emil had *done* it.

She swallowed down bile.

"Thank you, Elder Umar," Bren said. "Could you go sit with Meliya outside?" Kalina had only barely convinced Bren that Meliya shouldn't be in the same room as Emil right now.

Umar nodded and left, closing the curtain behind him.

Emil sat on the other side of the couch from Kalina. Shifted. Tapped his left foot. He fixed his eyes on the fireplace.

"I'm sorry for having to wake you at such a late hour," Head Mage Bren said from his chair behind her. "But I've heard some rather troubling allegations made against you, Emil, that we need to talk about."

"Oh?" Emil asked quickly. "What allegations?"

"Meliya told Elder Kalina tonight that you Compelled her to date you the past month and a half."

Emil blinked and his head jerked backward. "What?" His reply was instantaneous. As if he'd rehearsed it. "She said *what?*" His mouth dropped. "You...you can't believe that, Head Mage Bren, can you?" He swallowed. "She...she broke up with me earlier today and said she hated me, but..." His voice caught. "I swear, Head Mage Bren. I would have never done something like that."

"Meliya has brought several concerning things to us," Bren said. "I'm not sure what to think about it."

"What kind of evidence does she claim to have?" His gaze bounced between them.

Bren's careful tiptoeing around the subject won't get us anywhere. Emil will deny, deny, deny...and who knows what Bren will do with that?

"Emil." Kalina put on the mindset of a military commander and locked eyes with him. "Cut the dancing. We know you did it."

"I—"

She held up her hand to stop him. "You've looked like a terrified chicken since you entered the room. Meliya displays all the signs of a traumatic event...and she told us she's tasted sour cherries this whole evening. Now you and I both know Meliya. She's *not* someone who would know what the side effects of Compelling are. You did that to her.

She leaned forward. "It's only a matter of time until we can get a practicing violinist up here to check on the state of her brain, see whether she has the signs of being Compelled still evident in her mind, and if she does, compare the signature of the Compelling to your own magical signature."

Emil stared at her. And for a long moment, he said nothing.

Kalina held her breath, hoping Emil would buy into her lie. There unfortunately *wasn't* any way to see the signs of Compelling after the fact, only during it. But Emil hadn't done the in-depth study of magic theory she had over these past several months. He hadn't read the books inaccessible to students.

She wondered what Bren was thinking behind her.

Emil bit his lip. His breathing came out at the speed of a glissando.

Then he burst into tears.

"I-I-I'm so sorry." He bent over, and his body shuddered with sobs. "I'm so sorry."

Bren shifted behind Kalina. She said nothing. She'd expected to feel relief at his confession. Instead, her breath came out even heavier and her fingers itched to break something.

"I wanted to protect her," Emil sobbed.

"Protect her?" Bren asked. "From what?" Disdain poured through his voice.

"From Jacir! And all the other rotten boyfriends she's had," he cried. "You've seen this by now, haven't you, Elder Kalina? I wanted to show her what it might be like to date someone who respected her."

"You respected her by Compelling her to date you." Kalina had to work to keep her tone emotionless. Her hands itched to seize him by the collar and shake him.

"I...she was supposed to want me!" He lifted his tearstained face toward her. "How were the other guys better than me, Elder Kalina? They were dumb, they made fun of her, and they just wanted to take her clothes off. I didn't do any of those things!"

"You made out with her repeatedly."

He shook his head. "No. That's not true. Yes, I kissed her a couple of times. But that's *it*. And I didn't think it would be a big deal if we kissed once or twice." His lower lip quivered. "You know she's slept with half the kids in our Year already, right? Why would a couple of kisses bother her?"

"Meliya has slept with half the kids in your Year?" Bren snorted. "What are you talking about?"

Emil looked at him. "I'm not lying." Tears still slid down his cheeks. "I mean, maybe it's only a third of them, but ask Elder Kalina. Meliya hasn't been a virgin for a long time."

This is inane. "I don't care who she's slept with, Emil. It's not relevant *at all* to what you did to her."

"Elder Kalina." His voice choked up again. "I know that what I did was wrong. But I treated her so well. Haven't you noticed her grades improving in your class?"

Fury flared. Kalina stopped caring about her tone. "You took over her *mind*, Emil. Do you *know* what the law across the three kingdoms says about that?"

Terror crescendoed across his face. "But—but that's for people who try to *hurt* others!" He looked toward Bren. "You—you wouldn't give me the death penalty, would you?"

"How many other people have you Compelled?" Bren asked hoarsely.

Emil burst into tears again. His body shook with the sobs. "It..." His body continued to shake, and it took a minute before he could speak again. "Only Meliya, I swear."

Kalina's breath came out heavy. "And yet at the beginning of this conversation you said you didn't even Compel her."

"I was scared! I don't react well to stress. Check the minds of anyone else. I swear I only influenced her."

For a long moment, Bren said nothing. The moment stretched into eternity.

Then he cleared his throat. "We...we're not going to turn you over to the authorities for the death penalty, Emil."

Breath erupted from Emil's lips.

"But that doesn't mean there won't be consequences for what you did."

"I—I know. Just...please don't tell anyone. Does anyone else need to know? I need to fight for our country."

"I need you to leave the room," Bren said. "Elder Kalina and I need to have a conversation. Meliya is in the other room, so you need to wait outside."

"Emil shouldn't be left unsupervised," Kalina said quickly. She didn't like correcting the head mage in front of a student, but if Emil grabbed his instrument...

Bren nodded. "Let's get Elder Umar." He stood up. "Come with me, Emil. Elder Kalina, I'll return."

He walked out. Emil stumbled after. The curtain flapped shut.

The Ternion help us. Kalina leaned forward and rested her arms on her knees. She could hardly think coherently. *Emil did this.* She thought she knew who he was. *I thought he was heading in a positive direction.* But all this time...

Jadoni had been prophetic in her estimation of him.

The Ternion had chosen *him* to save Rizade?

And then there was Bren—

Before she could think any further, Bren came back through the curtain.

She glanced up. He trudged over to his armchair and sat down. His gaze rested on her as she turned toward him.

"Elder Kalina…we have a problem on our hands."

A laugh burst out of her mouth before she could stop it. "You think?"

He nodded slowly. "In all my years here…" He exhaled. "The Ternion help us all."

She waited for him to continue.

Finally, he opened his mouth again. "We…we're going to need to double or triple the time he's spending with you."

Kalina blinked. "I can't fix this."

"You have to." He spoke quickly. "This whole country depends on him. The Kaldians are only eight hours south of us, and unlike certain fatalists, I don't believe the Ternion will necessarily save us. The prophecy is conditioned on *Emil's prowess*. And so he's the only person who matters."

"We're keeping him as a *student?*"

"Kalina." Dissonance rang in Bren's voice. "We don't have other options."

"He's been *Compelling* a student for the past month and a half. Even if he's telling the truth that she's the only one, we can't have a student doing this. We need to notify the authorities. Let the king decide what to do with him. Just think about the parents. What would they say if they heard we allowed a boy to remain here after he Compelled another student?"

Bren bit his lower lip.

"We can't allow him to stay," she continued. "We can train Emil elsewhere." *Maybe while he's under house arrest.*

"And bring that kind of disgrace on him? There's no chance that Emil continues training under those circumstances. His resolve is tenuous enough, as is. No. Other people don't need to know about this."

"But—"

"What's been said in this room will stay in this room."

She choked. "What?"

"If this gets out there, we'll be ruined, Kalina. How will our troops keep the resolve to fight if they know they're doing it for a *Compeller?*"

"But we have students here! Who's to say Emil won't do this again and go further with the next girl?"

Bren shook his head. "You saw his tears. He won't do this again."

"Oh, cut the klyte." Kalina stood. "Don't you see how much he's lied to us? Those weren't the tears of repentance. Those were the tears of someone who's sad he got caught, if not an outright attempt to manipulate us. He spent all his time blaming Meliya, begging for mercy, and saying he wasn't as bad as other people. That's *not* repentance."

Bren's eyes flashed. "Sit *down*, Kalina. You will address your concerns to me *respectfully*."

He waited. She lowered herself into the chair, still quivering.

"Now." He spoke calmly, but she could hear the tension deep inside his voice. "Let's try to have this conversation like mature adults, not like hysterical students. I expect better from people I invite to teach here. The fact is, if we can't train Emil, our country will lose the war, and we'll watch as the Kaldians cut up and sacrifice hundreds to their pagan god. The Ternion never guaranteed our success."

"I know it didn't. But did you not *see* what he did to Meliya?"

"I'm not going to risk the well-being of an entire country because a girl got a few kisses she didn't want."

Anger bubbled up inside her. She choked it back down. "That's all this affair means to you?"

"It's a 'he said, she said' situation regarding how often they made out, and I'm going to grant Emil the courtesy of being innocent until proven guilty. The only strikes against him are a few unrequited kisses and his mental Compelling."

"A crime traditionally punished with death."

"Is that what you want, Kalina? You want to kill Emil for this?"

She swallowed. A picture of Emil in the jungle flooded her mind. She knew how much he'd been abused.

Bren shook his head. "He's a *kid*. If we don't extend grace to kids for their mistakes, what kind of school are we?"

Kalina cleared her throat. "I'm not arguing for the death penalty. I'm saying this isn't our call. We need to protect our kids, remove him from campus, and let the authorities handle this. This wasn't a *mistake*. He deliberately thought this out, and we need to treat it for what it is."

"And we'll set up means of protection. We'll do spot checks regularly on students' and teachers' minds, and we'll watch him carefully. Because he needs to be on campus. He needs *all* his teachers, and he needs those battle simulations. We can't risk losing because of a couple of kisses. What—are you willing to sacrifice your husband for that?"

She couldn't think about Riyad right now. She grasped for some way to show Bren the problems with his plan. "You expect Meliya to keep quiet about what Emil did to her?"

For a long time, Bren said nothing. Then he cleared his throat. "We have a relationship with a small mage academy north of here, closer to the Helgoland Sea. We'll transfer Meliya there."

She jolted in her seat. "What?"

"You will be incredibly careful with your words. At least if you want to have *any* ability to continue to influence Emil at this school."

She stared at him in shock. "You're going to expel Meliya for what happened to her."

"I'm going to *transfer* her to a place where she'll feel safer. I'm actually being *gracious* to Meliya considering the circumstances."

"*Gracious*? How on earth—"

Bren lifted a finger. "Did Emil lie when he said Meliya had slept with most of the boys in her year?"

Her eyes widened. "You would punish her for that, when—"

"I'm asking you a question. Has she been sleeping with the other boys in her class?"

"I've never personally seen her do anything. But even if she did, does it matter when—"

"Do you believe Emil lied when he said that?"

Kalina stared at Bren in disbelief. She knew Meliya's reputation. But why the klyte did that matter right now? She had been Compelled. She needed compassion, not a character investigation.

If she answered Bren's question honestly, he'd use it against her. She kept her mouth shut.

Bren nodded slowly. "And that's the truth. We both know the penalty for that is expulsion. She should be grateful that we're transferring her with a letter of recommendation. And if Emil really did all of this to her, it will be better for her not to be on campus with him."

"So you're going to punish the victim instead of her abuser." Her voice came out hoarse.

"I'm going to prepare our prophesied savior for battle, no matter what it takes." His eyes narrowed. "We need a champion, not a saint."

Words failed her.

Bren stood. "I'm getting Meliya. Support the school if you want to keep a job here." He brushed past the curtains in the doorway.

Her mind reeled. This couldn't be happening. Bren couldn't do this. *And with my support? I promised Meliya I'd protect her. I have to say something.* But...

Kay's words after the battle at Inlaru rang in her ears. *"Some people don't change."* And she couldn't deny the truth of that anymore. Mahd, Emil, Bren...she'd hoped she could change them. But she had failed every time.

She couldn't protect Meliya. She could say something. But then she'd be kicked out too. And there would be no one left with the leverage to restrain Emil.

Footsteps sounded and the curtain rustled. She glanced up to see Bren walking in with a nervous Meliya.

Kalina couldn't bear to look her in the eye.

"Thank you for your patience, Meliya," Bren said as he sat down next to Kalina. "I'm sure it's been a hard night."

Kalina studied the multicolored triangular-patterned rug in front of them. She was trying to think, but her brain felt like sludge. There was nothing she could say. Nothing she could do to stop this from happening.

"We will deal with Emil in accordance to what he did to you," Bren said. "But because we're a school that disciplines with an even, unbiased hand, we also need to discuss some other things as well. Emil says you've had sexual relations with a number of the boys in your class."

Meliya inhaled sharply. Kalina dug her fingernails into her palm. She could hear Meliya shaking. "But...but he—"

"And we're dealing with him. But right now, we're dealing with you. And so I'm asking if you can tell me the truth or if I need to investigate this."

Meliya began crying again. Kalina continued to stare at the ground. *How can he do this?*

"I didn't want to," Meliya sobbed. "But they kept pressuring me to do something with them."

"And you agreed."

"I didn't know what else to do."

"I see a clear common denominator in all of those relationships."

Meliya continued to cry. Kalina's heart broke.

"According to school policy, I ought to expel you and tell your father. He's one of the district magistrates, isn't he?"

"Oh, please no. My dad would kill me. You can't tell him! Please don't tell him what happened! I'll stop. I'll do whatever it takes to—"

"I won't tell your parents. But you can't stay here either. We're going to transfer you to Rayden Academy."

"But—but I don't know anyone there! Why can't I stay here? If—"

"You have two choices," Bren said. "You can go there without saying anything about what happened tonight and still graduate honorably from a respectable school. Or you can make a fuss about everything and be expelled with a letter explaining to your parents why we expelled you."

Kalina couldn't take this anymore.

She stood and, without looking at either of them, left the room.

28

I'M A COWARD.

And yet here Kalina was, standing on the top perimeter of seats in one of the outdoor classrooms instead of defending Meliya when she needed someone the most.

He expelled her. Wind blew softly through the onyx night. *I had promised her I would stand up for her.*

She swallowed and knelt. Jadoni was right. This school had so many problems. Now they would ruin a girl's life.

And I kept my mouth shut.

Emptiness rose inside her like the languishing sound of a minor chord.

Footsteps echoed through the blackness. Noise carried around this quiet enclave. She turned to see Umar and Meliya walking by the main academic building. Meliya cried as he held out a torch.

That wasn't a long conversation.

Am I a part of this now?

She had tried to stop Bren. *And I would have only gotten myself fired if I opposed him in front of Meliya.*

But deep down, she knew. She had become *that* teacher.

Umar and Meliya stopped in the middle of the central green, right before the male dorm would have blocked them from view. They talked in low tones. Then she went on alone to her dorm, and he walked back toward Bren's cottage.

Kalina stood and wiped her face. She needed his advice. Thank the Ternion he'd been on duty tonight. She ran to intercept him.

Her path intersected his at the side of the main academic building. "Elder Umar."

His aged face turned toward her. He smiled sadly. "Elder Kalina."

"What...what's going on?"

He sighed. "You know the situation. She's packing up while Bren writes a transfer letter, and then we're leaving."

She blinked. "Bren sent you with her?"

Umar shook his head. He gazed past her into the distance. Then he cleared his throat. "I'm going back to resign."

Kalina's jaw dropped. "You're what?"

"Remaining here means either staying silent and becoming a part of the problem, or speaking up and violating my pledge to support this school." Umar coughed. "I suppose I'm already disobeying Bren by not escorting her to Elder Suraya so she can supervise Meliya and make sure she doesn't talk to any other students. But that's why I'm resigning."

"But—but—" She scrambled to find the words. "We *need* you, Umar."

"Oh, Kalina." He smiled sadly. "You don't need me. You need someone competent in charge of the school."

She'd never heard criticism this biting from Umar before. "You leaving doesn't solve anything!"

"If everyone else left with me, we might wield some influence."

"But that won't happen. I'd be willing, and Jadoni, and maybe Suraya, but everyone else...?" Kalina bit her lip. "Even those who see the problems want to protect their jobs."

"I know. But sometimes in life, you don't make a decision because it's effective. You make it because it's the right thing to do." He shook his head. "I'm sorry. I don't mean to put an ethical burden on you. But tomorrow you'll walk into a classroom filled with Meliya's peers. You'll represent the school and everything it does. And because good teachers stay, students will continue to think this place can't all be *that* bad. Your presence will encourage them to remain at an academy where the Head Mage only values their dignity if he likes them."

"We could try telling the local authorities."

"The mayor of Chintor? He's close with Bren. And he's terrified of the Kaldians."

"What about the local magic task force? Surely they could revoke Emil's license to practice magic."

"Students don't need a license as long as they only practice on academy grounds."

Kalina grappled to find an answer. She knew better than to suggest telling General Mahd. "What if enough of us confronted Bren? At some point, he'd have to listen!"

He sighed. "Bren operates off a simple principle: If you allow people to vent, you don't need to fix the issues. That's why he won't fire you for everything you said tonight. When the daily grind of teaching begins again, you and everyone else will eventually shove this tragedy to the back of your mind. And when the emotions dry out, you'll stop pursuing change. Because that's how people survive working at this place."

He put a hand on her shoulder. "I need to leave this place with integrity. But you need to make your own decision. Don't let my conscience bind yours."

With that, he shuffled toward Bren's cottage.

Kalina tried to keep herself from staring as she stood, hands at her side, alone among the black winds. Umar couldn't leave like that. Whom else could she trust?

Was he right? The only two options if she stayed were to forget or be fired?

The gusts whistled behind her as she turned her options around. She knew the unwritten rules of the teaching profession. You always supported fellow teachers and administrators in front of students. If she wanted to keep her position, she had to stay quiet.

The image of her sister filled her mind. *Never again.*

What would Riyad do?

But Riyad had never dealt with this situation. He'd taught at a good school. He never had to deal with people like Bren. Believing the best about people may have worked in his situation.

But in this case, he was *wrong.*

She blinked.

In this case, Riyad was *wrong.*

"If grace was only for small mistakes, would it really be grace?" His words rang in her ears. *"What if grace is for the things we* can't *make amends for?"*

But what about the people who *refused* to repent? Or the people who *pretended* to repent?

What if grace let people like Emil continue abusing others?

Kalina heard voices. She turned to see people coming out of the girl's dorm. Umar was there with them. Had he talked to Bren already? He must have returned around the other side of the building. *How long have I stood here bogged down in my thoughts?*

She walked toward the girl's dorm. The muddy glow of morning rose over the side of the cliffs. As she drew closer, she could see Anvisa and Leneya, along with two other girls, hugging Meliya. Umar loaded her bags on a small handcart.

I should say something.

But Kalina halted in the middle of the central green. What would she say? What *could* she say to make this situation any better? That she quit as well?

That might be the ethical decision. But that wouldn't fix the problem.

Umar picked up the two handles of the cart and walked away with Meliya.

She still said nothing.

Because words would require commitment.

The girls noticed her. Anvisa dashed toward her, followed by the others.

"Elder Kalina," Anvisa wailed, "did you hear about what happened? What Emil did to Meliya? Why is the Head Mage doing this to her?"

Kalina snapped her mind into focus and zoned in on the distraught girl standing in front of her.

"I'm so scared, Elder Kalina. What if he comes after one of us next?"

Kalina could see the fear written across Anvisa's large eyes. The sweat plastering her thin black hair against her brow shone in the light of the muggy dawn. The anxiety written in the girls' tight postures and quivering limbs.

Meliya had told them everything. And now here they were, looking to her for help because they needed an adult to protect them. And the only other adult here had walked away.

Her heart thudded against her ribs.

Kalina could tell them everything was true and she was leaving with Umar and Meliya. They had to flee north before Emil Compelled everyone else.

But that would require parental permission. Otherwise, she'd get the Chintor Guard sent after them.

And even if they *could* ask permission over the few messenger pigeons Chintor had, too many of the students were nobility: Their parents might push for change, but they would never pull their students out of the most prestigious school in the country.

If Kalina left, they would still be here.

But she *wouldn't*.

"Remaining here means either staying silent and becoming a part of the problem, or speaking up and violating my pledge to support this school."

She wouldn't accept that. Because she had avoided problems before. And she had seen what that did to her sister.

I won't do that again.

She looked Anvisa in the eye. "I'm going to find a way." And she hugged her close. The other girls latched on to her. Kalina didn't know how to do this. But she felt the weight of their arms around her. They needed someone to give them direction.

Of course, I know whose arms are missing.

After giving them a couple of minutes, she peeled back from their embrace.

"Listen," Kalina said once she had extricated herself. "I know you have a lot of questions. But right now, I need you to be prudent. If it becomes campus gossip that I'm doing something about this, I'll be fired before sunset. What I say here *needs* to stay between the five of us. Understood?"

They nodded. "I—I understand, Elder Kalina." Anvisa still had tears in her eyes.

"This will be a long day," Kalina said. "But you still have two hours before classes begin. Right now, you need sleep. Or at least rest."

"But—" Leneya began.

Kalina shook her head. "I know it seems insignificant. But you'll need it for the day ahead. *I* need sleep. Because I know that I won't make good choices while I'm like this. You need that as well."

The girls reluctantly nodded.

Kalina had to do one last thing.

Saying her goodbyes to them, she headed toward the cliffs, first at a brisk walk through the gate, then at a light run down the winding trail that led to the city. Not only did Umar have a head start on her, but he had probably used his trumpet to make the cliffs lower them to the ground.

She intercepted them near Chintor's gates. Umar slowly pushed the heavy cart ahead of him. He was too old to do this. Meliya's shoulders hunched over with the weight of the night.

But she wasn't going to let them leave without saying something.

"Meliya."

She turned. The tears had dried on her face, but she could still see the tension in the way she held herself.

What can I say?

There was nothing left but the truth.

"I want you to know that everything that happened up there was wrong. Not that you didn't know it already. But I wanted you to hear it from me. And I'm so sorry for not saying so in front of Bren. I should have spoken up. I promised you I would protect you, and I didn't. That was so wrong of me to do. I failed you as a teacher. And…I should have known what Bren would do. I should have protected you. And I regret my cowardice. I'm not going to do that again. I'm going to protect your friends. And someday, I'm going to bring you back here. We're not going to forget what Emil did."

Meliya nodded. She looked lost for words.

Kalina had to pray that she would find someone at her new academy who could walk beside her after everything she had experienced.

We should have been that place for her.

Now, she had to find some way to protect the rest of her students from Emil.

29

ONE HOUR OF RESTLESS TURNING

in bed is far too little sleep for this conversation.

But Bren insisted that Kalina meet with Emil every day for two weeks, starting today. And these meetings needed to start off on the right foot.

Kalina actually felt somewhat hopeful for this conversation, though. Because somewhere between her bed and the winding trail back up to the academy, she realized what she did have.

Leverage.

Guilt whispered in the back of her mind. But she didn't care. Emil had Compelled a student. More important problems existed than making sure she followed traditional teacher ethics.

The moment she heard the knocking outside her curtain after her final class, she knew who it was. Even if he almost never knocked.

"Come in."

Emil slipped through the curtain. None of that swagger he normally had when entering her office. Only hunched shoulders, darting eyes, and a shuffle to his seat. The eight-stringed fiddle barely clinked when it touched the floor.

He sat down and looked up. "Elder Kalina...I...I'm so sorry about last night."

She elected not to respond.

"I...I don't know what to say," he continued. "I wasn't thinking about my actions, I guess. I thought I could give her a fresh start. But I realize now that I should have thought about the situation more."

The excuses have returned. No owning what he's done, no admitting of guilt, no honest recounting.

Kalina cleared her throat. "Who taught you how to Compel, Emil?"

"Um." His gaze flicked away from her. "I, uh, I read about it and figured out how it worked."

"Where did you read about it?"

"A book in the library talked about it. It...was pretty detailed."

The book she'd found didn't give enough detail to explain how to Compel someone. "Which book?"

He shrugged. "I don't remember."

"You expect me to believe that you spent weeks learning how to Compel someone and don't even remember the name of the book?"

Emil began to tear up. "What do you want me to say? I'm saying what I remember! I love you, Elder Kalina, and I love this school, and I love this country, and I—"

"Oh, please. Spare me the tears. Unlike Head Mage Bren, I don't care about your crying and moaning. To be honest, it makes you look pathetic."

Emil's head snapped up, and he stared at her wide-eyed. Were teachers supposed to say that to students?

Well, this teacher is an ex-military commander. She'd never exercised authority well on the battlefield. But she *did* know how to do so now.

Kalina leaned over her desk. The rough wood dug into her ribs. "Let's establish some ground rules here. I don't trust a word coming out of your mouth. I realize you won't tell me who taught you. But let's at least be honest with each other, because that's what I asked from the beginning. You are a manipulative, abusive young man who puts on a nice face because you know I can save your life. I'm here because I have students to protect. And it's become clear that right now, the greatest threat to their safety isn't the Kaldians—it's *you*."

She let the words hang in the air. He stared at her, dried tear trails evident on his face. *Interesting how he stopped crying the moment I told him they wouldn't work on me.*

"Bu-but Elder Kalina—"

"No. This right here? This isn't a friendship. And I'm tired of acting. So here's what's going to happen. Today, you're going to tell Head Mage Bren that you're resigning as head of your dormitory. And no matter how much he protests, you're going to make sure he accepts it. Starting today, you will also leave your fiddle here an hour before sunset and pick it up two hours after sunrise."

"But—but I need that to practice against the Kaldians!"

"And I need to protect my students."

Emil stared at her with widening eyes. Had no one at this school ever stood up to him before?

"Are you trying to make us lose?"

"Nope. I need us to win too. But you aren't following my advice anyway, so additional practice time won't make a difference. And it's more important to me that I protect my students."

"I'll borrow someone else's instrument if you won't let me use mine!"

She shrugged. "Sure. And the moment I hear you so much as touching another student's instrument after hours, I quit the school."

His open mouth snapped shut.

"Same thing goes for everything else. If you're still the head of your dorm tomorrow? I quit. If I ever catch wind of you dating a girl? I'm done. This is our deal. There aren't any witnesses. There aren't any counselors. There isn't anyone to tattle to. Because I'm not a real teacher. I'm a military commander. And I work out my problems in my own way. If you follow my rules, I'll stay and work to save your life. But if you break even one of them, I'm out. Because I'm done taking your klyte. Oh, and if you tell anyone else about this conversation? In that case, I leave too."

If he forced that decision on her, the consequences would be dire for her students, the nation, and her husband. But he needed her as much as she needed him.

Emil stared at her, his breath coming out in spurts.

"I..." Emil's voice faltered, and he took a couple more deep breaths. "I understand that you're disappointed in me." He stared at the ground. His lips moved, but no words came out. He looked back up and swallowed. "I..." He choked. "I thought that of all the people out there, you would understand."

Kalina's lip curled. "And why would I understand your decision to Compel one of my students?"

"Because...because you *know* me." Emil's lower lip quivered. "You know everything I have to give up. I just want one person out there to love me. And I thought..." He swallowed. "I thought you *promised* you'd always be there for me."

His words dug into her. Of course he was desperate for the unconditional love his parents failed to give him.

But she recognized his manipulation for what it was. "I've told you I'll stay if you follow my rules. But love doesn't force. Love doesn't manipulate. Love *does not* Compel. I care about you, but I *will not* let you hurt my students."

Emil quivered. "If you cared about me, your voice wouldn't have so much spite."

She rolled her eyes. "I'm treating you the way you deserve."

"And..." Emil's breathing continued in spurts. "And how do I know you're telling me the truth?" He stared at her with narrowed eyes. "How do I know you will try to save my life?"

"Because unlike you, I'm a woman of my word."

Emil swallowed, and he nodded slowly. "O...okay."

"Good." She kept her voice emotionless. "It's already nearly sunset, so leave your fiddle here on your way out. I expect to see you back tomorrow at the same time, per Head Mage Bren's orders."

"Okay." He stood, picked up his eight-stringed fiddle, and leaned it against the wall. "I..." He turned toward her slowly. "I tried to trust you." Tears sprang to his eyes again. "I *really* tried to believe that all women wouldn't turn out like my mom. But..."

The mask he had been using finally fell.

And he fled the room.

Kalina waited as she heard his footsteps pound down the hall. Then out the front door.

Her forehead pounded. She had become the tyrannical teacher she had always hated in school. The type of teacher who wielded power like a club, eschewed kindness, and enforced silence like a knife.

And it feels good.

A chill passed through her. She hadn't expected this satisfaction. It felt like power. She no longer had to wait and hope someone else would change. She could get things done another way.

Kalina understood now why those teachers handled matters the way they did.

30

KALINA COULD TELL THE MOMENT that Head Mage Bren stepped up to the platform for his end-of-week address that he planned on saying something about Meliya.

It would be hard not to. Over the past two-and-a-half days, news had spread like wildfire. Emil and his friends dismissed the claims and called Meliya a liar. Most students believed him. After all, "The administration would have punished him if he'd done that!" But rumors continued to spread.

And that, in turn, had led to the fistfight between Krem and Pesh yesterday afternoon.

The afternoon sun illuminated Bren's stern face as he stood in front of the wall. The students were unusually quiet as they took their seats on the central green. Everyone knew what he'd address. *But what will he say about it?*

Elder Toze walked past her bench. Thankfully, he *had* confirmed upon his return that no one else was being Compelled. Emil had seemed to limit himself to Meliya. Toze was deeply disturbed about the situation; but he had a family depending on his income and didn't feel like he could take a stand. Especially since it wouldn't make a difference.

Ashinara swept into the seat next to Kalina. "So sorry—I almost missed this!" She brushed her hair back from her face. "Couldn't stop talking with kids, you know? It's been an awful week for them with Umar quitting. They're so confused about why he left. Who does that in the middle of the school year?"

Kalina pursed her lips. On her other side, Jadoni fidgeted uncomfortably. She had been more reclusive than usual since Umar left.

Ashinara continued. "I had to lose a whole prep period to watch one of his classes while they scramble to find a substitute. I loved Umar, but this was such an insensitive decision."

Kalina stared straight ahead. Responding wasn't worth it.

"Umar was twice the teacher you are," Jadoni muttered.

Bren cleared his throat. "Good morning, Chintor Academy students." Kalina steeled herself. "I know it's been quite the week here, so I'll keep this brief: Two days ago, we discovered evidence that the Kaldians are sending troops from old Arditen toward the Great Steppes. We believe they hope to loop around the eastern Deep Jungle to attack us from the north and pin us between their two armies."

Shock thudded through Kalina's senses.

They hadn't worried much about that border since Inlaru and the Damanar River made attacking from the south the obvious choice for the Kaldian supply chains once they'd taken the Narrows.

But that was back when they only had one army to send to Chintor.

"General Mahd is rallying citizens in the northern villages to put up defenses at the border above us between Kaldia and Rizade," Bren continued. "Please know that we will keep you abreast of new developments. And we will do everything within our power to keep you safe."

Kalina shook her head. A citizen army would do nothing against the Kaldian guns. Sure, their mages could terraform the earth. But they didn't have enough mages to protect both fronts from full-fledged assaults.

Bren looked over the audience. "Crucibles like this reveal character. That means we all need to keep our eyes on the prize." Kalina could have sworn his eyes fixated on her.

"Some of you may want to take this opportunity to think about that," Bren said. "What matters right now? Rumors, gossip, and unfounded allegations? Or doing whatever it takes to beat the Kaldians?"

Jadoni began moving next to Kalina. Kalina glanced at her. The woman was shaking in silent laughter.

"I have high expectations for you," Bren said. "You are mages, after all, not simple farmers or artisans. Yours is the ability to control the world. And you represent the cream of the crop at the best school in the country. But the Ternion always gives us the freedom to choose. And you need to determine whether you'll commit to our country or to personal animosities." He surveyed the crowd. "We'll have to see who rises to become heroes and who remains children. The choice is yours."

He stepped off the platform. Kalina blinked. Normally he droned about virtue a lot longer than that.

Jadoni turned toward her. "The little bastard," she choked between her guffaws. "The little bastard really did that, didn't he?"

"Not here," Kalina murmured. She tried to ignore the sinking feeling in her stomach.

"Psh. Why not here? Like any of them pay attention." Jadoni waved at everyone else talking loudly around them. "That bastard is too good at what he does. Didn't you hear him? Anyone who cares about boys Compelling girls to make out with them for weeks on end is a prissy little schoolgirl."

"I don't think that's quite what he said," Ashinara butted in. "You might be reading into—"

"Oh, shut up." Jadoni glowered at Ashinara. "I don't have time for your excuses. This was about the fight yesterday and we all know it. Our duty is to tell our students to bend over and take Emil's abuse with a grin because hey, he's not sacrificing kids. He's just sticking his tongue down their throats."

Kalina grimaced. "I did not need that mental image in my mind."

"Right. You have more to say about my harsh language than his polite language covering up abuse." Jadoni laughed again, grabbed her cane, and stood. "Good to know some things never change."

A million responses jumped to Kalina's lips. Jadoni had no idea how she'd dealt with Emil.

But Ashinara spoke first. "I'm not trying to make excuses," she said quietly. "But I don't want to assume the worst about people until I talk to them first. Bren deserves that kind of decency before we gossip behind his back."

"Sure," Jadoni said. "You two do that and see where it gets you."

Kalina cleared her throat. "I think you should know my opinions about this."

"Yep. Speak the truth to your peers and shut up in the face of power.

The exact type of courage I expect from our military. Now if you'll excuse me, I have students lining up at my classroom. And the Ternion knows they need a teacher who will actually comfort them." Jadoni stalked off.

"Don't listen to her," Ashinara murmured. "She's upset that Umar left. Not that I blame her for her grief...the Ternion knows we all need someone to love us in life. But I don't assume the worst about you."

Kalina didn't answer Ashinara. Jadoni's words stung, but she didn't know Kalina's plans. That was probably for the best. The crone was unpredictable.

And Kalina doubted Jadoni would approve of what she planned on doing next.

When Kalina dismissed battlefield tactics class that day, most of the students immediately cleared out. Even Anvisa, Leneya, and Krem didn't stick around. Krem looked bashful about his black eye. But she'd see them again that night when she launched into the second stage of her plan.

One student dawdled, though, after everyone else left: Jacir.

The boy looked at her amid the brown hair that hung over the shaved sides of his head. His face was strangely blank as he made his way down the auditorium steps to her desk.

"Hey, Elder Kalina, can I ask you something?"

She studied his vacuous face. The boy never stayed after class. "Of course."

Jacir folded his arms. "I want to know the truth. I know you were there. Did Emil Compel Meliya to break up with me?"

She exhaled slowly. Bren had warned her to keep this quiet. When it came to Anvisa and students she trusted, she didn't give a second thought to disobeying him.

But with Jacir?

"Head Mage Bren has asked me not to answer that question," she finally said. "I think you're intelligent enough to know what that implies."

Jacir stared at her. And his eyes narrowed.

Then he looked away and slammed his foot against the floor. "That little piece of klyte!" He kicked his foot out again. "He said he was my friend. We were dorm leaders together!"

Kalina didn't respond.

He whirled around to look back at her. "*This* is the boy prophesied to save our country? A Compeller who steals girls from his so-called friends? And to think he ridiculed me for letting Meliya affect our friendship!"

A thought sprang to Kalina's mind, but she held her tongue until Jacir finished.

"And the Head Mage took his side. I can't believe it. He really does play favorites." His fists clenched. "Krem should have given Pesh a better pounding yesterday. How dare Emil do this!"

Kalina cleared her throat. "You think it was wrong for him to coerce her to date him?"

Jacir's jaw dropped. "Of course it was! He had no right to steal her from me. Every good person knows that."

She hardened her gaze. "Then why did *you*?"

Jacir stepped back. "Excuse me?"

"You heard me. Why did you coerce Meliya if you know it's wrong?"

"What are you talking about? I *never* Compelled her."

Kalina stood. "Because you didn't need to."

"I—"

"No," she said with the force of a military commander. "I'm talking now."

Jacir's mouth snapped shut.

"Meliya told us how you pressured her into sleeping with you. And don't even bother trying to deny it. I heard you bragging about this at the dance last month. What were your words? 'Ask enough times, and those girls get tired of saying no'? Quite frankly? I see through your rant about Emil. Yes, what he did was wrong, and sure, it may have been worse than what you did. But *both* of you used Meliya. The same rotten heart that motivated Emil motivated you as well."

Jacir sputtered. "But Meliya never did anything she didn't agree to."

"Emil could say the same thing."

"But I actually *cared* about her!"

"Then why have you complained a lot more about Emil stealing her from *you* than about what he did to *her*?"

Jacir opened his mouth. No words came out. He stared at her in abject shock.

Kalina was done trying to change bullies. At a certain point, they needed someone to tell them the truth about who they were. Maybe Jadoni was right. There was no point trying to build relationships they'd exploit for their own gain.

I'm sorry, Riyad.

With an incoherent mumble, Jacir slunk out of the room.

Seven students stood in her classroom when she returned after school hours. The four girls who'd been with her the night Meliya left, another girl, and two boys, including Krem. A few leaned against the pillars. A few awkwardly waited. Darkness had already fallen outside.

"I wanted to invite more people." Anvisa glanced at the door. "But after Head Mage Bren's speech…"

Kalina sat on her high stool. "I'm glad you seven didn't listen. We need to win the war. But you are *not* collateral damage."

The students here were all Year Six students except for one Year Five student. She had told Anvisa to give quiet invitations to trustworthy students concerned with Emil's behavior.

"I…I don't know what we can do," Anvisa said. "I know you said Elder Toze checks people's minds for a Compelling now…but what if he misses someone?"

The rules of teaching weighed on Kalina. *Always put on a unified front with other teachers and the administration. Don't talk to students about other students. Encourage peace at all times.*

Now, she planned on breaking all those rules.

"You need to be ready to defend yourself against Compelling," she said simply. "And if you see it happening…the law of the land allows you to kill the Compeller." She let the words sink in, watching all their faces become somber.

Good.

"I'm being frank," she continued. "And I'm trusting that what I say doesn't leave the doors of this classroom. If it does, the Head Mage will fire me and that's the end of my time here. But what the Head Mage said today? That was complete klyte. I don't care what anyone else says: You are *right* to fear, and it's *not* immature to wish the school would protect you from a Compeller. We can win this war without letting him treat you however he wants. Understood?"

They nodded but didn't speak. Her comment about killing Emil had apparently shut them all up.

"So here's the game plan. I'm going to teach you how Compelling works so you know how to break it. If you ever need to kill a Compeller and you get in trouble for it, you can blame it all on me, because I made this decision. But until then, you don't tell *anyone* about this or invite anyone else to these meetings. And I trust you will *only* use what I'll teach you if you see Emil Compelling someone again."

They all nodded again. They seemed scared. Like all this had become real. She had seen this look before. New soldiers had it the first time they saw a battle. There is a certain sobriety you don't learn in life until you come face-to-face with death.

Seeing that look in the eyes of kids...

It stabbed her. Even if they had to do this next year. *Why do I have to be the one pulling the veil away from my students?*

But she needed a multipronged approach to Emil. Control his behavior with threats. Train students to watch out. Deal politely with Bren so she could protect students behind his back.

Perhaps she should have taken the route of integrity like Umar. Perhaps Jadoni was right that her public silence was cowardly.

But Meliya's pleas filled her mind.

She cleared her throat. "Let's cover the basics. What do you already know about how Compelling works?"

They stared at her. A few exchanged glances.

"Look, I know students get expelled for seeking information about Compelling. But I also know that students talk. You won't get in trouble for anything you share."

After a long moment, Anvisa spoke up. "Um...I've heard it's done with bowed string instruments. But that doesn't make sense, since those affect the Fabric, and the Fabric doesn't exist within objects."

Kalina nodded. "Here's your first lesson for today. The Fabric *almost* never exists within an object. But there's one exception: our minds. Each mind has its own internal Fabric which musical instruments *can* affect."

Shock emanated from her students' stares. It spoke of lost innocence.

"Do *not* share this knowledge with any of your classmates," Kalina said. "It's kept under wraps for a reason. We don't completely understand how minds have their own internal Fabric. But they do."

"But—but that has a lot more applications than simple Compelling!" Anvisa said.

"It does. And all those applications also lead to the death penalty. The Fabric in another human's mind is sacred and should be treated that way, without *any* magical tampering."

"What other ways *can* you use this mind Fabric?" Krem asked. "If I can ask that..."

"I'm not sure," Kalina lied. "Dark mages likely have their own uses. But the only common use is Compelling, when mages manipulate the energy within someone's mind to force certain feelings or actions."

Lutists could use it to rip the brain into pieces. Few people did so due to how complicated it was. There were easier ways of killing someone, unless a mage wanted to covertly assassinate someone. But unlike Compelling, most mages didn't know about that use. Her students didn't need to know it either.

"So...it's up to our violinists to protect us," Leneya said.

"All of you will play a role," Kalina said. "Either in blocking the Compelling if you're a violinist or in attacking the Compeller if you're not. But yes, you two violinists—Anvisa and Andreya—play the most important part."

Anvisa exhaled slowly. "I...I'm kind of scared."

Kalina nodded. "It's scary to know what you can do with an instrument."

Teaching them all this brought its own level of terror to her as a teacher. If she misjudged any of these students' characters, the results could be disastrous.

But they had a dangerous predator in this academy.

She had to hope she wouldn't regret her trust.

Every single time. I try to trust someone. They tell me they'll be there for me. I reveal my secrets to them.

And the moment I make a mistake, they grind my face in the dirt.

Because that's what I deserve.

"That's what you deserve."

It's my mom standing over me with needled fingers planted on her nonexistent hips, telling me bastards aren't real children & I should be grateful I even get a bed at night. "You should be slaving out there in the fields. That's what you deserve." It's Elder Crayenda telling me my parents lied & I was never chosen by prophecy to save the world & how dare I ask her for extra training after hours. "I teach you every day in the classroom. That's all you deserve."

And now it's Elder Kalina. "I'm treating you the way you deserve."

Does she not understand?

I'm the only chance our country has. And I've given up so much to try to save it. A good childhood. The ability to have children who could know they always deserve my love. Even a normal social life chasing after girls, playing hooky & getting involved with pranks. Can't do that when I'm studying all day to beat the Kaldians.

I just want to be able to want something.

Does she not realize that if I actually had malicious motives in mind, I could have done so much more with Meliya? Because I did have standards. I made sure I didn't date her too long before letting her choose. And I never tried to have sex with her. I wanted to give her a taste of a better life.

Of course, she still rejected me.

Because no one really loves me.

Maybe my parents ruined me so much that my personality is irreparably broken.

I feel like a pariah. Somehow, the entire school knows about it, even though Head Mage Bren swore he'd keep it a secret. I got an anonymous note today during lunch. "Hey Emil! I heard the Kaldians want to kill a rapist this year. Guess there's something good about them after all."

Do I deserve this?

But even if I discover who sent me this note, we all know Kalina won't do anything about it. Because there's only one type of "victim" she cares about.

I don't know what to do.

I want to talk to Elder Mito. He would know what to do. But I believe Kalina's threat. She's the type of woman that would do that to me.

So yeah. I told Head Mage Bren I was resigning as head of my dorm. I'm going to leave my instrument in her room. I'm not going to date anyone. And if tomorrow she decides she also wants me scrubbing her floors, I guess I'll have to do that too.

Sixty years of life hang in the balance.

Of course, the most likely option is that I do everything she wants, she lets me die & then after my death goes around telling everyone I was some awful rapist who didn't deserve to live.

But I'm going to go out and die for her & everyone else, anyway. Because I actually believe in heroism. I'm *willing* to lay my life down so everyone else can live.

If only someone else here would sacrifice something.

BRASS MAGIC

Gremold physical objects

—> Trumpeters are used to sculpt houses,
furniture, weapons, dishes, fences,
walls, jewelry, etc.

SAW A TERIDEN
LAST WEEK!

—> Possible students to invite to our secret meeting:
Me, Anvisa, * Krem *, Andreya, Jez,
~~Marr~~, Carissa, ~~Jenasa~~, Ren

31

KALINA USED TO DREAM ABOUT

how exhilarating it would feel to stand up against injustice.

The reality of the three weeks since Meliya's departure felt more like exhaustion. Watching every word to make sure she didn't slip. Giving up a night every week to train her band of students. Feeling the weight of the country on her shoulders.

And remembering what it felt like to sit on Bren's couch next to Meliya and say nothing.

Some memories cling like vines.

She paused at the threshold of Ashinara's room. Kalina had stopped having lunch in the faculty lounge. Conversations with Ashinara and Mito reminded her how much she couldn't stand teachers who looked for ways to excuse bullies. So she'd done what she could to avoid them.

But earlier today, some students had shared with her that Ashinara's husband had been injured during the first skirmish on the northern front.

Kalina knocked on the wall outside of Ashinara's room, then poked her head in.

Ashinara sat behind her desk. Her elaborate shawl was nearly falling off her shoulders as she played a soft tune on her flute to water the ferns around the sides of her room. In the corner, Jacir sat eating a bowl of rice.

Kalina hadn't expected to see him in here. Had he been punished with a silent lunch today?

Ashinara's eyes lit up when she saw her, and she put her flute down. "Elder Kalina." Her eyes were red.

"I thought I'd come by to talk." Kalina glanced at Jacir again and nodded toward him.

Ashinara understood. "Let's walk outside."

She made her way through her garden of an office and joined Kalina. They walked outside where the empty outdoor classrooms awaited them. Wet season had begun a couple of weeks ago, but only a faint drizzle greeted them. The walk gave Kalina further time to contemplate what to say.

"I heard about your husband," Kalina said when they had cleared the academic building. "And...I wanted to say how sorry I am. I know how hard it is to be apart from a spouse in times like this." Her throat caught. "And I don't want you to be alone right now."

Ashinara sniffed. "Thank you. It...it means a lot. It's been so hard ever since he was drafted to stand against the northern army. He's never been a fighter. Every night, I worry about if he's still alive. And now to hear that he had a spear thrust through his side?" She paused on the edge of the jungle and swallowed. "I suppose I should be grateful he's alive. But I want to be there with him."

"I know. The war..." Kalina's voice trailed off. Too many emotions tangled up in her throat.

"I probably shouldn't be complaining." Ashinara wiped a tear from her eye and bent to pluck a few wildflowers. "You have it worse."

She shook her head. "I'm not here to compare sufferings. It's because of my husband that I know how hard this must be for you right now."

"Well, I appreciate you, Kalina. You're kind to think of me amid your own suffering." She put the wildflowers behind her ear. "I wish I did a better job of asking about your husband. I hate that it isn't until I experience what separation is like that I remember what you've dealt with this whole time."

Kalina bit her lip. "It's okay. My sister-in-law is a good help. You don't need to be bothered with my problems every day."

"But I should remember at least some days." Ashinara turned toward her. "I've missed seeing you at lunches, by the way."

Kalina avoided her gaze. "Yeah, I've had a lot of working lunches lately."

"I don't want the stress of the war to put divisions between us. Now is when we need each other more than ever."

She slowly exhaled. "Well, that's why I came today. Because I don't want you to be grieving your husband alone." A thought crossed her mind. "If you want, I can take Jacir for the rest of his silent lunch. You don't need to deal with him on top of everything else."

Ashinara laughed. "Oh, Jacir doesn't have silent lunch today. He just eats with me instead of with the students these days."

"You offered to let him eat with you?" A few teachers let their favorite students do that. But she offered that privilege to *Jacir*?

"I know you don't see things my way, Kalina. And that's okay. But the boy doesn't have anyone. Emil and the popular kids reject him because he's called them out, and the other kids reject him because he bullied them. I think he'd rather eat with me than deal with the embarrassment of eating alone. And I want him to know that at least there's someone in his life who doesn't hate him. It's what I'm called to do as a follower of the Ternion."

Kalina studied the wall of the small library ahead of them. It was hard to believe Jacir would gravitate to someone like Ashinara. She heard the kids dismissing Ashinara because they felt she was too mothering. For a bully who used to be one of the popular kids?

He must be feeling pretty desperate.

It was hard to pity him, though, whenever she thought about how he had pressured Meliya.

"I think I've had enough with kids who use our kindness to get away with crimes."

Ashinara nodded. "It's hard some days. Because they do sometimes use our kindness that way. But we never know what will happen if we refuse to give up on people." She smiled. "Krem is a good example of that."

"Krem?" Kalina turned toward her.

"Yeah. I know you spend a lot of time with him. First two years here? He wasn't a kind boy. But we had a lot of conversations during those years. And look at him now. Kindness and persistence turned him into a new person."

Huh.

"Sometimes change is slow. And that's what I need to remind myself every morning. I need encouragement from the Ternion to keep going, and our kids need encouragement from us to keep growing. Because if one of these kids continues to feel isolated and misunderstood..." Ashinara shook her head. "Sometimes when they feel like everyone assumes they're bad, that's who they choose to become."

The moon hung high in the sky by the time Kalina made her way back to her sister-in-law's house.

Of course, Chineya still had stew warming over the flickering fire for her.

"Mm, you're in for a treat tonight," her sister-in-law said. "Teriden cabbage stew. Brand new recipe to make do with what the rations allow me to buy—but I may have cooked up a new winner."

Kalina smiled as she sat on a bench around the firepit. "You decided to eat outdoors during wet season?"

"Oh, teriden stews are *always* cooked outdoors." Chineya ladled some into a bowl and handed it to her. "Besides, the rains stopped a few hours ago."

Riyad didn't care about the rain either.

Kalina blinked. *Where did that thought intrude from?* A small lump grew in the back of her throat.

She glanced back at the house and looked for a distraction. "Is everyone else asleep?"

Chineya nodded. "The boys didn't have much energy this evening."

"You didn't have to stay up for me."

"I wanted to. I know it's been a hard couple of weeks."

Kalina had broken that rule too—violating student privacy by unloading everything on Chineya. Because in the face of this threat, she needed to talk to someone. And she trusted Chineya's ability to keep things confidential.

This is probably why I shouldn't have become a teacher. I have no idea how to do the right thing while following all the rules.

"How did your meeting with the students after school go?" Chineya asked.

Kalina swallowed the mouthful of stew. "Fine. They're slowly learning what I'm trying to teach them." She paused. "They're still uneasy. I assume you've heard the second Kaldian army began crossing the border this week?"

Chineya nodded. "The skirmishes didn't go well."

She stared down at her stew. "I worry about what I'm doing." She sighed. "We need to beat these Kaldians. And Meliya is one girl. What if it's wrong to jeopardize the fate of this whole country over her? Because we both know our civilian army is going to do *squat* against the northern Kaldians."

The image of her comatose husband filled her mind. *Will I ever make peace with myself if Emil loses?*

For a long time, Chineya looked at her, rocking forward and backward on her seat. She scratched her chin. Kalina put another spoonful of stew into her mouth. *Feels wrong to eat after that kind of question. But I need energy.*

"Do you think that's what you're doing?" Chineya finally asked.

"Do I think *what's* what I'm doing?"

"Do you think you're jeopardizing the fate of this country because of what he did to one girl?"

Kalina considered that. "I think I'm trying to *protect* my students."

"Do you think he'd try to date one of them again?"

"I...I don't know. The boy feels cheated out of a good life. I don't think I can predict his decisions as long as he sees himself as the victim." Thoughts bubbled out of her quicker than she could manage them. "He has power at the school. And he knows that if not for me, he could do whatever he wants. And when you see someone with that much influence and ability with that kind of character..." Her thoughts trailed off. "I can't trust him."

Chineya nodded. "Well, there's your answer."

"But it's not." Kalina had to let her other doubts out. "Because the whole country lies in the balance. Even if he would abuse others...the Kaldians will sacrifice countless more if they take control."

Chineya looked past her in contemplation. "Are you preventing him from defending us?"

"I'm keeping him from using his instrument outside of school hours. Even though he probably won't even get his full four months at the school with the second Kaldian army approaching."

"And why are you doing that?"

"Because...because accountability matters." Kalina set her bowl down. Her hands shook. "I don't care how many random spot checks we're doing. He could still do temporary Compellings to get what he wants. I don't trust him with his fiddle if he isn't kept accountable."

"So you would allow him to use his instrument outside of school hours if he had someone supervising him?"

Oh.

She saw where this led.

Kalina looked at her.

Her sister-in-law put her hands up. "I'm not telling you what to do, Kalina. The Ternion knows I'm grateful not to be in your shoes. I'm saying you have options. You need to determine what you're willing to do to protect what you care about. That's a question you alone can answer. Of course, if you think he would Compel you while you supervised him…"

Kalina pursed her lips. She'd thought about that before. That's why she insisted Elder Toze check her mind for a Compelling every morning. But Emil already had plenty of time to Compel her if he wanted to during their private tutoring sessions.

She had three options—sacrifice her students, sacrifice this country, or sacrifice her time and safety.

These past few weeks have been so exhausting already.

But she could multitask while supervising him.

And by the Ternion, she still had too much of her husband in her.

32

The Sparkling Stone of the Temple

towered over her as Kalina walked toward the gaping entrance. A large triangle jutted out from the stone face over the entrance. And on either side, the various representatives of the Divine Council stood watch from the granite with cupped hands and solemn eyes—one fixated on the Ternion, the other toward the entrance. She hadn't seen many artistic depiction of a human—or any other part of the natural world—in Rizade other than the similar sculptures at the academy. But as members of the Divine Council, the figures certainly qualified as eternal and thus worthy of artistic depiction.

Kalina glanced at the towering cliffs of the academy and then walked up the three high stairs. She knelt at the entrance alongside some other citizen who had arrived at the same time. The stone behind her was worn with impressions from the worshipers who had knelt here before her. She lowered her head and pressed three fingers to her forehead. She could feel the expanse of the cavernous ceiling towering over her. *How small I am in the grand scheme of things.*

Footsteps padded on the ground nearby. The hem of the attendant's black robe swished around his feet just at the edge of her vision. A moment later, a drizzle of water hit the back of her head.

"The Ternion's grace is sufficient for you," the attendant pronounced. "Receive it and enter."

She slowly stood. The water slipped down her back. She nodded to the attendant with the silver bowl and stepped into the vaulted circular sanctuary of the temple. Frescoes of the Divine Council ran around the domed ceiling surrounding the tetrahedron hanging in the center. Kalina held out three fingers toward Fandola, the representative of the three kingdoms, and then turned her gaze ahead past the pews to the black-robed friar speaking in front. The temple was packed. The Kaldian armies had certainly affected attendance.

Kalina noted where Emil sat and took her own seat on a wooden pew. The friar was delivering some homily about the infamous "waterfall of grace" sculpture carved by the Ternion itself somewhere north of the Helgoland Sea and what every detail on that sculpture meant for them symbolically. She did her best to clear thoughts of Emil out of her mind. She could almost feel the tetrahedron at the top of the chamber staring down at her.

After the elegant homily and some congregational chanting, the friar instructed them to break into pairs to request prayers for each other. Kalina normally prayed with Chineya, but she had chosen a different parish this morning to try and intercept Emil on the holy day. So she gave the random worshiper she sat next to some generic requests she hoped the Ternion knew how to interpret before praying for the worshiper's rice fields.

The service wrapped up with a solemn blessing the friar uttered that the congregation repeated to each other to conclude the service. The tetrahedron above them glimmered in the light of the late morning sun. Kalina nodded solemnly toward it, then strode across the room to find Emil. She needed to talk before she changed her mind.

Emil was walking out with a few of his friends when she intercepted him.

"Emil," she said. His head popped up upon hearing her voice. "Can we talk?"

His eyes narrowed slightly. "In here?"

She shook her head. "The subject wouldn't be appropriate." Music was too earthly a matter to discuss in a temple. "Outside in the graveyard where we can have a bit of privacy."

Talking about music in a church graveyard still bent the boundaries of piety. But the Ternion would forgive her.

They walked out into the clouded sunlight and took a right to the graveyard packed full of triangular headstones and the occasional forsaken rectangular one. She hadn't expected this temple would bury nonworshipers. Most temples didn't.

"What do you want?" Emil asked, tone devoid of emotion.

She turned to look at him and hoped she wouldn't regret this. "I wanted to let you know I've thought about some of your complaints and have reconsidered what I told you last month. If you want, I'm willing to stay at school after hours and supervise you while you practice your fiddle."

He stared at her for a long moment, then rubbed his face. "You're going to let me practice again after hours?"

She could tell he didn't believe her. "With *supervision*." She rested a hand on the point of a nearby headstone.

Emil eyed her carefully. "And what if I don't want to?"

She glanced toward the noisy city beyond the low stone wall and played the dispassionate teacher. "It's your call, Emil. Believe me, I'm happy to go back to my husband."

He didn't respond at first.

Finally, he sighed. "I don't understand what the point of this is. If I was the person you say I am, I could use these opportunities to overpower you."

A chill ran down her spine. Being with Emil alone like this made her deeply uncomfortable—even with a whole city around them. But she tried not to let it show.

She looked back at him. "Maybe I think you know better than to Compel me."

"But you think I still might Compel others?" He stared at the ground.

"I judge people by their actions, not their words."

Emil continued to study the ground. She began to wonder if he planned on saying anything else. Then he sat on the pointed end of a gravestone. *That can't feel comfortable.*

"I'm not a monster." He looked up, and his eyes pleaded with her. "You have to believe me. I really, *truly* thought I was helping her after everything she'd gone through."

Kalina waved her hand. "Stop. I thought I made it clear that I was done with your excuses."

"Could you just listen to me?" he snapped. Then guilt flashed through his eyes, and he lowered his voice. "I know you want a perfect hero who would save his country. But I didn't grow up in a great home like Anvisa and Leneya. You know what my dad taught me? That women are there to be used and discarded. I've tried so hard *not* to fall into the mistakes of my father. And I guess I failed that here. But I'm never going to live up to the other perfect kids here. I thought you understood that."

Kalina inhaled. He wasn't crying. Perhaps he'd realized that tears didn't work on her. But his pain still screamed through.

Jadoni's words ran through her mind. *"That little bully will get you to like him so he can get out of trouble."*

But Ashinara's words also echoed. *"We never know what will happen if we refuse to give up on people."*

Kalina swallowed. *Whom do I believe?* Ashinara was wrong about a *lot*. But what if she was right that we shouldn't give up on trying to change people? Kalina had already put a plan in place to control his behavior. Would it hurt to at least try?

It's what Riyad would do.

She could almost see the tetrahedron in the temple hovering next to her. It aligned with Riyad.

"Listen, Emil," she said quietly. "I know you may not believe me. But I *don't* hate you. It's admirable that you don't want to imitate your parents' actions, and I *do* recognize that."

Emil sniffled. "Then why do you keep treating me like I'm no different from them?" He threw a pebble at the temple wall.

That isn't something I'd do to a temple, even with a pebble. But she ignored his mindless act.

"I don't," she said. "But I want to protect you from yourself. If you want to be that better person you've talked about, you need to realize power and freedom have not served you well."

Emil nodded. "I...I'll try." He swallowed and stared at the ground. "I just...I wish you would understand what I went through."

Kalina exhaled slowly. *It always comes back to him.* "Emil..." She paused. Should she really tell him this? Perhaps she could demonstrate that she did somewhat understand his experience.

"I have seen the effects of child abuse." Kalina paused again. But she had already started to share. "A friar abused my sister for years before anyone learned about it. I saw how much it hurt and changed her. Her abuse was different from yours. But I know that sort of treatment changes you."

"I'm sorry," Emil said, looking up at her. "I didn't realize that happened to your sister."

She swallowed. "Yeah." Coming to a temple for holy days like today reminded her of that.

"Were you the one who figured out what was happening to her?"

"I should have. The possibility crossed my mind. But she denied it, and I didn't push her hard enough to tell me the truth about her strange comments. I made a mistake. And I swore I would never make that mistake again." Kalina's fingers dug into her palm.

"That's also why I've disciplined you. Because you're not the only abused person here, Emil. You abused Meliya. And you need restrictions until you learn to treat people differently."

Emil swayed as he took this in. "Okay." He exhaled slowly. "Maybe you're right."

Kalina blinked. "Right about what?"

"About me. About what I did. About what I need. I don't know." He looked away. "I'm going to need to think more about it."

Only a baby step. *But that's far more than he's admitted to before.*

Unless it's just another manipulation attempt.

Emil cleared his throat. "I'll start practicing again, though. Obviously it will have to start after tomorrow evening. But the Ternion knows I need the practice."

Kalina breathed out. A success with Emil felt good. But she wasn't sure what he meant by his other comment. "What's tomorrow evening?"

Emil blinked. "Has Head Mage Bren not talked to you about it?"

"About what?"

"My dad's throwing a birthday celebration for me at the battlefield. And he asked that both you and the Head Mage speak at it."

33

I CAN'T HELP BUT HOLD A PREMONITION

that I'll regret this.

Their horses neared the tents of the front lines as the sun dipped toward the horizon. Bren rode on one side of her, Emil on the other. Their steeds had shortened the travel to the front lines from eight hours to four. *Good thing, given how much rain has dumped on us over the trip.*

A pit had rested in her stomach the whole day. She understood why General Mahd had planned this. Celebrating Emil's birthday gave him a great opportunity to encourage the troops. And who better to instill confidence in the prophesied hero's abilities than his personal trainer whom all the soldiers already knew?

But how can I praise Emil in good conscience?

If Bren hadn't ordered her to join him this morning, she wouldn't have shown up.

"Look at our troops," Bren prattled as they passed through the camps. "They look in much better shape than I thought."

Kalina glanced around with a commander's eye. She saw something different. More deserters hung on the gallows than usual. Lines creased the soldier's looks, and their shoulders sagged in a way indicative of defeat. *That looks like horseflesh on one of the spits.* The fires sputtered amid the falling rain.

They certainly needed a boost of morale. *Am I willing to sacrifice my integrity to provide that?*

"We'll be sure to tell your father how honored we are to be included in this celebration," Bren said.

Kalina shook her head. Mahd didn't invite them to honor them.

Emil looked around at the soldiers. "Sure."

She wondered what thoughts ran through his mind. Did he see what she saw in the faces of their men?

Or perhaps he interpreted it all as people waiting for him to save the day.

Her attention pulled back to the topic she'd contemplated amid the drenched journey: what she could say about Emil. He *was* a powerful mage. He *did* occasionally lead well. He *certainly* worked long hours. It left a lot unsaid—but she could at least testify to those attributes.

Of course, another voice whispered that she was betraying her beliefs. By standing up there and speaking, she would lend support to an unrepentant Compeller. *What would Meliya's reaction be if she saw me praising Emil for all his good traits?*

Maybe she was better off trying to get out of this entirely.

Like Mahd would let me.

Kalina pursed her lips.

They approached the crimson command tent in the center of the encampment. General Mahd stood with two advisers underneath the small canopy that jutted outside the main tent.

He looked up as they approached. "About time you showed up. I was getting worried you'd miss your own birthday celebration. We've got a lot of our commanders in the tent who are looking forward to talking to you, Emil."

Emil visibly swallowed. "Okay. Nice to see you, Dad."

"Yeah, you too," General Mahd said quickly. "We don't have a lot of time until the dinner starts, so let's get moving."

Emil slowly dismounted. The mud squelched underneath him. For a moment, it looked like he was going to say something else to his father. Then he shook his head and, shoulders slumped, walked into the tent.

"Stand straight," Mahd muttered as Emil disappeared. "Kids these days—they don't know proper manners."

Kalina suppressed a sigh as she dismounted, trying to avoid the mud as best she could. She joined Mahd and Bren underneath the small canopy. Rain tapped off the fabric overhead.

"After Emil meets our commanders, the whole army is coming together for a little presentation," General Mahd said. "They're pretty beaten down, and they need a spark of hope. I'll invite Emil up to say some words, and then I want both of you to talk about his accomplishments. A private banquet with the officers will follow. And don't worry, we won't follow ration restrictions." A rare smile slipped past his lips. "I treat my son and his trainers well."

Bren nodded. "I've already written speeches for both of us, based on what you requested. Your son is a treasure to our school."

Kalina inhaled sharply. *What?*

Mahd smiled. "Good. I'll see both of you shortly." And then he followed Emil into the tent.

She slowly turned toward Bren. He'd already written a speech for her?

"Don't look at me like that." Bren pulled a folded piece of paper out of his waterproof satchel and handed it over. "I understand your prejudices. But you saw those troops coming in. I talked them up for Emil, but they looked horrible. They *need* this."

She slowly unfolded the note and read the glowing words. This was a speech fit for a mythical hero, stuffed full of accolades about Emil's character, accomplishments, and nobility. Bren certainly knew how to pull out all the rhetorical stops. The only true sentence was the one saying she taught him.

Suddenly, partially praising Emil felt downright candid.

Kalina looked up at Bren. "I can't say this."

"Mahd told me he wanted speeches praising these parts of Emil. So we will."

"But—but this isn't true," she hissed.

"Does it matter? It will give the soldiers resolve to resist the Kaldians."

"Doesn't the Ternion command honesty?"

Bren pursed his lips. "The Ternion wants its people protected from heretical dogs."

Her heart beat fast. "Look, I knew the general wanted a speech. So on the road, I planned out some remarks that would encourage the troops while remaining honest. I can say those."

Bren stared at her. "Are you serious?"

She threw up her hands. What else did he expect her to say?

Bren shook his head. "Come with me." He walked through the tents.

She stuffed the speech into her satchel and slowly followed him into the rain. Where was he taking her?

The tents fell away, then all that was left was the wall at the edge of the cliffs. The wooden palisades had been replaced by firm stone. Mahd had at least successfully entrenched his troops.

Bren climbed the steps to the rampart of the walls. She trudged after him. A few guards farther down the wall looked at them, but neither spoke when they recognized her.

Bren gestured below. "Tell me what you see."

She glanced at him amid the drumming rain. Had he forgotten that she had served in the military? Of course she recognized the sight below. Columns of campfire smoke dotted the hordes of Kaldians assembled below, their crimson flags waving high. Guns boomed in the distance, no doubt used for target practice. And she could see several battalions performing drills, all done with perfect synchronization. The commanders' yells echoed over the rainfall.

At the foot of the hill, a row of impaled bodies lined the lower slope.

That's new. A deep shudder ran down her spine.

"I see our sworn enemies," Kalina said in a low tone.

"Good. Now I want you to keep looking at them and tell me, in all sincerity, that you think your moral purity—or making sure we properly punish some kisses—is more important than keeping these hordes back from massacring our students."

Her heart caught.

"Isn't this your whole moral crusade?" Bren asked. "It matters more that we do the right thing than that we protect our people from butchery? Well, tell me that right now while you stare at those godless pagans who would add both of us to their impalement lines. Your husband too, for that matter. Tell me that my embellishments are a bridge too far to cross."

Words escaped her. The stamping of the practicing Kaldians held her gaze. And all her thoughts followed with it.

After a long moment, Bren spoke. "That's what I thought. So let's focus on the things that count." He descended from the wall.

"It's all that I have," Kalina whispered.

"What?"

Kalina turned toward Bren, halfway down the stairs. Rainwater trickled down her forehead. "My integrity is all that I have." She bit back the sobs that threatened to rack her throat. "Because you know what I think of every time I consider giving in? It's Meliya, sitting on the couch and begging for help while we kick her out of the school. It's knowing that I watched her cry and said *nothing*. And look—I'm an ex-commander. I *know* what it's like to make hard decisions. But I could still sleep at night because I knew I had made the right decisions. Now? I *promised* to protect Meliya. And I *broke* my promise."

She stepped toward him. "You want to know how I can trumpet integrity in the face of *them*? Because if I go up there and read your saintlike speech about him, it's not just the soldiers who will hear it. That boy, who thinks heroism is a farce, will hear every word I say. He'll know that I don't mean it. And so he'll learn that I don't actually care about his behavior when push comes to shove.

"But our hope as a nation isn't in the resolve of our soldiers. It's in that boy admitting that he *isn't* a golden child and committing himself to change. As long as he shirks responsibility and uses everyone else to get what he wants, none of us should put our lives in his hands."

Thunder rumbled in the distance. Kalina stepped toward Bren. "Telling him he's already a hero would sign our nation's death sentence. Because if I can't model integrity myself, why would he respect anything else I say?"

Bren stared at her. And for one long moment, he gaped.

"Well," he finally said. "I guess you have a choice, Kalina. Because I'm here to win. You can either say the words I gave you, or you're fired. And I guess then Elder Mito will get that chance he's been begging me for and become Emil's tutor."

Kalina stared at the pages in her hand as soldiers gathered in the open clearing. The torrent had slowed to a drizzle, and trumpeters had already shaped the earth into a natural amphitheater. Drummers cast an aura of light around the covered stage in front of her. And the officers were drifting out of the command tent. Apparently they'd had their fill of time with Emil.

Mahd emerged with Emil, one hand securely on his son's shoulder while he guided him backstage. He nodded toward her as he approached. "You ready to speak after my son?"

Kalina swallowed down the lump in her throat. "Sure."

"Good." He clapped a hand on her shoulder. "The soldiers need *something* to get their spirits up, I'll tell you that." He continued forward, leaving her and Emil alone behind the stage. Bren had disappeared ten minutes ago to hobnob with the king's ambassador.

She could feel Emil's gaze upon her before she looked back at him.

"You...ah...ready to speak?" His forehead creased.

"Well, as you informed me yesterday, the general commanded me to do so."

"Right." He dug the tip of his boot into the ground. "Do, uh, you know what you're going to say?"

And that was the question of the hour. Bren's threat screamed in her ears.

But Kalina had already decided what sort of teacher she needed to be.

"You know, Emil, I would rather not speak. They want me to say you're a moral exemplar who's ready to fight the Kaldians, and we both know that isn't true. So I'll say what I can that will encourage the troops while being accurate. That probably means the Head Mage will fire me for not saying what he wanted me to. But I care more about the truth."

Emil stared at her. "They might fire you?" His voice quivered.

She knew what that look meant. *"I still need you."* And that's the only thing she could bank on. That even if she was fired, Emil would still come to her for private lessons because he needed her to save his life.

"I'll say something to my father. You won't lose your job."

She shook her head. "We both know how well your father takes advice."

Emil opened his mouth.

Then Mahd's voice boomed over the crowd. "Attention!"

The crowd hushed. Emil clamped his mouth closed.

"We all know what today is," Mahd said. "But more importantly, we know what we need. I know the state of our rations. I know the diseases that have swept through our ranks. And I know what lies beneath these cliffs. But despite all that, I have *no doubts* about our ability to win this war. Why? Because first of all, the Ternion always protects its people. And second, I know the caliber of the hero who's going to save us."

Mahd smiled and looked back at them. "Emil? Come show these men who you are."

Emil exchanged one last lingering look with her, then grabbed his fiddle and bounded on stage. "You called?" And suddenly, it was the smiling, confident Emil who had control.

A half-hearted cheer went up from the crowd. *Because of course war-hardened soldiers can see this whole event for the show it is.* The drizzle didn't help morale either.

Emil brought his fiddle up to his chin. Bren came up from behind, carefully avoiding the mud spots, and stood next to Kalina to watch the performance.

Then Emil began to play. A low, haunting tune rang throughout the amphitheater. And Kalina now noticed the metal poles set up around the amphitheater as multiple strands of lightning sparked from one to the other. The lightning bolts danced and crossed paths with each other.

She knew he inclined to theatrics. But she hadn't seen any of this before. *When did he practice this?*

He made use of all three of his melodies. And he gave quite the tour de force. She noted the raised eyebrows and large eyes of experienced mages like Padini as they watched the performance. They recognized his prowess.

Finally, with one booming finale, the performance was over. And Emil bowed to a much more enthusiastic cheer.

"Thank you," Emil said once the cheering died down. "I was asked to say some words today for my birthday. But I'll admit that I'm not much of a speaker, so I thought I'd show you what I can do instead."

Kalina shook her head. Emil could use his words well enough. He just wanted to show off.

Though from him, showing off is probably better than whatever lies he'd spin.

He scanned the crowd. "Now, I'm still a student. And so after me, you're going to hear from my personal trainer and my head mage about what kind of magic I can pull off. And yeah, they can tell you about a whole lot I've done."

Kalina's stomach knotted.

"But..." Emil cleared his throat. "Well, I know you're soldiers, and so you prefer raw honesty to polished blathering, right?" He grinned. "So let me be candid: I'm not ready to fight yet."

Kalina's head jerked up.

"I know." He took a step back. "That's not what you expected your future hero to say. And how could I say that after such an impressive show of force? But I'm not going to unload a bunch of klyte on you all. Haven't you seen enough new mages who talked a big game only to be caught with their pants down during their first battle?"

The crowd laughed. Bren stood stiffly next to Kalina. She leaned forward.

"So here's what you need to know," Emil said. "I may be powerful, but I need more time to learn what actually works on the battlefield. Good thing I have one of the best mage commanders your army has ever seen training me, right?"

A roar of approval went up from the crowd. From the stage, Mahd shot a glance back at her. She couldn't quite decipher what that look meant.

Emil continued. "She's still teaching me what works on this battlefield. As some of you may know, she's discovered this new way for mages to synergize with other kinds of instruments. And I, for one, am looking forward to learning how to master using my power to affect *all* kinds of magic."

Her heart leapt to her throat. *That* was a military secret that shouldn't have been shared outside the small group of mages she'd already talked to. There were certainly spies here tonight, and the Kaldians didn't need to know it was possible.

But that almost didn't matter. *Emil's willing to learn how to do this?*

"She'll probably have a bit more to say about that," Emil said. "But here's what you need to know. As powerful as I am, I'll only be able to beat the Kaldians if you keep them back long enough for me to learn all the techniques I need to know. So don't listen to the klyte some people will say about me already being perfect. And keep up the fight. Because every day you stand firm, the better my odds improve."

And with a theatrical bow, he was done.

She stood gaping as he said something to Mahd and then walked off the stage. *Did Emil really do that? Admit weaknesses in front of everyone and even pledge to learn synchronization?*

There was no way either she *or* Bren could give their original glowing adulations after that. Emil had enabled her to give a speech that was entirely honest without losing her job.

He just saved my teaching position.

It was the wee hours of the morning when the horses returned them to the gates of Chintor. Teaching after three hours of sleep would be a beast. But she'd done it before. Kalina's mind still raced at how that evening had gone. Even Bren had needed to change his speech so he didn't look like a fool. And despite Mahd pulling her aside to ask her what she'd said to Emil, neither of them had anything on her.

Near the gates, Bren went ahead to get the guards to open them. And she finally got the chance to ask Emil the question that had burned on her lips the whole evening.

"Did you mean what you said?"

Emil smiled. "I want to keep you as my teacher, don't I?"

That was all she got out of him before Bren returned and they had to go their separate directions.

34

SOMETHING ABOUT THE SLOW TRICKLING

of the stream always managed to put her soul in a state of calm. Kalina could almost forget about how close the Kaldian armies were.

She leaned back against a kapok tree at the edge of the grove. Its bark, damp from the morning rain, bent beneath her weight. The stream inched past her, waving this way and that before plummeting over the cliffs into the city of Chintor proper.

The wall at the front of Chintor Academy didn't extend to the edges of the plateau, giving her a full view of the Valan River valley. She could almost make out the farmers planting rice in the paddies below. Jungle cliffs on the other side of the valley hid behind the low clouds that drifted through the sky. Birds sang in the background. And the clouds beamed the colors of the setting sun.

A couple of open books lay next to her. She had come out here hoping to read them. But the trip to the front lines two days ago kept distracting her.

She'd decided after Meliya that she was done trying to change him. *Did I give up too easily?*

Of course, he had explained his reversal.

"I want to keep you as my teacher, don't I?"

She had made the mistake today of asking Jadoni about joining her in chaperoning Emil, though she left out the restrictions she'd placed on him.

Jadoni had refused. *"One of the best parts of this year is not having to see him each and every day."* And when Jadoni learned about Emil's speech, she had shaken her head even more. *"Don't believe an abuser's vain promises to change."*

Was this all a feint?

I need to see what choices he makes next.

"Elder Kalina!"

She looked up to see Krem and Leneya making their way toward her, hand in hand.

"Look at that face," Leneya said to Krem. "I told you she wouldn't want to see us outside of class."

Kalina laughed and shook her head. "You're fine."

"See!" Krem said. He glanced at Kalina. "It's not every day we see you out here in student territory."

"Student territory?" Kalina raised an eyebrow. "Since when was this whole plateau *your* territory?"

"I mean, you can go wherever you want," Krem said. "But we don't normally see teachers beyond the academic buildings."

Leneya giggled. "You're kind of in the kissing corner, Elder Kalina."

Kalina blinked. "What?"

"Well, you know, the place where you're sitting. It's the place couples go when they want to be together and away from other people."

She glanced around. The foliage *did* provide privacy.

"Hmm," Kalina said. "Maybe I should truck my husband's body up here so we can live up to the name." She squinted at the two of them. "Is that why you came here?"

"No," Krem said immediately.

"Well..." Leneya said at the same time.

"Lying to a teacher, Krem? I didn't expect that from you!"

Krem's cheeks reddened. "I mean, we hadn't *finalized* our plans. Someone else might be here—like you were! So..."

Kalina laughed. "Well, you both need to study, anyway. I heard you have a pretty intensive test tomorrow from Elder Toze."

"Yeaaaaah." Krem pursed his lips. "I mean, you're not *wrong*...studying would probably be a good idea."

"It's what I'm doing." Kalina tapped her current book.

"Oh, you're such a *teacher*, Elder Kalina!" Leneya said.

She snorted. "What did you think I was?"

"You're not like most teachers," Krem said.

"Yeah," Leneya said. "Most teachers wouldn't teach us how to fight back against Compellers."

Kalina glanced around. But they were alone. "Well, I never said I was a normal teacher. Nor a good one. But I *do* want you to succeed, whether in protecting yourselves or acing assessments."

"That's fair." Krem sighed. "Well, I guess we should be going."

Leneya nodded. "Thanks, Elder Kalina!"

Thanks for what? But they waved and departed.

She watched them leave. And then her eyes drifted back to the open book. *Strange & Amazing Tales of Great Mages: A Series of Tales of Unusual Magical Happenings and Occurrences.* She'd hoped to find someone in there surviving an instrument breakage. Unfortunately, those hopes hadn't come to pass yet.

To her right, leaves rustled and feet occasionally stamped somewhere in the jungle. Wings flapped and branches cracked.

Kalina picked up the book again, skimming past the story of a man whose arm shrunk every time he used a musical instrument. This was an old wives' tale—not a serious historical claim.

She flipped to the next page, ready to discard this book and call it a day. Then she saw it.

> *Eto Garrett may have the distinct honor of being the only man who cheated Death after an instrument breakage.*

She inhaled sharply.

Then she read on.

> *Eto was a normal flutist, who happened to also be the prince of Altonia. But he couldn't help himself. In the midst of a sordid affair with the queen of Denare (the details of which are far too steamy for these pages), he made enemies with the wrong people. And when a servant discovered his affair, he couldn't run fast enough to evade the irate king.*

The king caught up with him in the middle of the Helgoland Sea. If only you could have seen the battle. From everything our sources have told us, there was a terrific showdown to see which mage could display larger prowess over the water. But Eto, ever the sneak, had hidden on a passenger barge so he could try to capsize the king's trireme while the king's mages couldn't capsize his without harming innocent lives.

How did such a momentous battle end? A storyteller couldn't have imagined a better finish. A lone bowman on the king's ship, equipped with weapons forged of the unmusical substance, sent an arrow flinging into the wind. No sane archer would have taken such a daring gamble. The winds blew so fiercely that he had no guarantees of hitting Eto. But the Ternion must have smiled on the archer that day. The arrow, while pushed off course, still hit the end of the flute, and the whole instrument shattered. Eto fell back and the king's mages, satisfied to have hit the flamboyant womanizer, returned home.

But our story isn't over yet. Because what did the passengers discover when they surrounded the fallen Eto? That the man had revived! And after regaining consciousness, Eto boasted loudly of the triumph he'd scored over Death, who had admired his adventurous escapades enough to make Eto a deal. By besting Death in a duel of cards, Eto earned a return to life upon one condition: he never play music again. And so Eto kept his word. He returned home a hero and proudly wore the remains of his flute on a chain around his neck.

While it may be hard to believe for such a mischievous cheat like him, Eto remained true to his promise to Death. He never played a flute again. He didn't even have any other affairs! Which just goes to show that sometimes, all that's needed to cure a ruffian is a little run-in with death.

Kalina stared at those two pages for a long while. *Could this be possible?*

There were, of course, several significant problems, including the other ridiculous events in this book. It wasn't a rigorous historical text, even if it contained some true stories. The whole narrative—like the others—was written in sensational language. And some details, like this deal with Death, couldn't have happened. Not to mention the dubious bits like a whole barge of Denarian passengers not trying to stop Eto themselves.

But one detail caught her eye—the mention that Eto didn't use magic again after the accident. Was it a coincidence that a fictional story would contain eerie similarities to hers? Or was some truth buried within the myth?

She refocused on the text. The story claimed this flutist was a prince—and heir—to the throne of Altonia.

The library wouldn't stay open much longer.

Anvisa was packing supplies up by the time Kalina arrived at the library.

"I'm so sorry," Kalina said, aware of how flustered she must look. "I need to find something." She scurried over to the history section and began scanning titles.

The shelf had three books on the history of Altonia. Perhaps there were more in the basement, but she didn't have the patience for that today. She grabbed all three and returned to the desk for Anvisa to scribble dates in them.

"Elder Kalina, I had no idea you wanted to be a scholar of Altonia."

Kalina shrugged. She wasn't going to try to explain this. "Oh, you know me—I don't have enough to do with my time."

"I know what you mean," she chirped. "Right now I'm studying Endrish culture. It's not going to help me, but it's *so* fascinating."

Kalina didn't want to be pulled into a long conversation. She thanked Anvisa and rushed to her office, where she began skimming the contents.

The first book was compiled by the official Altonian biographer and had a timeline. Yes—Altonia had a king named Eto some four hundred years ago. She flipped to his section. It focused on political alliances, wars, and famines. Precious little about the man's personal life. Though it did mention a tense relationship between Altonia and Denare.

On to the second book. This one was an older work by a previous

Altonian biographer. It seemed less dry and politically focused—and yes, it had a section on Eto.

> *Eto is one of the most well-known Altonian kings. It becomes hard to distinguish truths from fables. Contrary to popular lore and campfire stories, however, Eto was never a mage, he never made a deal with Death, and he certainly never had an affair with a Denarian queen. He was simply a charismatic king who liked to make up tall tales at dinner parties that were further exaggerated by his bards.*

She stared at those sentences for too long. She tried skimming the rest of the section, but that was it. This history confirmed that Altonia and Denare were political rivals, but nothing else came close to the exploits claimed by the other book.

She opened the last book and scanned the table of contents.

No section for Eto.

Other kings had chapters in the table of contents, including kings she recognized from before and after him.

But no Eto.

Could he have been included in one of the other chapters? She flipped to the ones that seemed closest to his historical period. Nothing. This last book wasn't attempting to record a complete history of Altonia, just selections about key events from the perspective of a foreigner. And Eto hadn't made the cut.

The afternoon's hopes slid away like melting ice.

The book had a foreword. Perhaps it would mention why the author didn't include certain stories. She turned back and began skimming.

She stopped when she noticed a familiar name.

> *Certain readers will notice the absence of a renowned king of Altonia and question why I didn't deem him important enough to include.*
>
> *The truth, however, is that from everything I've found, the mythical king Eto never existed.*
>
> *I'm well aware of the torches and pitchforks*

Altonian readers will want to point my direction. But from the best research I've done, Eto was a folktale told by Altonian citizens during a period when they were ruled by a darker, more tyrannical king. Native Altonian historians, not willing to admit to the faults of the actual king (whose name has been lost) replaced him with Eto in their stories. More recent historians have rightly excised the most fantastical stories about Eto. But they ought to accept that the older notes scrawled in the margins of previous histories may have been correct—the whole narrative about Eto is nothing more than a historical fabrication.

There's some evidence from marginalia for a single rebel who won several victories against the tyrant through sheer cunning. And there are legends about this hero being so powerful, the tyrant had to kill him twice: once as a mage, and once again as a swordsman. Desperate populaces often imbue heroes with mythical qualities as a way of holding on to hope. Given these story similarities, I suspect this rebel is where the origin of the Eto myth came from.

The text went on from there to discuss other matters.

She stared and stared again at the section.

So...that was that?

Kalina knew the case she wanted to make from the last paragraph: there *was* some hero out there who survived his instrument breaking. That's why he "died twice"—everyone believed an instrument breakage led to instant death.

But she knew when she was stretching.

She'd spent months researching. One quasi myth was all she had to show for it. *Looks like I now struggle with researching as much as I do teaching.*

She played her cello for a while that evening, filling the empty classroom with languishing progressions.

35

$\mathcal{A}$ COUPLE OF DAYS LATER, $\mathcal{K}$ALINA found herself running late to her after-hours small group training. She'd tried chasing a few other solutions for instrument breakage. But still nothing. At this rate, she'd have nothing to show for her work when the armies eventually converged on Chintor. *Nothing that could motivate Emil to be better.*

The academic building was nearly empty. Rain beat on the roof. A flute squeaked from Ashinara's office. The teacher was working late with a struggling student. Kalina admired Ashinara for that. Let it not be said that she didn't pour into her students.

Kalina ascended to the second floor, headed down the hall, and entered her classroom to join her special cohort of students.

There was one more than she expected.

"Hanodoi?" She furrowed her brow as she stood at the top of the auditorium stairs. "What are you doing here?"

The gangly boy looked up at her with widening eyes.

"Oh, I asked him if he wanted to join us," Anvisa said.

"Join us? This isn't a party!"

"I-I'm sorry," Hanodoi stuttered. "I didn't realize I wasn't supposed to be here."

"We were talking a couple days ago, and Hanodoi was worried about

Emil," Anvisa said. "You know what Emil did to him. And so...well, I thought maybe I should invite him." She mouthed the final words. *"He needs friends."*

Hanodoi was still a Year Three student. He could work some magic, but not a lot—and he was pretty young. Would he know how to keep his mouth shut? Of course, he *had* done that for a while with his love of old Kaldian culture. And he hated Emil. He could likely stay quiet, even if he couldn't work much magic himself.

"I can leave." Hanodoi began walking up the steps.

Kalina sighed. "No, at this point you should stay." Goodness knew the boy needed some friends. And if Anvisa and her buddies wanted to befriend the Kaldian boy, she should encourage that.

She looked at Anvisa. "Just make sure you don't talk to anyone else. The more people who know, the more dangerous this becomes."

"Oh, we know," Krem jumped in. "And we don't. Jacir also keeps trying to befriend us, but we know better than to trust bullies like him."

Interesting. She mentally filed that for future contemplation, then clapped. "Let's practice."

Competing tunes filled the room as Anvisa and Andreya tried to practice mental Quelling.

Kalina had taught the violinists enough for them to put pressure on a mind—in this case, the mind of the turtle sitting confused in the middle of the classroom. What they knew could give someone a terrible headache, but nothing more than that.

She didn't dare teach them how to turn pressure into control.

But while they could apply pressure, they couldn't Quell pressure yet. And that's what they really needed to learn.

Kalina gestured with her baton toward Andreya, motioning for her to narrow her focus. Her Quelling reach was too wide. For something as precise and targeted as a Compelling, she needed to zero her Quelling to that specific region of the brain.

Andreya narrowed her focus. But unfortunately, she couldn't find the exact spot that Anvisa was putting pressure on.

"All right." Kalina gestured for them to stop. *We've tortured the turtle long enough.*

The two students put away their instruments. Kalina rested her chin in her hands as she watched them trudge back to the other six. *What am I doing wrong?*

Krem turned toward her. "I'm sorry, Elder Kalina. I don't know if we can do this."

She shook her head. "Nope. You're not giving up that easily."

"I mean, we haven't made progress for weeks."

Leneya walked to him. "You're too hard on us, Krem." She wrapped her arms around him.

Kalina waved Leneya off. "You know the rules, Leneya. No physical contact within my classroom." They reluctantly separated.

She looked back at the eight students. *Krem didn't speak for himself.* "You're trying to learn a difficult skill. It may take you more time, but Anvisa almost has it and Andreya will get there."

Admittedly, though, Andreya hadn't made any progress over the past few weeks.

Krem shrugged. "I don't know how this will help."

"What do you mean?"

He gestured with his thumb at Anvisa. "They can't even beat Emil when they duel. They can mitigate him, sure. But he still overpowers them."

"Our goal isn't to stop him ourselves, though," Anvisa said. "It's to slow him down so that everyone who isn't a violinist can fight and incapacitate him."

"I guess I'm worried the couple of extra seconds you'll buy for us won't do anything."

Kalina bit the inside of her cheek. She had the same worry herself. Anvisa and Andreya could only slow him down so much. And if Emil started Compelling students to fight against each other...she shuddered as she envisioned Krem fighting Anvisa.

Working with Emil this past week had given her one idea.

"What do you all know about mages synergizing?" she asked.

"Um...that's really hard to do," Andreya said. "I know you have a lot of confidence in us, Elder Kalina, but I definitely can't duet and Repose with someone else."

Anvisa looked at her quizzically. "I thought only experienced mages could synergize with others."

Kalina nodded. "That's what's generally accepted." She paused. "But there's a lot we don't know about how synergy works. I discovered that firsthand when I achieved synergy with my husband on the battlefield."

Anvisa cocked her head. "But I thought he played the lute."

"He did."

Shock rippled through the students. Hanodoi's eyes were perhaps the largest of them all.

"You synergized with someone using a different kind of instrument?" Leneya asked, dumbfounded.

"This is why I've gotten on you so much about why you can't rely on textbooks." Kalina stepped down to the main floor of the classroom. "There's so much more about music."

"I thought you couldn't mix different types of magic!" Anvisa exclaimed. "What does it even mean to mix Substances together? They're all different uses of the Fabric."

Kalina waved a finger. "Synergy doesn't mix Substances. But achieving harmony with another instrument can amplify the effects of the leading instrument, even if you don't have the same magic."

"But if someone doesn't have experience with a Substance, how can they direct their instrument to do the same thing?" Anvisa asked.

"That's what I'm trying to say. All the books out there say that if mages want to synergize with each other, they need to artistically blend their music and then direct their minds at doing the exact same things. And so without time to plan your exact moves to the minutia, you can't have that sort of synchronization. What my husband and I discovered, however, is that it doesn't have to be that hard. A mage can direct his energies toward his *partner* while in Repose."

They all focused on her.

"That's possible?" Anvisa asked, eyes wide.

"Don't get me wrong. That doesn't mean it's easy. You still need to hear and harmonize with someone's beat in a chaotic battlefield, and that takes concentration. It helped that we were married. For our purposes, however, you wouldn't need to harmonize during the noise and chaos of battle. Just here at the school."

"So you want us to harmonize with Anvisa and Andreya," Krem said.

"If you can, that changes the entire game here."

"We're not going to be able to live up to you and your husband." Krem frowned. "You know that, right?"

"I do." Kalina brushed her hair behind her ear. "But thinking like a soldier isn't about achieving perfection. It's about doing your best with what you have."

"How would we even harmonize?" Leneya piped up.

"That's what I'm here to teach you."

A couple hours later, only Anvisa, Krem, and Leneya remained. The others had all gone to their dorms after an unsuccessful night.

"I don't think we can perform at the same level that you and your husband did," Anvisa said. "The medley sounded awful."

Kalina reflected on the day's results. Emil had done better his first day, but it wasn't fair to judge them by his standard. "We need to give it time. It's only your first day."

Krem kicked at the ground. "I don't know. We're not very good."

"Stop." She fixed her gaze on Krem. "That kind of attitude won't get us anywhere."

"I'm trying to be realistic," Krem muttered.

"And maybe that's why we're losing this war."

All the kids looked at her. Thunder blared outside.

"Look," she continued. "We can blame it on poor generals—and let's be clear, that *is* a problem. But we also need a transformation. We're failing because we're still trying to win the last war."

"I'm confused," Anvisa said. "I thought you disagreed with everything Elder Mito said. Was I wrong?"

Normally Kalina held back her critique of Mito. But the kids had caught on to her beliefs, anyway. And this group needed her honesty. "I don't mind that Elder Mito wants to improve our tactics. He's right. Our culture shouldn't believe that valuing stability means rejecting innovation. But Elder Mito doesn't have enough experience to innovate well. Think about it for a moment. What's given the Kaldians the upper hand in this war?"

"Their guns," Krem said.

"Exactly. They discovered new, proven technology from over the seas, and used it to revolutionize their warfare. And they're winning. Because armies win when they're experienced enough to know *how* to innovate well."

"Learning new kinds of magic is a bit different than using guns," Krem said.

Kalina shook her head. "Look, when my husband and I began experimenting, if we had given up at our first obstacle, we wouldn't have ever succeeded. You need to try new things, fail, and try again to protect yourselves and others from a prophesied hero."

"If he even is the chosen one," Krem mumbled.

She cocked her head. "I'm sorry?"

"Have you not heard the rumors?"

"What rumors?"

"This whole 'an elf came up to my dad after my birth and chose me to save the country' deal. Doesn't it sound convenient? It makes some of us wonder if his dad made the prophecy up."

Kalina furrowed her brow. "It wasn't just any elf who gave the prophecy. It was Zedin, who's been a conduit of the Divine Council for *centuries*."

Leneya shook her head. "There weren't any witnesses, though. I dated Emil for eight months, and he's always said Zedin came from the middle of nowhere while his dad was at the edge of the Deep Jungle. *No one else heard Zedin*."

Kalina scrunched her lips. "That doesn't make any sense. The whole leadership of this country clings to the prophecy. They wouldn't believe it based on General Mahd's word alone."

"People doubted the general at first," Anvisa said, jumping in. "At least here they did. When Emil first joined the school, teachers disagreed about whether they believed him. They only started believing it when the war started and they *needed* something to hope in."

"I understand what you're saying. But our military leaders don't depend on unproven miracles."

"Even if the king assured them it was true?" Anvisa asked.

Kalina bit her lip. *Yes, we put too much trust in the king's claims. An unbroken six-hundred-year-old dynasty grants that kind of credibility. But this much?* "They wouldn't take it on the general's word alone."

"But how many people know there weren't witnesses?" Krem asked. "My dad serves as a low-level adviser to the king, and when I mentioned

Emil's story to him a couple months ago, he had no idea Mahd didn't have witnesses."

She stared at Krem. The whole idea was ludicrous: The entire leadership of a country wouldn't pin their hopes on this one boy on General Mahd's word alone.

Of course, if everyone assumed someone else had verified it, given how *desperate* everyone felt...

"I—I don't know." She glanced at the seat Emil normally took in the classroom. "I mean, he's an *excellent* mage, and we have all seen that."

"He also received private training before coming here," Anvisa pointed out. "And he always had teachers giving him special attention. Maybe he's the chosen one. But maybe he's reaped the benefits of early training."

The suggestion sounded ridiculous.

But good researchers didn't reject far-fetched ideas without investigating them first.

Silent Arcane Society Notes

The Silent Arcane Society vs. Emil. If we can learn to synergize like this, he won't know what hit him!

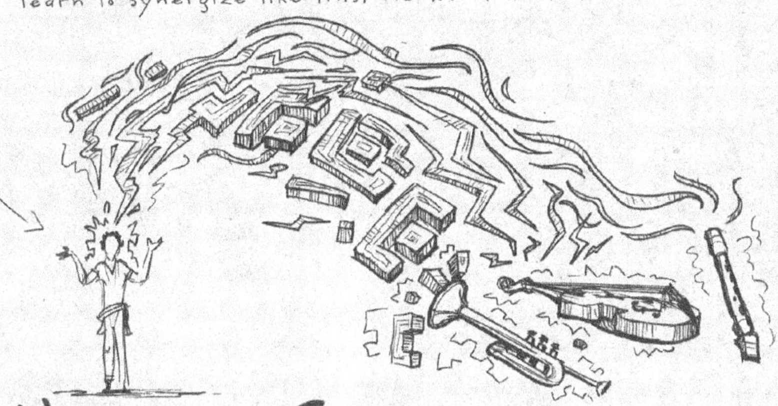

Normal Synergy

↳ Identical instruments + mages harmonizing + exact same Substance control = multiplied effect.

*Expert skill is needed to prevent chaos!

The New Synergy

↳ Different instruments + one mage directing magic to the other + harmonizing = super multiplication!

*This eases coordination by bypassing direct Substance control. Elder Kalina is so smart!

RatClam Vine —
Twisting rodent trap.
atracts and eats rodents.
(Gross!)

36

THE STUDENTS' ANNUAL FORJEN

tournament meant another weekend at the school. This time, Umar wasn't here to add his wisdom or his dry sense of humor. *He was my guide...until he wasn't.* She swallowed back the lump in her throat. Hard to believe it had almost been a month.

Now, Kalina stood alongside Elder Suraya surveying the game. She had never played sports much as a student. But it was quite something to watch sweaty teens kick a ball up and down the hummocks of the playing field while standing next to a woman with finely done hair, perfectly applied red lip paint, and a carefully curated outfit. *Should I expect anything different from Suraya?*

Near the edge of the forest, Emil stood playing his fiddle. Kalina had encouraged him to take the day off. But he had begged her to let him play his fiddle within eyeshot of her so he could get some additional practice hours in.

Of course she couldn't refuse that.

"I swear I have never had students this lazy before," Suraya was saying. "I don't know where in Rizade Head Mage Bren recruits from, but I'll tell you, the standards have plummeted. If I have one more student tell me they don't know how to clean a trumpet properly, I'm grilling Bren about what teachers do in earlier years."

Kalina laughed. "They *do* seem to have trouble with that."

"I caught a whole cheating ring going on too," she continued. "Thought they'd perfected a subtle tapping code, so I made the four of them unique multiple-choice tests for a month and watched their grades plunge. And they thought they could get away with cheating in *my* class."

Kalina glanced at Emil. The question her students had raised yesterday about his prophecy rolled around in her mind. Was Suraya a safe person to discuss that with?

The kids stopped for a break. Krem was drinking an absurd amount of water. Jacir hung around him and Leneya, trying to talk with them only to be rebuffed. It didn't seem like he had many friends after everything that went down with Emil.

But that distracted from the matter at hand. "You were here when Emil first showed up, weren't you?"

Suraya rolled her eyes. "I tried to ignore him. He got enough attention. And the students I had that year were already a handful."

"My kids told me some teachers didn't believe the prophecy when he first arrived."

"Yep." She popped her *P*. "Pretty crazy."

"Do you know why they didn't believe him?"

"It was a dumb gossip circle. You should ask Jadoni. She hung around that circle for the longest time before admitting the prophecy was real."

Kalina blinked. *Jadoni once believed that?* "Do you know what changed?"

Suraya laughed. "Rumor says Bren fired all the teachers who didn't believe the prophecy. I don't believe that. But people got scared, and I think Jadoni decided to shut up to keep her job. The woman doesn't listen to many people, but she listens to money."

The kids resumed their game. Krem gave a yell as he chased up a hummock after the ball.

"Why were kids talking to you about that?" Suraya asked.

Can I trust her? Kalina shrugged. "I don't know. I think they're wrestling with how someone prophesied to save our country could act the way Emil does."

"Well, nip those rumors in the bud. We don't need a return to that drama."

"Sure. They were just asking questions."

"Who was?"

Kalina didn't like this line of questioning. But it would look suspicious to not answer. "Anvisa and a few of her friends. Krem, Leneya...you know the lot."

"Yes." Elder Suraya pursed her prim lips and looked out over the field. Her gaze focused on each of the students Kalina had named. "Those were the students Meliya told before leaving, weren't they?"

Her tone put Kalina on edge. "I think so? I don't know for sure."

"Umar did his best to make sure these last several months of the school year will be miserable." She shook her head. "I could have done with a different farewell present."

Don't engage. But Kalina did anyway. "You don't think the students should have known what Emil did?"

"I've had quite enough of student drama, and that's all this is."

Kalina blinked. *I expect this rhetoric from Bren. But from Suraya?* "I thought you recognized Emil's issues."

Suraya glanced toward her. "Sure, but let's not pretend like everyone else here is a perfect little angel."

Beyond them, the kids cheered about some recent score.

"What do you mean?"

"Look, I know you're new here, but Meliya has been *the* drama queen of the past six years. I'd take anything she says with a grain of salt."

"I heard Emil admit to what he did," Kalina said curtly. "That's not debatable."

"Oh? And what did he do? Because I've heard five different answers."

"He Compelled her to date and make out with him for two months."

"Ah." She chewed her lip and then shrugged. "See, if the rumors that he'd raped her were true, I'd stand with the kids. But that's different."

Kalina scrutinized her. "You don't have a problem with what he did?"

"Of course I do! Who do you think I am? It's wrong, it's immoral, and it's disgusting. But Emil is also a stupid teenager, and boys do dumb stuff all the time. And let's not pretend like Meliya was a pure victim. I warned her about him. But if she wants to flirt with every guy in the school, she can't be surprised when she reaps what she sows."

Kalina winced.

"Oh, don't look at me like that," Suraya said. "Yes, I know what that face means. It means you think I'm terrible, and how dare I say this as a teacher? But we all know this situation would have been different if Emil had Compelled Anvisa instead of Meliya."

Kalina bit her lip. "I'm not going to deny that Meliya made foolish choices. But you can make foolish choices and *still* be victimized by someone else."

"Mm. But when the livelihood of this country is on the line, I won't risk that for a girl who couldn't keep her skirt on. When you dress for attention, you get attention, and girls need to take responsibility for that."

Hot rage boiled up within her. "She didn't deserve that from Emil."

"The girls can be as bad as the boys can be, Kalina. But you can believe what you want." Suraya eyed her. "You're not encouraging the kids' gossip, are you?"

Her pulse quickened. "No. They asked me some questions, but I defended the prophecy."

Suraya's eyes narrowed ever so slightly. She wore the same expression she had when she'd described hunting down cheaters.

"Well, I'm glad to hear that." But her tone didn't change. "Some of us can't risk losing our families to the Kaldians."

Suraya knows.

Kalina stared at her husband's rising and falling chest. Ruddy moonlight from the open window illuminated his dark face. And the night breeze whispered against her folded arms. The problems at Chintor Academy apparently didn't stop at Bren. Nor at Mito. *Does anyone other than Jadoni see the problems?*

But now Suraya knew how Kalina felt about Emil. *And I know what that look on her face at the end of our conversation meant.* She was suspicious. And she always dug until she found answers.

Kalina had told the group of eight she couldn't have them gossiping around campus about what they were doing. But could she trust them? They'd told Hanodoi already.

*If Suraya corners one of them...*Worry knotted deep within her stomach.

"I need you here with me." Kalina squeezed Riyad's hand. "You always knew what to do. And I need help right now. You know?" She blinked back tears. "A year is too long without you. And...um, it's been more than that at this point. So could you just come back and help me?"

His tranquil face stared back at her.

She glanced away from Riyad toward the blood moon hanging low in the sky. *To think I once didn't believe it was an omen.* Her hands itched. *If only…*

But those thoughts didn't lead to a good place.

"I can't keep doing things alone." Whether it was getting up with the empty spot in the bed every morning, talking with others without her trusted confidant by her side, or closing her eyes without someone to unpack the day with. *I need someone who can help me right now. And Chineya doesn't understand school politics.*

Who else was there?

Jadoni.

Kalina blinked. Jadoni was erratic. Judgmental. A gossip. *She'll find something to criticize me about. And I could do without another long lecture about why everything I do as a teacher is wrong.*

But who else did she have? Umar had left. And everyone else either had red flags or she didn't know them. The alternative was dealing with Suraya by herself.

And she needed someone else in the hole with her.

Even if that meant going to her faithful critic.

37

As soon as Elder Toze had
checked her that morning to make sure she wasn't being Compelled, Kalina
headed for Jadoni's office. She was still drenched from the morning rain,
but she at least tried to dry her shoes off before entering the room.

Jadoni was writing a letter. "Can I help you?" She didn't stop writing.

"I have a question for you if you have a moment."

"Sure." She put her fountain pen down with a clink. "My niece somehow
thinks I can solve her marriage problems. Which is ridiculous. My husband
and I struggled before he died, the Ternion keep his soul. And so my
children know better than to come to me with their marital problems. But
apparently she thinks my advice helps, and so here we are writing letters
to each other every other week. You didn't come here to listen to me rant,
though." She took Kalina in with her gaze. "What can I help you with?"

Jadoni stayed uncharacteristically quiet as Kalina explained the
situation. She didn't even ask clarification questions. She just took it all in.

Finally, Kalina finished and leaned against the back of her chair, waiting
to hear Jadoni's response.

The elderly woman stared at her through the stacks of papers and books
piled on the desk. Kalina couldn't tell if her face spoke shock or disapproval.

"So...let me get this straight," Jadoni said. "You're putting a bunch
of restrictions on Emil and threatening to leave if he disobeys or talks
about them."

Kalina's gaze flicked from the overflowing bookcases to her. "Yes."

"And you're also teaching students how Compelling works so they can defend themselves."

"A group of eight students I trust, yes."

"And those students also think Emil might be lying about the prophecy."

"Yes."

"And because you blabbed about this to Elder Suraya, now she's suspicious and coming after you."

Kalina sighed. "That's why I came to you."

"Of course." Jadoni stared at her wide-eyed. "Because when people make moronic choices and realize it, they come to me for help."

Kalina bit back her knee-jerk response. Her foot nervously tapped against a nearby stack of books.

Jadoni sighed and bent over, putting her head in her hands. "I don't know whether I should be glad you take Emil seriously or if I should yell at you for your naivete."

"With all due respect, Elder Jadoni, I don't think I'm naïve."

Jadoni jerked her head up to look at her. "Right now, half the student body knows about your Silent Arcane Society."

Kalina blinked. "What did you just call it?"

"The Silent Arcane Society. That's the name all your students are using for your group. Stupid name, if you ask me. But this secret society you're leading is all the rage among our students. They don't know *what* you're doing. But they know it exists. When Suraya goes snooping, it won't take her long to discover this."

"I swear I did not come up with that name." But Kalina could see it now; Anvisa convincing Leneya and Krem how fun it would be to say they were a part of a secret society and coming up with some impressive-sounding name for it.

Klyte.

"Doesn't matter if you named it or not," Jadoni said. "It proves my point—students can't keep a secret to save their life, *especially* when it has to do with gossip. That's your first problem. The second problem is that you're pitting students against the school."

Kalina frowned. "I don't think that's a fair way of putting th—"

"Yes. It is. I'm not going to report you because I know you had good intentions. But you don't *ever* work with students against the administration.

You might think you can trust them, but they don't think rationally like we do. And they will let their stupid drama get in the way. You come to other adults for help. *Not* students."

Kalina exhaled slowly, unsure of what to say.

"But you didn't come here for my lecture," Jadoni continued. "And you're right: You need to get Suraya off your tail. If Bren kicks you out, we all suffer. Because you might be the reason Emil has acted halfway decently the past couple weeks. And while I'm sure he's doing the Ternion knows what with his dorm leaders in dark corners at night, I could do with fewer issues in the daytime."

At least she sides with me? Kalina shifted in her seat. She had a difficult time making herself comfortable when she had hardly enough space to put her feet down without hitting a stack of books or papers.

"That's the other problem with your plans, by the way. Sure, Emil might not be the official head of his dorm. But I keep my ears wide open and he's the leader in all but name. He got his whole dorm to remove Jacir as a leader and he holds all the cards. Sure, you're kind of controlling him. But you can't force him to be good."

A deep sigh welled up within her. Kalina nodded and avoided Jadoni's gaze.

"I'm not going to lie," Jadoni said. "You're in hot water. With someone as observant as Suraya, your only chance is to pretend you were giving extra group lessons and then shut down your meetings immediately."

Kalina tilted her head. "I'm sorry, don't these kids *need* a way to protect themselves?"

Jadoni pushed a pile of books aside to get a better view of her. "I don't get this about you. You know Emil's actions were wrong, but you're teaching your students to do the same thing."

"I'm not teaching them all the steps."

"You've given them enough!"

"By that logic, no one should know how to fight against Compelling."

Jadoni shook her head. "There's a difference between teaching mature *adults* and teaching *students* how to Compel or break a Compelling."

Kalina pointed to a few of the textbooks on the desk. "We teach them how to kill."

Jadoni smacked her hand down on the book stack. "Because one is far less tempting than the other. People don't have a natural desire to kill most people they meet. They *do* have a desire to get others to do what they want. Why do you *think* this isn't a part of the curriculum?"

Kalina swallowed. "I trust my group of kids."

"Oh, because you've been around them for decades to understand their character?"

Kalina shook her head. "That's a high standard to judge this situation by."

"Because these are *students*." Jadoni's eyes looked about ready to bulge out of her sockets. "They don't have the mental development and foresight to think these things through well. Even the mature ones. You're thinking like a commander who works with adults, not like someone who works with children. What if Anvisa decides to Compel a bully to keep him from hurting other people? *We* bear the responsibility of protecting students from Emil. Not them."

Kalina exhaled slowly. This fight wasn't worth continuing. "I understand where you're coming from."

"No, you don't. You still think that kids really aren't *that* immature. I've seen it all before. Every teacher gets their naivete hammered out of them within four to five years. But most of them aren't stupid enough to teach kids about Compelling."

"Okay. Point taken." *Whether I made the right decision or not, I can't take it back now.* Kalina racked her brain, trying to figure out how to get the conversation off this thread. "Did you have any thoughts about what the students claimed about Emil?"

"That Mahd made the whole prophecy up?"

"Yes."

"It's a stupid idea. That's why you don't go to kids for advice."

Kalina chewed the inside of her lip. "Suraya told me you had believed it once?"

"Yes. Then I looked into the matter—because unlike kids, I'm a mature adult—and Zedin confirmed to me that the prophecy was real."

Kalina stared. "You talked with Zedin?" The prophet only rarely emerged from the Deep Jungle.

"Old women have their ways. He also confirmed that while he may have first spoken alone to Mahd, he also went and told the king and his counselors the same thing. Our royalty isn't that inept. Emil may not be a good person. But he *is* the chosen one."

Well, there goes that idea. It had been nice for a moment to consider that she might have additional options for how to handle Emil. But no, she had put herself in Suraya's path for nothing.

Jadoni eyed her. "Have you found out how to save his life?"

Kalina sighed. "No luck."

Jadoni snorted. "Or maybe it is. Bullies don't change. Doesn't matter if they're Emil, Jacir, or anyone else. And if they don't...well, perhaps we're better off without them."

38

BELLS RANG. PEOPLE DANCED.
Drums beat. Flames rolled into the air.

It was the Festival of Nafti, celebrating the completion of the sowing and 713 years since the first follower of the Radian Way came to the three kingdoms preaching the grace of the Ternion. For a moment, they could forget all the cares of the world.

Kalina watched as a couple of Chineya's older sons danced gaily with a few of the local girls around the roaring fire. Dozens of fires lit up the city, each with similar crowds packed around the open dance ring. The fires all had a smaller burning basin elevated above them, with embers occasionally spilling from that basin into the ring below. It symbolized the way the Ternion's grace poured out onto believers. While the feasting had died down, the aromas of roasted teriden still wafted through the evening air.

Chineya touched Kalina's arm. "Oh, look at the two of them: proud as zeletors out there."

Kalina laughed. "They look happy."

"I tell you, one of these days, those two boys of mine will have the guts to propose to those girls. And I don't know I'm ready yet to be a grandma. But spoiling them will turn out better than spoiling my kids, so..."

Kalina elbowed her. "Oh, come now. You're not that lenient with your kids."

"No. But it's a real struggle not to be. I was made to be the cheerleader. Maybe the coach. But that's about it."

"Well, you've done a fine job raising young men."

"They're better than I had any right to have. I had always thought I'd relate better to daughters than sons. But the Ternion gave me five sons and one daughter, so perhaps it knew better than me."

Chineya's husband, Raz, came up on the other side of her. "Well, isn't this a sight to see?" His gray-freckled beard shook as he laughed. "A welcome relief from my conversations with citizens today."

Kalina nodded. "Worries about the Kaldians?"

"We're still waiting for news about how the second skirmish between our volunteer troops and the northern army went," he replied. "We outnumber them. But those troops aren't trained. And I can see worry on the faces of everyone who visits the shop. Yet this...for a moment, I'm getting a glimpse of what this town used to be like."

Kalina's eyes flitted from the figures who increasingly looked like silhouettes against the flames to the pure delight in Chineya's face as she watched her children. A trio of younger students stood near one of the nearby shops and laughed while they finished the roasted teriden kebabs. And other students blissfully drummed away. Not all the fires had mages on the drums. But the school had obtained temporary licenses for students to use magic outside of academy grounds.

She'd even spotted Hanodoi with Leneya and Krem having a fun time. Jacir looked rather lonely here, and she was almost beginning to pity him. But everyone else reveled in the festival.

She couldn't help but remember when she and Riyad had twirled around the fire. They always danced at the Festival of Nafti. *What blissful days we lost.*

"Elder Kalina!" Leneya and Krem split off from the dancing. "You're here!"

"I'm here! Is that a surprise?"

Leneya gestured at her. "I mean, you're not in your teacher robes."

She snorted. "Some of us try to have some semblance of a life outside of school."

"It's...very *strange* to see you outside the academy," Krem said with a cheeky grin. "That's all."

They weren't the first students to say that tonight. Kalina smiled and shook her head. "Is Anvisa here with you?"

"No..." Krem said slowly.

Leneya sighed loudly. "We tried to get her to come! But she was being all moody and saying it would be weird to come without a partner. And we tried to tell her she doesn't need a partner for the Festival of Nafti! But she wanted to stay inside and study like Emil does. Can you believe it, Elder Kalina? We even got Hanodoi to join us!"

Kalina frowned. Anvisa was a brilliant student; she hated thinking of her feeling lonely and single.

"I'm sorry," she said. "Sometimes people want their space."

"I guess." Leneya shrugged.

Kalina gestured to the drummers. "Are you listening to them?"

Leneya looked at her oddly. "I mean, I hear them."

Kalina smiled. "That's not what I mean. *Listen* to them while you dance. It's like I've told you a dozen times in class: Music can be beautiful, not just powerful!"

Krem grinned. "I like the way they make the flames dance."

"Of course you do. Because none of you care about the beauty of music." But Kalina smiled regardless. "If you at least try to pay attention, you might surprise yourselves."

"We'll do our best, Elder Kalina," Leneya said. And then she and Krem spun back into the dance.

Kalina nodded as they left. They were good kids. They'd have to have a talk about their secret society next week. But for now, she could hold her tongue.

"You know, I think you do yourself a disservice when you talk about how terrible you are as a teacher," Chineya remarked. "I've seen quite a few of your students coming up to you over the course of the evening."

Kalina shrugged.

Chineya's husband nodded. "While I don't know everything about what's going on at your school, I know enough to be grateful you're there. We need good teachers, especially now."

Kalina felt that knot in her stomach again. *Because Emil is my responsibility.* "Let's hope we're up to the task."

Chineya laughed. "That's not what my husband means." She looped her arm through Kalina's. "You don't need to bear the weight of the world on your shoulders. You can't control your students. Fight for the things you can influence."

Kalina exhaled slowly. "Maybe."

"Sorry if my words felt pressuring," Raz said. "The Ternion knows you hear enough of that up there. But perhaps tonight we can forget about the Kaldians. Tomorrow we'll worry. Tomorrow we'll fight. Tomorrow we'll make decisions. But today we can thank the Ternion for its grace."

Kalina nodded. "May the Ternion give us mercy."

She watched the flames for a long time as they crackled and danced, spurred on by the energy of the mages. Fire was a fickle element. You could never quite predict its movements—even as a mage. You could only light it, give it fuel, and see where it went.

Perhaps I can use that as a reminder. A living symbol of where my responsibilities begin and end.

She meditated on that as the fire burned through the ink-splattered night.

ℐnterlude:
FROM THE JOURNAL OF EMIL MAHDSON

Well, I'm doing what Elder Kalina wants right now. I'm learning how to synergize, practicing her techniques & doing a great job of sacrificing my dreams for a legacy.

If I had only known at the beginning of my time here how much I'd have to give up.

She's also been making me read biographies of heroes. "Great men from Rizade's past" and that kind of stuff. I think she's hoping reading them will encourage me in my resolve.

Honestly? These stories scare me.

Take Eru. Pretty much a guy with no family from the middle of nowhere. Comes in, fights some battles & saves the country from destruction. Then he's captured & tortured for over a month without giving up information before dying in a grisly fashion. That's his life.

Or consider Kade. Not as well-known or famous as Eru. He was a random guy at a random village who single-handedly defended his neighbors from a pack of ravaging razdas. I've never seen one before, but they've got the body of a monkey and the claws and teeth of a leopard and lurk in the deepest parts of the jungle. The man lost both his arms, but all well & good: he's celebrated in the songs, right?

I don't think Elder Kalina thought this through.

Because, yeah, she looks at them & expects other people to aspire to be like these heroes.

And I know I should as well, but I just want to be happy.

The words of Elder Crayenda from my first year ring in my ears. "Emil. It's okay to want something for yourself." Sure, when I started following her advice, she changed her mind about me. Everyone loves the quiet, selfless kid who soaks up abuse & never burdens anyone. They change their mind when they need to sacrifice to help him.

But even if she eventually took back her words, I still cling to them.

It's okay to want something for myself.

I'm just asking to have some semblance of a normal life: friends, happiness, acceptance, fulfillment, love. That's all I'm looking for.

Not die a Ternion-accursed virgin.

If I follow Elder Kalina's rules, she'll help me survive. So I'll learn how to synergize & let other people steal my legacy if it allows me to have that long life I'm pining for. Anything to get her to trust me again.

I even got the other dorm leaders to join me for my experimental magic studies. Not with Elder Mito, since he doesn't like the other guys in my dorm. But it turns out that strong-arming people works. And I finally have them practicing obscure types of magic with me. Elder Kalina should be proud of me—I really can motivate & work together with people when I need to.

If she can just see who I really am, maybe something could change.

39

RAIN POUNDED THE CANOPY OVERHEAD.
Kalina watched Emil's team coordinate their defenses against the other team's attack. They weren't working together as well as Anvisa's group. There was still awkwardness, miscommunication, and missed opportunities.

But for the first time in a battle simulation…they *tried* to work together. And Emil was *synergizing*.

After two-and-a-half weeks of strenuous work, he had pulled it off. He used one of his melodies to bolster the work of his allies while his second and third melodies channeled his own lightning. *The boy's a legend.* While her group of eight still couldn't perform even rehearsed synergizing, he perfectly improvised to match the students he supported.

Kalina watched in admiration as Emil and his forces handily beat Anvisa and her companions.

Emil's team packed up their instruments. Kalina met Emil's gaze. "Good work. You all looked like a team for once."

He grinned at her. "Don't we always, Elder Kalina?"

She opened her mouth to correct him. Then she stopped. She saw the gleam in his eyes. And his teammates' vigor. He didn't need someone getting on him for every minor issue.

So she smiled. "Like I said. You played like a team out there." She turned to Anvisa's team. They'd need encouragement as well. Out of the corner of her eye, she spotted Jadoni talking with her students. Jadoni was beaming as she praised their performance. Kalina grinned. *So she can gush on occasion.*

Then behind her, Kalina heard Emil's low voice. "Next time, Zeldara, cut it with the dumb attacks. Can't do anything to help you when you're being an idiot."

She turned to see Emil facing one of the weaker drummers in his class. *He must think I'm out of earshot.* She opened her mouth.

Then Jacir stepped next to Zeldara. "Leave her alone, Emil."

Kalina blinked.

Emil snorted. "What, is she your girlfriend now?"

"I don't need to be dating someone to stand up against a bully," Jacir said. "We won. So leave her alone."

"Sure, if you like defending people who need to practice more, go for it. Probably fits you." Emil walked away.

Kalina suppressed a sigh. Just when she had hoped Emil was turning a corner. *Two steps forward, one step back.* At least he was synergizing. Maybe that was all that mattered. If he could beat the Kaldians, she had at least managed one success.

At some point, though, she might need to ask Jacir where this new side of him had come from.

"I can't believe Emil figured it out so fast!" Anvisa groaned as she lay on the wooden floor of Kalina's classroom. Rain rattled the roof. Kalina probably should have told her not to lie on the floor. But she had accepted that conversations with Anvisa, Krem, and Leneya were more casual.

"You should be glad he's synergizing," Kalina said. "It gives us remarkably better odds against the Kaldians."

"I know," Anvisa said. "But do you know how frustrating it is to play games against a hero chosen by prophecy?"

"On the bright side," Krem said. "At least we know it's possible to synergize." He looked at Kalina. "I mean—not that we didn't believe you, Elder Kalina! We just hadn't seen it before."

Kalina nodded. "I understand."

Anvisa glanced at her. "Do we still need to speak in code when the Silent Arcane Society meets again?"

Kalina rolled her eyes. "Once again—this is *not* a secret society, and I *never* agreed to that name."

"Emil has his own secret society," Anvisa claimed. "How can we stop him if we don't have our own?"

"Emil has a *study group*." He'd told her about it multiple times, probably to get in her good graces. "He doesn't have a name for it, and it's not a secret."

"They never share what they're studying, though."

"Because it's weird, obscure magic techniques that are hard to use and rarely work. Go ask him yourself if you must. But it's not a secret society."

"That's why we have to have a better one!" Anvisa grinned. "I think you secretly like the name."

"You know what I like? Not having to speak in code because the school now thinks I'm running a secret society." Kalina shot her a look. "To the original question, I haven't heard anything from the person who might be spying on us. So yes, you still need to speak in code, and that includes *not referring to our meetings as a secret society.*"

Her attempts to shut down their name for the group hadn't turned out very well. Though she had at least impressed on them that they might have someone listening in on their meetings.

She hadn't taken Jadoni's advice to stop working with them.

"It would *really* be great if you told us who you thought was spying on us," Anvisa said. "Because if it's someone we know—"

A yell snapped through the building. "Where is Head Mage Bren? I need to speak with Head Mage Bren!"

Kalina would have recognized that voice anywhere. *General Mahd.*

She shot up. Her chair fell over. "Hold on," she said to Anvisa. Kalina walked out of the classroom, moved for the stairs, and quickly descended them. General Mahd stood in the vestibule, water dripping from his soaked body.

She strode down the hallway. Why were no other teachers around?

"General Mahd." She saluted out of habit. "Can I help you?"

He whirled to face her. "Commander Kalina! I need to see Head Mage Bren right away."

"Of course." She stopped in front of him. "Is anything the matter?"

"The Kaldians routed our southern defenses. Our army will arrive at the city within the hour, the Kaldians tomorrow. We need to prepare for a siege."

40

"So...let me get this straight."

Bren sat at his desk in a state of shock. "The southern army broke through our defenses."

General Mahd nodded. "And the northern one isn't far behind. With their combined armies, they have a force of eleven thousand. We have six thousand. And they have five mages to every three of ours. I've sent messengers to the other two generals, but they're still in the south. It will be weeks before they could arrive. We're on our own."

Kalina sat with General Mahd, Head Mage Bren, Commander Kay, and Emil. She had no idea how she'd earned an invite to this meeting. *Maybe I still have privileges as Emil's trainer.*

"A true siege." Bren chewed his lip. "It's been hard enough cut off from the rest of the country these past four months."

"They ran through both our northern and our southern defenses on the same day," Mahd said. "We can set up camp outside the city, but we'll be overrun in no time if we're pushed behind the walls. We need to beat them outside the city, and that depends on the decisions we make right now in this room."

She noticed the way Emil stiffened. *Did anyone else see that?*

"Decisions about Emil?" Bren asked.

Mahd nodded. "I believe this may be the time foretold by prophecy for him to take his stand and break their might."

"And so we're here to assess his skill before settling on a plan," Commander Kay added.

Emil looked about ready to flee the room. And Kalina felt a jab of pity for him. *This is his death sentence.*

Bren fixed his gaze on Kalina. "I understand the...concerns...Emil mentioned in his birthday speech have been addressed."

Kalina saw the look hiding behind his genial eyes. *"Don't mess this up and humiliate me."*

She also had an obligation to the truth. And as complicated as her feelings were about Emil, she did have a stab of compassion for him. "Emil has improved," she said carefully. "But I'm worried about sending him to battle this soon."

Mahd curled his lip. "Are you telling me you didn't do your job?"

"Elder Kalina is an excellent teacher," Bren said. "While the two of us may have...differences...regarding Emil's current abilities, I can assure you they don't stem from any faults in her teaching."

Kalina blinked. *Bren defends me?*

"Let's put it to my son directly." Mahd turned to Emil. "Son, are you strong enough to beat the Kaldians?"

Emil's eyes widened. His muscles tensed, and his gaze flashed around the room. But then he leaned back in his chair and laughed. "Wasn't I born for this?"

The fear still flashed in his eyes.

"As his personal instructor, I maintain that Emil needs more time," she said. "If he has the rest of the school year, I'm sure he'll rise to the challenge. But I planned on getting another three months with him."

"We don't have three months," Mahd snarled. "Didn't you hear what I said? Eleven thousand men tomorrow. And this village *can't* withstand a prolonged siege."

"Wasn't this academy originally built as a fortress?"

"For a small hamlet—not the city Chintor has grown into!"

"What if we moved him closer to the capital?"

"How? We're about to be surrounded."

"I'm not saying it will be easy. I'm saying we have talent and ingenuity. We can leave today before we're completely cut off and sneak around the edges of the jungle. Send me and another teacher with Emil and some of his friends to the capital and give us till the end of the school year. With all due respect..." She tried to find a more tactful way to say this. "I mean, we know what the prophecy says. Letting him finish out the year with his friends would be good for him, and I need more time to save his life. I'm thinking about Emil here."

"What—because I don't care about my son?" Mahd turned toward her with quivering lips. "Believe me, Kalina. I *know* the prophecy. But I care about the kingdom and my soldiers' lives as well. Emil knows how much I care about him and his future. Just ask him!"

Silence fell upon the room like a thick blanket. Kalina glanced at Emil. He sat frozen like a rabbit caught by a ravenous teriden, staring at the floor.

"Emil?" The edge in Mahd's voice could cut a cord. "Do I care about you, boy?"

His head popped up. "Oh—of course, Father. I know you've always cared about me."

"There we go." Mahd rolled his eyes. "Come on, son. It's like you want to embarrass me in front of these adults. You could show a little more respect." He turned back toward her. "Emil and I aren't going to sacrifice soldiers' lives for a harebrained stalling act. The Ternion made Emil its hero, and real heroes don't run from the fight. You're not a coward, are you, Emil?"

"Absolutely not."

"Well, there you go." If eyes could burn a hole into her, his would have. "See, I thought I gave you a gift, Kalina—a break from the stress and terrors of the battlefield. Of course, I thought you would use that time to properly train my son."

Kalina's eyes widened. *Does Mahd know even an ounce of what I've done here?* She opened her mouth.

Bren spoke first. "Elder Kalina has been an invaluable asset to the school. I understand your concern, General Mahd, but you must realize that she's committed to excellence. And so when she says Emil needs more time, it's not that she hasn't worked. It's that she'll always have more she could teach him." He smiled at her. "As is, though, I think you're right, General. Emil is ready. And we can't let a desire for perfection prevent us from recognizing the excellence we have here right now."

Kalina bit her lip.

"I would like to get a word in here." Kay turned his piercing eyes toward her. "Elder Kalina, could you share more about your concerns?"

"Oh, come off it," Mahd snapped. "I don't care if the king promoted you as representative or whatever klyte title he gave you via messenger pigeon. You don't call the shots."

Kalina blinked. Kay had received a promotion?

"I have the gravity of the king's ambassador," Kay said tersely. "And on behalf of him, I'd like to say—"

"You are *not* the general," Mahd erupted. "And in this city, I have authority. We will follow the Ternion's appointed plans for Emil. Know your place, or I will make sure you're nowhere near the command tent when the battle begins."

Kalina's gaze met Kay's. She saw the fury in his eyes. But she also saw the fear. The position of the king's ambassador stood outside the military chain of command and on equal footing with the generals as an adviser. But Kay didn't have enforcement power. And, cut off as they were, there was only so much the king would know.

His eyes turned away from her to the floor.

"Thank you," Mahd said. "To think that my son had to see all this. If adults can't respect each other, how can children be expected to?" He turned to Bren. "I would like to talk with you privately about a few matters related to the defense of the school. I trust our ambassador here has the prudence to remain with us."

"Of course," Bren said, smiling. "I would be honored to do so." He turned to Emil. "You can go now, Emil." He glanced at Kalina. She stood up.

Mahd gave neither of them a second look as they left the room. Emil walked with her into the empty vestibule where rain splattered the stones outside.

He grabbed her in an embrace.

She gasped. But then he collapsed to his knees, clutching her calves, as his whole body shook.

"Elder Kalina," he sobbed. "I'm not ready for this. I'm not ready for this."

She blinked. For once, his tears actually seemed genuine.

"I can't go up against the Kaldians," he gasped. "Not now. I still have friends here. I'm not done living."

"I...I know." She knelt and put her hands on his shoulders. "I tried to help you, Emil."

"I know," the boy cried. He looked up at her. "Why can't my father understand that? Why did he have to make me lie in front of you all? We all know he doesn't care that I'm going to die. Not one bit. I'm going to *die*, Elder Kalina."

"I...I know," Kalina repeated, conscious of the tears brimming in her eyes. *When did I start caring again about this boy? I told myself I was done with him.* But no matter his faults, he seemed to *want* to do the right thing.

"I'm trying to find an answer," she murmured. "I'm not giving up yet, Emil. You shouldn't either."

"I'm only barely beating Anvisa and her classmates in our games. How can I go out there and save our nation?"

"You won easily today. Your synergizing will help you turn the tide."

He turned his tear-filled eyes up to her. "Is there *any* way you can save my life?"

She swallowed. "I'll do whatever I can."

41

@KALINA'S WHOLE BODY FELT NUMB

when Bren addressed the student body the next morning. They stood outside before the wall, with only a faint drizzle falling. The laughter and frivolity normally present before an assembly had vanished. If you went up to the wall behind Bren, you could see the approaching masses of Kaldians. Hordes of human-sacrificers ready to terrorize the city.

All eyes glanced toward Emil. He stood like a violin's E string—thin, stretched near to breaking.

"I know you're frightened," Bren said. "I don't know how the next several days will look. Some of you Year Five and Six students may be called to join the fight. But it's at times like this that we need to pray. The Ternion still influences the world's events, and while we can't predict what it will do, our prayers do make a difference. So let's take some time to pray together."

The Year Five and Six students certainly will be called into battle. She knew how the army worked. Any license requirements would be waived in light of this threat.

By the time she shook away her thoughts, people were already pairing off to pray together. Unlike the heathen Kaldians, they didn't believe in praying alone. *You don't approach a god without someone to represent its grace to you.*

She stood and looked around. Ashinara had split off with Mito. Jadoni had gone with some other teacher she didn't know. *Who else is still free?*

"Elder Kalina."

She turned to see a man with graying hair. He taught Year Two students, but she couldn't remember his name.

"Do you want to pray with me?" he asked.

"Sure." They moved to an open place in the field to sit down. The wet grass poked against her legs.

"Do you want me to ask the Ternion's grace for you first, or do you want to ask it for me first?" he asked.

"Um." Kalina was still trying to remember his name.

"I'll go first." He put his hands on her damp shoulders, and she followed suit.

"Framer. Supplier. Illuminator," the man prayed. "Today I beseech you to let your grace flow down through me to your daughter Kalina. I know that neither of us knows each other well. But I've heard what she's going through. I know the immense weight she bears training Emil. I know he needs spiritual growth more than he needs magical growth. And I know Kalina needs your help for that. I thank you for how you have used her here to help Emil understand what he truly needs. And I pray that whatever she needs from you, you would grant it to her bountifully over the next several days. May your grace flow through her to Emil, and may you give her the strength she needs to be your conduit."

Her eyes opened before he finished. She stared at him. "You...how did you know?" Her heart was awash and her voice thick.

"People talk," he said. "I don't know everything. But I know enough. You're not alone. Other teachers have also been upset about Emil for a while and want to support you. May the Ternion provide you with the answers you need."

Kalina was leaving the gathering when Bren called her. "Elder Kalina."

She turned. He bustled up to her in his bleached robes. Wearing white during wet season was a bold move. Good thing for him that today came with a mere drizzle. "Can I walk with you on the way to class, dear?" he asked.

She wrinkled her nose. *Why did he call me that?* "Sure." Students parted around them as they moved toward the academic building.

"I was curious why Emil leaves his instrument in your room every evening."

Her gaze narrowed in on him, and her heart beat fast. *How much does Bren know?*

"Oh." She kept her voice calm. "He was asking you questions about it?"

"Elder Suraya approached me," he said. "Apparently some students told her, and she wanted to know why we had limited his ability to practice. It took me by surprise since I never put that restriction on him."

Suraya. Kalina focused on keeping a calm face. "Oh, I see. Yes, I asked Emil to leave his fiddle with me at the end of each day."

His gaze drilled into her. "Could you explain why you made that decision?"

"Sure. I worried about other students, given how few teachers we leave up here in the evenings. And so I decided that as his mentor, I would set some boundaries for him."

"You did not have the authority to make that call." The rhythm of his voice came out brisk and fast.

She feigned ignorance. "I didn't? I thought we had certain disciplinary authorities as teachers."

"You have authority over your classroom. *I* have authority over the campus."

So that's why campus protection doesn't exist.

But she didn't say that out loud. "Oh," she stammered. "I hadn't realized that. Guess you skipped that part of teacher orientation."

Bren halted and pivoted to her. They stood right next to the pillars of the main academic building. "I'm sorry?" His words were calm, but icy tones slipped through them.

That was not the time to be snarky. "I'm sorry. That came off too harsh. I meant I didn't get the rule overview all the other teachers here got."

Bren's eyes narrowed. "You know, I've believed in you, even when no one else would. And that means I've stood up for you when no one else did. I'm not going to publicly mention your obvious inadequacies as a teacher, your failures as a researcher, or your questionable judgments in front of General Mahd because we're on the *same team.* But if you would rather throw barbs in my direction, there's no need for you to step in this building again."

Her cheeks burned. "I...like I said, I'm sorry. I shouldn't have said that last line."

"No. You shouldn't have." Bren glanced back at the students still milling around the fields. "I will inform Emil that he can use his fiddle wherever and whenever he wants. We will *not* lose to the Kaldians because of you."

Kalina bit her lip and nodded.

"While we're talking," Bren continued, "is there anything you'd like to tell me about why Emil resigned as the head of his dorm two months ago?"

She cleared her throat. "I encouraged him to resign. It was a distraction from his studies."

"So you got him to step down from the dorm to focus on practicing at the same time that you forbade him from practicing outside school hours."

"Emil needed to stay away from the student drama circle. And the students needed a better leader. Just so you're aware, I've stayed here after the official end of the school day for hours the past four weeks to give Emil time to practice."

Bren narrowed his eyes. "How did you convince Emil to step down from his dorm position?"

"I persuaded him."

His eyes drilled into her. She could see him mentally chewing over what she said. "You're a good woman, Elder Kalina," he finally said. "I just wish you could get off your high horse of moral purity every once in a while to love your students for the people they really are."

He turned and walked inside.

The rest of the day went as badly as it started. The Year Three students still weren't practicing enough. Nor could they remember to loosen their bows without her reminding them. Her Year Six students then proceeded to know nothing about how topography affects battle tactics. Even Anvisa.

Kalina finally got back to her room and went straight to her cello. She needed to try to relax.

She had just lifted her instrument when Emil rushed in. "I didn't tell him, Elder Kalina, I swear I didn't tell him." His eyes were wide, and they fixed on her with an intensity worthy of Kay's.

"What are you talking about, Emil?" But of course, she already knew.

"Head Mage Bren. He told me he wants me to use my instrument after hours. But I don't know how he found out about it. Please don't leave. I *need* you to stay here and to—"

Kalina put down her cello. "Slow down, Emil, I—"

"I *need* you to figure out how you can save my life." Emil halfway collapsed on the desk in front of her. "I *swear* I told nothing."

"I know." She returned his gaze. "I *know*, Emil. I'm not going anywhere."

Emil staggered back into the chair. "I...I was so scared when he told me. You're the only person who can save me."

"Someone else told him, Emil." He had probably let the rule slip at some point—which he wasn't supposed to do. But she wouldn't judge the kid for that. "You're fine."

"I...I don't get it. Why does he trust me when you don't?"

Kalina studied him carefully. Bren's last words had haunted her all day. Emil had the face and characteristics anyone could trust.

But his natural trustworthiness also enabled his bad behavior. And while he's begun to change, he hasn't owned his crime against Meliya yet.

"You want my honest answer?" she asked. "It's because he doesn't think what you did to Meliya was a big deal. But I've seen how devastating it is when a girl is manipulated and forced to do things she doesn't want to do."

Emil met her gaze and slowly nodded. "I want you to know you can trust me. I know you've talked before about what you think happened to your sister, but most men are trustworthy."

She blinked. "What I *think* happened to my sister?"

Emil looked away. "Oh. I'm sorry. I didn't mean anything by that."

But he had. "Emil Mahdson. What are you implying?"

"I'm sorry." He glanced back at her. "I'd heard some different things from Elder Mito about what happened."

Kalina stood. "What did Elder Mito tell you?"

He jolted in his seat. "I'm sorry. I shouldn't have said anything."

"What did Elder Mito tell you?"

His eyes widened. He opened his mouth, but words failed to come out. "Emil."

He sank into his seat. "He told me he had known someone who was falsely accused by your family of doing something with one of their daughters."

Fire snapped inside her. "My sister was *raped*. Not once. But for several years as a child—and we found out because my parents *caught* him doing it. He *only* escaped justice because he bribed the magistrate and our wretched culture values the stability of an unbroken line of 'pious friars' more than it does actual piety. Nothing else."

"I'm sorry. I'm sorry. I shouldn't have said anything."

"Why the klyte were you talking to Elder Mito about this?"

"I...I don't know..." Emil swallowed. "I—I shouldn't have said anything. It sounds really bad. What happened to your sister, that is."

"Yes. It was." Kalina leaned over the desk. "And you want to know why I take what you did so seriously, Emil? Because even if you didn't do anything as bad as that friar, what you did comes from the same mindset— the mindset that views women as objects. And until you can confess that, the pernicious lie still settles deep within your heart. Because people don't change until they admit the truth. The full, ugly, uncomfortable truth. Do that, and maybe I might begin to trust you."

Emil bit his lip and glanced at the floor.

"That's your lesson for today." Kalina stormed out of the room to find Mito.

42

THE HALLWAY PASSED IN A BLUR.

Kalina knew she should take a moment to plan out her strategy. But the time for being a respectful colleague disappeared the moment Mito crossed *that* line.

Right now? She went for blood.

She threw the curtain aside without knocking. Mito lounged against his chair, feet propped on his desk, with a large book in his hands. He looked at her, running a hand through his unkempt hair. "Elder Ka—"

"How dare you."

He raised an eyebrow, as if oblivious to what he'd done. "I'm sorry?"

"No." She lifted a finger. "You don't get to claim ignorance after what you've told Emil about me and my family."

"I hate to disappoint you," Mito said slowly, "but I've never claimed to be able to read a woman's mind."

"You just claim to be the judge of what happened to my sister."

"Ah." Mito nodded slowly. "That's why you're finally talking to me again."

Crimson filled her vision. "I've held my tongue about you and your stupid ideas for so long. Because why should I care about a fool who would wet himself at the first sight of battle? But snooping into my family's past? Feeding lies to a Compeller? I don't know who you think you are, but your career is *over*. And the moment I'm out of here, I'm making sure Head Mage Bren knows what you've done."

He stared at her with a smug look of haughty disinterest.

Kalina spun to leave the room.

"And what will Head Mage Bren say when he hears about how you're blackmailing Emil?"

She froze. *Mito can't know.* "Lie about me all you want. I don't care." She stepped toward the entryway.

"Are you saying you *didn't* threaten to leave if Emil didn't resign as head of the dormitory and start giving you his instrument after hours?"

Kalina paused at the entrance. Could people in the other rooms hear them? Sure, Mito spoke in his stereotypical quiet drawl. But...

She turned to look at him.

"Sorry." A small smile slipped past his otherwise apathetic expression. "I wasn't supposed to know about that, was I?"

"I don't have time for this."

"No. But you looked. And so we both know you did it." He shrugged. "How about you come in and have a seat?"

She wavered. Mito was a snake.

But he also *knew*.

She let the curtain fall back across the entry and sat.

Mito stared at the bookcase ten feet from her. "You know, Elder Suraya was sniffing around here earlier for you."

Kalina kept her mouth shut. *He wants me to beg him to tell me what he told Suraya.* She wouldn't give him the pleasure.

"I never could quite understand why Bren hired you," he finally continued. He leaned his head against his left hand and glanced back toward her. "We talk a lot, you know. Pretty sure he trusts me the most." He snorted. "Yet somehow he decided to hire a failed commander with no teaching experience. Though I must say, even I didn't predict you would blackmail students."

"Listen." Kalina chose her words carefully. "I don't know what you heard—or what you think you heard—but I *never* blackmailed Emil."

"Oh, stop." He rolled his eyes. "The boy came crying to me a month and a half ago about what you were doing. Begged me not to tell anyone because if I did, you would abandon him. That's blackmail."

Kalina stared at Mito. Emil had told him *a month and a half* ago? That would have been immediately after she had laid down the law to him.

"I gave him reasonable consequences for Meliya, and I told him that if he wouldn't comply, I would leave," she said. "That's hardly blackmail."

"Yeah, but you also swore him to secrecy. And when you hold the boy's life in your hands...that's about the cruelest thing I think a teacher could do to a student." He glanced back at her again. "Wouldn't you agree?"

His words thudded into her. "If you think I'm that awful of a person, why haven't you talked?"

Mito smirked. "Right. Because we all know you—holy crusader that you are—would have in my shoes." He leaned back in his seat. "Maybe I care for Emil's life and well-being. I know a dangerous woman when I see one and know when to advise a boy to play the long game."

Her lip curled. "I think you misunderstand which of us poses a threat."

"Do I? Because in my book, threatening to let a student die is far worse than making a student kiss you."

"It..."

It's not about a simple kiss. It's about forcing others to pleasure him.

But for a moment, all of that disappeared under the weight of Mito's insinuations.

"Of course, it's not like it's the first time your family has done this," Mito continued. "You see, I grew up in the Metsan District, and my father knew Friar Qel. Took me a while to recognize you. But when I saw the pattern of how you treated men you don't like..."

Kalina's gaze hardened. "Friar Qel raped my sister."

Mito rolled his eyes. "Oh, stop. Friar Qel overflowed with the Ternion's grace more than anyone else I knew. And he was one of the only friars willing to think for himself instead of blindly following centuries of dead tradition. Forgive me if I don't throw a role model to razdas because an eleven-year-old decided it would be fun to tell some stories."

"We had eyewitnesses."

"Oh?" Mito snorted. "Like the invisible witnesses in Emil's case that made him guilty on one girl's accusation?"

"Emil confessed."

"To *a few kisses*. No one ever saw him do anything more." His mouth hung open in contempt. "And then Meliya played the rape card, and you backed her up."

"Meliya never said he raped her." Her body shook. "Neither did I."

"Maybe not in public. But Suraya told me about what you say to students in private. You should thank the Divine Council I decided not to tell her everything I know." He sighed. "I shouldn't have to be the one keeping this school together, but if I must, I guess I have to."

So Suraya *had* listened in on her meetings. *But I've never said that to my students.*

"Have you ever heard of a suicide pact?" Mito asked.

Kalina glared at him.

"Even someone as dull brained as you should be able to figure out how it works," Mito said. "If you don't like what I told Emil, go tell Head Mage Bren what *terrible* things I've done." He rolled his eyes. "But then I tell him *everything*. And who do you think he'll side with?" He smirked. "We'd better stay quiet."

He leaned forward, and his traditional drawl vanished. "But I'll tell you this, Kalina. I'm *only* staying quiet on the condition that you save Emil's life. If you fail to do so...well, I think I'll tell General Mahd what you did to his son. And if Mahd decides not to have the Arditen mages revive your husband as a result, well...that's on *you*."

Kalina's heart pounded. "I don't know if there's an answer to how I survived."

Mito shrugged and leaned back in his seat. "Not my problem." He twirled his feather pen between his hands.

Kalina stared at him. He returned her gaze, a wry little smile still on his face.

"So, Elder Kalina. Was there anything else about my mentoring philosophy you wanted to complain about?"

She swallowed. "I think you've made yourself quite clear."

43

THE CANDLE BURNED LOW IN THE
iron holder as Kalina flipped the pages of the book in front of her. She
should thank the Ternion that her final book request had come in a mere
two days before the Kaldian army did.

If only the books gave me what I need.

The text swam in front of her. She knew scads more about the fine
details of magic theory than she had ever expected to know. None of it
was helpful.

In mere days, Emil would go out and fight.

And according to the prophecy, the nation rose or fell based on his
mastery *that day.*

Kalina tried to concentrate on the detailed diagram of magical flow
around an instrument. Her husband's face filled her mind instead.

She pounded her fist against the desk. "The blood moon take you,
Mito." She should have talked with Jadoni before the crone left for the day.
Not that Jadoni could help at this point.

Kalina homed in again on the circles of magical energy the drawing
showed emanating from the musician's fingers as he played.

> *Some mages theorized that any part of the human*
> *body—or even the instrument itself—could unleash*

magic. But further research shows it only emanates from the hands. Brass and woodwind instruments utilize the breath, but the magic itself comes from the manipulation of the fingers.

Like any of that helps. She flipped to the next page, hoping to find something about instrument breakages.

While the instrument itself may not emanate magic, it serves as a container for the magic. One might compare it to a water pipe. The pipe doesn't produce the water, but it channels and funnels it to its specific purpose.

Basic information. Kalina had learned that years ago. She flipped a few more pages. This was reportedly the most advanced book on magic theory out there. But this last chapter had felt pretty basic.

Her eyes zeroed in on the heading. "Instrument Breakages." *Finally.*

Why does instrument breakage inevitably kill its user? That question has been asked countless times, and we will only attempt to outline a bare structure of what happens. For understandable reasons, this sort of incident is hard to replicate as a result of the casualties incurred.

She snorted. *If they think replicating a normal breakage is hard, try replicating one while surviving.*

Popular opinion holds that a breakage causes the mage's concentration in Repose to be redirected into himself, leading to instant death. However, tests on captured enemy mages reveal that what actually happens is more complicated than that.

She read on with interest.

As a result of the immense amount of magical energy flowing through the instrument, any damage to the instrument creates a leak that prevents the instrument from directing the energy toward the Substance. When magic erupts through that leak, two things occur. First, without a container to hold the magic, the vacuum rips the magic being used and the mage's own internal magic out of his body. This has been observed multiple times by mage observers of these tests.

Huh. She reread that part. Was that what prevented her from using magic anymore? The vacuum created by the breakage drew the innate magic out of her body?

Second, that energy then hits the air in such a high concentration that it tears the Fabric itself. While the Fabric will reweave itself together quickly, this momentary fracture creates an eruption that destroys anything nearby.

The size of the magical eruption is determined by two things. First, the size of the instrument fracture. Larger fractures create larger eruptions. The second factor is the distance between the fracture and the mage's hands. The longer the distance, the more the energy becomes diluted. This means that fractures closer to the mage's hands will create a stronger explosion.

It is this rupture of the Fabric that creates the destructive explosion. The size of that explosion determines whether it only kills the mage playing the instrument or also several others around them.

The book moved on to other topics.

Kalina sighed and stared at the text. It certainly expanded her understanding about what had happened to her in those brief seconds. But in terms of giving her the answers she needed…it made no exceptions for the mage's death.

She flipped the page.

Then she stopped.

Memories of that day flew vividly through her head. The arrow ripping through the end of her cello. The energy destroying her instrument and sending magic-encrusted pieces ripping into her husband. The explosion shattering her consciousness. And yes, now that she had read the section of the book, she could also remember a sucking feeling at her fingers, as if the instrument was pulling her whole body into it.

But Kalina kept thinking about where that arrow had hit: at the end of a large cello.

If the fracture didn't kill the mage by redoubling the magic back on itself but by the nature of the explosion…and if her explosion had been a small fracture at the very end of the instrument…

She pursed her lips. *That can't be all it was.* Even if that led to a smaller explosion, certainly other mages had experienced minor eruptions. But they still died.

Kalina finished turning the page.

Then she could see it again as if she were reading it for the first time: *The arrow, while pushed off course, still hit the end of the flute.*

The character of Eto from the book.

It wasn't just that he couldn't do magic afterward. Legend said the arrow hit the instrument at its extremity.

She bit her lip. That story was a myth. The history books made it clear. Maybe something inspired it. But the similarities between their stories were a coincidence.

Right?

Of course, she and Eto also shared something else in common. Klyte arrows had damaged both their instruments. Not the more common pike or sword. How many mages had died from klyte arrows that created small punctures at the instrument's extremity?

And how much of a coincidence could it be that the only other story of someone surviving happened in a way eerily similar to her own?

Sure, Eto may not have existed. But even if the story had been taken from another hero, the facts all fit too closely together.

She ran her finger over the lines again. According to this book, nothing about an instrument breakage necessitated the death of the mage. It necessitated an explosion. It *normally* killed the mage, but it didn't have to. Not with a small puncture.

Kalina pushed the book aside, bewildered in the shock and grandeur of the moment. Had she unlocked the mystery? Had she discovered the great exception behind centuries of mage theory?

But...

It had been nothing she'd done. Nothing Emil could imitate. Nothing that could save his life.

What had saved her from near-certain death had been nothing more than a stroke of luck.

Percussion Magic

summon what passes
through the fabric.

↳ (light & flames)

→ While doing percussion magic seems really easy compared
to mine, drummers insist it's actually "Very Hard"

→ The Light Network is a series of river outposts
using colored light codes for messaging across the
kingdom (the messages are public).
Most percussion mages serve either
the network or the army.

My FAVORITE TEACHER

PERSONAL GOAL FOR THE YEAR:

↳ Find a dashing young man
for Anvisa to fall for

↜ Don't you <u>dare</u>, Leneya.

→ You can't be the only matchmaker in Chintor!

44

@KALINA COULD SMELL THE SMOKE
of a thousand army campfires the following morning. And she could see
worry in the face of every student she walked past.

Head Mage Bren had called an emergency teacher meeting to inform
them that the military had called the Year Five and Six students to join the
front ranks and the Year Three and Four students to stand in reserves. The
Year Three and Four teachers had been livid.

She understood it, though. Even if she hated the idea of students that
young fighting, they faced overwhelming odds. The students would all be
sacrificed if the Kaldians broke through the gates. *If we can fight first, we
have to take the opportunity.*

Today, then, was her last day with the Year Six students.

She looked over the field as the lutists finished moving the last of the
sand and blocks into position around the arena's pond for the upcoming
battle simulation. At least it wasn't raining.

This time, all types of mages would duke it out at once. Ambassador
Kay had returned to observe the fight, along with Padini. They had stood
beside her instead of Head Mage Bren. Which, of course, had led to Bren
moving down from his own hill to join them.

Kalina felt the weight of all their eyes on her. And if she felt that, she
knew the students did.

"All right." She clapped. "You have five minutes to put together your plans. I know you're nervous about everyone watching, but welcome to war. I'm sorry that life dealt us these cards. But I *have* told you that mages must perform under pressure. Remember your lessons: The battlefield isn't about waiting for the perfect opportunity. It's about taking the best available option and working together as a *team*. May the grace of the Ternion be with you all."

She stepped back.

Anvisa took the lead among her team as she always did, calling the leaders of the different mage groups together and explaining her plans and strategies. And while Emil paused for a moment to glance up at Kalina, he did the same. He imitated Anvisa's lead by talking with his own team—and it looked like he even listened to them. He kept stealing glances at Kalina, as if looking for her approval. She smiled at him each time he did.

Emil was *doing it*.

After five minutes, she blew her whistle and watched as the students entered their final simulated battle.

The cacophony of instruments buffeted the air. Lightning shook the field. Trumpeters ripped cubes into pieces. And fires blazed among Emil's cubes. She tuned them out to enter Repose. And blinked as she felt how much was happening. She hadn't had to track so many types of magic in a while.

Emil began barking orders. Kalina raised an eyebrow. He almost never did that. A moment later, a thin wave flew out from the arena's pond to douse the flames burning his cubes. His magic synergized with his flutists in order to help them break the Quelling.

Emil *had* been learning.

The ground underneath Emil's side shook. Even Kalina could feel the tremors. She steadied herself. Emil yelled again at his mages. Although this looked less like guidance than like frustration.

Then two pieces of sheet metal flew into the arena.

Kalina stepped back, startled. She hadn't been following the actions of the lutists. Where had those come from? They landed on either side of Emil's area of the arena, but Anvisa's team had made them. Had their trumpeters flattened other metal objects into these sheets?

The two metal sheets wedged vertically into the ground. Anvisa's lutists tried to move one toward the other—presumably to sweep Emil's cubes away.

Kalina's eyes widened. That wasn't all. Anvisa's violinists were also creating an electrical difference between them to create a magnetic effect. Kalina had only recently taught them that. And when the growing magnetism between the two metal sheets combined with the efforts of the lutists—

A thunderclap blasted through the arena. Not any lightning. The kind that melts metal. The kind that could only come from Emil. Lightning struck a stationary piece of metal and sent it flying.

The boy knew what he was doing.

Anvisa's team tried a few other creative attacks. But Emil overpowered them—either by himself or by synergizing with his mages. He worked together with his team.

And so he won easily.

Kalina's heart pounded as she released herself from Repose and watched the kids talk with, praise, and console each other. She walked up to greet and congratulate them all.

She nodded toward Emil. "Excellent work."

"That match was far too close. If other people did what they should have, we could have won *much* faster, and I could have spent more time on my magic!"

"But you led," she said. "And you were fantastic! That extra time you've been spending studying with your dorm leaders has really paid off."

He grinned. "Well, I *am* trying to follow your direction, Elder Kalina."

She couldn't help but smile. What had changed in Emil? He had actually become a team player.

"Kalina, that boy has grown by leaps and bounds," Commander Kay said once Emil left. "You taught him well."

Kalina looked back toward him. "I don't know what I did."

"But you did *something*. And for us right now? That's what matters."

It took Kalina longer than expected to clean up after the battle simulation, which in turn made her late for her final class with her Year Three students. She had only begun to dismiss them when her small band of students made their way into the room.

"Ooh," one of the Year Three students said. "Is this a Silent Arcane Society meeting?"

"It's a *study group*," Kalina said. "If you would like to study with me after hours, you're always welcome to do so."

But of course, the student shook her head and left the room.

"Elder Kalina!" Anvisa exclaimed as the last of the Year Three students left. "Did you see what we tried to do out there?" The girl gleamed.

Kalina smiled. "You were very creative. Emil might have prophesied abilities. But your strategies were excellent."

"I was *so* proud of my team," Anvisa said. "They did well even if we lost."

Kalina nodded as the rest of the students shuffled in behind Anvisa. "You...you're as ready as you can be." She felt that lump in her throat again. They were still kids! They shouldn't have to enter the battlefield. But all of them except Hanodoi would learn what it's like to kill someone. What it felt to normalize that. And even Hanodoi might by the battle's end.

She'd fought alongside mages this young before. But after living with them in a school environment for months...she saw them differently.

She cleared her throat. "Thanks for coming by on short notice. I wanted to work with you one last time to make sure you're ready to work together as needed out there on the battlefield."

"So..." Anvisa took a deep breath. "Do we still need to learn this, Elder Kalina?"

"You need to be strong warriors," she said. "And this could turn into a prolonged military expedition if you're drafted and have to go farther south with the army. In that case, you need to be ready for anything—whether on *or* off the battlefield. Just don't use experimental techniques unless you absolutely *have to*."

She studied each of them closely, meeting their gaze to make sure they understood what she meant. Maybe she should give Emil a bit more trust. He *had* made tremendous progress over the last month.

But he still hadn't truly repented for Compelling Meliya.

"Let's get into position," she said. "Leneya, I want you to mold the dirt in the front of the room into a pillar. Sez, I want you to work against her with the rest of you assisting." While neither Leneya nor Sez played the right instruments to stop a Compelling, she wanted to give the students the chance to practice synergizing. Last week, they had figured out how to direct their energies to other people in Repose. But blending their tunes together posed more of a challenge.

Kalina had made at least one breakthrough when she realized they needed to maintain a simple beat in the same key as the lead player—not an identical melody. She and Riyad had always improvised harmonizing melodies since traditional synergizing required that. That's what she had taught Emil to do. But traditional synergizing also required both partners to do the exact same thing with their magic. Without that requirement, they could afford a simpler approach.

That alone made synergizing *startlingly* easy to pull off if you knew what you needed to do and learned how to direct your energies to the other person. Of course, it still required students to keep on the same beat—a skill rarely practiced.

Leneya picked up her trumpet while Sez positioned his own. They began to play.

Brass created a cacophony of noise within the narrow room as the two beats clashed. The pile of dirt Krem had transported into the room earlier began to form into a pillar. The other students tried to play to a simple beat along with Sez. But Sez and Leneya played on two different tempos. And it became immediately clear that the students weren't able to tune out Leneya's melody to focus on his. A myriad of competing beats overwhelmed the room.

After two minutes of their failed attempts to join Sez's rhythm, Kalina waved her hands to stop them. A five-foot-tall pillar of earth stood in the front of the room.

"Okay." She tried to think through what she should recommend. Something wasn't working, but she couldn't quite put a finger on what it was. Maybe another round would clarify the problem. "Let's try that again."

The second time didn't go any better. If anything, it went worse.

"It's the room, Elder Kalina," Krem said after she stopped them again. "I can't concentrate on a beat when the music echoes like this!"

She shook her head. "You have to. You won't get to choose where you need to defend yourselves."

Anvisa sighed. "How do we even have a chance at doing this, then?"

"Practice." Kalina stood up from the desk she'd been perched on. "We're going to learn how to make sure we're counting each beat equally." On a whim, she grabbed her fountain pen. "Here. I'll signal each beat so you can practice beforehand."

Krem rolled his eyes. "That's Year Three level stuff! We know how to choose the right tempo."

"But you need to learn how to do it *together*," she replied.

"Is this how you learned to do it with your husband?" Leneya asked.

"No...we knew each other so well, we could pick our melodies out of the cacophony." Kalina shrugged. "We also didn't have five people blending their music. So let's try it." She waved the pen up and down. "Count together with me."

"One. Two. One. Two," they reluctantly chanted as she waved out a simple beat.

Kalina motioned to Krem with her free hand. "Play along while the others chant." The plucky sounds of the lute aligned with the chanted beat.

She signaled him to pause. "Hold the beat in your head," she said and then nodded to Sez. Soon his trumpet played in tune with the beat. Then after him, Anvisa. Then Carissa. Then every other student in the room. Even Hanodoi kept up with the rest of the older students.

Finally, when they each had matched and now stood silently with the beat in their head, Kalina put the pen down. "Okay. Let's try that again."

Music again filled the room. But now everyone except for the opposing Leneya played on the same tempo. Six musical streams blended into one. And the pillar in the front of the room was driven back into a pile on the floor.

Kalina looked at them. "Wow!" *They did it! Even Hanodoi! If they can keep that while Anvisa or Andreya play...*

"I mean, if we had you guiding us through a four-minute exercise beforehand, we wouldn't have much to worry about," Anvisa said.

"If you practice it enough, you won't need me. We may not get there tonight. But you could continue to practice this at camp if you're drafted."

Krem groaned. "Why couldn't the Ternion have given one of *us* the powers Emil has?"

"Apparently the prophets prefer living trash," Hanodoi remarked.

Kalina raised her eyebrows. Hanodoi rarely joined in critical talk.

A knock sounded at the doorway.

Her head whipped in that direction. Had Suraya finally intruded? Kalina's heart beat faster. "Come in?"

But it wasn't Suraya who entered the room.

No, the tall figure with a wobble to his normally confident stride was none other than Emil himself.

She tried to keep her jaw from dropping. *How much did he hear?*

"Elder Kalina," the boy said. "Could we talk outside?"

45

HOW MUCH DOES EMIL KNOW?

Kalina shook away her questions and met his gaze with the confidence of a teacher.

"Of course, Emil." She strode up the stairs, ignoring her students' stares. Following him outside, she let the curtain brush shut behind her. "How can I help you?"

Emil looked down at her. Nervousness bled through his gaze, and he twitched. "I...um, I wanted to talk about the upcoming battle."

She exhaled and nodded. "What about?"

"Well, really, it's about your research." Emil shifted his weight. "I'm scared, Elder Kalina. And I know you still don't like me. I heard what your secret society students were saying. And maybe you don't care if I live or die, but I need to know if you've figured out anything about how you survived. Because I want to live." He swallowed.

"Oh, Emil." Kalina looked up at him. "Of course I want you to live." That's what made her discovery so crushing. She could hide the truth from him. Perhaps form some lie to protect her husband from Mito.

But Emil deserved to know the truth. And Kalina had also begun to understand him. Despite all his deep faults, he desperately *wanted* to be a hero. And so she would choose to trust him.

"I think I found something last night," she said. "I want you to know up front that it isn't a pleasant discovery."

He swallowed as he looked at her.

She continued. "I think I found one other person who survived an instrument breakage. I can't be sure he actually lived. But I suspect someone like him did. If so, we both share something in common: Our instruments were broken by a klyte arrow hitting the tail end of them."

She walked Emil through the magic theories she had learned and what they meant.

"I wish I had more I could tell you," she said after explaining it. "Or that I had something you could use to survive. I haven't stopped researching yet, and maybe the final tomes will give me something. But I don't want to give you false hopes. It seems the only thing that saved me was where the enemy hit me. And I'm so sorry, Emil. Because I know you've been hoping I could save your life. But...that's what I found."

Emil stared at her. Time stretched between them like a musical string stretched taut.

Finally, he spoke. "That...that's *it*?"

"I'm so sorry, Emil."

His breathing came out heavy. He broke away and stared at the wall. "You knew this all along, didn't you?"

Kalina shook her head. "Emil, I didn't—"

His head whipped back toward her. "You *promised* me that if I did everything you asked, you would save my life." His eyes reddened by the second.

"I told you I would do whatever I could to find the answer. I tried, Emil."

"Oh, you tried all right. You tried everything you could to lead me on." Hot air blew out of his mouth. "Do you *really* expect me to believe that you only discovered this right before I left this place?"

She opened her mouth to defend herself. Then she paused. *Does he need to hear a defense right now? Or does he need my sympathy?* The boy had heard a death sentence.

"I'm so sorry, Emil," she repeated. "I know this has to be hard for you."

"Really? You think you know what it's like to experience this? I'm sure you think that. Because Kalina knows everything. She knows how to read people and who's the epitome of 'living trash' and who isn't. She knows how to win wars even when she's lost every battle."

Kalina inhaled sharply.

"Do you know how much I sacrificed and groveled these past six weeks? Trying to trust you. Putting away my instrument even when I needed it. I spent so much time trying to synergize with my teammates and sacrificing my potential so you could save me. I even wrote in that stupid journal every day so you could see my thoughts."

So I could see his thoughts? Kalina cocked her head. "I...I never read your journal, Emil."

"What?" For a moment, his rant broke. "But that's why you wanted me to write in it."

She shook her head. "I *told* you that it was just for you."

"Oh yeah. What they all say before they come after hours to riffle through my journals."

Was this something else his mother did to him? But she continued to shake her head. "Emil, I never read your journals."

He rolled his eyes. "Whatever." His words came out like water kicking back from the bottom of a waterfall. "That's not the point. I did every single stupid order you gave. And now you're going to tell me you failed and I'm going to die, and whoops, you say you tried, but we all know exactly what you thought about me."

"I stood up for you in the meeting with your father to buy you more time," Kalina said quietly.

"Yeah?" Emil sputtered. "Well, we all know that's because you never believed in the prophecy. If you had *really* cared about me, you wouldn't have blackmailed me."

She grappled to find the right words to say.

"You know what?" Emil said. "You can do what you want. It was a mistake to ever listen to you. Thanks for ruining the last couple months of my life." He turned on his heel and stomped away.

A dozen responses leapt to Kalina's lips. None of them would make the situation any better.

She watched him leave and tried to keep back the tears that sprang to her eyes. *I shouldn't cry over a Compeller.*

But he'd become more than just a Compeller. And she'd been so close to breaking through to him.

She had to hope that after the shock wore off, he'd come back.

46

KALINA HAD BEGUN TO PACK UP

for the day, still thinking about her conversation with Emil, when Elder Suraya strode into her room. "Head Mage Bren would like to speak with you."

Suraya has discovered something. Kalina tried to ignore the fears slipping underneath her skin. "Okay." She put her books aside, straightened, and followed Suraya.

The woman said nothing the entire way to Bren's cottage. She walked intentionally, her perfectly red lips pursed, as she escorted Kalina like some kind of unruly student.

Kalina hadn't thought much about Suraya after Mito's threat. Was this just about the students denigrating Emil in her study group? Or had Suraya overheard something else? She tried to swallow back her fears. *Act naïve.*

Suraya brought her into the room Bren always used for disciplinary conversations. He stood next to the chair he usually sat in, and his eyes lit on Kalina when she entered.

Kalina nodded toward him. Then she saw Emil sitting on the couch next to Bren's chair. Tear streaks lined his face. A large red welt covered his left cheek. Elder Ashinara sat beside him, a reassuring arm on his shoulder.

"Thank you for coming here, Kalina," Bren said. "Please remain standing. I have asked Elders Suraya and Ashinara to remain here for protection."

For protection? Kalina stared at Bren in confusion.

"Emil and I had a long conversation about what's been happening the past couple of months." Bren fixed his gaze on her. "I haven't been this disturbed in a long time."

Kalina inhaled sharply as she felt a pit forming in the bottom of her stomach. *So this isn't about Suraya's investigation. Emil decided to out me. But...why are Suraya and Ashinara here for "protection"?*

"When I asked you about your rules for Emil yesterday, you weren't completely honest with me," Bren said. "Would you like to add to what you said then?"

Kalina could feel her cheeks beginning to redden. "I'm happy to talk further, Head Mage Bren," she said. "But with all due respect, do we want to have this conversation in front of a student?"

The Head Mage's gaze could have burned a hole through her. "I think you lost your ability to make requests. Please answer my question."

She swallowed. But she returned Bren's gaze without flinching. "I have a duty to protect my students. I could only protect them if Emil had more limits on what he could do. And so I told him that if he wanted me to stay here, he needed to follow my rules. Because if he could not be controlled, I could not keep teaching in good conscience."

Bren's expression didn't change. "And so you told him you would only save his life if he followed your every instruction."

"I told him I would stay here as a teacher if he did."

"But you would only try to save his life if you stayed here, right?"

I know how this makes me look. "He Compelled a student. That made him dangerous, and so I acted accordingly."

"You believe Emil is dangerous?"

Kalina glanced at Emil. This was why she didn't want him here. Ashinara's eyes pleaded with her.

She chose her words carefully. "I do not believe he is a monster. But I do believe he did something terrible, and until he fully admits to and repents of that, yes, he's dangerous."

"But you also threatened to leave if he ever told anyone what you were doing to him, correct?"

Kalina thought about her words. "Because I knew that you didn't care about the well-being of your students, Head Mage Bren. And so I needed to do whatever it took to protect them myself."

And there it was. *I've revealed what I think of the man. Time to pack my bags.*

Oddly enough, though, Bren didn't blink. His pale lips parted once more. "And how about your other punishments for him?"

Kalina frowned. "My other punishments for him?"

"Yes. Would you like to explain to us how those protected our students?"

"I...I'm not sure what you're referring to."

"I'm referring to the *beatings*, Kalina. Could you please explain how beating him every other day protected my students?"

For a moment, the whole world seemed to freeze. A myriad of bodily feelings hit Kalina at once. The heart caught up in her throat. The soreness of her muscles. The adrenaline coursing through her veins. And then she remembered the welt on Emil's face and the comment that Suraya and Ashinara should stay for protection and—

No.

She could feel her face paling. "I...I don't know what—that didn't happen."

Emil sniffled. Ashinara hugged him.

"Really?" Bren stepped toward her. "He has witnesses, Kalina. A couple of other students told us earlier that they saw him with fading bruises on a regular basis. And we can *all* see the welt on his face today."

Fear rushed through Kalina like spring floods pounding through a gully. "Head Mage Bren, I don't know what Emil told you. But I have never laid a hand on that boy."

"Because you've always been completely honest with me about what you've done with Emil."

"I have *never* directly lied to you."

"Then why would Emil and these other students lie to me about this?"

"Listen," Kalina said quickly, "I told Emil the results of my research earlier today. I survived because of where the arrow hit my instrument, nothing else. I can't save his life. He exploded when I told him that. I understand he's hurting. But this story here? The boy wants revenge, and he and his friends have every reason to lie about me. You know me—I would *never* do something like this."

Bren studied her carefully. "I don't think I knew you at all before today."

"Why would I beat Emil? It makes no sense."

"It seems to me that you have impossible standards for men," Bren said.

"You don't believe in the Ternion's grace. I told you yesterday that you needed to get off your high horse if you wanted to love students for who they really are. But I hadn't realized how much your past has twisted your view of the world."

Her skin crawled. She wanted to run. "What do you mean?" Her voice came out hoarse.

"Emil told me about what happened with your sister."

"My sister didn't lie," Kalina spat.

"No." Bren nodded. "She didn't. I knew people involved with the case, and I know for certain that Friar Qel did everything your sister said he did. I told Emil that. But I hadn't realized how guilty you felt about your inability to protect her."

Unease coiled around her ankles. "I don't understand why this is relevant."

"I'm so sorry, Elder Kalina," Emil burst out. She turned to look at him sitting there on the couch. "It must feel awful to know you're responsible for not helping your sister escape. But I'm not Friar Qel." Tears began spilling down his cheeks again. "Why can't you see that not everyone is like him? All men aren't scumbags!" His body shook with his sobs. "I didn't want to tell all this to Bren, because I know you're hurting, and I know you only beat me because you thought you were loving me. But I couldn't take it anymore."

No. No. No.

Kalina whirled back toward Bren. "He's lying. I never laid a hand on him. And I have never suggested that he was the same as Friar Qel."

"I've seen how little grace you have to show for others," Bren said. "You don't need to say it for me to know it."

"Do an investigation. I'll answer any questions you want." She stepped toward him. "But—"

"Elder Suraya!" Bren barked. Suraya stepped toward Kalina and put her trumpet to her mouth.

"Make one more threatening advance, and we *will* take action," Bren said.

Ashinara looked at Kalina with a strange look in her eyes.

Tears rushed to Kalina's eyes. *I won't cry in front of Emil. Ternion forbid—I will not give him that satisfaction.* "I'm *not* threatening you, Bren. I can't even practice magic."

"The boy has welts all over his body," Bren said. "And contrary to your insinuations, I *do* take the well-being and protection of my students *very* seriously."

Kalina breathed in and out slowly, trying to hold back her tears. She glanced toward Ashinara. At one point, she had been one of her few friends here.

"Ashinara," Kalina said. "You can't believe this...can you?"

"Elder Kalina..." She had a conflicted look. "You've always been a friend to me. I don't know what to believe. I only know that I trust Head Mage Bren. My husband's going to be out there on the front lines this week. We *need* Emil to win this battle for us."

Her words should have stung. But right now, Kalina felt nothing.

"This is a school where we show grace to others," Bren said. "Which means it's clearly not the place for you. I've already sent messengers to the city authorities to lock you up for the next week. They'll be here any moment now. I recommend you don't make a fuss about this. If I need to get the general involved, I will, but I know what he'd do to your husband, and I'd rather he not pay for your deeds."

Kalina's tongue loosened. "Head Mage Bren, please, investigate this first. Yes, I did some things that maybe a teacher wasn't supposed to. But I never hit Emil, and if you could look into this, I'll—"

Bren waved his hand. "I've heard enough. Elder Suraya, please escort her to the authorities and inform your colleagues about her departure. She won't abuse my students anymore."

47

KALINA WOKE TO THE BARE
stone walls of the prison surrounding her like the thick trees of the Deep
Jungle. Water dripped somewhere in the distance, and moisture collected
along the moss nestled between the stones. Dim light from a torch flickered
through the small, barred window. There were no doors.

She sat up, trying to recall how she got here.

Then all the memories of the previous evening flooded her mind.

She stared at the wooden bed beneath her. How had she slept? But
then she remembered all that restlessness...she couldn't have slept for more
than an hour.

Just enough to momentarily forget my humiliation.

The guards hadn't allowed her to keep her old clothes. They'd forced her
into this rough sack that she supposed technically constituted as clothing,
then shoved her in here and sealed the wall with trumpets.

Here she was, the once-promising mage reduced to a prisoner hung up
on allegations that she beat kids. This was how her students and colleagues
would remember her.

Emil's words echoed in her mind. *"Why can't you see that not everyone
is like Friar Qel?"*

Kalina shook her head. She had done what any decent person would
have done.

But...

Jadoni didn't like how you handled things.

Emil's words weren't the only ones that slunk around her mind. *"All I'm asking you to do is to love your students for the people they really are."*

If she had been a little more caring in how she talked to him...

A little more loving...

A little more like Riyad...

"He still wouldn't have changed!" Kalina cried.

Right?

She stood, shaking. The hem of the burlap dress fell around her ankles. Images of her sister sprang back into mind. The vague, concerning comments she had made, even though she denied Kalina's direct questions. Everything she went through for years because no one knew...even when they should have.

Every time I find myself face-to-face with abuse, I fail. Even when I try my hardest. I only find new ways to let everyone down.

Ashinara's conflicted gaze loomed over her.

I'm not a teacher anymore. It was odd how much that recognition hurt. She had never wanted to be a teacher in the first place. She rarely knew how to do it well.

But she had gotten to work with *students*. Anvisa and Leneya and Krem and Meliya and Hanodoi all held a special place in her heart. Even Emil, for all his faults. They were *her* students.

Chineya had claimed the Ternion had sent her to teach these students. But now here she was, forever exiled from doing that.

Footsteps sounded through the prison. Her head turned to the barred window. Who was coming?

A trumpet played and the stone near the window peeled back. Anvisa stepped through. Then Leneya and Krem and two other students from her training group.

Kalina blinked.

"You have five minutes," a gruff voice said outside. "Then you're leaving." The wall closed behind them.

She searched for the right words to say. "I..."

"Elder Kalina!" Anvisa ran over and hugged her. Kalina started.

"I'm so sorry!" Anvisa said. "We all know Emil lied about you."

Kalina breathed in and out. Tears sprang to her eyes. "I..."

Krem's lip curled. "I heard his friends joking last night about all the lies they spun about you."

Kalina tried to slow her breathing and focus. "It's the morning?"

"It's almost noon." Anvisa pulled back from her. "Head Mage Bren announced today that General Mahd has placed Emil in charge of all the mages. Emil only submits to Mahd. And he put all his dorm leader friends in charge underneath him."

What does Emil have planned?

"Emil told us he's setting all the terms of our engagement," Anvisa said. "Whatever he says goes, and he doesn't want to hear anyone questioning his decisions."

Kalina tried to imagine Padini and the other battle mages listening to Emil's commands. "The boy's never fought on the battlefield before. There's so much more than I can portray in a simulation."

"I know," Anvisa said. "But he says he's the chosen one and so he's going to know the right calls to make."

Something tells me he doesn't plan on synergizing anymore.

"Okay," Kalina said slowly. "It's possible to work with bad commanders. You need to be clever enough to slip under their radar, and—"

"You don't understand." Anvisa's breath came out fast. "He says he wants us students to fight out in front, not hiding in the back lines."

She blinked. "What?"

"He says that's what heroes did in the epic works of old. He won't ask the experienced mages to do this, but with us students...he wants us with him on the front."

I really failed with him, then. All that time and work for nothing. A chill danced around her fingertips. *My students will be massacred.*

"We need you, Elder Kalina," Anvisa said. And Kalina could see the fear nestled in her eyes like a dog cowering before a razda.

"You need *me?*"

"You're the only teacher who understands Emil," Anvisa said.

Kalina shook her head. "You have other teachers who know what he's like. Go to Elder Jadoni. Or..." She racked her brain to remember the name of that other teacher who had prayed with her.

"But you're the only one who does anything about it."

"And look at me now." Kalina gestured around her. "I couldn't stop him; I only made things worse."

"This...this isn't your fault, Elder Kalina," Krem said. "We all know you're only here because of Emil's lies."

"Exactly. I failed." She considered shutting up, but these kids looked at her like she was a savior. She wasn't. "I didn't stand up for Meliya. Nor could I lead him down a better path. I know you all look up to me like I'm some kind of great teacher. But I drove Emil further down his destructive way."

"Elder Kalina, he was *always* like this." The quiet Leneya spoke now. "I *dated* him for eight months. I know. He always acts kind and considerate, and he pretends to change, but when you refuse his demands, it's always about how hard he's had it and how bad you are. He'll do whatever he can to force you into doing what he wants. And if he can make your life miserable...he will."

Kalina bit her lip. "You don't understand. I should have gone about this differently." *If I had, I wouldn't have found myself here.*

"But isn't that what you always tell us?" Anvisa asked. "The battlefield isn't about waiting for the perfect opportunity; it's about taking the best available option."

Of course, my kids would use that against me now.

She looked at them. Here they were again. Looking to her. Waiting for her. Because she was the adult in the room.

Kalina wiped her eyes. "I don't know how I can help."

"The guards said you could be bailed out," Anvisa said. "We don't have much, but maybe if we cobbled enough together from different students and teachers, we could pay it? It won't be easy, but if it's what we have to do..."

Kalina blinked. "They told me last night that they wouldn't post bail for me."

Krem coughed. "Well...we may have gotten some help."

She cocked her head.

"It was Jacir," Anvisa said. "He talked with his dad, and his dad used his influence as mayor to get bail posted for you."

"*Jacir?*" She'd seen improvement from him the past couple of weeks. But the last serious conversation they'd had was when she'd called him out for using Meliya. *He's trying to free me?*

"Hard to believe," Krem said. "But we told him to stay away. We don't need him for more than bail."

Kalina shook her head. "I want to talk with him when all this is over. But the guards will return soon. How much is the bail?"

"Fifty silvers."

"You're not going to get that from your teachers and classmates. Go to the villa near the fountain square in the sixth quarter. Raz and Chineya are relatives of mine. Explain the situation and they'll help. And...do me a favor and bring Jacir along with you."

The wall opened behind the students. "You're out of time," the guard said.

She looked at them. She couldn't believe she was doing this. Was it arrogant to think she could still fix things?

But I've seen what happens when good people do nothing.

She might not have stopped Emil as a teacher.

But she *was* an ex-military commander. *I have contacts. I have allies. I have knowledge.* And maybe the Ternion was still with her.

48

KALINA SURVEYED THE BATTLEFIELD
from the top of Chintor's walls, Chineya and Raz beside her. As soon as
they had heard about her predicament, they had come. And of course they
had paid her bail, no questions asked. Raz had even used his connections
to get her to the top of the walls.

The scene wasn't promising.

Both forces stood on rice paddies the mages had formed into artificial
hills with a valley in the middle. Technically, Rizade had the advantage.
Tomorrow, the current drizzle should escalate into a downpour from the
looks of the weather patterns, and the valley would turn into a muddy
pool of sludge. But the Kaldian numbers spoke for themselves. Sure, Mahd
could play defense, and the enemy mages would have to work to keep back
the mud. But she'd seen his textbook tactics too many times before. And if
Emil fought on the front lines in some vain show of bravado...

Kalina swallowed. "That's a lot of Kaldians."

"It is," Raz said. "I'm disturbed to hear about what Emil has done to
you. If he's our only chance..."

That recognition had slowly crept in over the course of the day. If Emil
couldn't be forced to act strategically...

We're going to lose.

"Don't let it get to you," Chineya said. "The Ternion put you here for a reason. I've always known that. And if you need to stand up against the entire military to save us, the Ternion will give you what you need."

If only I could believe that. But Kalina had seen too many people claim the Ternion was behind everything when it clearly *wasn't.* The Ternion gave people free will. And that meant that their choices made a difference.

She studied the situation. "I need to talk with Commander Kay."

They met at twilight on a small hill. "Commander Kay," Kalina said as his shadowed figure approached. The rain continued to drizzle around them.

"It's actually Ambassador Kay," he said. "Don't you remember my promotion?"

Kalina had fuzzy memories of that conversation. "Remind me what exactly that entails?"

"I represent the king." He stopped in front of her. "Mahd is supposed to listen to my counsel as an independent adviser. Of course, we both know what kind of klyte he is. He's betting the king won't care about his disrespect when his son wins this battle. And he's probably right."

She sighed. "I'm impressed you got this position in the first place."

"There are perks to having a father who knows how to play politics." He laughed. "And I *did* work in court myself before the war started, so I know a thing or two about the king's preferences. But we're not here to talk about my promotion. What's this I hear about you getting kicked out?"

Kalina took a deep breath. "Emil is crazy, Kay. The performance he did for us in my simulation? It was all a show, and he doesn't plan on working together with other mages on the battlefield. Once he realized I couldn't save his life, he made up a story about me abusing him and got me kicked out."

"What?" Even in the darkening shadows, she could see Kay's face wrinkle. "But that's ridiculous!"

She shook her head, flicking off some raindrops. "He plans on fighting on the front lines too—him and all the other students from my school."

A laugh burst out of Kay's throat. "I thought we'd gotten past this!" Thunder boomed somewhere in the distance. "I'm sorry, we need to back up. He's claiming you beat him? What kind of hero is this?"

Kalina bit her lip. *May as well spill everything at this point.* "He

Compelled a girl to date him for a month and a half before I caught him. He may have a prophecy. But he's no hero."

A hollow laugh. "This can't be true."

"I'm sorry."

Kay stepped back. Mud squelched. "If I didn't know you, I'd call you a liar. But...klyte, how long have you known?"

"I caught him Compelling his classmate a couple months ago."

"Then what was that whole birthday speech about?"

Kalina pursed her lips. "I thought he was changing."

"But you *knew* he was a Compeller."

"And I was sworn to secrecy. You know as well as I do that I couldn't have gone up there and told the army that."

"But you could have told me." Even in the darkness, she could see his face pleading with her. "The king had appointed me as his ambassador. I could have written to him and tried to do something about it. But you went up there and suggested that everything was fine!"

I can't deal with this right now. "We need to focus on the present. The boy doesn't have good intentions. And he's bent on putting my students on the front lines. We're going to lose this battle if Mahd doesn't control him."

Kalina wished she could read the expression on his shadowed face. "I don't know what I can do. Mahd doesn't listen to me."

"And if Emil goes to the front lines with all my students, we lose. Look, Kay, Mahd's an idiot, but you know how much he hates risks like this!"

"He cares about his reputation more." Another distant blare of thunder. "Besides, we're talking about the prophecy now, and that means 'it's all up to the Ternion' to save us."

"I *know* the challenges you face." Kalina wiped accumulating rain from her brow. "But what's the alternative? At least keep my students from going up there." *Even if we lose, maybe I can at least save them.*

Kay shook his head. "I can't believe this. We're *desperately* outnumbered right now. If Emil tries to use fictional battlefield strategies, it won't even matter where your students fight."

"Why do you think I'm here?"

"We have to pray the reports you've heard are wrong," Kay said. "I'll try to break through to Mahd. But if this is his plan...even the Divine Council may not be able to save us."

WOODWIND MAGIC

↳ control, move, and shape liquids

—> Flutists help us irrigate & water the rice paddies, move water across towns and cities, and keep the rivers down when they flood

—> Flutists probably don't deserve to be made fun of as much as they are, but they really do drink a lot!

* Mages on mountains can kind of control the rain, but not enough to stop it from raining during wet season, which is a big letdown.

Interlude:
FROM THE JOURNAL OF EMIL MAHDSON

So, I'm a villain.

I can see the charge every time Leneya, Anvisa, or one of the members of their stupid Silent Arcane Society look at me.

What else is new?

I'm not sure why I'm still writing in this thing when Kalina isn't here to read it anymore. Maybe I like getting my thoughts out on paper.

I love how sure Leneya & her friends are that I'm lying about Kalina's abuse. They believed Meliya's charges based on her word alone. But now they insist they need more than my word. Because men need proof, but girls can say whatever they want.

Kalina is exactly where she deserves to be after waving my life like a carrot on a stick. She may have doomed this country by not allowing me to train properly. I wasted all this time learning how to synergize because I trusted her.

I should have known from the beginning. Women never care about me. They just want to use me. Because that's all that men of high ideals deserve.

But now she's gone & all Anvisa & company can do is complain about my battle plans.

How horrific they are.

Because yes, I'm going to ask other people to risk their lives alongside me. The horrors. I thought I was the only one supposed to risk my life for these lazy freeloaders.

But no. Mages moved to the rear guard because they were cowards. So if they're going to preach the importance of selflessness, they're going to live it out beside me on the front lines.

And who knows, maybe I'll have to use my backup plan and call the Year Three & Four students to make some sacrifices too.

Everyone will hate me if I pull *that* move. But I'm tired of the hypocrisy. Because I shouldn't be the only one forced to give up my life for the greater good. If I'm going to go out there & make sacrifices, everyone else needs to as well. Whether they want to or not.

49

Kalina sat squeezed around the kitchen table with Chineya, her husband, and the eight students who'd worked with her after hours along with Jacir. Rain continued to drizzle outside. The students had decided to come back here instead of the school tonight. Amid the rest of the chaos, she couldn't imagine Bren would notice a few missing kids. And with the battle tomorrow, they needed something more than the school would offer.

"So your commander friend may *not* be able to override Emil?" Krem asked.

She shook her head. "I'm sorry. He'll try. But the general has a lot of power and he rarely backs down."

"Well, maybe I shouldn't go," Krem said. "Maybe none of us should go up to the front lines! Who cares what Emil tells us? He doesn't understand how brass instruments work. He and all his dorm leader lieutenants are stupid violinists because he thinks his instrument is the best. So we don't need to listen to them. And, uh, violinists like Anvisa and Andreya don't need to because Emil's a fool. We can stay with the other mages and do what we want."

"What he said." Jacir slurped his stew. "I'm not following Emil." Hanodoi nodded vigorously.

Kalina exhaled slowly. *I appreciate their resolve. But...* "You know you'll get yourself executed if you disobey orders mid-battle, right?"

Krem put down his bowl of stew on the table with a clatter. "What should we do then? Go out there and die?"

"Listen." Pain gripped her heart. "I know. I hate this. But you need to disobey subtly, not blatantly. Not by running back to the rest of the mages, but by keeping a couple rows of soldiers between you and the enemy. Think about what I did at the academy. Resist quietly, not openly."

Krem exhaled noisily. "Didn't turn out well for you."

Kalina swallowed. "No. It didn't. And...I'm not going to sugarcoat things. You may die." Tears brimmed on her eyelids. "If I could do anything to keep you from that, I would. But it's the moments like this that determine whether you're the hero or the coward." She looked around; she had their full attention. "Maybe the Ternion has a plan. Maybe there's something I don't know about how heroes fight. But even if we lose, I'm going to be so proud of you." She laughed as a tear slipped down her cheek. "Maybe you really did live up to your name as the Silent Arcane Society."

Anvisa looked up at her and sniffled. "I don't know what we'd do without you. Previous teachers *tried* to tell us about the battlefield, but you know what it is actually like. I don't know where we'd be without your training. We'll make you proud."

Kalina shook her head. "You already have."

When the conversation finally died out and all the other students had retired, it was only Jacir and Kalina still sitting at the table.

Kalina studied his posture and face carefully. She had already been backstabbed by one bully who faked repentance. She didn't need a second.

"So," she finally said, "are you here because you hate Emil? Or did something else bring you?"

Jacir stared at one of Chineya's tapestries. "Maybe I just don't want to be like Emil in any way, shape, or form," he finally mumbled. "I've been spending a lot of time at the temple lately."

"Does that help?"

Jacir kicked at the ground. "I mean, the friars say some helpful things. But I don't know if I belong." He turned his gaze toward her. "You don't really believe what you said to me the last time we talked...do you?"

Even in the gloom of the sputtering candles, she could see the anxious lines around his face. Could those be the signs of someone who actually wanted to be a better person?

"Jacir...the grace of the Ternion doesn't say that the bad things we do aren't actually that bad. It says we can be forgiven for the awful things we've done. But you need to repent first. So no, I can't take back what I said before. And you shouldn't want that."

His fingers thudded against the table. "What about days like today, though? Don't they prove I'm not the person you think I am?"

"If you want to fully abandon your past, you need to own it. You were a bully. Not just to Meliya, but to many of the students you ate with tonight. Lying won't remove your guilt."

"Well. Klyte." Jacir stood up. "Guess I'm just like Emil then." And he walked off into the night.

Kalina bit back a sigh. *No matter how many times I try to explain the truth, people don't change.*

She wanted to reform at least one of her students.

But perhaps she needed to focus on saving their lives.

She couldn't sleep. And so, she found herself beside her husband's comatose body. She stroked his hand as she meditated on the day to come.

"Maybe I'm a coward," she whispered. "And I should tell Mahd what his son wants to do. I know you'd tell me that. Don't worry about you and go out there and do what's right."

Kalina breathed in slowly. And then out again. Years' worth of memories with Riyad flooded through her. And with them, the pain of loss. *Calm.* She had to keep her calm. The Ternion may not control everything, but it seemed to care about this war. It had given them a prophecy after all, through the Divine Council.

But did they have to choose the worst person possible?

"If the Ternion asks me to give you up, I'm not going to do it. You have to come back to life."

But what if it wasn't the Ternion asking her to do this?

What if it was her students?

She thought of Anvisa and her infectious enthusiasm for life. That funny smile Leneya had when she was sarcastic. Krem's facade of seriousness when he really wanted to enjoy being with others. Their torn, discarded bodies littering the battlefield.

At that moment, she knew what would break her more than anything else.

"I...I can't let them die." And she gave herself a moment to let that seep in. "I can't let my students die."

Kalina stared at Riyad, well aware of her words. Because if that were true...

Where did that leave him?

If only I was one of those heathen Kaldians who can pray to the Ternion directly. No one else was awake at this hour. If she would even feel comfortable sharing these thoughts with someone else.

"If you can hear me, please pray," Kalina said to Riyad. "Ask the Ternion for both of us if it can save my students without forcing me to visit the battlefield myself."

Not that praying has done much good for me lately.

She punched the ground. "Haven't I sacrificed enough already?" Her lip quivered. "Why do I need to give you up too?"

She'd already given up the inventor job she loved. Then her ability to use magic. The companionship of her husband. Her reputation in this town.

And now...

Her breath choked.

But her students' faces filled her vision again. It was Anvisa talking excitedly about the latest book she'd read. Krem awkwardly admitting his feelings for Leneya. Leneya breaking out of her shell and gently teasing her.

They were what she had *gained* these past five months.

A sob tore through her body.

Because what if sacrifice wasn't about seeing what you lost but seeing what you gained?

It comes at such a high price. But was being there for others only about giving up the things that were easy to live without?

What if being there for them was actually about giving up the things you really wanted to keep?

Kalina's heart broke. "I love you, Riyad."

But she felt his approval. Because he'd always told her she didn't need him to make a difference in others' lives. *"You're human—which means you're entirely unique, entirely valuable, and entirely full of potential."*

She set her jaw. Tomorrow would be hell.

But she could sacrifice every time duty called because she knew whom she fought for.

And whether she went up against the Kaldians, Emil, General Mahd, or anyone else, she wouldn't let them take away the people she loved without a fight.

50

T**HE DAWN CAME UP A MURKY RED.**
The skies were clear again, which only added insult to injury.
They wouldn't even have the advantage of rain and mud clogging the
Kaldians' advance.

Kalina stood on the hill north of the city walls. It towered over the
artificial hills beyond the river, giving her a clear view of the valley between
both camps. She eyed Mahd's crimson command tent.

Her bow and quiver rested on her back. Her backup plan in case the
Kaldians overran their defenses. Earlier that day, she had also replaced one
of her arrowheads with the klyte one she normally wore. *In case their mages
try to go after me.*

Two hours after sunrise, the Kaldian troops descended into the valley
between enemy lines. They raised long shields to ward off arrows. Kalina's
fingernails dug into her palm. *So it begins.*

She entered Repose. It was hard to track everything from this far away,
but she could sense how the Fabric was stretched taut with Quelling. No
one had made any magical attacks yet, though.

Emil and his group of students stood on their own lookout hill near
the other mages. There were about as many student mages as trained battle
mages. Only a few had been tapped to act as medics instead. Of course, the
students had nowhere near the experience the other mages had.

At least Emil stood in the back. Had Kay convinced Mahd to override the plan? Who knew? But that kept her on this side of the river. *No point risking my husband's life if I don't have to.*

The Kaldians made it halfway across the rice paddies. Arrows fell around them, but their shields covered them. *Why aren't the Kaldian mages diverting the arrows?* She didn't like this.

Then she saw the boulders sailing through the air.

They came from the Kaldian side. Four massive boulders thrown and accelerated by powerful lutists. Rizade's mages attempted to resist, but the boulders had gathered too much momentum.

On the field below, Kaldian soldiers broke into a jog.

The boulders had just sailed above Rizade's lines when they exploded.

Enemy brass instruments split the boulders into shards. A boom shook the air. And the pieces rammed into Rizade's lines. Dozens of men hit the ground. Screams rang through the air. And the Kaldian pikemen ran up the slope.

Kalina glanced at Emil's hill.

It was empty.

A chill ran down her spine, and she stepped forward. *Please don't let my students be where I think they are.*

A barrage of lightning shot into the enemy lines advancing up the slope. More screams rang as fried soldiers crumpled to the ground. *I know that lightning pattern.* And she could sense with her Repose where that energy came from.

Kalina raced down the hill. There wasn't time to think. One of those boulder shards may have already killed a student. She ran over the rickety bridge spanning the river. The wood creaked. She got to the other side and began climbing the hill. *When Bren sees me...*

But she wouldn't find her students' bodies broken on the front lines.

She struggled over the top. The high ground had been leveled except for a ten-foot hill where the crimson canopy of the command center loomed. The Year Three and Year Four students stood in reserve on her left. Nearby guards approached her. Then a couple of them recognized her and nodded. *At least the news of my firing hasn't spread this far.*

Screams and thunderclaps continued to fill the air. She came within a hundred feet of the command tent when Kay hurried toward her. She stopped, panting.

"I tried." Kay locked his gaze on her. "I swear I tried. But Head Mage Bren assured Mahd that Emil has received expert training, and Mahd won't hear any contrary opinions. If your presence could make Bren ruin your husband's life, don't do it."

"I can't let my students die."

"I'm telling you to use your brain." Kay smacked his fist into his hand. "If you go up there, Mahd's guards will cart you off."

Kalina stared down the hill at the battle. The Kaldians still charged up the slope. But before they got halfway, lightning struck them, pits opened under them, or they got thrown twenty feet in the air. Most of the Rizadian arrows were deflected now. But they hardly needed it when they had that kind of magical defense.

Emil and the student mages stood between the blocks of pikemen. These were impressive results for mages in their first battle. Playing magic this close to the front lines certainly had its advantages.

But mages had abandoned this technique centuries ago for a reason.

The ground at the front lines shook. Several Rizadian pikemen fell, including several student mages. *Is Emil not directing some mages to Quell attacks?* Her gaze darted back to the slope. The Kaldians were getting closer.

"They've already planned for this defense," Kalina whispered.

Their front lines burst into flames. It didn't quite reach the mages. But the screams of burning men filled the air.

Of course. Because Emil had been appointed commander of the mages. And he wasn't coordinating the mages to make sure they Quelled every section of the battlefield.

The pikemen broke formation to avoid the blaze. And now the Kaldian troops crossed the distance to smash into Rizade's chaotic front lines.

"Don't throw away your husband's life for nothing," Kay said. Then he sprinted toward the command tent.

Kalina stood, caught in a moment of indecision. She had made her choice the previous night. But Kay's warnings rang in her mind. If her interference wouldn't change anything, why risk Riyad?

Down on the battlefield, Emil retreated. Her other students did the same. Was he recognizing the folly of his choice? She watched as they gathered a hundred yards back. Two makeshift hills rose. Emil stood on one with half of the mages, Anvisa on the other with the rest. So he was compromising.

Is he far enough back? Her fingernails dug a groove into her hand.

The Kaldians had pushed their disorganized front lines back. Kalina entered Repose. Rizade's mages were trying to attack, but all the Quelling prevented them. *A few more minutes of this, and we'll be in full-out retreat.*

A thunderclap broke the tense air. And a barrage of lightning charred the Kaldian ranks. Men fell by the droves.

The Kaldians faltered. Rizade's pikemen took the opportunity to rebuild formation.

Kalina let go of the breath she'd been holding in. *So Emil hasn't forgotten everything I taught him.* Of course, the Kaldians had already gotten a foothold on the high ground. More men surged up from the valley to replenish their ranks.

The pikemen ranks tore into each other. Emil tried to find more openings. But the Kaldian violinists were Quelling the area more heavily now. Emil could only take out a few troops at a time. *You need to synergize and surprise them!*

For twenty minutes, the battle went back and forth. The students stood far enough back that she wouldn't interfere. But the mounds of bodies only grew.

And one-on-one losses benefited the Kaldians.

Pressure was building in her chest. Was this what losing looked like? *We need to change our strategies.* The Kaldians focused so much on blocking Emil's fiddle that he would have an opening if he synergized with another kind of instrument.

Why can't he see that this matters more than his so-called reputation?

Hope slipped through her fingers. And a deep numbness welled up inside.

Then gun cavalry descended the opposing bluffs.

Kalina ran up the hill. Maybe Mahd had already seen what would happen. Maybe he cared. Maybe he didn't.

He stood with Ambassador Kay, Head Mage Bren, and a couple of other advisers under the canopy surveying the battlefield. Kay saw her and tried to signal her with his eyes. *"Don't come up here."*

But she'd already decided what she valued in life.

"General Mahd!" Kalina cried.

The man turned to look at her.

"Those gun cavalry will aim for your son and my students. They need to move back."

Mahd's lip curled. "Mind your business and let us deal with this. They're outside range."

Bren had turned toward her, too. *"Do you know what you're doing?"* his expression asked.

"They won't need to take out too much of our front line to get within range." Kalina kept walking toward them. "Maybe Emil will take down two dozen of them. But that's it. Can you afford to have his instrument breaking this early in the battle? You know what the textbooks say about having mages this close to the front lines!"

Mahd's eyes were a burning inferno. She could only imagine the thoughts going through his mind.

But he knows I'm right.

Mahd turned toward the signal drummers. "Call the mages back," he growled. The drummers beat the taut skins. Kalina glanced back toward the battlefield.

Just in time to see Hanodoi running toward the battle lines.

Kalina stared. Where was he going?

Then another student ran after him. Elrenda.

She turned to see several other students trickling out from the reserve and running like they had little care for their lives.

Bren had come up behind her and was trying to hiss something at her, but he didn't matter anymore.

Kalina scrutinized the reserves. "Are the Kaldians behind us?"

A sergeant ran up the hill. Blood trickled down his forehead. "General Mahd!" he yelled. "I tried to stop them."

A terrible "if" filled her mind.

"What are they doing?" Mahd snapped.

"I don't know! They kept yelling about needing to go to the front lines and make some sacrifice to protect Emil from the guns!"

"No." Kalina took a shaky step toward the battle lines and entered Repose. "By the Ternion."

She could feel not only Emil but *three other* violinists all playing similar melodies.

Half their melodies extended toward Anvisa and her classmates, who frantically played in harmony to block their attempts.

And the other half reached the reserves. She saw their streams of magic flowing over the troops. And she saw what they were doing.

How their magic Compelled the fourteen-year-olds to move.

What had the students called it?

"Our sacrifice."

51

EMIL WAS COMPELLING FOURTEEN-
year-olds to run to the front lines and draw the attention of the cavalry.

Everything became clear.

This was who Emil was.

This was who he *always* had been.

What had Krem said yesterday? Emil's dorm leaders were all violinists. Memories flashed of Emil bragging about how he'd gotten them to study "experimental magic" with him. *Klyte.* All these months where he'd seemed to be making progress...he'd been secretly training his friends to Compel at the same time.

He would do whatever it took to become the hero he believed he deserved to be. No matter who that meant trampling on. Even if that led to a pile of children's bodies on the front lines.

Kalina's frozen world spun back into reality.

"I told you what would happen," Bren was saying, "and this is your last chance. If you don't leave right at this moment, I'll—"

She ran past him. "Emil's Compelling those students!" she roared.

Mahd and Kay turned toward her. Kay's eyes widened.

"I told you I didn't need your input!" Mahd snapped. "This isn't your place!"

"Your son is *Compelling* children!"

"The Ternion chose him! Guards, take this fool woman away from here."

Kay stepped forward. "I invited Kalina here as the king's ambassador. She's outside of your jurisdiction, General. And I demand that we stop Emil from doing this *right now*."

Mahd wheeled on him, spittle flying.

Kalina looked at the field. Her students were getting closer to the front lines.

And the cavalry had arrived.

They ran their circles behind their pikemen, pistols blazing. Emil picked off a few with lightning. And Rizade's pikemen stood bravely. *But we all know they don't stand a chance.*

Kalina remembered Kay's words yesterday. He had no real power in this situation. Only words.

"What will you do to protect what you care about?" Chineya had asked her that. And that was the only question that mattered now.

For a moment, Kalina's gaze met Kay's.

"Stop him," Kay mouthed while Mahd yelled at him.

She looked again at the students running toward the front lines. And in that moment, she knew exactly what she had to do.

Bren was coming up behind her again. But her legs had already started moving. She raced down the hill toward the battlefield.

She ran past the few scattered tents on the plateau. Past several students. Unreal fervor filled their eyes as they ran toward the front lines. She kept her gaze locked on the twin mage hills as she dashed between the battalions. Her lungs gasped for air.

People will hate me for what I'm about to do. Riyad would never come back. *Neither will I.* Perhaps that was best. Together forever, even in death. *Who knew what I signed myself on to that day I said my vows to him?*

But if Riyad could see her right now, Kalina knew he would be proud.

The twin hills loomed ahead. The frantic melody Anvisa and her mages played stood out from the clamor. Emil had stopped trying to electrocute the cavalry and had gone back to trying to Compel her students. Only three of her group were in tune enough to synergize, and they barely resisted. Kalina could see the terror on Anvisa's face as she played, and the tears streaming down the faces of her fellow students.

Between the hills, Jacir socked Hanodoi in the face.

There were four or five of the younger students there, dazed and stumbling, as Jacir grabbed their instruments and threw them to the ground. A surge of relief rushed through Kalina. *They aren't at the front lines yet.*

But another student was approaching. It was only a matter of time before Jacir couldn't keep them all back. Or until Emil noticed him.

Emil stood on his hill in the middle of dozens of students. Kalina almost considered calling out to him. But he wouldn't hear anything aside from the din of the battle. *And all my words to him are just words.*

Kalina grabbed the klyte arrow from her quiver. How ironic that the object that destroyed her would save her students.

She whipped out her bow and fit the arrow to the string. She thought she had failed when she discovered that luck had saved her life. But perhaps she never needed to save Emil. She only needed to stop him.

I'll be the biggest traitor in the annals of our country.

But who cared?

All that mattered were the Year Three students piling on top of a flailing Jacir and Hanodoi running past him toward the front lines blaring with gunfire.

Ternion, forgive me for what I'm about to do.

And please give my students enough time to escape.

Kalina put the end of Emil's eight-stringed fiddle in her sights. There was no wind. It was just her, the bow, and Emil. His hands played close to the body of the instrument, away from the scroll.

Her heart broke one final time for everything Emil could have been.

She released the arrow.

It sang through the air as it drove toward its target. There was no question about its accuracy. She had practiced on targets for a year. And she and Emil were a mere hundred yards apart.

The arrow hit Emil's fiddle below the scroll.

Her view of the hill disappeared in the explosion of light.

52

A **BOOM SHOOK THE BATTLEFIELD.**
The force slammed into Kalina, and she stumbled back, shielding her eyes.
Please be right about how instrument breakage works. She didn't know if
she would forgive herself if she'd killed Emil. Sure, he deserved the death
penalty. But she didn't want to be his executioner.

The clearing smoke revealed a desolate hill—presumably the students
were unconscious. Several mages around the edges bent over and coughed.
Kalina ran to the hill where Anvisa's mages stood, hoping the pikemen next
to her were in enough disarray not to notice her involvement.

All eyes pivoted toward her when she ascended the hill. Some of them,
like the seven students she'd worked with, understood. Others looked at
her in terror.

"Anvisa and Andreya!" Kalina ordered. "Our students are Compelled
until you break their mental bonds. You need to do that *right now*!"

They immediately began playing. Kalina glanced toward the battlefield.
Their front lines were collapsing. Another volley went off. Kaldia's
pikemen pushed.

They'll be on us within the minute.

She whipped back around. Several students had large drums. *We don't
have time to run.* And Anvisa and Andreya *needed* this height to see the
Compelled students and break Emil's magic.

"Leneya!" Kalina yelled. "Form a wave of earth against the cavalry. Everyone else, harmonize with her, just like we practiced!"

"We don't have time to practice our counting!" Sez lifted his trumpet.

He was right. And only three of them had managed to synergize a few minutes ago.

Another volley. And suddenly Rizade's pikemen collapsed.

Kalina dropped her bow to snap up a broken stick from the ground. "I'll signal. Same tune we practiced. Play!"

She began waving it in a brisk four-four movement. The earth shook as the cavalry surged forward. They weren't even attempting their circle formation—all the gunmen charged between their ranks of pikemen to take shots at them.

Ternion, help us.

Leneya blew her trumpet. The simple melody rang through the air. Then Sez's trumpet came alongside it. Then Carissa's drum, pounding out a basic beat. Kalina entered Repose as the final students joined in. And she felt it. Their magic synergizing with Leneya's to reshape objects within the Fabric.

A wall of earth plowed out of the ground that used to be their front ranks.

The Kaldian mages tried to Quell it. But while Leneya had never been her best student, the Kaldians couldn't stop the might of five students working together. The wave of earth pummeled down on the horde of gun cavalry, breaking horses' legs, throwing riders from their steeds, and swallowing the rest.

All the other students on the hill stared at them in shock.

Kalina's heart pounded.

That had *worked*.

A thought bubbled its way to the surface.

Kalina spun back toward her students. "Don't stop playing! Leneya, take out those Kaldian pikemen. My band, support her. Everyone else, keep doing what you've been doing." She began signaling again with her makeshift baton—one eye on the battlefield, one eye on her students.

The ground around the Kaldian pikemen leapt up and grabbed a whole regiment by the ankles, pulling them into the dirt. Rizadian troops surged forward to spear the half-buried soldiers.

Kalina glanced at Leneya. Sweat dripped down her forehead. Kalina knew from experience that she couldn't keep this up for long. But Anvisa and Andreya were still breaking the Compellings on the other students. *Please get them all in time.*

With her free hand, Kalina gestured to Carissa. "Take up the lead," she mouthed. Then she motioned to the other four students before pointing to Carissa. As Carissa changed her playing to a louder, more vigorous beat, Leneya switched to a basic beat and their energies shifted to Carissa.

Kalina glanced back at the battle. Four beats later, a massive sheet of flames erupted underneath the Kaldian front ranks.

A chill ran down her spine. She'd only ever seen a flame attack this large when one of her best drummers had gone up against an amateur Queller. Now, a perfectly average student had done it against experienced Quellers.

It almost scared her. *This will change our entire approach to warfare.* The old "normal" would never return. Because she had just blown up the magical paradigm of the past few centuries.

She kept directing. Sez's music had gotten off beat. She indicated with her free hand for him to speed up his tempo. She had forgotten those signals before teaching at the academy. Before, she'd always run from one mage to another whispering directions. Teaching had reminded her of the whole repertoire of signals that had been forgotten on the battlefield.

A violin entered the melody. "We did it!" Anvisa yelled. "All of them are free."

Kalina straightened and put a hand to her chest. It was like a hundred-pound weight had fallen off her shoulders.

And then Andreya's violin joined the song. Kalina inhaled as Carissa's drums burst with energy.

We've already won.

She glanced toward the other hill. A couple of Emil's buddies were beginning to stand. They looked dazed.

She whipped her head back around. Looking back and forth from the students to the battlefield, she continued to lead them.

Their music is beautiful. The realization came in like a jolt. She had become so accustomed to the musical chaos of the battlefield. But for once, seven conflicting tunes didn't compete for dominance. Instead, their instruments blended into a gripping harmony.

A tear slipped into her eyes.

She shook it off and put her mental commander hat on. How far could their influence extend?

Kalina scanned the battlefield. The right flanks were weakening. She signaled for Anvisa to take up the lead, then pointed her to it. As Anvisa took over from Carissa, she directed her energies there. The Kaldian Quelling failed in an instant. Lightning devastated Kaldia's ranks. Lines of men crumpled to the ground.

She pulled out perfect harmonies from her students and watched as, under her direction, they rained fire down on Kaldian troops, swallowed others up in the recesses of the earth, and sent lightning deep into their ranks. Other magic still happened on the battlefield, worked by the more experienced mages in the rear guard. But the most powerful displays? *My students did that.*

Months of hard work and training and education and research finally paid off.

Innovation has returned to the battlefield.

Kalian wanted to laugh. This battle...they were *winning* it with beautiful music. It sounded majestic and artistic—no longer a cacophony of divisive melodies. They all combined into a symphonic performance.

Movement caught her eye. Another stream of gun cavalry—this one larger than the last—came down from the bluffs. She could feel all the Kaldians Quelling the area around the cavalry. *Do they really think they have a chance of hitting us?*

She turned to signal Anvisa to shift her focus.

Something slammed into her.

Kalina spun through the air. Ground rushed below her as her thoughts only began to catch up. Had there been another explosion?

She crashed into Emil's hill.

Kalina gasped. The ground tore into her. For a moment, she couldn't breathe. She skidded over the earth and then rolled down the slope. Her body hit the base of the hill hard.

She wheezed and sucked in air. What...who had attacked her? *My students!* They still stood on the other hill. Still exposed. With a much larger group of gun cavalry coming. And now without anyone to direct them.

She forced herself up to her knees. And the wave of pain hit her. She felt the blood running down her elbows. And her knees. And she was pretty sure her back from the trickle she felt.

Her head spun. There weren't many people around; their soldiers had all moved their ranks forward. But she had to move. She'd seen how quickly her students got off rhythm without her direction. If she didn't—

A lute strummed a dark melody.

Kalina was thrown back against the sharp incline of the hill.

Then she saw Head Mage Bren walking around the curve of the hill. His normally pristine bleached robe fluttered in the wind, spotted with flecks of dirt. His hands strummed his lute.

And for once, lines of anger crossed his face.

"Please," Kalina gasped. "Do whatever you want to me after the battle. But my students are *winning* for us. If you let me go back there and—"

He played a few higher notes. Forces pressed her head back against the dirt.

"I invested so much in you," Bren said in his low, quiet voice. "So much in Emil. I trusted you, Kalina. When everyone else told me I should have never hired you, I gave you grace. But you got me. I was wrong. And to think you had the gall to claim you weren't abusive."

Kalina could hear the pounding of cavalry echoing across the battlefield.

"The Kaldian cavalry are coming!" She strained against the forces pressing her against the hill. "You need to let me go."

"Oh, I don't think so." Bren stepped in front of her. "I'm sure it makes you feel righteous to help the put-together students and throw away the ones with more mess in their lives. But your days of picking favorites are over."

"What are you talking about?" she gasped. It was hard to breathe with this much force pressing on her. "If you want to know which students had messes in their lives, look at Hanodoi, whom Emil almost *murdered*. Or Leneya, who has never been the same since Emil got his claws into her. You need to let me go so I can help them survive."

Bren's lip curled. "And that's why you shot an abused boy who was trying to save this country."

Kalina laughed. She shouldn't. Her whole body was bruised and battered. But it was so funny—Bren *really* thought he was a good judge of character.

"What's so amusing?" Bren snapped.

"You've been a head mage for twenty years and still don't know when students are manipulating you!"

His face darkened. "I'm sorry that you're unwilling to show your students the Ternion's grace. It's going to hurt you. Who knows what Mahd will do when I drag you to him? I tried to protect your husband."

I've already given my husband up for dead. She tried to look back toward the battlefield but couldn't see past the hill. The field still shook from the pounding of the approaching cavalry.

"Let me finish winning this battle with my students and then you can do whatever you want to me."

"What—because you want to share in their fame?" Bren's eyes flashed. "You don't deserve it. Some of us have worked years to make this moment happen."

He continued strumming his lute and her body jolted forward to hover midair in front of him. "It's time to return you to the general." He turned to leave.

But there, on the other side of the hill, stood Jacir with her bow, arrow notched and pointed at Bren.

"Hey, Head Mage," Jacir said. "This is the klyte arrow Kalina used to shoot Emil. I don't know if this makes you or me the bully, but I'd love to see what it does to you."

Kalina's mouth dropped. *Has Jacir even used a bow before?*

"Jacir! Put that bow down right now," Bren snapped.

"I sure will, as soon as you let my teacher go."

"Her?" Venom dripped from Bren's lips. "Don't you know who she is, Jacir? Do you know what she says about you?"

An uninterpretable expression crossed Jacir's face.

"This woman sees demons in every man around her," Bren said. "Including you. Is this *really* the woman you want to stick your neck out for?"

Jacir gave a half shrug while keeping the arrow aimed at Bren. "Maybe I don't care what she says."

"You don't care? Really—you're fine with her believing you're an awful person?"

"Well..." Jacir exhaled. "Maybe I need to admit she was right."

Kalina stared. *Did Jacir just say that?*

Bren sputtered. "She was right?"

"Yeah. I ran with an awful crowd. I did stuff I'm ashamed of. And my old dorm leader friends? They're all knocked unconscious up there because they're bad kids. And...I used to be one of them. There's something about seeing their fate that's pretty unnerving." He flashed a grin. "Plus, telling the truth allows me to point bows at my favorite head mage."

Bren stepped closer toward him. "That...that isn't a klyte arrow."

And now, Kalina saw that the arrowhead was the dull gray of any other iron tip.

"Oh." Jacir smirked. "Yeah. I'm still a liar. But I distracted you."

A symphony burst out on the hill above them.

And a boulder slammed into Bren.

The forces on Kalina's body vanished. She dropped to the ground, gasping for breath. Then she turned back to the hill.

There they were. The seven students she had trained. Anvisa waved her bow like a baton to signal time for the six students behind her. Ambassador Kay stumbled down the hill to come and stand next to Kalina.

"It's okay." Kay helped her to her feet. "We have you now."

"But the cavalry," she gasped.

Kay shook his head. "Your students decimated them."

Kalina turned. In the distance, she could see recognizable signal lights from the Kaldian drums. They were calling a retreat. A *retreat*.

Kay laughed. "You see, Kalina? You won the battle for us."

She was still trying to catch her breath. *We...we've won?*

"Your students are safe and the Kaldian forces have broken. You *won*, Kalina."

And right there on the battlefield, she broke down and cried.

53

KALINA COULD FEEL EVERYONE staring at her as she ascended the command hill alongside Ambassador Kay and her students. The army reserves, battle mages, and advisers alike all stood watching. She could only imagine what must be going through their heads.

General Mahd descended to meet them. His face screamed the fury of humiliation.

Kay snapped his fingers toward two nearby commanders. "Arrest the general and put him in chains."

They looked at him in surprise.

"He allowed a commander to Compel soldiers in clear violation of military law. And you all heard him send the Head Mage to take out the woman who massacred the Kaldian troops. When the king hears about what went down today, whose side will you want to be on?"

After a moment's pause, the commanders ran to intercept the general.

"Kalina."

She turned to see Padini moving toward her from the crowd of mages. "What...what was that?"

How do I describe what my students did? "I guess I learned a couple things during my time as a teacher."

"I...I've never seen anything like that." Excitement dripped through her voice.

Another mage burst out from the group. "How did you learn to do that?"

Kalina glanced at him. She didn't recognize him—he must have been a recruit. "Hard work and the blessing of the Ternion, I suppose."

"She's the best teacher we ever had," Anvisa put in. "She knew exactly who Emil was from the beginning. And she gave us all the training we needed to stop him and the Kaldians!"

No, that isn't me. Kalina shook her head. *I didn't know who Emil was from the beginning. Meliya gave evidence to that. And—*

"We hardly need a prophesied hero when we have a leader like this on the battlefield," Kay said.

Kalina tried to meet his gaze, shaking her head more vigorously.

"You see this woman?" Kay grabbed her arm and held it up in the air. "This woman led seven mages to single-handedly turn the tide of this battle. And that's only the beginning of what she'll do for us!"

The crowd roared in approval.

"I know you hate attention," Kay murmured, "but you know how much the king values tradition. To remove a general? You need a completely loyal army behind you."

She looked at all the people cheering around her. Her students even joined in. They were the real heroes of the day. And Kay wasn't wrong— they had unleashed a military revolution. War would never be the same.

I don't deserve all this.

But together with her students...and Riyad, who had first discovered this with her...maybe she had gotten something right.

It took far too long for Kalina to get back to Chineya's house and away from the crowds. First Kay sent off the rest of the army to pursue the fleeing Kaldians. Then Kalina had to leverage her influence with the mayor to put Bren and Mahd in prison for enabling Emil's Compelling; Jacir helped with that. And then she had to deal with the crowds.

There were *so many* people.

She did what she could to escape them. She didn't need their praise and gifts. Her students *certainly* didn't need the attention, as much as they reveled in it. That sort of fame at their age would rot them. If she hadn't had the good luck to run into Jadoni—who foresaw the same dangers and shuttled the kids away—Kalina didn't know how she would have gotten them out of there.

But now I'm here. The doors to the courtyard were locked behind her. The sun had begun to set. Light rainfall sounded in the distance. And she was...she was safe.

Chineya ran out of the house with a grin. But Kalina leaned against the courtyard wall, slid to the ground, and let the tears flow freely. They were safe. Anvisa, Krem, Leneya, Hanodoi, Elrenda...they were all safe.

Except for one.

54

RAYS OF THE LATE MORNING SUN

painted the walls yellow. Kalina stared into the small hospital room where Emil lay on a wooden cot. The doctors said he would regain consciousness eventually. His left arm had been amputated at the elbow. *The cost of playing a fiddle instead of a cello; his playing hand was closer to the explosion.*

Kay planned on putting him and his Compelling friends up on trial. Who knew if the king would allow the death penalty? But they would be held accountable.

What did all this mean about the prophecy? The words rang through her mind. "On the great day when you enter the battlefield, whether your nation rises or falls will depend on your mastery in war." The Divine Council couldn't give a false prophecy. But as several friars had already pointed out, the prophecy didn't technically say he needed strong mastery to win. *Perhaps Emil needed to show poor mastery so I would act.*

It explained the last line at least. "On that day, your instrument shall be broken as a reminder to all that the Ternion raises up and uses whom it chooses."

Kalina still didn't know what to make of the prophecy. She knew they finally had hope as a country again...and it wasn't in Emil.

The words she had spoken to him so long ago drifted through her mind. *"I won't abandon you—even if you fail to stop the Kaldians. I promise."*

She studied the look on his face. Did it speak of peace or unease?

Why did you need to try to kill my students?

Part of her wanted to walk out the door right now and not return until the trial. Meliya deserved her support before Emil did.

Another feeling tugged on her at the same time. It was the other set of memories. The hours of working with him to learn how to synergize. The way he stood up for her at his birthday celebration and admitted his failures. Those battlefield simulations where his strength and charisma had made him such a joy to teach.

I was so, so close to breaking through.

But she just hadn't had what it took.

Kalina sat in the temple next to the hospital for a good while afterward. The wooden pew dug into her back as she stared at the tetrahedron hanging from the ceiling. Eventually, she'd have to ask the friar to pray for her. But how did she explain everything in a way that made sense to a total stranger?

There was a movement nearby, and Chineya slipped into the pew.

"Thought I should find you," Chineya said. "The doctors said I could find you here."

Kalina exhaled. "Have I been gone that long?"

"I finished my errands an hour ago. Sent the boys back to the villa with all our produce and everything. You should have told me not to wait for you." She smiled and then put an arm around her. "Still thinking about him?"

"It's dumb." Kalina shook her head. "He made his own decisions. It's just..."

Half a year's worth of memories flashed through her mind.

She cleared her throat. "It's the ache of taking him out because I knew he wouldn't stop hurting others. The confusion thinking back to all those times when I was *so close* to persuading him to stop. The second-guessing of what words could have pulled him back from the edge. And the remorse of accepting that I couldn't change him."

The morning sun gleamed off the candlesticks around the temple. "I keep comparing what I said to him and what I said to Jacir," she continued, "and I can't find anything. I barely said anything to Jacir, and somehow he was the one who pulled through. And I *know* that it's because one of them wanted to change and the other didn't, but..."

She turned toward her sister-in-law. "When you care about a student, it's really hard to accept that the person you so badly *wanted* them to be wasn't real."

"I know." Chineya hugged her. "The grieving process can be complicated."

"I'm not grieving for him."

"No. But you are grieving for the person he could have been."

Kalina sat beside Jadoni on the edge of one of the fountain basins, watching the students sit and talk on the central green as dusk fell over the school.

"A lot of stories have come out today," Jadoni said. "Some of the students are exaggerating so they can join the drama. But others?" She shook her head. "He did so much to our students. I hadn't heard everything he'd done to Leneya during and after the time they dated. And many others are finally beginning to open up."

"You knew about this all along," Kalina said.

"I'm not the Ternion," Jadoni scoffed. "I knew he was a rotten apple. But not how many kids he'd hurt."

Kalina looked around at the buildings. They didn't seem as glorious as they did when she first joined the academy. "What's going to become of this place?"

Jadoni snorted. "We'll assemble as teachers tomorrow to vote on deposing Bren. I'm not good with politics, but those who have skills in that arena tell me we should have barely enough to vote him out. I'll move to kick out Mito as well. Emil had to have learned Compelling from him. Either way, I'm sick of his tomfoolery. We'll see. If we gave it a month, people would stop caring and we wouldn't have the votes to do either. But in the aftermath of yesterday? I think we'll pull out a squeaker. And then we'll take the rest of the school year to clean up this mess." She eyed Kalina. "Are you coming back?"

Kalina had considered that. "I don't think the army will let me. And if the Year Six students get permanently drafted...I need to be with them."

Jadoni nodded. "I suspected as much. You were never that great of a teacher. Courageous and ingenious? Sure. But your gifts were more as a commander."

Kalina coughed. "Thanks for the honesty."

"You know I don't have the patience for anything else." But then a look of guilt crossed her face. "You did the right thing out there."

"I should have listened to you earlier."

"You're not the first who should have done so. I should have listened to myself earlier as well."

Her heart twisted inside of her. She didn't want to say these words. But Jadoni knew who she was. "I...I wish I had stood up for Meliya. She should be here right now."

"You're not the only one with regrets." Jadoni paused, and for a moment, it looked like she was going to share something specific. Then she shook her head. "We'll leave it at that. I want to bring her back once Bren's deposed." She coughed. "If we can only do something about her work ethic."

Kalina smiled and then turned back to watching the students. Jacir was talking with several of the Year Three and Year Four students. Earlier today, he had made his apology rounds. He had a long journey of change ahead of him. But he seemed to have finally begun it.

On the other side of the green, Ashinara sat with Mito. She had sought Kalina out earlier that day. But while Kalina's actions had saved her husband's life, she couldn't get over Kalina's decision to imprison Bren. *"He's a good man, Kalina! How could he have known that Emil lied about you?"*

Her silence the night of her accusation still burned.

But between her and Kalina were all the students she'd fought for. And that was what mattered right now. Not the divisions that still existed. But the lives they had saved.

Kalina hadn't slept long before messengers arrived from Ambassador Kay, calling her to report at dawn.

She met him on the city ramparts beneath the watchtower. The remains of the battle spread out before them. The mages would restore the natural environment at some point. There would certainly be a cost to the village, though, in the ruined rice paddies.

Kay turned to her as she approached. "How do you like the sight?" Rain pounded the watchtower above them.

"The sight of a decimated Kaldian army?" Kalina smiled. "I like that rather much."

"I always told you that you kept us alive in battles. Who knew you would win them too?"

She shook her head. "You know I wasn't alone out there, right?"

"Oh, stop the false humility. An army fights as a team. But we all know the role a good commander plays." He eyed her. "This isn't just about this battle. If your mages can keep doing this, we've won this war."

"At least until the Kaldians learn how to do the same."

"Already planned for that. Right now, our spies are spreading rumors that we lied about which student was the prophesied hero. As long as we keep that up, they won't realize they can replicate our tactics. Today we saved Chintor. Tomorrow we save the rest of Rizade."

Kalina exhaled slowly. She doubted they could keep that feint for long. But it was a start. She let his last words seep in. *We can actually win this war.*

"You do know this means we're going to need you back on the battlefield, right?" A sly smile played across his face.

"I had guessed you would ask that."

"We need your students too. I know how protective you are of them, and I know they should have two and a half months until graduation. But we don't have the time to train other mages to do what they did. And we need to keep up the facade that this is all a student's work."

She didn't love the idea. But they'd fight in the rear guard and they'd be safe. She could finish their training on the battlefield.

"Are you acting general, then?"

Kay cracked his neck. "Well, that's the position I'm carving out for myself right now. We'll have to see what the king says. But most of Mahd's old commanders back me."

She laughed. "You always were a favorite among them."

"I know how to play the game. And when I coupled myself to your success, it's hard for them to resist." He grinned at her. "See, I'll make a good politician yet."

Kalina rolled her eyes. "You think you're ready for the demands of being a general?"

"Psh. Of course not. But my job's easy. You'll win all the battles for me, and I'll get all the victories."

"I see. Well, I look forward to seeing you taking the credit for my accomplishments."

"You know it." Kay stretched. "We're going to turn the tide of the last four years. There's a lot more outdated tactics for us to replace. And I think I've found a third member to round out a new trio of leaders."

"Oh?" She raised an eyebrow.

Kay nodded. "The Kaldians fled so quickly, they abandoned all their prisoners. Found some rather interesting captives, including a mage from Arditen."

"What—" Her stomach leapt and caught itself in her throat.

Kay looked at her. "Oh, yes. And I asked him that question first: Can he break a magically induced coma? Well, we're bringing your husband back to the land of the living."

And for what must have been the hundredth time over the past week, Kalina broke down in tears.

55

CHINEYA'S COURTYARD BUSTLED
with activity that evening. Smells of roasted teriden wafted through the courtyard. Drummers in the city continued to celebrate the second day of postvictory festivities. And people milled around Kalina. Her sister-in-law's friends talked alongside her students, which made for an odd mixing of worlds.

It's all I wanted.

Leneya ran up to her. "Elder Kalina! Did you hear? Krem asked me this morning to marry him!"

Kalina jolted. Hard. It wasn't unheard of for Year Six students to marry, but these were *her* students. And they hadn't even seemed all that serious.

"He still needs to talk with my parents," the once-quiet Leneya continued. "But he pointed out that if we're going to war, we don't have any time to waste. And I know my parents will say yes to someone like him. Can you believe it, Elder Kalina?"

Kalina looked at her and laughed. "No...no, I can't. That's amazing, Leneya."

"I'm so excited to meet your husband, Elder Kalina. When Krem and I get married, I want us to be like the two of you."

She blinked. *Like the two of us?*

Carissa pulled Leneya's hand. "I have to go," Leneya said. "See you on the battlefield!" And then she left.

Kalina's head spun.

Anvisa ran up to her. "Elder Kalina! Did you hear about Leneya and Krem?"

"She just told me. It's...quite something." She laughed. "What a two days it's been."

"I know. People in the streets are coming up and congratulating me! Not to mention the ways the other students look at us. We...we're heroes!"

"Try not to let it go to your head."

Anvisa laughed. "We're going out on the battlefield again and getting an early graduation. Can you believe it?"

At least she was taking it well. Kalina worried for them. But they still had the thrill of victory. And maybe that was for the best.

She smiled. "You've shaped the course of this country."

Anvisa shrugged. "Oh, we all know it's you, Elder Kalina. We're just your minions." She grinned. "I'll see you around." She danced off into the crowd.

"You've certainly made an impact," Chineya murmured from behind.

Kalina glanced at her. "Didn't see you there."

"I've enjoyed listening. Hard to imagine that this is the same woman who told me she could never be a successful teacher."

"Pretty sure I got lucky."

Chineya shook her head. "Call it luck if you must, but I know the Ternion's plan when I see it."

Kalina laughed. "You're a better follower of the Radian Way than I am."

"I've lived by it my whole life. And look at us now."

Kalina looked back at the crowd. Her students danced in the middle of the courtyard. They moved with passion, following the centuries-old dance with perfection and poise. Around them, Chineya's friends feasted and stole glances at them. Would they finally bring this war to an end?

For the first time in a long while, they had hope: a hope not resting on a manipulative abuser but on symphonic community.

A gray-haired man dressed in a golden uniform stepped up to her. She'd only met him twice. But she'd remember that face anywhere now.

"It took several hours." His voice had a lilting Arditen accent. "But your husband will wake up any minute if you want to come see him."

For a moment, time seemed to slow around her.

My husband. Riyad.

Kalina had thought when she went out on the battlefield to stop Emil that she had lost him forever.

But the grace of the Ternion had finally poured itself into her again.

She met the mage's gaze and smiled. How could she put everything she felt right now into language? Music was the only medium that could express this kind of emotion.

She followed him back into the corner room of the house. And there she saw Riyad, with more color in his cheeks than she'd seen for a while.

Kalina watched as his cheeks continued to redden. After so many nights spent quietly here with him...was she really going to receive him back from the dead?

She could suddenly see everything she'd gone through over the past thirteen months in a new light.

Riyad took one more breath. And then his eyes flickered open. As his gaze focused on Kalina, he flashed her that trademark grin only he could give.

And she knew what he would say before he opened his lips.

"Hey, human."

Kalina was right.

You don't really know what a battle is like until you're in it.

The authority to snuff out lives. The power of the Fabric in the palm of your hand. You feel like a god. Like not even the Ternion itself could stop you if it tried.

Of course she wanted to seize that for herself. Even if it doomed our nation.

She used her time well while I was unconscious to convince the town that I was losing the battle. Even though, blow for blow, more Kaldians were dying every minute than our own troops. I was overpowering the Kaldian mages. Sure, the gun cavalry had posed a problem. But the Year Three and Year Four students were about to protect us. I had the battle under control.

We would have won without her seizing the reins of fame for herself.

And now, here I am. Being carted along with the head mage & my dad to the capital to await some trial. Because it's not enough to steal my fame. Not enough to destroy my left arm. Not enough to kill my magic. I need to be sentenced to the death penalty as well.

Elder Mito warned me.

But I wanted so badly to trust her that by the time I realized who she was, it was too late.

This was her plan all along. Waste my time on synergizing so I couldn't actually achieve mastery in war. And then replace me with her favorite students.

Well, I've learned my lesson.

I find her second lie amusing. The one she's used to cement her power, claiming that the prophecy actually required me to have poor mastery in war for us to win.

But I suppose it's not surprising that everyone has bought into it.

Hope makes us desperate.

At least the king knows the truth. He heard Zedin's desperation when he delivered the prophecy. The prophet practically begged the king to make sure I received the right training.

I think even Kalina knows the truth at the bottom of her heart, beneath all the lies she spins around herself & her students. We're now destined to lose.

So I welcome the chance to be put on trial in front of the king & make the case for who really betrayed our nation.

Because if the shroud of darkness is going to spread over our land, at least the architect of our destruction will be the first to fall.

THE STORY OF *CHINTOR'S LEGACY*
WILL CONTINUE IN 2027

GLOSSARY OF MAGIC

From Pahr's *Introduction to the Musical Arts*

SUBSTANCE	MUSICAL INSTRUMENTS	WHAT IT IS	WHAT IT CAN DO
Space	Plucked string instruments (lutes, dulcimers, harps)	The distance between the Fabric	Telekinetically move objects
Energy	Bowed string instruments (violins, cellos, fiddles)	The power of the Fabric	Endow objects with energy and create lightning
Solids	Brass instruments (trumpets, tubas, horns)	That which the Fabric bends around	Mold and shape solid objects
Liquids	Woodwind instruments (flutes, clarinets, oboes)	That which fills the Fabric	Mold and shape liquids
Light	Percussion instruments (drums, bells, cymbals)	That which passes through the Fabric	Summon light and fire into existence

Acknowledgements

This book has been years in the making. And I have a lot of people to thank for their role in helping me to get to this point where I could publish this first novel.

My School Inspirations: To my students during my four years at MCA: I first started teaching because I loved literature; I kept teaching because I learned I loved you all more. Thank you for inspiring me. To my fellow teachers at MCA, especially Eric, Antonio, Annaley, DJ, Maria, David, and Erick: Thank you for teaching this fresh-out-of-college guy what it means to be a good teacher, and for always supporting me.

My Writing Mentors: To Caleb and Mr. Jones: for taking me seriously as a high school aged writer and investing deeply in me as a storyteller. To Christine: for helping me really grasp themes and character arcs for the first time.

My Story Developers: To Brett and Kara: you were the individuals who first grasped my vision for this story and helped me understand how to tell it effectively. This story would not have been the same without your encouragement and insight. To Mel Hughes, Lauren Hildebrand, and Claire Tucker: each of you made a permanent imprint on this story through your sharp editorial insights and your persistence in helping me elevate my writing.

My Beta Readers: To Elisha, Zachary, Kara, Isabela, Hannah, Val, Coralie, Carolyn, Bethany, Laurel, Morgan, Nicole, Taylor, Cissie, and Daeus: for reading a very rough second draft and giving me awesome feedback that helped shape this story into what it is now.

My Art Team: To Abian van der Meijden: for visualizing this story better than my mind could. To Jamie Foley: for the beautiful chapter headers. To Rachael Ward (CartographyBird) and Aaron Williams (AaronMaps): for the amazing maps. To the team at Damonza: thanks for the sick cover. To Cheryl DeGraaf: for the incredible special edition designs. And, you know, for being my mom.

My Cheerleaders: To my students at the Young Writer's Workshop: thanks for your enthusiastic support for me and my writing. To my Young Writer coworkers: for the encouragement, suggestions, and flexibility you provided that enabled me to write this book. To my friends at Lorehaven:

for your enthusiasm and rich discussions on the nature of fantastic stories. To my Story Embers team: for letting me roleplay as Emil during a writing therapy session. I hope it wasn't too scarring. To the Order of the Oxford Comma: thanks for your accountability and ideas whenever I got stuck along the way. To my church community at New Life and at Covenant Reformed: for always being there for me as a person. To Brock and Brendan: for the many conversations we had over the years that influenced this book in a variety of untold ways. And to my family: thanks for being the first people who believed in my writing dreams.

Finally, to the Creator who never let me go. I couldn't tell stories if you hadn't first allowed me to live some.

S.D.G.,

Kickstarter Acknowledgements

The illustrations in this novel are only possible because of the 501 supporters who came together on Kickstarter and other platforms to crowdfund this project. Thank you to everyone who believed in this vision and helped make it possible:

A.M. Denelsbeck, Aaron Kamakawiwoole, Abian van der Meijden, Abby Burrus, Abby Henderson, Abby Jo Hansen, Abigail E., Abigail H, Abigail Matthews, Abigail Pelegrin, Adam David Collings, Adam Wilson, Adia Snyder, Aeriana Brentlinger, Aileen, AJ Elliott, Alannah Williams, Ale Sogn, Alex Harlequin, Alexandra Corrsin, Alia, Alicia Kay Sproul, Althea Damgaard, Alyssa G., Alyssa Grant, Alyssa Savident, Amanda, Amanda Godbey, Amethyst, Amy, Amy Ullrich, Anastasia Ericson, Andrew Furstenberg, Angelique Stefanelli, Anica, Ann Marie Stewart, Anna, Anna, Anna Beth Harrison, Anna C., Anna Gruber Kiefer, Annabelle Richardson, Annarose Willhite, Anne, Annika, April Choate, Ari, Ashlynn, Ashton Reynwood, AslansCompass, Audrey Freund, Autumn Acosta, Ava Hope, Aviela, Ayomide, Bailee Werner, Barbara Carpenter, Bella Raine, Benjamin Brown, Beth, Bethani Theresa, Bethany Fehr, Betsy Jones, Bill & Sue Mendenhall, Billye Herndon, Blessing Hope, Brandi, Braxton French, Brendon Marotta, Brett Adams, Brett Harris, Bronte Clarke, Byron Spear, C. L. Mullikin, C.J. Milacci, Caleb "The Shrubbery" Renich, Caleb Barley, Caleb King, Calvin Beideman, Camy Tang, Cara Peregrino, Carly Hunt, Caroline Swayze, Carolyn Givens, Carolyn Leiloglou, Cass Medcalf, Cassandra Wilkinson, Cathy Smith, Cecelia Hill, Celeste, Celeste Baxendell, Chad Bond, Chantelreadsallday, Charis Mace, Charissa Chi, Charlie Banders, Charmaine Nicholson, Chase McGlinchey, Chloë Mali, Chris Frank, Christiana Blake, Christiana Kranich, Christopher D Shramko, Christopher Holtery, CJ, Claire, Clare Caughron, Cody Davenport, Cole Walker, Corinne, Cristina Flores, Crystal Mims, Curnock Moore, Daeus Lamb, Dan Daetz, Daniel Amador, Daniel DeGraaf, Daniel Lewczuk, Danielle, Darlene N. Böcek, David Bock, David Holzborn, David Lapp, David Matsumoto, David Stertz, Diana Crowe, Dimi D., Dorothy E. Carlson, Dr. Chriss Gregory,

Dylan, E. A. Hendryx, E. Leet, E. N. Manning, Ed McKeogh, Eddie Joo, Eileen Coxe, EL, Eli Carnley, Eliana Plumb, Eliana the Writer, Elias Gannage, Elisabeth Starling, Elizabeth, Elizabeth Dowdell, Elizabeth Farquhar, Elizabeth Semkiu, Ella Peterson, Ellie Duprix, Ellyana Howell, Elsa Sturm, Elysia, Emily Gellhaus, Emily H., Emma, Erin, Erin Dydek, Ethan DeGraff, Ethan Eshleman, F. Ted Atchley, Faith and Neil David Mangrobang, Faith Drake, Frederick Perillo, Freya Chi Vevette, Gabriel, Gabriele Areolite, Gabrielle, Gabrielle Schertzer, Gaja Renier, GASIWAC, Gayle Veitenheimer, Gianna Christopher, Ginny Priess, Grace Livingston, Grace MacPherson, Grace Taber, Gracie, Gracie Perry, Grandma & Grandpa, Gregory Butt, Gwyneth Wise, H.M. Hershberger, Hannah, Hannah, Hannah Kyle, Hannah Marie, Hannah-Abigail Toth, Harlie Roark, Harrison Tu, Hemlock, Holly Knight, Hope Ann, Hope Flinchum, Horatio Astor, Hudson & Rebecca Schrock, Irinel Finco, Isadora Dunham, J. A. Webb, J.R. Brady, Jack Baer, Jada Morrison, James, James Noller, James R McGinnis Jr, James Richmond, Janeen Ippolito, Janine B, Jenn Shackelford, Jenna Snaer, Jenni Lee, Jessica A. Tanner, Jessica Meuth, Jessica Moore, Jim Waters, Jimmy Bui, Joanna Peng, Joel Crumbley, Joelle Behrens, Joey Hedrick, John DeGraaf, John Idlor, John Powell, Jon & Ashley Stauffer, Jonathan, Jonathan Stanhope, Josephine Scheffrahn, Josh MacDonald, Joshua & Corine Kauffman, Joshua Parker, Josiah Smith, Julia, Julian Douglass, Juliet Artman, Justin D. Joy, K Hendrick, K Werntz, K. D. Lynn, Kal Tomson, Kalina Delacruz, Kara Matsumoto, Karl Crary, Karmen Adaire, Karyne Norton, Kate Franc, Kate Goforth, Katherine Briggs, Katherine Shipman, Katherine Vercouteren, Kathy Brasby, Katie Carter, Katie Handel, Katie Hay, Katie McLean, Katie W., Kayla Bergen, Kayla Maurais, Kelly Jo Wilson, Kelly L Clark, Kellyn Roth, Kenyon Wensing, Khylie M. Small, Kiersten, Kim, Kimberly Cornelius, Kirk Lundby, Kirk Rokey, Kirsten, Kirsten, Krisalyn, Krisan Marotta, Kristin Flanagan, Kristyn Brendle, Krys Galvez, Krystal Bohannan, Larisa Ignacio, Lark Cunningham, Laura Mayfield, Laura VanArendonk Baugh, Laurel Burgess, Laurel Stein, Lauren, Laurie Christine, LE Vandehey, Lee Anne Womack, Lee Brock, Lily, Lilyanna Dunlap, Lilyanna Grace, Liz Hutchings, Lorelei, Lorien Cord, Lucia M, Luke Crouch, Luke Genter, Lydia Dummermuth, Lydia Lewis, Lydia Lobb, Lydia-Faith Toth, M. Kincade, M. Weedin, M.J. Cossel, MadiJoy, Maggie Woods, Mahina K, Malcolm Coon, Mandy, Mandy Smith, Margaret Willinsky, Marie Wells Coutu, Marissa Geddes, Marlene Simonette, Martin Nordeman, Mary

Frances Pickett, Marybeth Davis, Matt & Sarah Scales, Matt Swinnerton, Matthew Sampson, McKenna Hubbard, Melissa Graham, Melissa J. Troutman, Melissa Matos, Meredith Carstens, Meshia, Michael Bello, Michael Dubost, Michael Evans, Michael Fulk, Michael Somerville, Michelle and Lee Sharp, Mihir W, Mike Hodder, Minde Artman, Miriam, Mitchell Bluestein, Mollie Feldman-Adams, Molly Hackett, Morgan, Myra Szobody, Nancy B. Yee, Naomi Sowell, Natalie Walsman, Natalie Williams, Nathan, Nathan Covington, Nathan Keys, Nathan Morgan, Nathan Spear, Nathanael Planalp, Nathaniel Paslay, Nellie Peters, Nena Yochim, Nicholas Stephenson, Nichole Heydenburg, Nicole Sanders, Nicole Niemiec, Nicole Walters, NIsaac, NJ Basel, Noah Scherer, Onika Howdyn, Owen, Owen Tillerman Adams, Pamacii, Paul M Green, Peter Schott, Peter Van Liew, Philip Bunn, Polina Bazlova, Rachael Dahl, Rachel A. Greco, Rachel Ann Naisbett, Rachel Feeck, Rachel Leitch, Rachel Lowe, Rachel Scheller, Ramel Austin, Raquel Branchik, Raymond Keith, Reagan Roberson, Rebecca, Rébecca Boileau, Rebecca Fay, Rebecca Mieczkowski, Rebecca Todd, Rebekah Doose, Reida, Renata Hornshaw, Rick & Barb Beideman, Robert Battle, Rolena Weber, Rose Hales, Rose Sheffler, Ross & Rebekah Allen, Roy Orbach, Ruston Ropac, Ruth Nguyen, RuthAnna, Ryan Alford, Ryan Mendenhall, Ryver, S.D. Smith, Sage, Sam Sleep, Samantha, Samantha Curran, Samantha Martin, Samantha Newberry, Sangeetha, Sara Francis, Sara Twinkle, Sara Wilde, Sarah E. Hamilton, Sarah Hickner, Sarah Marson, Sarah Pagel, Sarah Ritchey, Sarah Romanov, Sarah Sax, Sarah Spradlin, Scott Minor, Sebastian Stephens-Young, Selina Oliver, Sereena, Shanon M. Brown, Shiloh Pennings, Signe, Sophia Sc., Sotiris Karras, Stephanie Kwong, Stephen Bushmire, Stevie Ray Wunder, Story Warren, Sydney Leeson, Sydney Newman, Tamara Heiner, Tania Ibrahim, TechnoTiger, Tee Hongsieng, Terri Schwomeyer, Terry M Hulett, Thad Hoskins, Thane Merrick, The Burk Family, The Cooper Family, The Gomez Family, The Presson Family, Theresa Williams, Thomas Umstattd Jr., Tiana's Pocket, Ticia Messing, Tiffany, Tiffany Goldman, Tiffany Raven, Titus, Trisha Sparrow, Tyler Petrich, Tyson Daniel Freshour, Valari Westeren, Valerie Jo, Valerie Sizemore, Vanessa, W. Sim Davis, WaterNai, Webb, Will, 'Will It Work' Dansicker, Xavier Schwindt, Xiomara Reyes, Ysabel D, Z.R. McCormick, Zach Burnham, Zach Sollie, Zachary, Zachary Holbrook, Zackary Russell, Zoe Anastasia, Σου Αδελφός

About the Author

Josiah DeGraaf taught high school English for four years in the small North Carolina town that inspired the Andy Griffith show. During that time, he learned what normal schools were like (he was homeschooled as a child), which helped to inspire this book. After helping high schoolers enjoy Homer & Austen, he moved to small town Pennsylvania, where he currently resides as a writer and writing teacher. He loves crafting fantastical stories about characters who face the same dilemmas we do when we try to do the right thing.

Outside of work and writing, he enjoys engaging in lively intellectual discussions, playing board games, hiking to gorgeous overlooks, and hanging out with his eight younger siblings (yes, you read that correctly). He is the Program Director of The Young Writer's Workshop and the Features Editor for Lorehaven.

You can learn more about him and his future projects at JosiahDeGraaf.com

OTHER WORKS BY THE AUTHOR

A forgotten widow who can change the future must choose between two terrible options.

An idealistic guard has to destroy his reputation to stop a murderer.

A plucky shapeshifter has to save a man he accidentally incriminated.

These are the god-blessed of Morshan. And they're about to learn how supernatural powers can be both a blessing and a curse.

Living morally was easy when their lives were normal. But now that they're gifted, they carry additional responsibilities–and face impossible dilemmas. How far are they willing to go to save lives?And whose visions of grandeur will turn into fruitless dreams?

Medieval superheroes face a variety of heart-breaking dilemmas in this illustrated short story collection.

Download your free copy at JosiahDeGraaf.com/Free-Book/

No instruments were harmed in the making of this book.